THE
LENSKY
CONNECTION

CONRAD DELACROIX

Matador
9 Priory Business Park,
Wistow Road, Kibworth Beauchamp,
Leicestershire. LE8 0RX
Tel: 0116 279 2299
Email: books@troubador.co.uk
Web: www.troubador.co.uk/matador
Twitter: @matadorbooks

ISBN 978 1800465 275

British Library Cataloguing in Publication Data.
A catalogue record for this book is available from the British Library.

Printed and bound in the UK by TJ Books Limited, Padstow, Cornwall
Typeset in 11pt Adobe Jenson Pro by Troubador Publishing Ltd, Leicester, UK

Matador is an imprint of Troubador Publishing Ltd

For my grandfather, Ivar Bisgaard Throndsen, and to those who have inspired me on my journey which I hope has been worthy of their creative counsel (aka Stuart Adamson, Joe Strummer, Alistair MacLean, Frederick Forsyth, Robert Ludlum, Martin Cruz Smith, Robert Harris, Lucinda Williams, John Sturges, Jean-Pierre Melville, Eric Ambler, Walter Mosley).

PROLOGUE

The burial at the Serafimov Cemetery in the Primorsky District was a small gathering, barely a dozen people.

Major Valeri Grozky of the Federal Security Bureau (FSB) had not expected to bury his elder brother, Timur. The coffin rested on his left shoulder, Grozky's left hand braced around the upper arm of his father, Keto, who had made the journey from Batumi, Georgia. Keto had been a soldier before he'd joined the Georgian KGB. Even in retirement, he had lost none of his military bearing, holding his son at arm's length in a rock-steady grip.

Though Grozky did not know this cemetery he knew the trees, for the maple, pine and cypress surrounding the graves were all to be found in the Batumi Botanical Gardens where he and Timur had played hide-and-seek as boys. Instead of the subtropical plants of the Caucasus, Serafimov's ranks were filled by silver birches, lime, linden and thickets of black alder.

They reached the burial plot and put the coffin down. Across the ground, a carpet of tousled green plants butted up behind the gravestones as ferns mingled with pilewort and ground elder. Timur's final resting place resembled a small square of cleared earth in a wooded glade rather than a grave. Grozky took small comfort that Timur would have liked his shaded plot, though it could not ease Grozky's anger at the manner of his brother's death.

A fifteen-year veteran of the KGB, Grozky kept his emotions in check. A combat death he could have accepted, but Timur had not died in battle. A decorated soldier, Timur had survived the Afghanistan war unscathed except for his mind. A year ago, with Grozky's support, Timur's decline had stabilised and he was fighting his demons to rediscover the man he had been. Grozky did not know when his brother had turned to heroin but the opiate had stripped Timur of his resolve. An overdose was not the inglorious way Timur would have chosen to go. A tarnished veteran was being laid to rest alongside those who had given their lives in a ten-year campaign the Soviet government had never publicly acknowledged. Had Grozky not been serving in the Third Directorate during the war, he might have ended up the same way as Timur.

His brother's funeral was, Grozky thought, an occasion for the grieving and the angry. For Grozky's wife, Marisha, now crying uncontrollably into Keto's chest, it was enough to cherish Timur's memory. She had loved Timur and mourned him like a sibling. Grozky could not accept Timur had to die.

Grozky walked over to where his father had taken charge of comforting Marisha. Several yards away Dr Anosova, from the clinic, was talking to a pretty girl Grozky didn't know. In a smart two-piece black suit, she was the best dressed of all of them. Timur had always had an eye for the girls.

"I didn't raise a son to die a junkie. He should have died in Afghanistan," Keto said. His sadness could not hide his disgust.

"I remember Timur for the brother he was. You raised a good man. He didn't deserve this," Grozky said.

It was harder for Keto, for the son he had nurtured and prepared for life with the soldier's code had succumbed to despair and died a degenerate. Timur's death was too raw.

They were joined by Dr Anosova and the pretty girl.

"Valeri, I'm so sorry about Timur. You did everything you could," Dr Anosova said.

"Perhaps, perhaps not."

"My sister, Roza, is a recovering addict. There isn't a day that goes by when I wonder what else I could do," said the pretty girl. "Trust me. What more could you have done?"

Grozky heard the pain in her voice, the anger too.

"Valeri, have you met Natassja?" Dr Anosova said.

"Natassja Petrovskaya," Natassja said, extending her hand.

"Valeri Grozky."

After a firm handshake, Natassja said, "Roza would have come today. She was too upset."

"It's very good of you to have taken the time," Grozky said.

"It's the least I could do. If it wasn't for the damned gangs polluting the city with drugs, Timur might still be alive," Natassja said.

Grozky nodded. Where once the heroin supply had been restricted to the opium crop from the poppy plantations of Kyrgyzstan, St Petersburg was overrun with heroin. The Soviet Union's decade of occupation in Afghanistan had enabled the country's drug lords to profit from new supply routes to the West. Farmed opium sold for US$25 a kilo was worth US$1,000 a kilo wholesale by the time the morphine base had been turned into heroin, and US$50,000 a kilo wholesale when it arrived in Western Europe. Grozky felt Natassja take his hand and press something into his palm.

"I work for the *Kommersant* newspaper. I'm writing a piece demanding the government does more to tackle the drug gangs. I'm very sorry about Timur. If there's anything I can do to help, please call me," Natassja said.

"Thank you."

Grozky looked down at her card. His brother would not have wanted his legacy to be reduced to a drug addict with a criminal record for petty theft. Grozky chose not to recall what Timur had become. He had been found dead on a park bench. The autopsy report highlighted a purity of heroin in his body well beyond the fix he could have afforded. Timur had died of an overdose or perhaps it had been made to look like one. That Grozky doubted he would ever know only added to his anger.

They gathered at the grave's edge to lower the coffin. Grozky's face betrayed no emotion as he held the tension on the rope and lowered Timur's coffin into his grave. It was as the chunks of earth battered the top of the polished wood that the finality of his loss hit him, no longer sadness but fury at his failure to save his brother.

Standing opposite Grozky, one long gaze from Keto was enough to tell his remaining son the account must be settled. Timur might have survived were it not for those who were making millions of dollars from the misery of addicts. There was a debt to be paid for those who had taken his life. Grozky turned to the assembled group.

"Thank you all for coming to say farewell to Timur. He was a good man. I know it would have meant a lot to him to have you here and it means a lot to me and my father. Before we go and toast Timur, I give you my word, he did not die in vain."

Grozky wasn't one for empty gestures. In the calm of Serafimov Cemetery, amidst the cover of the trees, he had made his pact with Timur.

1

The sniper lay on the frozen grating of the metal walkway. It was the fifth day of his vigil. He didn't know this city. A vantage point, a line of sight and he was set. The faded grey/white camouflage of his thick winter suit might have been aged to match the scuffed paintwork of the abandoned gantry crane. Except for the wind it was a good position, over fifty feet high with a 180-degree view across the railway yard and beyond. He was losing the light. Another hour at most.

He was a late addition, one of eight sharpshooters now spread above the city and supported by two jeeps. Like the others, he was concerned with the practicality of the mission. They could cover the assigned ground, but the chances of spotting the target seemed slim, not that any of them would dare tell Ivan the Surgeon. Ivan told them daily that the longer it took to find the target, the longer it would be before they could all get back to Chechnya. He hadn't served with the colonel before and he was grateful for that. With Ivan's reputation for slaughter, he should have been Ivan the Butcher, except he was too clinical a killer. It would be warmer in a jeep, but it was better not to be around Ivan. It must be a big job though, to select a dozen Spetsnaz troops from the Chechen front line. At least in Yekaterinburg he didn't have to worry about the wretched counter-snipers. Chechnya was becoming as bad as Afghanistan, worse if you were a conscript. Even the damn Afghans were rallying to the Jihadist black flag of the 'Arab Mujahideen in Chechnya' to fight for the separatists.

The sniper carefully stretched his body, holding his muscles firm to stave off the cold seeking to invade his insulated suit. Through the PSO-1 scope on his Dragunov rifle he scanned the railway yard and the streets, ignoring the vehicles. The sun was a token in the freezing gloom, softening the glare from the snow and the silhouettes of the pedestrians. He saw a shape by the railway yard fence which had not been there a moment ago. The sniper picked out the standing figure. Compared with the shrouded walkers in heavy coats, their thick hats bandaged tight against their heads by long scarves, the man's bare head marked him out and he wore no gloves. In this temperature it was madness. The man slipped on the frozen pavement, flinging his arms outwards to recover his balance. He steadied himself, looking hurriedly around him. The sniper noted the absence of boots. Even the fur collar on the dark overcoat was incongruous in this working part of the city. The man stepped off the pavement and started walking across the street. The illuminated 'café' sign and the bright lights within might have been a beacon. The sniper watched the man's movements, pulling at the trim on his upturned collar before thrusting his bare hands back into his pockets to salvage some defence against the vicious wind. The man glanced frequently behind him as he stumbled across the road. The sharpshooter slowly reached for the radio handset next to him.

"This is seven, I have a target."

*

The fugitive crossing the street shivered as he eyed the hurrying figures nearby. He yearned for the cover of dark though the sub-zero temperatures were worse, bullying his mind into delirium. The image of sitting next to a hot stove in the corner of a warm room taunted him, even the impossibility somehow a comfort. During daytime he could not dispel his sense of pursuit, yet he saw no sign. He could not countenance another night in the railway yard.

He skidded on the frozen slush churned up by the vehicles, walking faster than his brogues would allow. His shoes were permanently damaged, cracked and dulled to a filthy grey except for the resilience of the hand-stitched contours. The artful patterning might have been etched into the Italian leather.

Reaching the café, he discovered there was a small convenience store adjacent, its meagre glow hidden by the sacks of coal stacked on a worn wooden trestle table outside.

Surveying the café through its bright windows, he envied those at the tables enjoying alcohol and hot food. He could easily have afforded these prices. He checked the luminescent dials of his chunky stainless steel watch. The café would close in twenty minutes. He wished he dared chance it.

Crossing the few yards to the store he peered through the panes, dusty with dirt and frost. He used the sleeve of his coat on the glass and made out dark rows of shelves. The reflection from the shabby window was poor, making his decline even more abstract, the features lost under several weeks of a grubby salt and pepper beard while his thick hair sat lank and tired. Only the quality of his clothes remained proud. The black cashmere scarf and overcoat were a present from Irina. He recalled the warmth of the central heating in their Moscow apartment, the memory immediately banished as the wind whipped around his head and freezing wisps of icy powder tore at his legs and feet. He had to escape the godforsaken cold.

The man opened the shop door, ignoring the pressure of the spring holding it. The joyous warm air against his face was spoilt as the noisy ring of the bell above the door announced his presence. Ignoring the stocked shelves, the man hurried to the back. He took his hands from his pockets and rubbed them briskly together to restore his circulation. Even the faint scent of oily diesel infusing the warmth was welcome after the hideous cold. Amidst this unfamiliar place, he became aware of another foreign smell: his own, rank odour.

Reaching the end of the aisle, he spotted the old shopkeeper who waited behind an ancient cash register. He saw the shopkeeper's expression change, his greeting for a derelict restricted to a nod of suspicion. The fugitive felt for the wads of notes in his coat and thrust a thick handful of crumpled roubles on the counter.

"Please, for God's sake, hide me."

The fugitive tried to smile, his entreaty as pathetic an appeal as he could manage. The shopkeeper looked at the money, his hands hidden in the pocket of his apron.

"*Please*," the fugitive said, his face ragged with desperation.

The shopkeeper looked up, paused, then gestured towards the door behind him at the end of the counter.

"Go in there. It leads to the storeroom and out to the

back. There's a yard outside with no access onto the street. Use the yard if you want to. Help yourself to anything you need for now. I can bring you some hot food later after I've closed."

"Oh, thank you, *thank you*," the man said, grasping the shopkeeper's hands and feeling the warmth so absent in his own.

The fugitive hurried to the stockroom entrance, lifted the latch and entered, closing the door behind him. The smell of fuel receded and the room was cooler, although a sauna compared to the hellish conditions outside. In front of him a long row of shelves, from floor to ceiling, seemed to block access to the rest of the room. Bars of strip lighting illuminated upper shelves dominated by tinned food, before fading to leave the contents of the lowest ones a mystery. He was in a cave of food except he had no opener. He was about to return to the store when he saw a paper bag wedged between some tins and the shelf above. Inspecting it, he found a small loaf. He tore off a crust and felt the softness of fresh bread. He bit through the crust, the plainest nourishment a luxury.

Browsing the shelves, he reached the end to find a gap which became the start of the next aisle. He walked the length of the room again until he reached the next turn. Tearing off another chunk of bread, he chewed it as he continued the zigzag path of discovery until, after a final loop, he found the outer door. Set in a corner, it was a few yards from the stockroom entrance. The man avoided the icy draught, walked halfway down the aisle and sat on the floor. He took another bite of bread and considered his situation. If the shopkeeper was amenable, this could become an ideal arrangement.

In front of him, he saw a row of boxes hidden on the bottom shelf. Leaving the bread on his lap, he pulled one of the boxes half out and tore open the top. Inside, the ends of packets of biscuits fitted together like a puzzle. He had always scorned biscuits, yet this was a treat. He was using his fingertips to prise out a packet when he thought he heard a scraping noise from the far side of the room.

Had he heard something? He would have registered the sound of a door opening. He listened, hearing only the low hum of the electric lighting. Reassured, his fingers returned to the box.

The shout from behind the rows of shelves was so sharp it took him a moment to register his name.

"Tomarov."

The verbal assault was repeated.

"Tomarov."

They had found him!

Damn. Tomarov pushed himself up, the bread rolling to the floor. He lightly ran the few yards to the outer door.

Praying for his salvation, Tomarov carefully released the lock and quietly pushed the door open, immediately feeling the freezing air encroach into the stockroom.

"*Tomarov.*"

His name resounded like a denouncement. Tomarov eased himself around the side of the door and then pushed it to as quietly as he could, the lock gently re-engaging.

He stood in the yard, expecting to have to climb out. He saw a scrubby patch of ground and, to his relief, its boundary was little more than a thin wooden fence whose uneven staves were held together by wire both top and bottom. Past the fence, was a road.

Tomarov praised his good luck as he ran forwards, the frozen, uneven terrain making him stumble. He cursed the shopkeeper and the leather soles that gave him no purchase on the ground. He was yards away from the road now, the only obstacle the flimsy wooden fence. He could flag down a vehicle. He still had plenty of cash.

Dashing towards the thin fence, he realised there was no gate. It made no difference. As he forced himself over the posts, using them for support, there was a sudden splintering as a weaker stave gave way to his weight. He felt his leg catch and, unable to stop himself falling, he felt something stab deep into his left calf. He screamed at the pain as he hit the ground. Looking down he saw a shard of wood embedded in his leg. He cried out again as he pulled his leg free and, as he did so, the outer door of the stockroom flew open. Tomarov did not look towards the figure. He stood up, trying to block out the searing agony in his leg and hobbled forward into the road, desperate to escape.

"*Tomarov.*"

He limped hurriedly, distracted by pain and panic, and turned too late to escape the jeep bearing down. He could not believe it could get so close without him hearing it. He tried to jump aside as the jeep struck him.

2

Sidelined from the maelstrom of drinkers, Grozky perched on a plain stool at the corner of the Imperial Hotel's long bar, browsing the *Kommersant* newspaper laid out in front of him. Sitting at an angle to the grand room provided the best vantage point. Rising behind the plethora of bottles, the bonus of a mirror offered the backdrop to the room's activities. Off duty in a black roll-neck jumper, he didn't need to glance at the tattooed fingers to distinguish the gangsters from the businessmen. Even when he sought to relax, the little details around him trickled through his mind.

Grozky's calm features belied his irritation with his surroundings. The bar's fabric had been updated along with the hotel's clientele, the oak panelling sacrificed for a modern invasion of pastel colours and stainless-steel fittings. The metalwork extended to the ceiling where cavernous lamps with the presence of searchlights were embedded like shrapnel. Amidst the floodlit excess, waiters moved amongst the wealthy crowds, glowing in white tuxedos, their foreheads glossy from their exertions.

This was not the type of place he and Marisha would have come to even before she had left him a month ago. Timur's death had changed him more than he cared to admit. Georgian families were tight-knit and the pact Grozky had made in Timur's memory was his penance to bear. Marisha could not accept he had to fill the void left by his elder brother by putting his own life on the line. He knew, though, his way of dealing with Timur's death was only part of the reason why he and Marisha had separated. They had married in 1988 when his authority in the Third Directorate's Naval Counterintelligence section gave him a dark kudos and the security of a steady income. Back then, criminals knew their place and crossing the KGB was reserved for the desperate. Since the KGB's disbandment, five years previously, the privileged life the Soviet system could guarantee him was long gone. Facing off against the drug gangs was a step down from the livelihood he had known. As his status eroded, so had their relationship. He could no more save his marriage than his brother.

Within arm's reach, several bottles of the finest Russian vodka tempted him. Fermented grain had been as much a part of his daily mantra as black coffee and sixty knuckle press-ups until his last medical, two weeks ago. The FSB's physician, Dr Feliks Fedorov, had advised him that, at forty-four, he would be in better shape if he 'drank grape not grain'. A fellow KGB veteran, Fedorov's knowledge was as extensive as it was economically dispensed. But for Fedorov's care in removing a bullet from his right thigh six months previously, Grozky's limp might have become permanent. In his youth, growing up in Batumi, Grozky had been a useful wrestler in Georgian Chidaoba, his foot sweeps made lethal by the power in his legs. He was still building the strength back up in his right leg, lucky to have avoided serious muscle damage.

Grozky's eyebrows furrowed as a small glass of Napoleon brandy appeared on the bar in front of him.

"Thank you," Grozky said without looking up from his newspaper.

The double-page spread laid bare the Kizlyar-Pervomayskoye hostage incident, outraged that the Chechen war of independence was spilling into Russia. After crossing the border and raiding the Kizlyar aircraft base, Chechen separatists had escaped to the village of Pervomayskoye with over a hundred hostages. Spetsnaz forces had encircled the village, yet after several days of intense bombardment, the guerrillas had escaped. It was the latest debacle in a war Russia had been struggling with since December 1994 when General Pavel Grachev, Yeltsin's Defence Minister, had boasted Russian paratroops would seize the Chechen capital, Grozny, in two hours. The victory had taken two months and cost 25,000 civilians their lives, many of them ethnic Russians.

Since May 1992 Yeltsin had entrusted Grachev with the reorganisation of the Soviet Army into the Armed Forces of the Russian Federation. It was Grachev's Directorate of Military Reform which had cut over two million personnel and left the military ill-prepared for the current conflict. The army was now as much a casualty as the disbanded KGB, depleted by restructuring and rebranded. President Yeltsin's popularity rating had dropped below five per cent. His record on the war was as poor as it was on organised crime. At this rate Yeltsin wouldn't survive the summer's election.

Grozky's change arrived in a small, highly polished steel saucer while the barman hovered, expectant of a tip. Grozky ignored both.

"Those bloody Chechens. We'll sort them out," the barman said, stabbing his finger onto the page.

"Let's hope we will," Grozky replied, without looking up.

"Never trust a black bastard," the barman said, asserting a belief he expected to endear him to a new customer.

Grozky curtailed a smirk as he turned a page. Born in Tbilisi, the Georgian capital, he would be considered 'a black' by the barman. Instead of inheriting the swarthy features and dark hair of his father, Keto, Grozky bore the pale skin, blond hair and steely blue irises of his Cherkessian mother from the north-west Caucasus. In his youth, his Slavic resemblance had been betrayed by the narrowness of his face. His hair was thinner now, his cheeks thicker and the Georgian renegade blended into White Russia like the chameleon he was. Keto had seen to it his son would have opportunities outside Georgia. Grozky's flair for languages had seen him excel at Kiev University at a time when the KGB sought able students. Grozky's fifteen years with the KGB's Third Directorate were roll-of-the-dice military counterintelligence postings across Georgia, Armenia, the Ukraine and finally the Kronstadt naval base in St Petersburg. Five years on, a passed-over major was fortunate to have state employment.

The barman departed and Grozky sipped the brandy, the sweetness still alien to his palate. It tasted like a soft drink. He'd have to watch that otherwise he couldn't see Fedorov's advice making much difference.

A clock chimed eight, barely audible above the drunken cheering of a group of inebriated men. Grozky glanced at the mirror. Amidst the crowd he could not at first pick her out. He watched until he saw her smart bob and the face that smiled at him across the glass. Natassja Petrovskaya had a journalist's discipline for timing and a model's sense of style.

He turned to watch her final approach, the leggy stride, the short black mackintosh and the long legs encased in sheer black stockings. She made everyone else look dull in comparison and heads turned, the girls envious and the men lusting.

Natassja eased herself down on the stool next to him. There was no handshake, no peck on the cheek, just a demure smile and the rich, physical scent of her perfume. She placed her small black handbag on the bar and stockinged flesh stroked itself as she crossed one leg over the other.

"Hi, Natassja, as I recall a gin and tonic is your preference. Or would you prefer something else?"

"Hi, Valeri, a good choice. Thanks."

Grozky ordered her drink and used the moment to withdraw a square of paper from his trouser pocket. He discreetly unfolded it and placed it on the bar, protected from view by Natassja's handbag. A small table of numbers ran across the page.

"These are the latest official figures from the MVD, the Russian Ministry of the Interior, covering 1993 to 1995. It lists the number of organised crime groups uncovered, number of members, ties to criminal groups within Russia and to international groups," Grozky said.

Natassja rang her finger down the numbers and he saw the alarm in her face. But for Timur's death, Grozky would not have countenanced divulging such information to a journalist. Now the terms of engagement had changed. St Petersburg could not stem the rise of the criminal classes any better than other cities across the Russian Federation. This was their fourth meeting. Natassja hated the drug gangs as much as he did. The Russian government had underestimated the corruption its nascent capitalism would breed. The rewards of crime had seen an explosion of criminal entrepreneurs. Now the thieves had to compete with the *sportsmenny*, the 'gangster

12

athletes', drawn from the ranks of ex-Soviet sportsmen whose endurance and competitiveness were ideal qualities for the street gangs. At the top of the hierarchy the oligarchs made the serious money in whatever business they chose to pursue. The old criminal codes held no significance to the new breed of felon; 'silver or lead' was the choice on offer.

"Over the last two years, the number of gangs has increased from over 5,500 to almost 14,000. Their membership has doubled from almost 27,000 to over 57,000," Grozky said.

"This would indicate you're losing the war?" she asked.

"I prefer to think we're winning some of the battles."

"That's what the Americans said about Vietnam," Natassja said as she studied the figures.

Grozky nodded; her comparison was truer than she realised. With the collapse of communism, St Petersburg faced a battle against the drug gangs of a kind not seen since the German siege from September 1941 to January 1944. Grozky's grandfather had defended Leningrad only to die within weeks of the Nazi blockade being lifted. He was buried in Piskarev Memorial Cemetery, a city of the dead, where half a million lay. Grozky never forgot his grandfather's sacrifice. At the heart of the cemetery the words of Olga Bergholz, the Leningrad poet whose radio broadcasts had symbolised the city's resilience, were memorialised: 'Nobody is forgotten, nothing is forgotten'. Grozky would avenge Timur's memory. A phrase from the poet Mikhail Dudin on a wall in the cemetery was etched into his mind.

Your own lives align with the lives of the fallen.

In his otherwise unremarkable career, Grozky was making a stand against the scourge of addiction that had claimed his brother's life, just as his grandfather had stood against the Nazis. It was a piece of redemption Grozky clung to.

"I really appreciate this. The stock answer from the Russian Ministry of the Interior is complete denial that organised crime is rising," Natassja said, refolding the paper and placing it inside her handbag.

"It would be. The presidential elections are coming up in June. The Kremlin has the big stick out for results. That's forcing better coordination across the District Security Council. The level of small arrests is endless, the challenge is getting close to the organisations behind it," Grozky said.

He spun the stem of his glass, the thin residue of brandy barely reacting.

"It's no wonder you're tired," Natassja said.

Grozky felt her hand brush his forearm. It stayed there longer than it needed to. She was skilled in how she used empathy. If it wasn't for their shared goal, her gesture might have been a ploy to retain a source.

"It's what I do," Grozky said, conscious there was no end to the fight. The reality was that the gangs replaced their criminal infantry while they used their funds to infiltrate the Internal Security Services. At the start of January an FSB captain on the fifth floor had disappeared. Two weeks later his headless corpse had been pulled from the Bypass Canal at the heart of the city. His scalp was a warning; in the choice of 'silver or lead', he should not have decided he was owed gold. It was better he be remembered as a hero. Grozky would never entertain such an offer. These days, he never left his apartment without his pistol.

Natassja's drink arrived along with another metal saucer. Grozky pocketed the change and stacked the saucers on top of each other.

"*Nastrovje*," Grozky said, raising his glass to take a reluctant sip of brandy.

"*Nastrovje*. So, you've read my article?" Natassja asked.

"I haven't got that far."

"What *do* you do all day?"

"You mean other than chase down drug gangs? Try and avoid getting shot by them," Grozky said.

Natassja leant across and turned a couple of pages.

"There," she said, pointing to a few paragraphs at the bottom of the page.

Grozky read quickly. Yuri Tomarov, once the head of the privatised Yanusk Oil Company, was the victim of a hit-and-run in Yekaterinburg. She had vilified Tomarov as a greedy, immoral businessman and then redeemed him as a victim dispatched by unseen hands even more ruthless than his own. Grozky smiled, for her article would never have made the reactionary *Izvestia* or *Sankt-Peterburgskie Vedomosti*. In the new order of Russian journalism, *Kommersant* often crossed the line. For someone as driven as Natassja, it was not difficult to be righteous in a country crippled by corruption.

"Natassja, I'm sure you've considered this could have been a traffic accident on a frozen road?"

"It could have been except that the local newspaper, *Uralsky Rabochy*, reported Yuri Tomarov to be the only hit-and-run in Yekaterinburg in the last nine months. Hit-and-run implies carelessness like a drunken driver who loses concentration and registers their mistake too late. Tomarov's pelvis and thigh bones were shattered. There was also reference to 'massive trauma to the brain'. Then there's the small matter of the compression to his arms and torso. If he was hit that hard, it was a high-speed impact, so how can he also have been run over? When you consider the facts, this was a deliberate hit rather than a hit-and-run."

For a journalist, Natassja possessed the instinct of a policeman. Grozky wondered at the substance behind her assertion.

"I didn't read that medical evidence in your article," Grozky said.

"It was in the police report. I left it out to protect my sources."

"How did you get the official police report?"

"A fax."

"Any witnesses?" Grozky asked, looking again at the article. Natassja knew her craft and how she liked to apply it. Deaths were a steal for her, he thought. She mined her information until she found the nugget she needed. However Tomarov had lived, it was how he had died which would define his legacy.

Natassja laughed.

"Currently not. That's a product of the snow and the sub-zero temperatures. If anyone did see what happened, they're probably too frightened to report it. I'd tick all the above. Predictably, the police report concluded there's nothing to indicate this was more than an accident. Instead of making it a priority, they accept it as an unsolved case. That tells me they either don't care or they're party to the cover-up."

Grozky listened. Accident. Disinterest. Scandal. Amidst the choice, she drew her readers to follow the thread of a conspiracy.

"Natassja, you know inflammatory speculation could get you into trouble. Be careful."

She smiled ruefully, as if she expected no less from an FSB officer. When she replied there was steel in her eyes.

"The Russian people have a right to know. Even for a scumbag like Yuri Tomarov."

"What's your next story?" Grozky asked, glancing down the bar. Several yards away, an almost familiar face had appeared amidst the scrum, except the longer hair didn't fit with the face. Grozky struggled to place him.

"Not so much a next story as a continuation of the current one. I was in Moscow last week. I interviewed Andrei Simonov from the Ministry of Fuel and Energy for some background on Tomarov. I asked Simonov several times why Tomarov wasn't under investigation. All he would say was 'no comment'. How can he think that's an answer? By evading the question, he's admitting the Ministry are doing nothing to draw attention to Yuri Tomarov. They've closed ranks on one of their own. I don't suppose you feel like asking a few discreet questions?"

"Natassja, unfortunately I'm knee-deep in criminals," Grozky said.

"I know I shouldn't ask."

"No, you shouldn't." Grozky was conscious her conviction was the reason for their collaboration. While he defended the authority of the state, she attacked the government's inability to stem the corruption that had killed his brother.

"If Tomarov was as guilty as you say he was, I can't imagine the Ministry wants to be reminded of that," Grozky said.

"Exactly. This is what makes me think I'm onto something. Who do you think I bumped into when I was leaving Simonov's office? Yevgeny Kochenko and his entourage. Simonov saw I'd recognised Kochenko and he flipped. He literally pushed me out of his office and slammed the door."

"Perhaps you caught him on a bad day."

"It was more than that. Simonov became furious when I tried to speak to Kochenko. Anyway, I waited for Kochenko in reception and he gave me a lift to the Metro station in Lubyanka Square. I even got his card."

Grozky listened. Natassja's charm belied her industrious pursuit of a story. A St Petersburg oligarch like Yevgeny Kochenko wouldn't have realised a lift gave Natassja her chance to harvest a new contact.

"You should watch who you get into cars with, Natassja. From what I've heard, Kochenko's wealth came at a price."

Amidst the hubbub of the bar, habit caused Grozky to glance at the opposite end of the room. He noticed a man on his own and wondered why he sat alone, smoking his cigarette with such intent.

"I know. All Kochenko would say was 'he had some business at the Ministry'. I've done some digging since I got back. Kochenko is now the majority investor in the Yanusk Oil Company. How did that happen? Why did Kochenko have to go to Moscow to meet Simonov? Something's going on," Natassja said.

Grozky recalled Yanusk, the backbone of the Soviet oil industry. It was one of the first state privatisations, the symbol of how the wealth of the state would become the wealth of the people. Kochenko's business interests were extensive. He might be respectable now, but everyone had heard the stories. The racketeers who had crossed him in the early 1990s were no longer to be found. That was reason enough for a bureaucrat like Simonov to be uneasy.

Iakov Osin. The name of the man on the far side of the bar popped up in Grozky's mind. Osin had been a member of the KGB's Sixth Directorate, responsible for Economic Counterintelligence and Industrial Security. Their paths had crossed during an investigation into Baltic Fleet sailors withholding foreign currency to deal on the black market instead of spending it in the Soviet Beriozka stores. Grozky had been assigned to assist Osin.

"If you're interested in Tomarov, there's a man over there who might know something. I can introduce you," Grozky said.

"Thank you, Valeri," Natassja said, finishing her drink and slipping from her stool.

Grozky led the way through the crowd, making a mental note to suggest one of the decent, crowded bars on Middle Avenue near where he lived for the next meeting.

At the height of its power, the KGB was known as the *Kontora Grubykh Banditov*, the 'Office of Crude Bandits', with good reason: its methods were answerable to no one. Grozky had run a small network of informers within the Kronstadt naval base. The KGB relied upon everyone knowing they were watched, including KGB personnel. An entire country had to assume their business was known. After Grozky threatened several sailors with immediate dismissal from the navy and a spell in jail he obtained the names of their civilian contacts and passed them to Osin. The fear of being caught was how the Soviet state had enforced servitude to communism amongst its citizens. Giving up a name to a state bogeyman to keep the Ministry of Fear at bay was the lesser of all evils. The Sixth Directorate had infiltrated the black market operation and netted several hundred thousand US dollars, a small coup for Osin. Grozky's reputation as a 'fixer' had not survived the KGB's passing. He hadn't run across Osin since then.

By the time they reached where Iakov Osin had been, he was gone. Grozky glanced around until he saw Osin leaning against a pillar talking to a petite girl who was wearing too much make-up.

"Iakov, it's Valeri Grozky. A long time no see. You always knew where to find a good bar," Grozky said.

Osin looked at him, his face hazed in inebriation, while the girl smiled at the interruption.

"Valeri. What the…? Valeri Grozky," Osin said, fumbling with the name as he repeated it.

"It was a while ago. Kronstadt naval base. I won't keep you, Iakov. I was on the other side of the bar. Let me introduce Natassja Petrovskaya," Grozky said.

"Kronstadt, of course," Osin said, almost with conviction.

"Natassja," she said, extending her hand.

Osin shook it while he grinned at Grozky.

"You're working an angle, Valeri?" Osin asked.

"An angle?" Grozky queried.

"Trying to get laid."

Osin laughed, clapping Grozky hard on a shoulder. His escort's grin widened.

Grozky saw Natassja bristle at the inference. He doubted Osin was in any shape for a conversation.

"Iakov, it's good to see you. What are you up to these days?" Grozky asked.

"Same old, except worse," Osin said.

Grozky nodded. In a Russia distilled into the quickfire option of wealth or death, the safety net had been cut from under the investigators of economic crimes.

"You haven't been working on the Yuri Tomarov case, have you?" Natassja asked.

"Tomarov? Why would anyone care about a shit like Tomarov? He's dead, isn't he?" Osin said.

"That's what I've just read," Grozky said, holding up his folded paper.

"There you go. Fuck Tomarov. Let me buy you both a

drink," Osin said, turning towards the bar before Grozky could respond. Grozky felt Natassja's signal as she gripped and released his forearm.

"Iakov, we have to go. We should catch up another time," Grozky said, placing a hand on his acquaintance's shoulder.

Osin turned, handicapped by his stupor. Grozky reached into a pocket, retrieved a card from his wallet, and handed it to Osin.

"What's the best number to reach you on, Iakov?" Natassja asked.

Osin, battling to stuff Grozky's card into a back pocket, struggled with the question.

"So we can meet up for a drink," Natassja added.

"Great idea," Osin said. Still clutching Grozky's card, his hands clambered over his trousers, checking his pockets until he conceded defeat.

"Why don't you write it down?" Natassja suggested, producing a small notepad and pen.

Osin opened the notepad and looked at a blank page for several seconds before scribbling a set of numbers.

"Call me at work. It's where I am most of the time," Osin said, handing back the pad and pen.

"Thank you, Iakov," Natassja said, grinning at her success.

"Have a good evening, Iakov," Grozky said, shaking his hand as they left.

"You too," Iakov said.

They fought their way across the floor of the Imperial Hotel bar.

"I can drop you back at your apartment?" Grozky asked.

"I'm on Mendeleev Street, opposite the Vyborg Metro station."

"It's on my way home," Grozky said.

"Liar."

"It's close enough."

At the doorway to the bar, Grozky glanced back across the room. St Petersburg had survived so much, yet with the demise of communism, the criminals openly competed with businessmen in their rivalry for wealth. Grozky was living in a country he barely knew. He noted the lone smoker who might have been watching them was no longer there.

3

Grozky was in his office at the FSB's headquarters, the *Bolshoi Dom*, 'Big House', checking his AS Val semi-automatic rifle when the telephone rang.

"Valeri, it's Iakov Osin."

Grozky heard the slurred names. It wasn't yet 4 p.m. and Osin's weekend had started early.

"What are you up to? Let's meet for a drink," Osin said.

"I can't tonight."

"Seeing that skirt again? Bring her along."

"It's not that. I'm working."

"Working? On a Saturday? That's not an excuse, that's sad. Come on, let's go out for a drink."

"I'd like to, Iakov. I can't make it tonight."

"Valeri, your hot friend called me," Osin said.

"I thought she might."

"Why is she interested in Yuri Tomarov?"

"Tomarov turned up dead. She's reporting on his death," Grozky said.

"She shouldn't be trying to dig up Tomarov's past."

"I'm sure she'll move onto something else soon," Grozky said.

"I don't know why Tomarov's become such a focus since he died. I've heard the GRU are asking questions. When the GRU become curious, it's never a good sign, know what I mean?"

Grozky knew. With the dissolution of the KGB's 600,000-strong *silovye ministerstva*, 'power ministry', in November 1991, the price for supporting the coup against Mikhail Gorbachev, Russian Military Intelligence (GRU) had become the unrivalled alpha male of the Russian Federation's Security Services. Quite what the GRU's interest was in Tomarov was anyone's guess. If the GRU were asking questions, they had a reason.

"You didn't tell Natassja about the GRU, did you?" Grozky asked.

"Of course not."

"Out of interest, Iakov, was Tomarov under investigation for economic crimes? What charges were pending against him?"

"Valeri, we're not short of people we could investigate, but Tomarov didn't make the list, not in St Petersburg anyway. I'm not aware he'd been charged with anything. Enough about Tomarov. Life's too short, know what I mean? Give me a call when you're free and let's meet up. Bring Natassja. We'll make a night of it."

"Sure, Iakov. Take care of yourself."

Grozky hung up, conscious Tomarov had sidestepped Osin's purview, yet attracted the GRU's. Natassja might yet find she had a bigger story than she expected. Compared to the criminality of organised crime, Tomarov was part of a deeper corruption which had taken root, he thought. In a country where State Security had enforced communism since 1917, suddenly the government had demanded its citizens embrace capitalism. During the mass privatisation from 1992 to 1994, the State Property Committee had valued the Russian Federation's state industries at 150 billion roubles, divided that figure by the country's population of 150 million, and allocated every citizen a voucher for 10,000 roubles. The voucher could be sold, invested in a fund, or exchanged for shares at auction. Grozky's own brush with capitalism had been brief; with inflation surging in 1993, his voucher's value had nosedived and he had felt fortunate to have traded it for a set of second-hand tyres for his car. Marisha had sold her voucher on the Moscow Commodity and Raw Materials Exchange for less than its value, but it was still free money. Soviet values, which had dictated Russian lives for so long, had been upended to drive free enterprise and become a breeding ground for greed where a few, like Tomarov, had seen the opportunity for plunder.

Of late, amidst the chaos which Russians struggled through every day, Grozky had started to feel irritated by his circumstances. That he was better off than many could not console him. He walked to the window of his office and looked out across the Neva river where in the distance a tall tower and spire dominated the skyline. A mile away, surrounded by water on the tiny Hare Island, stood the golden belltower of the Peter and Paul Cathedral. He preferred it in the dark when it glowed in the distance, like a thin flame. There was a reassurance about the glistening steeple, secure on its island, defiant against the night.

It was uncharacteristic, this dissatisfaction. His father would have cursed his melancholy. Keto came from a generation who knew the sacrifices a soldier made, never knowing the outcome of a battle. Keto's own father had been killed at forty-three, among the nine million Red Army personnel killed during the Great Patriotic War. Keto had instilled in his sons the creed that a soldier always embraced his survival, only for his eldest son to become overwhelmed in his struggle to live, killing himself at forty-seven. Grozky was resilient enough not to let Timur's death and a failed marriage chip away at his psyche, their impact was more subtle; his mishaps felt as if they were crystallising the creeping claustrophobia of middle age and the realisation that, at forty-four, his best years were now behind him.

*

A little after 2 a.m. Grozky walked across the floor of the Big House's garage, his footfall masked by the rubber crepe soles of his worn, blackened shoes. He'd taken time to craft his appearance into a composite of partial care. The dark slacks and navy open-necked shirt were offset by a grey sports jacket, thinned by age, and a day's growth on his jaw. To those he met he would appear a man of limited means who had made the effort to make himself presentable. Initially, he would be unarmed and after that limited to only his P-9 Gyurza pistol, but the firepower of the criminal brigades required a weapon in reserve.

Going head-to-head with the gangs was a dangerous endeavour. His peers distrusted his zeal. Such purpose could get you killed. He did not blame Marisha for leaving him. The odds were against him.

With the rewards at stake the gangs could afford to be ruthless. There were huge profits to be made in Europe and America. The gangs sold guns for drugs. With the cuts to the army, the Russian Federation was awash with guns. If it wasn't Kyrgyzstan it was trading with the Mujahideen in Afghanistan. Grozky was not an embittered man, reserving his rage for the enemy who scorned his stupidity in accepting the paltry state salary. Timur might still be alive except for the availability of heroin. In the moments when he wondered at the futility of his endeavour, his fury stoked his resolve.

Since the start of the year the frequency of FSB raids had increased as General Donitsyn, the Deputy Head of the St Petersburg FSB, responded to the Kremlin's demands for results with the zeal of an NKVD kommissar. Donitsyn was rumoured to be seeking officers for a new, specialist unit to target the drug gangs. Grozky hoped it was true.

Ahead of him, the garage resembled a hotel forecourt with a line of a half-dozen taxis standing in front of a pair of unmarked cars. In contrast, the FSB men who moved around them looked anything but civilian, garbed in black and the heavy jump boots favoured by the paramilitary. He'd handpicked his squad. On their heads full-face balaclavas were rolled up and worn like caps. They focused on their weapons, checking the silencers on semi-automatic rifles, adding magazine clips to their harnesses and securing pistols in holsters. If there was one saving grace to the army's decline, it was the quality of candidates desperate to join the FSB. Across the Baltic, Military District personnel had applied in their thousands from northern outposts like Arkhangelsk, at the edge of the White Sea, to those units cast out from Lithuania, Latvia and Estonia.

Grozky was noticed and heads turned. The largest man in the group hurried to meet him. Senior Lieutenant Dmitri Borzoi had been with the 37th Motor Rifle Division under the 30th Guards Army Corps stationed at Vyborg, eighty-five miles to the north-west of St Petersburg, before his division had been disbanded. Though the clothes could not disguise the discipline in his stride, his furrowed brow betrayed the anxiety behind his grin. When Borzoi half raised two hands in a conciliatory gesture, Grozky knew an explanation would be forthcoming.

"We're ready except we're waiting for Stepan Nedev," Borzoi said.

"What's his reason?"

"I don't know. I've tried calling him. No response."

Grozky frowned. Nedev was his liaison with the OMON, a special-purpose militia of the Russian Ministry of the Interior, the MVD. Without a tip from Nedev, he would not have identified a quayside warehouse on Gutuyev Island being used to distribute drugs. Grozky knew Nedev should have notified the MVD's Department of Extradepartmental Protection, the OVO, of the FSB's surveillance at the docks and he hadn't. The grand-sounding OVO were little more than moonlighting policemen for whom the sale of information represented a lucrative sideline. Nedev's absence was out of character.

"Nedev is very late. We don't have time to wait. We go without him and we go now," Grozky said.

"Understood."

Borzoi turned, raised his arms over his head, his double clap echoing like staccato across the garage. He shouted the order.

"Time to go."

Immediately the men moved to their vehicles, faces stern with anticipation. Engines started, disturbed by the rapid percussion of slamming doors as the men embarked. The taxis and their casually dressed FSB drivers were a nice touch, Grozky conceded, as commonplace as drunks in the early hours of the morning.

Amidst the scramble Grozky saw Borzoi ahead, holding open a rear door of an unmarked, white Lada Riva estate. It was ironic, Grozky thought, that five months earlier Borzoi had been reluctant to serve under a passed-over ex-KGB major still fortunate to have a livelihood. Grozky paused at the door. Borzoi might have been on parade, his brow intense with purpose.

"Dmitri, there's no need to stand on ceremony. You owe me nothing," Grozky said.

"Far from it and you know it, sir," Borzoi said, grinning.

"Rubbish. All I did was put in a good word for you."

"A good word, indeed."

"Listen, Dmitri, all that matters is you passed the FSB's new Certification Programme for Honest Officers. You weren't to know we were using agent provocateurs from the MVD to offer bribes."

Grozky had no wish to be reminded Borzoi had passed with such flying colours they bled.

"I allowed myself to be provoked. You got me off the hook. I can't thank you enough," Borzoi said.

"Don't blame yourself. An MVD operative baited you about your honesty. It was a fair fight and you left him with concussion and two broken ribs. The MVD demanded your dismissal because you embarrassed them. All I did was point out the MVD is applying a double standard. How can they criticise the FSB when they're expanding their own organisation without any comparable honesty programme? We'll say no more on the matter, agreed?"

"Very well. If there's anything I can do for you, you're to let me know. I owe you my career," Borzoi said.

"Good, let's go," Grozky said and got into the car. Amidst a country facing moral collapse, the Russian Federation had never needed men of principle more. Borzoi was worth saving, though the senior lieutenant had a lot to learn. If there was one constant since the fall of communism, it was that everyone was watched. It was a deterrent the government relied upon.

It was too bad about Nedev, Grozky concluded as his driver, a young corporal named Pasha Fett, touched the horn and the Lada pulled away, leading the small convoy.

At the entrance to the garage, an FSB guard, his head previously barely visible from the window in his office, appeared at the doorway, his hand raised in an informal salute. Fett acknowledged him with a wave before his hand flicked to the dashboard and the bright beams of the headlights illuminated the short ramp.

As the Lada passed through the open gates and into the night, Grozky caught a glimpse of a darkened figure on the opposite side of Zakharyev Street.

"Who the hell is that?" Borzoi said.

Grozky leant forward. Swathed in the headlights, a silhouette in blackened camouflage made no attempt to move until the Lada neared, when he stepped back, absorbed into the night.

"Pull up," Grozky said.

Fett's face was hard as he stopped the taxi against the kerb, the Lada's engine idling. The line of vehicles drew by before the brake lights on the last taxi brightened and the column halted, ahead of them.

"Wait here," Grozky said, checking the ceiling light was off before he opened the door.

He felt the freezing damp embrace his skin through his

thin clothes. He closed the door quietly as Borzoi joined him. Around them the darkness was undisturbed, the handful of streetlights isolated in shadow.

They walked in silence, the mist from their breath barely visible. Ahead, the sudden flare of a match illuminated a dark form lighting a cigarette. A greeting followed.

"Good evening. I hope I didn't startle you."

Grozky recognised the voice of Stepan Nedev. He sounded tired.

"Stepan, it's good to see you. We didn't think you were going to make it. What happened?" Grozky asked.

Nedev walked up to him and extended a gloved hand. As Grozky shook it he saw Nedev's face was strained. Behind Nedev, Grozky noticed the outline of a second man.

"I'm sorry I'm so late. There's been a lot going on," Nedev replied.

"I'm sure," Grozky said.

"My superior asked to join the operation tonight. It was a sudden decision otherwise I would have raised it with you."

"I see," Grozky said.

From out of the shadows, the man stepped forward. He was shorter than Nedev and wore the same darkened camouflage, his partially rolled-up balaclava reducing his face to eyes, nose and mouth.

"This is my superior, Major Emile Rastich," Nedev said.

"Gentlemen," Rastich said. His poker features could not hide the irritation in his voice.

Grozky's wariness turned to unease. Were it not for the time, he would have challenged Rastich's presence, for the OMON were renowned for their brutality. During *zachitsya*, or cleansing operations against Chechen rebels, an OMON unit had been implicated in the massacre of 300 civilians in the border village of Samashki. In the new Russia such paramilitary excess went unchecked.

"Well, you're dressed for the occasion. That's as much of an invitation as you need from me, Major Rastich. There's space in our car. You can both ride with us," Grozky said.

"Thank you," Nedev said.

They returned to the car and drove north, across Foundry Bridge, to be absorbed into the industrial hinterland of the Vyborg District. The vehicles split up, taking separate routes to their destination.

"Major Rastich, I'm indebted to Stepan. His assistance has helped us identify the Red Star Bar as a major distribution point," Grozky said.

Grozky heard the sigh before Rastich responded.

"I only heard about this raid from Stepan a few hours ago. Why so late? Why didn't the FSB communicate it to the District Security Council?"

Rastich made his question an accusation. Next to him, Grozky sensed Nedev's discomfort at the situation.

"This has primarily been an FSB surveillance operation. There are so many of those I doubt it warranted any special mention. The District Security Council will be fully debriefed after this operation," Grozky said.

"I'm sure I don't need to remind you the FSB has a responsibility to keep the MVD informed," Rastich said.

"You do not," Grozky said, in the spirit of understanding. This was not the time for inter-agency squabbling. Despite the Kremlin's renewed pressure for results, the sharing of information remained a pissing match between the FSB and the MVD, depending upon when each decided to cock its proverbial leg on the other's patch.

Glancing behind him, Grozky was reassured to see a

distant set of headlights. His team, including the vans from the detention facility on Tapestry Street, would converge near the Red Star Bar. The club was typical of the new breed, a converted warehouse a few miles from St Petersburg's centre. South of Muzhestva Square Metro station stood the Red October machine plant, hemmed in between Avenue of the Unvanquished to the north and the railway yard to the south. Amidst the faded industry the private club offered cheap alcohol to those for whom the expensive nightspots were beyond their means. The formula of partying, booze and drugs offered a cocktail of addiction to those who could least afford it.

The journey took less than twenty minutes, the vehicles converging again at the side of a derelict factory.

"What happens now?" Rastich asked.

"You and Stepan stay with Dmitri's squad," Grozky said and got out of the taxi. Around him the FSB teams disembarked. Soon Grozky was surrounded by the half-dozen FSB drivers and the dark shadows of armed men in full-face balaclavas. But for their shoulder flashes even the OMON pair would have been indistinguishable amongst the armed men.

"Right, you know the plan, let's get this done," Grozky said. "Use your silenced weapons as a last resort. Unless there are final questions, I'll see you inside."

"Good luck," Borzoi said.

Grozky left the group and walked back to his taxi. From inside his worn sports jacket he took an unopened half-bottle of cheap brandy, broke the seal and took a short slug. He gargled and then spat the coarse liquid across his hands, wiping them across his cheeks and finally running them through his hair. Satisfied, he left the bottle in the glove compartment of the Lada.

The faint luminosity of his watch dial showed 2.35 a.m. As Grozky walked, he focused on his gait becoming less steady and forcing the muscles of his weakened right leg to take the pressure. He was good at balance from years of shifting his weight in the five-minute wrestling bouts. A man at this hour in the morning would be expected to be tipsy. His limp only showed when he walked fast, his dominant left leg compensating for his right. Any sign of an injury would attract questions. He must avoid that.

Slow and unsteady, Grozky inhabited his persona, welcoming the release the good-natured drunk provided from the tension of his existence. He'd visited the bar enough times, clapping the security personnel on the shoulder and been warned not to, that he'd be remembered. Tonight, he'd behave and trade on his familiarity.

Ahead, the long hulk of the warehouse came into view, the doors at the gable end lit up beneath a brazen neon red pentagonal star. Emblazoned under the Soviet icon, the English words 'THE RED STAR BAR' in a gaudy Cyrillic typeface denoted its new purpose. Grozky saw the strobes piercing the first-floor windows like haphazard searchlights before he heard the thump of the bass through the walls.

Even at this hour the club's entrance was a portcullis of security, the two guards at the bottom of the steps matched by a pair above.

"Evening, friend, I'm just stopping by to have one for the road," Grozky said.

The body search by the first set of doormen was brief and thorough. The second, faces set like alabaster, ignored him as he passed through the phalanx of defence.

Inside, a sea of patrons swelled between the brick walls, leaving those seated as copses of humanity compressed against stained pine tables masquerading as oak. Pretty waitresses dropped their grins as they fought their way through the drinkers. The shoals of noise and movement were his ally, absorbing the attention of the barmen who doubled as security guards.

Battling his way through the crowds, Grozky reached the short queue where another pair of goons vetted anyone wishing to go upstairs. A skinny man in front of him was refused access, his protests ignored as the broad arm of a guard funnelled him to one side.

"I'm not here to dance," Grozky said, the folded 10,000-rouble notes inconspicuous between a thumb and forefinger. He felt the glare of their challenge before the cash was slipped from his hand. It was a routine he'd been through before.

Grozky walked up to the landing, the banisters splitting to form a balustrade overlooking the ground floor. In front of him a double set of swing doors struggled to mask the din from the disco. He'd recced the layout of the upper floor on a previous visit. To his right, the corridor led into what looked like a dead end, except for the metal door embedded into the inner wall, the club's drug-dealing room. Behind that was the room he could not have hoped to reconnoitre, the hidden heart of the castle.

Grozky shuffled forwards, as if he was about to enter the disco, but then turned left, like a man remembering something. He reached the end of the landing and turned the corner. Ahead he saw the emergency exit signs from the disco's toilets and, at the far end, the fire exit door. Grozky expected the single guard by the fire exit, a precaution to prevent the clientele from letting their friends in via the external stairwell. Grozky pottered towards him, ignoring the egress from the men's room and pausing to consider the door to the women's toilets before discounting it. By the time he reached the guard, his disorientation was a matter of record.

"Hey, my old friend, where did the girls go?" Grozky asked. He wobbled, finishing his question with a chuckle of revelry.

"You're not going to find any here. Go back to the disco and you'll find plenty," the guard said.

"Good man."

Grozky considered a short jab to the throat or a knee to his testicles. Instead, he half turned and slipped against the fire door, catching the release bar as he fell. Lying on the floor he felt the cold breeze of success.

"You idiot," the guard said, his bemusement vanishing as the suppressor on Borzoi's 9A-91 compact assault rifle punched into his chest.

"This is an FSB raid. On your knees and keep quiet if you want to stay in one piece," Borzoi said, driving the guard against the wall as the FSB squad entered.

The guard was gagged and handcuffed before being marched down the fire escape.

Borzoi handed Grozky his P-9 Gyurza pistol and holster.

"Thank you, Dmitri, I feel better dressed already," Grozky said. He quickly attached the weapon to his belt, resting it at the back under his jacket.

Grozky led the FSB team along the corridor, the casually dressed men in front masking the black-clad ones behind. The exit from the women's toilets was secured by a wedge under the door and then the FSB men disappeared into the men's room, leaving Grozky to continue alone. The infiltration of the disco had started.

On the landing, Grozky saw a young man stumble from the other corridor, his face blushed with euphoria. He supported himself against the wall until Grozky helped him to the stairs and propped him against the balustrade. Grozky checked the ground floor below. He saw the crowds drinking, swearing and singing, disassociated from everything except enjoying the moment.

When Grozky entered the disco, his senses were seared by the repetitive beat of techno music. His eyes struggled in the dark, finding a dim light from the bar near the entrance before he realised he'd been surrounded by three of his civilian-attired FSB vanguard. He heard Kostya Gagolin's voice in his ear.

"We're all good, sir."

"Good work, Kostya," Grozky said.

He walked to the bar, accompanied by Gagolin. Behind the counter stood his driver, Pasha Fett, and, when Grozky glanced over the top, he saw two security guards sitting on the floor, cuffed. The younger of the pair looked terrified, as if he might be abducted without trace.

Grozky left Gagolin at the bar and made his way back through the shadow towards the glow of the sign to the men's toilets. The urgency of the music was not matched by the activity on the dancefloor. He estimated twenty-plus bodies, their exhaustion frozen into snapshots by the strobe beams dissecting the crowd. At every pulse of light, Grozky could not dispel an irrational fear the illumination would betray him.

When he entered the toilets, the brace of FSB men loitering by the door ignored him. The smell of fresh disinfectant could not disguise the stench of vomit, while the rhythmic thump of the music intruded through the walls.

Grozky walked to the back and found Dmitri Borzoi in discussion with Rolan Gubanov, his plain clothes anomalous against the masked squad in black.

"Well done, Dmitri," Grozky said.

Borzoi looked up, his face taut.

"We have a problem, Valeri," Borzoi said.

The armed men stepped aside and Grozky saw the floorplan resting on top of a sink.

"Your reconnaissance was good. We've secured the disc jockey's booth. It's what's behind it," Borzoi said, handing Grozky the floorplan.

Grozky saw the fresh pencil marks on the plan where a pair of lines now joined the rear of the disco to the club's hidden room. Where there had previously only been one entrance, through the drug-dealing room, now there was a second hidden access point from inside the disco.

"What is this?" Grozky asked.

"Who knows," Borzoi said. "Rolan secured the booth and saw a curtain hanging at the back. He checked it, expecting to find a cupboard and found the corridor. It leads to a door."

"Guarded?" Grozky asked.

"No, but the hinges are recessed and there's no handle," Gubanov said.

"We were just planning to work around that. We have a pair of skeleton keys," Borzoi said and reached across to relieve a man of a squat hand-held battering ram. Borzoi swung it, making the twenty kilograms of steel look like a plastic plank.

Grozky nodded, considering the situation. He felt cheated to have secured the dancefloor only to discover the flaw in his planning. If a new door had been added, what other changes had been made to the upper floor? The floorplan indicated two rooms adjacent to the disco. Now he could not be sure.

"It's only a door. We take it out and we take down whoever's behind it. We're as ready as we're going to be," Borzoi said.

"Agreed, except once that entrance is compromised, the occupants will likely use the other to escape. Dmitri, your team will start the assault and I'll cover the dealing room from the other corridor. We'll still keep a lookout at the top of the stairs," Grozky said.

"Understood," Borzoi said.

"Rolan, go ahead and evacuate the dancefloor as we rehearsed. It's for their own safety. They go down the fire escape and you can hold them in the vans for now. Take the captured security guards with you."

"Yes, sir," Gubanov said.

"Stepan and I will give you a hand," Major Emile Rastich said.

"I appreciate your assistance, sir," Gubanov said.

"Dmitri, taking the upper floor is now a pincer movement. Give me five minutes to get into position. Look after yourself," Grozky said.

"Sure, Valeri, you too," Borzoi said, pulling his balaclava over his face.

Grozky left the toilets, relieved to leave the rancid smell. The dance floor was now blasted in permanent lighting, while the music continued to pummel the partying incumbents. Awoken from the numbing reverie of the strobes, the revellers' discomfort was compounded by the heavily armed men who surrounded them.

On his way out of the disco, Grozky poured himself a double vodka and took it with him. When he reached the landing, he found Kostya Gagolin smoking, his jacket over one arm to shield his pistol. Gagolin ignored him, the image of a man cooling off from the disco, while his vantage point gave him a clear view of the disco's entrance, the ground floor and the corner of the corridor to the drug-dealing room.

It was when Grozky reached the dead end and stared at the closed metal grill of the door to the drug-dealing room that he felt the palpitation start in his chest. He took a nip from the glass, enjoying the alcohol resting on his tongue and the tingling warmth soften his palate. He yearned to drink, yet defied the urge, instead allowing the fumes to embrace his throat and creep up the back of his nostrils. In that moment he dispelled any self-doubt, swilled the vodka around in his mouth and spat it out onto the floor where it shrank into the stained carpet. He felt under the back of his jacket, familiarising himself with the location of his pistol's grip.

He knocked on the grill, the laconic double tap of absent-minded purpose. Nothing happened. Grozky gave it a few seconds and when he rapped again, it was slower and harder. This time the grill was drawn back and a pair of eyes scowled at him from behind the door.

"I came for a little taste of heroin," Grozky said.

"Wait."

The eyes watched him for longer than Grozky cared for. Then the face behind the door moved back and, as the grill closed, Grozky caught a glimpse of a fat man sitting behind a desk.

The door opened a crack and the unsmiling face of the gatekeeper surveyed him. He was a couple of inches taller than Grozky and with a presence marking him out as more than just muscle.

"It's been a great evening," Grozky said, exhaling vodka fumes with a fatigue he did not feel.

"Leave your drink outside," the gatekeeper said.

Grozky allowed himself a few seconds, shrugged and then deposited the glass on the floor outside with theatrical care for its meagre contents.

He returned to the small room and heard the door spring shut behind him with a loud click. Conscious of the gatekeeper's scrutiny he did not turn around, instead he kept his eyes on the squat thug behind the desk counting rouble notes, a pistol beside him, the blare of the music an intrusion in the confined space. To his right Grozky saw another door, its handle protected by a keypad. This drug den was the last gatehouse behind which lay the throne room of the Red Star Bar. Was it one room or two? He was on his own until Borzoi's team reached him.

"I've not seen you before. You don't look like a user," the gatekeeper said.

"I've been downstairs a few times. All I'm after is a little heroin."

"You seem too relaxed to be a user."

"Relaxed? I should hope so. I've been drinking since five."

There was a pause as the gatekeeper reflected on his response and the fat thug continued to count the money. Grozky waited, his listlessness passing for patience.

"I'm going to have to disappoint you. We're out of heroin," the fat thug said, without looking up from his task.

Grozky allowed himself a quizzical expression at the news.

"Not even…" Grozky said.

He didn't get to finish the sentence.

"So, come back next week for a taste, eh?" the fat thug said and Grozky saw his eyes move to the gatekeeper. Grozky's audience was at an end.

The metronome in Grozky's mind counted down the fuse to confrontation.

"Pah, if you've got no heroin, what about some amphetamine?"

Grim-faced, the thug behind the desk shook his head.

"No? What about some dope? I could really use a good smoke." Grozky half turned, bringing the gatekeeper into the exchange. The man's neutral expression gave Grozky no insight as to whether his request would be considered.

"I can pay," Grozky said. With a hint of hope, he held up a hand to postpone the decision while his other reached for the pocket of his jacket.

The thug behind the desk suddenly glared at him. Grozky didn't wait for the man's ire to manifest itself. When his hand emerged from his jacket it held his pistol. The fat man behind the desk gawped in shock while the gatekeeper squinted in anger.

"You won't get away with this," the gatekeeper said.

"With what? You don't know what I want," Grozky said. On top of the desk, he saw the thug's hand creep towards the pistol.

"Don't do it," Grozky said.

The gatekeeper stayed still with the poise of a reptile preparing to strike, while his subordinate's hand inched across the desk. *The man has no choice*, thought Grozky.

"What do you want?" the gatekeeper asked.

The question was redundant for at that moment the gatekeeper hurled himself at Grozky. Grozky fired at the most immediate threat and his bullet took the thug behind the desk in the shoulder, spinning him as he fell backwards to the floor with a cry of pain. Then the gatekeeper was upon him.

Forceful hands clawed for his pistol, the gatekeeper's fingers binding around Grozky's with the grip of a python.

Grozky yelped as an index finger was crushed against the trigger guard. He grappled against his opponent, stepping inside to brace his shoulder against his adversary's chest and pivot the man's weight against him. The gatekeeper compensated in turn, using the momentum to twist Grozky, so that they both stumbled. Off balance, Grozky took the initiative and countered again, prevailing until his weakened leg failed to hold his foe's weight and they both fell to the floor.

Winded, Grozky found himself pinned beneath the gatekeeper, their hands still bound together around the weapon which would determine the victor. Grozky brought his left knee up sharply, connecting with a thigh. The gatekeeper grunted at the impact and then retaliated, using his weight to force Grozky's arms against his chest, the purchase enabling him to push himself up and get his knees either side of Grozky. There was the dampened staccato of muffled shots in the next room. Grozky rallied to the sound, his arms twisting with a feint to the left before thrusting to the right. The gatekeeper struggled to contain him and then suddenly he was knocked sideways as the stock of a 9A-91 compact assault rifle butt connected with his head. Grozky saw a masked head above him and the grinning face of Pasha Fett behind.

"I'm sure you'd have had him, eventually," Borzoi said as he retrieved the pistol from the desk.

"Timing is everything, Dmitri," Grozky said.

From the floor, the thug moaned.

"It looks like that one needs some attention," Borzoi said.

"He'll live. How did you fare?"

"It was one room. There were four of them, one's dead and one's wounded. None of ours were hurt," Borzoi said.

He used a pair of handcuffs to secure the unconscious gatekeeper's hands behind his back.

"Good. I want a full inventory," Grozky said.

"Of course, Valeri," Borzoi said.

"Leave a handful of your squad here and then take the rest down the fire escape with Pasha and our plainclothes men. You take the front entrance as planned. I'll take Kostya and secure the stairs."

"See you shortly," Borzoi said.

Fett manhandled the moaning thug to his feet and Borzoi picked up the unconscious gatekeeper, putting him over a shoulder. They left the way they had come.

Grozky checked himself, relieved his finger was not broken and only his right thigh was sore from the tumble. The main casualty was a large tear on the back of a jacket sleeve. He returned to the landing, clapping Gagolin on the back and relaying his order as if it were a greeting. Gagolin smiled back.

Keeping one hand on the banister, Grozky ambled down the stairs. As he reached the pair of guards at the bottom, Gagolin came alongside him.

"My friends, I hope you had as good an evening as I did," Grozky said loudly. "Alas, all good things must come to an end."

"Indeed, they must," Gagolin replied.

The guards ignored them until Grozky spoke quietly.

"Don't be alarmed, but if you glance down at the jacket my friend is carrying, you'll see the barrel of his pistol. He won't give you any trouble, providing you stand there as if we're having a few words, which we are."

Grozky saw the guards' faces bristle at his effrontery while Gagolin covered them with more than a disarming grin.

"What the hell do you want?" a guard asked.

"I'm waiting for some friends," Grozky said.

He watched the chaos around him; the bar's clientele, inebriated by liquor and narcotics, sat, stood, cheered and sang to get through the marathon of their evening. He caught a glimpse of the casually dressed FSB men enter the room, filtering into the crowd. He could not see them secure the bar, but heard shouts at the cessation of service.

Borzoi appeared at the entrance, a megaphone in his hand and flanked by several of his squad, their automatic weapons readied. The revellers closest to the doorway turned to wonder at the armed men. There was a short pause then Borzoi's voice boomed out.

"Ladies and gentlemen, this is an FSB raid. The Red Star Bar is now closed. Please finish your drinks and leave the premises."

The lights in the room suddenly came to life, bright illumination broadcasting the end to the evening. The chattering hubbub stuttered. Borzoi repeated his command, the message reinforced by the pairs of the FSB squad who moved among the crowd, tapping the tables with their guns' suppressors. The timbre of muddled conversation stalled.

"It's time to leave. Now," Borzoi said.

Slowly, the Red Star Bar's customers responded, several supporting each other as they stood up. Most shuffled and staggered towards the entrance while a few stood, their reluctance etched in angry stares at the armed spoilsports.

"You bastards won't get away with this," one of the security men said as Gagolin handcuffed him.

4

G rozky found Nedev in the hidden operations room of the Red Star Bar, taking photographs of maps on a wall. Of Major Rastich there was no sign.

"What happened to your boss?" Grozky asked.

"He left with the others," Nedev replied.

"What have you found?"

"More than we expected, but not what we were looking for. A fair amount of cash, plenty of dope and pills. Barely a trace of heroin and we've turned the room over a few times. Unless it's stashed somewhere else, that's our haul for tonight."

Grozky heard the disappointment in Nedev's voice.

"Well done, Stepan. A good night's work," Grozky said. He looked at the maps, noting the largest one where several routes across the city were highlighted.

"What do you make of it?" he asked.

"You'll see most of these routes end up at or near to the docks on Gutuyev Island. That's close to commercial freight routes and the Gunboat Shipyard. Different routes, same destination. Based on the surveillance, I would say the distribution network supplies St Petersburg as well as shipping overseas," Nedev said.

Grozky looked at the map and the organised pattern of lines across the city. There would be other clubs and bars.

"Look here," Nedev said, pointing to where the Red Star Bar was highlighted by an 'x' in red biro. It was the only location marked on the map.

"Do you think if we checked out the other bars and clubs on these highlighted streets we'd find other such maps?" Grozky asked.

"We might. At least this helps to narrow down the other areas of search. We can start by cross-checking establishments on these streets with arrest and criminal records."

"Good work. I'll impress upon Major Rastich how much you've contributed to this operation," Grozky said.

"Thank you. I appreciate that."

Grozky sensed Nedev wanted to say something else, but at that moment Borzoi entered the room, rattling a set of keys.

"Unless you're keen to stay in this shithole, we're ready to go," Borzoi said.

"Anything else you need up here, Stepan?" Grozky asked.

"All done, except the maps. Then we can go," Nedev said.

Grozky helped Borzoi and Nedev take down the maps and place them on top of the box of evidence. Nedev carried it downstairs.

The ground floor was empty, reeking of smoke and sweat. Empty bottles and discarded glasses covered the tables and, on the back of a chair, someone had forgotten a coat.

"I'll be glad to get out of this dump. I'll lock up," Borzoi said, holding up his keys.

"That's thoughtful of you," Grozky said.

Outside, it was fresh and cold, the air damp from the earlier rain. Parked in front of the club were the taxis they had arrived in, the illumination of their fare lights redundant. Grozky saw Rastich talking with Nedev by the first of the taxis. Rastich was smiling, his mood improved from the man Grozky had first met.

"Valeri, over here."

Grozky turned to see Pasha Fett, waving at him, his head half out of the Lada. Grozky walked towards the car and saw Borzoi relieving himself against the side of the club's steps.

Getting into the back of the car, Grozky's relief at the end of the raid was tempered by the outcome. The intelligence would be useful, yet their haul was low-grade marijuana and pills for the dance crowd. There was a sudden rap on the glass of Fett's window and then Kostya Gagolin opened a rear door and sat next to Grozky, grinning with a lit cigarette clamped between his teeth.

Fett started the engine as Borzoi arrived, eased himself into the passenger seat and slammed the door. Moments later the Lada moved slowly forward, following the taxi in front. The Lada had barely done twenty yards when the brake lights of the taxi ahead of them glowed and Fett braked sharply. His passengers rocked forward, a shower of sparks scattering from Gagolin's cigarette as his hand clipped the back of Fett's headrest.

"Shit, what now?" Fett exclaimed.

"A fare can't pay," Gagolin said, to muted laughter.

Grozky opened his door, securing a foot on the cobbles and a hand on the roof. Half out of the car, he could see nothing ahead except the headlights of the lead vehicle staring into the blackness. The engines of the vehicles were still idling when the firing started.

*

Grozky heard Fett calling for support on the Lada's radio. Ahead of him, pinpricks of light lit up the dark followed by the cacophony of automatic gunfire. The muzzle flashes flicked on and off, masking their origin. The noise and bluster seemed unreal until flames emerged from the first taxi and the cab's silhouette erupted in an explosion, the pyrotechnics illuminating prone figures inside.

The FSB men scrambled from the vehicles, the open car doors forming shields as they returned fire. Grozky pushed himself from the car, ran to the boot and grabbed his AS Val assault rifle and ammunition, the belt becoming a bandolier. Borzoi was already shooting back, his 9A-91 compact assault rifle wedged between the door and the chassis he crouched behind.

Grozky threw himself down, wincing as his elbow clipped the curb and then the stock of his AS Val found his shoulder and he aimed into the darkness. He saw a pair of gun flashes, winking together, and fired, the recoil from the heavy 9x39mm rounds banished by the stab of pain from his damaged trigger finger. His bullets powered into the night, muted by the integrated suppressor while the spent casings jangled against the ground.

Another ignition rose above the gunfire, the cracking explosion of a grenade. The second taxi took the brunt, fragmented shards from its shattered windscreen clipping across the cobbles like fractured ice. Grozky cursed as an FSB man by the vehicle slumped to the ground.

Amidst the noise and the dark, Grozky struggled to get his bearings. Illuminated outside the Red Star Bar, the line of taxis was the underdog in the exchange. Twenty yards to his right he saw the outline of a narrow alley between two buildings. He racked his memory, recalling a group of four workshops converging on a small quadrangle. To stay pinned down was madness. Their attackers would pick them off and, at this hour, Grozky and his men were on their own until help arrived.

From the opposite side of the car Grozky heard Pasha Fett and Kostya Gagolin firing like trigger-happy cowboys. Grozky made his decision and shouted to them.

"Pasha – Dmitri and I are going to try and work our way round. We can't all stay here."

"Okay," Fett shouted back, then fired again.

"Dmitri – follow me," Grozky said and began to crawl towards the back of the car, ignoring the discomfort every time his raw elbow scraped the cobbles. He reached the back of the taxi, stopping to fire at the bright lights at the top of the lamp posts. Borzoi followed his lead. The bulbs shattered, and the light fell away, leaving the fluttering glow from the bonfire of a taxi.

On the other side of the car Grozky found Gagolin, crouched behind his door and reloading his 9A-91. Fett was still blasting away.

In the sudden darkness Grozky's vision struggled to adjust, the thin wedge of the dark alley barely visible. At least their silhouettes would be masked.

"There's no point both of us getting killed. I'll go first," Grozky said.

"I'll cover you," Gagolin said, lining up his 9A-91.

Fett fired another short burst as Grozky and Borzoi crouched, like sprinters taking their marks. Gagolin fired a thunderous salvo and Grozky ran, tearing across the open ground. His ragged breath and running feet seemed to broadcast his position. He reached the gap unscathed and, as the firing ceased, Borzoi joined him.

Standing in the alley, Grozky struggled to catch his breath. His right leg ached. He could not recall the last time he'd been for a run. Probably before Fedorov had stitched up his thigh. He waited until his panting lungs recovered, supporting himself against the wall, his hand feeling the damp brick and mortar. Once these buildings might have been home to industrious artisans, now they were dark and derelict. Borzoi's hulk crouched next to him.

Grozky inched forward, the buildings on either side compounding the night, a faint stripe of dark grey ahead at the end of the narrow alley. Behind him the gunfight was now in earnest, a furious exchange of rapid fire.

He reached the end of the building and crouched down. Ahead, Grozky was relieved to make out a small piece of open ground around which buildings clustered. He was where he hoped he would be. He did not hear Borzoi next to him, there was just a light squeeze from the powerful paw on his right shoulder. Despite his size, Dmitri Borzoi could be surprisingly agile.

His orientation re-established, Grozky estimated their assailants must be firing from the embankment above the railway lines. It was a strong position, providing a wide field of fire, the gunmen shielded by the lie of the land. Grozky kept still as he surveyed the darkened square lest he attract a lethal burst of bullets from an unseen gun. He spoke to Borzoi, his voice low.

"Dmitri, this quadrangle sits in between four buildings. We can cut left and come out opposite the railway embankment. We can fire once we get to the top of the next alleyway."

"Sounds like a plan," Borzoi said.

"I can only hope that they haven't got infra-red sights," Grozky said.

"Christ."

"We need every gun we've got so take it slow."

"Understood. I'll follow you," Borzoi said.

Grozky lay on the ground, his AS Val held out in front of him, and started crawling along the edge of the square. Every minute he delayed would be taking its toll on his men, yet caution was a necessity. He felt the cold seep through his thin clothes, his breathing regular and calm.

The gunfire became more muted as they skirted the side of the small square. Wedged against the wall in the still air, Grozky smelt the sweat and cordite on himself. Confined in darkness for several minutes his night vision was improving. He made out a low outline at the centre of the quadrangle that might have been a small fountain or a well.

They reached the start of the next alley. Grozky paused, hearing the gunfire pick up, the source their assailants' weapons. Ahead he made out the edge of the building beyond which their enemy waited. His eyes strained, seeking any movement which might indicate a hidden figure.

Satisfied, Grozky crawled forward cautiously. Progress was slow; his adrenaline was fading and the icy stones harbouring him sucked the heat from his body. He focused on the image of the bodies in the burning taxi, feeling his anger rise. He crushed the AS Val between his hands, forcing the heat into his muscles. Slowly he felt the warmth creep back.

Ahead, as the sound of heavy gunfire raged, Grozky wondered how his adversaries had found them. This was no opportune ambush. Behind him, Borzoi's presence was as silent as the stone.

Grozky inched closer until he reached the corner of the building. He felt a careful nudge against his arm – Borzoi signalling he had brought his 9A-91 to bear.

Together they listened to the gunfire, watching the muzzle flashes now no more than forty to fifty feet away, making out the ground and seeking any marker which might improve their aim. When they opened fire, their bursts were targeted and accurate, hammering the edge of the embankment.

Grozky heard shouts of alarm from their attackers. Seconds later, a hail of bullets peppered the wall above Grozky's head, scattering shards of brickwork. Grozky winced as something sharp clipped his forehead and then he felt the blood sliding down his skin. He wiped it away, trying to keep his vision clear.

Shielded by the edge of the building they held their position while their attackers' guns sought them out. Grozky was grateful for the AS Val, its integrated suppressor reducing his footprint. He and Borzoi alternated their muted bursts, taking it in turns to reload and rake the ground. Once, Grozky heard an attacker cry out.

To his left, disciplined calls from his men reached him, rallying each other as they pressed forward. Grozky fired a long burst and then reloaded. He paused as the faint sound of sirens became audible.

"About bloody time!" Borzoi said and fired again.

The gunfire from their attackers faltered momentarily, accompanied by several shouts and then a stream of bullets tore into the wall behind them. Suddenly, the muzzle flashes ceased.

Grozky watched the blackness as Borzoi finished firing and reached for another magazine.

"Hold a moment, Dmitri," Grozky said.

The FSB men defending the taxis continued firing for several more seconds, then they ceased. The eerie silence was filled with a growing wail of klaxons.

They stayed where they were until the first FSB Volvos roared into view, sirens blaring, then they screeched to a stop and armed men disembarked. The fight was over.

Grozky's worst fears were soon confirmed. Their enemy had inflicted a heavy toll: all four occupants of the first taxi were dead, including the OMON's Lieutenant Stepan Nedev, and two men in the front of the second taxi had been killed. Three more FSB men were wounded, one seriously. Despite the hundreds of rounds fired by the FSB, of their assailants there was not a body to be found.

Surveying the outcome, Grozky cursed his luck. The blackened bodies inside the charred taxi were indistinguishable from the men they had once been. The area outside the Red Star Bar no longer resembled an industrial suburb of St Petersburg, it could have been a street scene from the Chechen war.

5

Grozky marched through the open door of General Donitsyn's office in the Big House, the epitome of a parade ground poster. Even the five stitches above his left eye were masked by a flesh-coloured plaster. His attention to detail was a distraction from his state of mind. Shock manifested itself in very different ways as did a man's ability to cope with it. He felt no euphoria at his survival and could not post-rationalise his guilt, haunted by the faces of the six men who had died under his command. There was nothing to link the club's owners to the ambush and the drugs haul was low grade. Minor charges at most. Once repaired, the Red Star Bar would reopen in a matter of weeks.

Despair would have overwhelmed him except for the revenge he craved. By the time he stopped in front of Donitsyn's desk, his black leather wallet case under his arm, and clicked his heels sharply together, it was as much as he could do to stop himself from shaking.

"Major Grozky reporting, sir."

Grozky unzipped his wallet case and extracted his six-page report, the product of his previous night's work. He'd known this gang was well organised but failed to anticipate their capacity for violence. Worse, when he considered the timing of the events, there was the sickening probability he had been betrayed. His actions had cost his men their lives. The words of the post-mortem were redundant. He was culpable.

General Donitsyn looked up from the paper he was reading.

"My report, sir," Grozky said, offering the pages to Donitsyn.

The general took the report and put it on his desk. Until now, barring his run-in with the MVD over Borzoi's suitability for the FSB, Grozky had avoided Donitsyn's scrutiny, which he reckoned was attributable to his steady trickle of results and rarely being in the Big House during normal working hours.

"No need to stand on ceremony. I can imagine you had a rough weekend. Please take a seat." Donitsyn gestured to the two chairs in front of his desk.

Surprised by the civility of his reception, Grozky sat down.

General Donitsyn's hand reached out. Instead of picking up the report it rested on the top page, his fingers splayed wide as if trying to exorcise a bad spirit. He spoke slowly.

"I want you to know I do not hold you responsible for what happened at the Red Star Bar. We must fight each battle as best we can. When we're up against heavily armed criminals, we can't expect it to be on our terms. The violence confirms the FSB is getting close. It's inevitable we're going to incur losses. You are not to blame yourself."

"Sir, my report makes it clear I am fully accountable for the deaths of my men outside the Red Star Bar. I must also report that, having considered the scale of the ambush, my assessment is there was an information leak," Grozky said.

Donitsyn's eyes met his and the Deputy Head of the FSB studied him.

"I can see you blame yourself for what happened. Any responsible officer would. Have you really considered all the possibilities? Your vehicles would have been parked up for over an hour. They could have been spotted. It only takes one phone call to raise the alarm. I will, of course, have all those with knowledge of your raid interviewed and checked."

Listening to Donitsyn, Grozky's vacant stare hid his numbness. Understanding was not what he expected or wanted. He waited for the general to scream and curse him. He deserved to be savaged. More than that, he yearned for the punishment which might somehow give him some small absolution for the death of his men.

"The Head of the St Petersburg MVD called me yesterday to express his regrets. He asked me to pass on his appreciation at your diligence," Donitsyn said.

Grozky was still expecting him to explode into a tirade. The quiet delivery of the next sentence tripped him up.

"I have received a request from Moscow, top priority. A call to arms. You have been selected."

"Selected, sir?"

"Moscow has a fight on its hands. The request for assistance from the St Petersburg FSB came direct from the Kremlin," Donitsyn said, putting Grozky's report to one side.

"This seems very sudden, sir. If I have a choice, I'd prefer to stay in the fight in St Petersburg."

Donitsyn nodded.

"You might have had a choice, except that you were personally selected by General Anatoli Koshygin of the GRU Second Directorate."

Grozky listened, his face stern. He did not know Koshygin, but he knew of the Second Directorate, a close-knit group who saw themselves a cut above the other security agencies and whose dark reputation rarely surfaced to see the light of day.

"I understand, Major Grozky. You want to get back in the ring. I can see that. Trust me, you'll get your shot, but a request at this level from Moscow takes priority."

"May I ask how I was selected?"

"You may. I can see you're not convinced. In short, Moscow needs someone resilient. You take a bullet in the leg and you get back up. You get ambushed and fight back, turning what probably would have become a slaughter into the loss of six men. That's the type of resilience Moscow is after."

Resilient. Donitsyn was being too generous. The brothel of the capital's politics was a far cry from St Petersburg.

Donitsyn beckoned Grozky closer.

"I know you're angry. Save it for when you get back from Moscow. I'm letting you know that in the next few months there will be a new specialist FSB crime-fighting unit. It will be referred to as 'the Division for Investigation of Criminal Organisations' or URPO. It will be an elite unit, developing its own techniques and fighting the criminals by whatever way works best. This is unofficial so keep it to yourself for now. You want to get back at someone, I can see that. Go to Moscow and get back at whoever they're after. Impress Moscow and there'll be a place waiting for you in URPO. I need officers who can keep their heads."

So, it *was* true. Donitsyn was a fox when it came to selling bad news. Grozky's disappointment at being seconded was compensated by the lure of serving in a specialist unit. Donitsyn's black humour in his coded reference to the decapitated FSB captain found floating in the Bypass Canal hid the seriousness of the situation.

"What is the effective date for my transfer to Moscow, sir?"

"This is a top priority. Both you and Lieutenant Borzoi will be flying to Moscow tomorrow morning; there you will be briefed. You know St Petersburg as well as anyone. Effective from tomorrow, you will both be on secondment with the GRU. General Koshygin told me it will be for no more than two to three months."

Grozky was surprised by Borzoi's inclusion.

"I would have expected…"

Donitsyn raised a hand and cut him off.

"I can spare Borzoi. You two work well together."

"Yes, sir."

"Of course, after what happened at the Red Star Bar, there can be no let-up in the fight against those responsible. I've informed the District Security Council I need to raise the ante in the fight against organised crime in St Petersburg. You were building a good working relationship with the OMON. Out of respect for the death of Lieutenant Nedev, I have agreed to strengthen our partnership with the OMON. For that reason, Major Emile Rastich will temporarily replace you and take on the role of central coordination in the ongoing investigative work."

Grozky hoped his face did not show his disquiet. There was no need for such a gesture, yet Donitsyn would have his own reasons. Sitting on the seventh floor, Donitsyn was tipped to succeed the current head of the St Petersburg FSB, General Viktor Cherkesov. The ebb and flow of the games between the agencies was a sign of the times. The KGB's mandate was now splintered across fourteen separate intelligence, security and law enforcement agencies. Amidst the new order of tribalism, distrust reigned. The brotherhood of the wolf had been reduced to a pack of dogs.

"Of course, General," Grozky said.

"There is not much time before you leave for Moscow. The OMON are sending over Major Rastich at 3 p.m. this afternoon. Please ensure you walk him through your operation and hand over copies of relevant information."

"I'll go over everything with him, sir," Grozky said.

"Thank you. The FSB appreciates your commitment." Donitsyn reached down to withdraw a file from his drawer. He handed it to Grozky.

"I was asked to give you this by General Koshygin. It's the GRU file on Yevgeny Kochenko. You can read it on the plane."

"Thank you, sir," Grozky said, taking the file and placing it in his wallet folder. He stood up, snapped to attention and left Donitsyn's office. He was lucky to be alive and that Donitsyn still seemed to have faith in him, yet his new assignment left him uneasy. What could Moscow want with a St Petersburg oligarch? Donitsyn had the cunning of an NKVD kommissar. Instead of giving him the beating he deserved, he'd cast him the bone he craved, except to earn it he'd have to jump through hoops for the Moscow circus. Prove your worth and you can come back for your reward. That seemed to be the bargain.

In the chaos of the last few years Grozky had been transferred from the Ministry of Security to the Federal Counterintelligence Service and then passed to the FSB for the last nine months. Instead of feeling grateful, he couldn't

shake the feeling he was being given up for adoption once
more.

*

It was shortly after 3 p.m. when Grozky received the call from
the security desk advising that Major Rastich had arrived
and was being escorted up. Grozky stood up from the desk
which was too big for his office and stretched. The twinge in
the trapezius muscle in his neck reminded him he had been
sitting too long. He felt tired. He looked at the open file on
his desk, several fresh pages scattered on top from two hours
of typing. Grozky sat again and collated the papers, tapping
them into line against the worn wood before clipping them
inside the cover of the file.

He sensed he was being watched and looked up to see
Rastich leaning against his doorframe. He was dressed in
blue/grey combat fatigues, his black beret the mark of the
OMON as much as their motto, 'We know no mercy and
we do not ask for any'. Grozky wondered how long he had
been there. Only the toothpick twitching from the corner of
Rastich's mouth betrayed his archetypal militia image.

Rastich entered without a greeting, his eyes hard as he
met Grozky's. Grozky recalled the OMON major's cold
reticence when he had first met him before the raid.

He blames me for Nedev's death, Grozky thought.

"Major Rastich, it's good to see you. I'm very sorry about
the death of Stepan. He was a good man. He will be missed,"
Grozky said, standing up to greet his guest.

"Indeed," Rastich replied.

Grozky extended his hand and sensed Rastich's
reluctance to reciprocate. After the briefest of handshakes,

Rastich pulled up a chair and sat down in front of the desk. Grozky handed across the file which Rastich placed on his lap without acknowledgement.

"Where would you like me to start?" Grozky asked.

"Stepan, God rest his soul, kept me informed of the generalities of what he was up to. I would prefer to take your file, read it in detail and then meet with you if I have any questions," Rastich replied.

"Of course."

"It would be useful if you could summarise your own conclusions," Rastich said, opening the file's cover and staring at the pile of pages.

Grozky nodded.

"Most of the local gangs are involved, to varying degrees, in the drugs trade. This gang uses the port both to supply St Petersburg and ship overseas. With the loss of the Soviet ports in Estonia, Latvia and Lithuania, St Petersburg has returned to becoming the gateway to the west, particularly for heroin. The volume of sea freight passing through the port is huge. Aside from the occasional spot check, the containers are as anonymous as the bills of lading and documentation accompanying them."

"Indeed. The challenge we face is that these marine processes exist primarily for the benefit of commerce, not control," Rastich said.

"Exactly. With the maturity of their distribution network and organisation I believe this gang reaches well beyond St Petersburg. Recent arrests included a national from Turkmenistan. Their contacts likely extend to the Golden Crescent," Grozky said.

"I didn't realise the St Petersburg FSB's remit extended as far as Afghanistan, Pakistan and Iran," Rastich commented.

"It doesn't, directly. I'm familiar with the region."

"Really, how?"

"I spent some time there. My Farsi is better than my Turkmen," Grozky replied without being specific. Rastich's eyes narrowed as he looked at him.

"Ah, the old days. Which Directorate were you with?"

"The Third."

"Well, I suppose someone has to cover military counterintelligence," Rastich said. "I was fortunate enough to have been with the Fifth Directorate."

"I hope you disclosed that before you joined the OMON," Grozky responded, for the KGB's Fifth Directorate was considered the poor cousin of the Second. Grozky took silent satisfaction as Rastich's eyes blazed at his remark. Aside from harrying political and religious dissidents, the Fifth were known for supplementing their income through the pilfering and resale of religious icons.

"From what you'll read in the file, you'll see we're up against a very well-run criminal organisation," Grozky said, returning to the purpose of the meeting.

"Based on what you've outlined, I would agree. And what is your take on the raid at the Red Star Bar?"

"I've already told General Donitsyn there must have been an information leak. It was a very professional ambush. To pull that off required funding and preparation. In my view, this is much more than a local St Petersburg gang. It's all in my report."

"What was the general's reaction?"

"He thinks we could have been spotted. He's going to follow up."

"Interesting," Rastich said.

Grozky saw Rastich's hard eyes briefly scan the freshly

typed pages. Then Rastich closed the file and kept it clasped between both palms, seeming to covet the information which was now the preserve of the OMON.

"I have a small favour to ask," Grozky said. "In my absence, would you be able to debrief the District Security Council on the Red Star Bar?"

Rastich's eyes looked at him blankly.

"Of course, I was there. The raid wasn't unsuccessful. You were unlucky, that's all," Rastich said. The words would have had empathy except for the viciousness in Rastich's delivery.

His next question took Grozky by surprise.

"I hear you're off to Moscow to work for General Koshygin?"

Grozky's face betrayed no emotion. Word would inevitably slip out at some point about his reassignment. However, even with Rastich's new responsibilities, it struck Grozky as odd the OMON officer should be aware of his situation.

"You seem very well informed."

"It pays to be well informed," Rastich said, the toothpick at the corner of his mouth twitching.

"When were you told?"

"After you were. A decision was made. It affects you. It affects me."

Grozky nodded. Rastich's parries were reason enough to doubt his answers. It would be out of character for Donitsyn to share such information. He wondered at Rastich's inclusion.

"It only remains for me to wish you the best of luck, Major Rastich. If there's anything I can do for you, please let me know," Grozky said, standing up and offering his hand.

"I'll be sure to do that." The hard eyes made no such promise.

Grozky took Rastich's cool hand, applying unduly firm pressure. On releasing his grip, Grozky took satisfaction from the way the OMON major's cold expression had waned to a taut wince.

Rastich departed with the file, leaving Grozky with a sense of unease. It was more than irritation at Rastich's officious self-belief. Grozky couldn't decide whether the man's arrogance had been brutalised into him by the OMON or whether the flaws in his character had given way to their own excess. Either way, there was something about Major Emile Rastich he did not trust.

6

It was a little after 10 a.m. when Grozky and Borzoi stepped off the aeroplane at Sheremetyevo airport. The Tupolev Tu-154M was a three-engine workhorse as good as any Aeroflot could offer. The sub-zero temperature embraced the thin telescopic walls of the passenger airbridge and Grozky, clasping his small black wallet case, turned up the collar on his overcoat.

Their uniforms and peaked caps set them apart from the hurried mix of humanity in the arrivals hall. After several yards they were accosted by a swarthy GRU sergeant. He blocked their path, the heels of his boots snapping together as his right hand shot up to his Ushanka fur hat.

"Sergeant Rakhimov. At your service."

Rakhimov's deference did not pass for a welcome. Grozky returned his salute without comment. With his angular nose and thin face, Grozky placed Rakhimov from one of the Central Asian republics, most likely a Tajik or possibly a Kazakh. He considered his features too hard for a Turkmen.

As they entered the sudden chill of the car park, Rakhimov paused to retrieve a packet of cigarettes from a coat pocket. His offer to Grozky and Borzoi was declined. Rakhimov lit his cigarette with a lighter and led the way across the frozen tarmac, smoking in silence. The GRU sergeant stopped in front of a black 4x4 Niva jeep, unlocked the vehicle and got behind the wheel. Grozky opted for a rear seat, placing his wallet case on his lap, and opened a sliver of window to ventilate the smoke. Borzoi sat next to him and clapped his bare hands together several times to warm himself.

The jeep pulled onto the highway and Grozky saw the airport complex replaced by a flat hinterland of whiteness, barren but for a handful of wispy birch trees. The thin traffic barely challenged one lane on the dual carriageway and Rakhimov kept the jeep at speed, his mute presence compounding the empty vista.

Four hundred miles from St Petersburg, Grozky pondered his reassignment. His selection still troubled him. For a three-month secondment to Moscow there would have to have been a shortlist of candidates. Grozky would like to have seen the names. Had Koshygin read his file? What was it that had caught his attention? In an unspectacular KGB career, Grozky's final promotion in the Third Directorate had been in one of the *osobye otdely* or 'special departments', reviewing the security clearances for the Baltic Fleet. Only the most zealous could be trusted to intercept the mail of the men who defended the country. It was, he knew, his zeal which had ultimately cost him his marriage. Marisha could accept his anguish at the loss of his brother, not how he could find such purpose in putting himself in the firing line against the drug gangs. Yet 'resilient' was the word Donitsyn had used. It was a favourite term amongst old Soviets for something hard-wearing and trustworthy. Perhaps Donitsyn saw him for what he was, a Soviet throwback used to taking punishment. It made no difference, Donitsyn had assigned him to Moscow to earn his day of reckoning in St Petersburg.

The onset of faint music from the front of the jeep intruded on his brooding. Grozky listened to the faint trill of a snake charmer's flute. This was not the Georgian *zurna* played at Chidaoba wrestling bouts. It had been a long time since he'd heard the music of the Ferghana Valley where Uzbekistan, Tajikistan and Kyrgyzstan intersected. The simple notes were from a conical oboe fashioned from copper, called the *karnay* in Uzbekistan and known as the *dilli tuyduk* in Turkmenistan. When the hypnotic rhythm was joined by the percussion of strong fingertips against a taut membrane, Grozky recognised the higher pitch of the *doira*, a small drum favoured by the folk musicians of Uzbekistan over the Georgian *doli*. Grozky reclassified Rakhimov from Tajik to Uzbek as the desolate countryside swept by.

Grozky picked up his wallet case and unzipped it. He looked up and caught Rakhimov's eyes watching him in the rear-view mirror. The man affected a quiet intensity on the road which failed to disguise his interest in his passengers. Grozky was glad of Borzoi's company, he would need to keep him close.

Extracting the thin dossier he had received from General Donitsyn, Grozky passed it to Borzoi. There was a single name in neat black typeface: 'YEVGENY KOCHENKO'.

"You read this on the plane. What do you make of Kochenko?" Grozky asked.

Borzoi opened the file, the papers inside bound by a thick rubber band. On top, tucked under the band, were a pair of A5 photographs in glossy black and white, someone's final selection from recent surveillance. Borzoi dismissed the first photo, a head and shoulders shot which looked like an enlargement, and handed across the second.

The monochrome captured a smartly dressed man walking down the steps of a building surrounded by the dark shadows of men in overcoats. The zoom lens had captured Kochenko's features in forensic detail, an adjacent face was in soft focus and the rest were blurs. Unsmiling, the oligarch projected intensity. Even preoccupied, Kochenko's face had an intelligence that belied the ruthlessness Grozky knew he was capable of.

"As if he needs any introduction, that's Yevgeny Kochenko," Borzoi said. "Despite his military background, you'll notice his naval-style overcoat and the eight brass buttons. It's as much a trademark as the heavy security presence. The taller man next to him is Sergei Malievich, his business partner and right-hand man who reputedly served under Kochenko in Afghanistan."

Handing back the photo, Grozky noted the single page clipped inside the cover, the jagged scribble of Borzoi's notes, occasionally peppered with double question marks.

"What's your read on Kochenko?" Grozky asked.

Borzoi put the photo to the back of the folder and picked up his page of notes.

"Kochenko is forty-two and one of St Petersburg's more resilient entrepreneurs. He's well educated: a degree in economics from St Petersburg University, followed by a year's postgraduate course at the London School of Economics. He returned to the Soviet Union in 1980 and joined the army, likely influenced by his father, who graduated from St Petersburg's Nakhimov Naval Academy and was a career officer. Although he has become the leading local oligarch, he strikes me as a man very much connected to his past. Even his choice of overcoat has a significance," Borzoi said.

"Everyone has a past, just as they have a future. What makes you say that?" Grozky asked.

"Until he was dishonourably discharged in July 1988, towards the end of the Afghanistan war, the assessments on file indicate he was a talented officer – strong discipline and excelled at whatever role he was given. On his return to St Petersburg he dropped off the radar for almost a year. No record of employment. Nothing. What was he doing? A pivotal point is when he resurfaces and sets up the Lensky Security agency in April 1989. This wasn't racketeering of the kind that has made several gangs very rich. Kochenko recruited ex-military types and provided a professional protection service. He went back to what he knew."

"I agree. What would you say are the significant events which shaped him?"

Borzoi looked again at his notes. "It went wrong for him in Afghanistan. He was posted with his unit to the garrison town of Charikar in August 1985, running a Spetsnaz unit. By all accounts he did well in the first two years and was regularly commended, but by early 1988 conditions had deteriorated. There was a huge surge in Mujahideen activity and the Americans were spending a fortune backing them. He also fell out with his commanding officer, a Colonel Koshygin."

At the mention of the name, Grozky saw Rakhimov's eyes switch to the rear-view mirror again.

"It happens," Grozky said.

"Sure, it does. There's friction and then there's *friction*. In this case it resulted in a serious assault against Colonel Koshygin. Kochenko was discharged on medical grounds."

"You don't sound convinced."

"I'm not." Borzoi pointed to a pair of question marks on the page. "It meant Kochenko stayed below the radar. There was none of the procedural attention a court martial would have attracted."

"Very good, Dmitri. You're learning. However, given the conditions in Afghanistan, battle fatigue was to be expected. Kochenko was under a lot of pressure and it sounds like he cracked. A lot of men got screwed up by that war." Grozky paused, momentarily, recalling Timur's death. He did not allow himself to dwell on the memory.

"Why do you think what happened to Kochenko was unusual?" Grozky asked.

"It's everything about his character up until this point. Kochenko was an experienced officer with a strong track record. He's disciplined and decisive, someone who makes living by a code a personal mantra. To go off the handle and strike his CO seems out of character. He must have known the consequences. Colonel Koshygin should have thrown the book at him, so why didn't he? A court martial was avoided. From what's in the file, Kochenko got off lightly," Borzoi said.

"What caused the confrontation?"

Borzoi pointed to the last page in the file.

"That's also odd. You'd think there'd be a detailed explanation of why Kochenko snapped. Instead, the medical report is light to the point of omission. Everything else in his file indicates a man who excels under stress, even thrives on it. My read is Kochenko developed some sort of grudge against his colonel. He did more than strike his superior, he beat the crap out of him. Kochenko must have known the consequences. If he had a case against Koshygin, he could have reported him, except he didn't. Perhaps battle fatigue did have something to do with it. Either way, it finished his military career."

Listening to the events, Grozky did not discount stress, it corrupted the mind in different ways. Timur had survived the Afghan war, it was the memories he could not endure. The Mujahideen persecuted the Soviet soldier with a medieval barbarism – the hidden knives on every street and the shopkeepers who offered poisoned food with open smiles. Once the paranoia of his mind set in, it ate into his sanity like cancer. Kochenko did not strike Grozky as an officer in despair. This was the behaviour of a rational man who had lashed out for a reason. Grozky also wondered at the cause.

"You'll make a good analyst yet, Dmitri. Anything else to add?"

"Not on Kochenko. That's as much as I can establish from what's in the file. I did note that the colonel who was assaulted was recalled shortly afterwards. It's possible this episode may have contributed."

"Do you know where he is now? Grozky asked.

"Who?"

"That colonel, Koshygin."

"No."

"Well, Dmitri, I'll tell you. That ex-colonel is now General Anatoli Koshygin of the GRU's Second Directorate. Isn't that so, Sergeant?" Grozky asked, meeting Rakhimov's eyes in the mirror.

Rakhimov nodded.

"Whew, someone who knows how to take advantage of a situation," Borzoi said.

"Clearly. Your post-war insights into Kochenko?" Grozky asked.

"He's become successful. Very successful. You've probably heard the same stories I have, never proven but which now serve as a myth to warn off his competitors. Kochenko established the Lensky Security agency after a local gang lord, Vadim Vogorov, and several of his henchmen disappeared. Kochenko's finger was rumoured to be on the trigger. Suddenly, Lensky Security was protecting the businesses Vogorov used to threaten. Kochenko hadn't broken the rules of the *vory v zakone*, the 'thieves in law', because he hadn't stepped on anyone else's turf. If it's true, he's as smart as he is ruthless."

"And his business interests?" Grozky asked.

"Kochenko used his profits to invest in the enterprises he was protecting. Given the state of the economy in the early 90s it was a smart move. The success of his Lensky Group has surprised everyone. Those who crossed him did so to their cost. When a couple of the local gangs tried to extort some new clients, the businessmen went to Kochenko for protection. A feud ensued and a couple of Kochenko's men were ambushed and killed. Kochenko found those responsible, shot them and then went after their gangs. The gangs didn't realise what they'd started. Kochenko's security teams hunted them down."

"Kochenko learnt how to hunt the Mujahideen on unfamiliar ground. A city he knew would have been easy."

"By the end, the gang leaders were lucky to escape with their lives. No one has crossed Kochenko since. Even the bigger crime syndicates stay clear of him, although they'd like to see the back of him. Whatever Kochenko did to get started, his investments seem legitimate. With the loss of the Soviet Baltic ports outside Russia, Kochenko saw the opportunities for St Petersburg. He took a lead when others were reluctant to, buying up long-term charters on second-hand ships and establishing a fleet to take advantage of the demand for freight shipping."

As he listened, the image of a dockside warehouse struck Grozky.

"I didn't know his investments included shipping."

"You think he's involved in shipping drugs through St Petersburg?" Borzoi asked.

"He has the capability, doesn't he? But I interrupted you, Dmitri. Please continue."

"Aside from security and shipping, his varied interests include a banking operation, and fifteen months ago, the Lensky Group acquired the majority share in an oil company, Yanusk, which was in financial trouble. He's discreet with his wealth and how he spends it. For instance, he doesn't broadcast his support of several veterans' charities. From what I hear, he commands extreme loyalty," Borzoi said.

Grozky remembered Natassja mentioning Kochenko's stake in Yanusk.

"That's a thorough assessment and one I agree with. On the one hand, Kochenko is the antithesis of what the Soviet Union stood for, while on the other he is everything the new Russia should be embodying: a successful investor who supports veterans in a way the Russian state has failed to do."

Borzoi nodded, returning the papers to the wallet case.

"Thank you, Valeri. Any ideas about what Kochenko has to do with our briefing in Moscow?"

"I know as much as General Donitsyn told me, which is 'All will be revealed in Moscow,'" Grozky replied.

At the mention of Moscow, Grozky saw the excitement on his protégé's face. Grozky did not exude the same enthusiasm. He had not been to Moscow since the disbanding of the KGB and even then, the capital had been a high castle of intrigue.

With the chaos following the collapse of the USSR, it was now a political minefield.

Ahead, Grozky saw the thin funnels of light industry melding with concrete blocks of workers' housing. Their progress on the outskirts of Moscow slowed as a series of junctions and traffic lights hindered their path. The volume of traffic grew heavier and the jeep was absorbed into the impatient stream of vehicles heading into the city. If Rakhimov was frustrated by the delay, he did not show it.

They turned right at a set of lights and Grozky saw the familiar sight of the Birch Grove Park, a meagre wood of scrubby trees compared to the grand parks like Gorky Park or Filev's Park in central Moscow. A district like Khodynka was unpretentious and industrial, save for the presence of GRU headquarters and the 2,500 military intelligence operatives based there.

A few minutes later Rakhimov joined the Khoroshev Highway and the trees could no longer camouflage the approach to the old Khodynka airfield complex. Rakhimov slowed, indicated and then the jeep turned off the highway.

Ahead Grozky saw the GRU headquarters, the *Steklyasha* or 'piece of glass', a nine-storey block clad in glass panels which had once been a military hospital. A few hundred yards later, their journey came to an end as they stopped in front of a pair of metal gates embedded in a windowless two-storey building running along the perimeter. The armed guards who approached either side of the jeep showed no signs of familiarity. It seemed to Grozky that Rakhimov's identity card received as much scrutiny as his own. The guards disappeared behind the gates. For the first time, Grozky saw a hint of dejection in Rakhimov's expression. Shortly afterwards the guards returned to wave the jeep through.

Inside the perimeter, the jeep sped past a long blockhouse while Rakhimov's eyes scowled from the mirror. The jeep turned once more before Rakhimov pulled up, deposited them in front of the GRU headquarters and drove off. Grozky spoke quietly to Borzoi.

"Remember, avoid asking questions until you have to. In these circles, questions have a habit of turning on the originator. If you're required to provide an answer, be direct and to the point and if you're unsure, bring me into the conversation. Got it?"

"Trust me, I understand," Borzoi replied.

"Whatever's going on, we need to be careful when dealing with a man like General Anatoli Koshygin. You don't reach the heights of Military Intelligence unless you're either very astute or very well connected. Koshygin is one individual you do not want to cross."

7

The transparency of the building's exterior belied the ultra-tight security inside. Their FSB identity cards were rechecked before their names were matched to an authorised list of visitors. Successfully authenticated, a young GRU soldier escorted them with the same cold deference as Rakhimov. He carried an electronic swipe card, without which they could not have passed through the security doors which seemed to pervade every corridor. Even by the FSB's standards, trust was very secondary here.

On the third floor their GRU escort left them in a large meeting room containing a highly polished wooden table around which were, Grozky estimated, some thirty armchairs. At the far end of the room, behind the table, five men stood talking together: four uniformed GRU officers and a thin civilian wearing a well-cut suit. On the far end of the table, except for a carafe of water and several glasses on a tray, the only item was a stack of thin manila dossiers.

The small group turned to meet the new arrivals. General Anatoli Koshygin stood out, his ample chest dominated by the multicoloured embroidery of his medals. His grey hairline had receded, leaving his face a balloon of flesh. He smiled, creasing his heavy jowls.

Grozky and Borzoi were a yard away from the group when the door at the other end of the room opened. Grozky did not allow his surprise to show at the besuited man who strode into the room. Aleksandr Metzov, Deputy Chief of Staff in the Presidential Administration, was rarely sighted outside the Kremlin. He had oversight for government operations in the regions and was as close as Moscow came to royalty, denoted by his moniker of the 'Grey Cardinal'. His white shirt and red tie made him look more businessman than politician, yet the expensive sheen of his dark grey suit could not hide the power in his shoulders from his days as a construction foreman with Yeltsin in Yekaterinburg. The Grey Cardinal's shaved head and eyebrows disguised his age as much as the black dye of the thick moustache camouflaging his mouth.

General Koshygin stepped forward and the Grey Cardinal received him like a senior courtier. The initial handshake swelled into a double embrace as Metzov's other hand clasped the general's forearm. Metzov relinquished his grip and turned to face his small audience. His left arm encircled Koshygin's shoulder like a paternal strongman, while the grin on Metzov's face was not reflected in his dark eyes. It struck Grozky that Metzov could easily crush Koshygin's neck if the mood took him.

"Gentlemen. Welcome. Please sit down," Metzov said. He waved them towards the table, pulling Koshygin with him in conspiratorial camaraderie. Metzov made a point of seating Koshygin immediately on his right before he sat at the top of the table.

Grozky offered the chair on Metzov's left to the civilian and waited for him to sit down before he took the next seat. As Borzoi joined him, Grozky found himself looking across the table at the cadre of three GRU colonels clubbed together on Koshygin's flank.

The civilian stretched out to retrieve the pile of folders from the centre of the table. He wore his thick hair swept back in a bouffant coiffure and sported the thinnest of pencil moustaches. His patterned silk tie and blue suit looked expensive. Grozky saw the small typeface on the top folder: *SOVERSHENNO SEKRETNO*, TOP SECRET. The civilian's hands rested behind the thin pile of manila folders, one finger picking absently at the skin surrounding the cuticle of his thumb.

"Grigori, please distribute the materials," Koshygin said.

The civilian stood up, taking care to place the first file in front of Metzov. As he handed the files out, Koshygin stood up and extended a florid hand towards the Grey Cardinal sitting at the top of the table.

"Gentlemen, Aleksandr Metzov needs no introduction. I am indebted to him for asking me to lead this select group. Before we continue, I must emphasise this is a matter of state security and you are not to discuss anything you hear today with anyone except those in this room."

There were nods from all around the table, except Metzov who sat motionless, his eyes narrowed. But for the absence of hair, Grozky saw the mask of Stalin.

"Good. We are fortunate to have with us Grigori Zotkin from the Prosecutor-General's office. Grigori will brief us all shortly. He is working closely with the GRU operation," Koshygin said, finishing his introduction with a flourish of a ringmaster's hand and resting his fleshy paws on the top of his chair. He took another breath as he held court, the patchwork of medals on his chest stretching with the exertion.

Grozky watched as Zotkin distributed the folders as if he was laying plates. His round face and short chin were given definition by the dark frizz on his upper lip.

Metzov turned to address Koshygin.

"General, before you introduce everyone, I'd like Colonel Ekomov to tell us what he has found in Washington and why we need to be so worried."

"Of course," Koshygin said, momentarily placing a hand on the shoulder of the colonel sitting next to him. Ekomov had the youthful face of an athlete crowned with parted blond hair. As he started talking, Grozky recognised an emotional undercurrent beneath the measured delivery and listened with keen attention.

"The GRU monitors all American government Senate hearings for any topics of interest to the Russian government. In late January, we saw the Senate Permanent Subcommittee on Investigations had scheduled a hearing on the security of America's oil supply. It's a topic which comes around every few years. What we have now learnt is that the Subcommittee's focus is as much on the threat that Russian organised crime presents to America's ability to import oil. They have picked what they consider to be an example of such a threat. The Yanusk Oil Company."

Yanusk! Grozky's interest sharpened as Ekomov continued.

"What we could not have known is just how much the American Senate has found out about Yanusk. You may be aware that Yuri Tomarov, the man who oversaw Yanusk's privatisation, was recently killed in Yekaterinburg. Tomarov committed a huge fraud when he ran Yanusk, something which was uncovered after he lost control of the company.

That was bad enough, except we now know that Tomarov colluded with the St Petersburg oligarch, Yevgeny Kochenko, enabling Kochenko to take control of Yanusk. You can imagine how the public exposure of this information in an American Senate report will jeopardise President Yeltsin's chances of re-election."

Ekomov finished his last sentence as if someone had died. Grigori Zotkin remained tight-lipped as he placed the last of the folders in front of Grozky and sat down. Grozky recollected Natassja's suspicions. He had discounted her intuition, yet her insights had been more accurate than she knew.

"Let's get down to business so everyone understands their role in this operation," Metzov said.

"Of course, of course," Koshygin said, still standing. He extended a brusque hand in Grozky's direction.

"First, I must welcome our friends from the St Petersburg FSB who have flown in at short notice to assist us. Major Valeri Grozky, whose experience and knowledge of the city's organised crime scene will, I am sure, prove invaluable. Welcome, Valeri," Koshygin said.

"Thank you, General. I am grateful for the opportunity to serve," Grozky said, avoiding Metzov's glassy stare.

"Next to Valeri is Lieutenant Dmitri Borzoi who has proven himself to be an officer of the highest integrity. I appreciate you making the effort to join us, Dmitri," Koshygin said.

"Thank you, General," Borzoi said.

Koshygin turned to Colonel Ekomov and clapped a hand on his shoulder.

"Colonel Ilia Ekomov has held postings across Europe. He is now based in Washington DC. He is fluent in English and has authority for all our activities in the United States. As you heard, we owe it to Ilia for alerting us to the threat we face."

Grozky heard the pride in Koshygin's voice. He might have been congratulating a favoured son for spotting the danger before anyone else.

"Thank you, General. I look forward to working with the team," Ekomov said in flawless English. He smiled at his own joke revealing white teeth as shiny as his hair. Were it not for his uniform, Grozky imagined he would be equally at ease as a playboy.

Koshygin moved to stand behind the next colonel.

"Colonel Arkady Dratshev is a twenty-year GRU career officer. With Ilia focused on Washington, Arkady is responsible for coordinating the overall operation from Moscow, particularly with Grigori and the Prosecutor-General's office. Arkady is also responsible for providing additional resources any of you require. I expect each team to provide detailed daily reports to Arkady," Koshygin said.

Dratshev's curt nod was his only acknowledgement of his role.

Koshygin stood behind the chair of the last colonel in line and clapped both hands on his thick shoulders.

"The last member of my team is as skilled a soldier as I could hope to find for this operation. Colonel Ivan Palutkin. Recently transferred back from Chechnya, he has made many personal sacrifices for his country. As head of Operational Security he is accountable to me alone."

Ivan Palutkin chuckled, while the fresh scar on his cheek winced.

"With a man like Ivan watching our backs, we can all sleep more easily," Metzov said.

Grozky looked across at Koshygin's ranking flush of colonels, hand-picked men who would obey him unquestioningly. The one who concerned him the most was Palutkin, his head shaved to the scalp and the angry slab of a pink scar a fresh memento of Chechen resistance. Grozky did not need to meet the wild eyes from across the table to know which officer was Koshygin's best *pistolero*. With the Kremlin's backing, Koshygin and his cronies would take no prisoners.

The introductions finished, Koshygin sat down, the springs in the chair creaking under his weight.

"Grigori, please brief us," Koshygin said, opening the cover of the file in front of him. He reached for the carafe and poured two glasses of water, placing one in front of Metzov.

Zotkin glanced around the table before he started speaking. He spoke slowly, as if wary the complexities of his subject might be lost on the assembled company.

"Thank you, General. Since 1990, Russian oil production has fallen by forty per cent. Some of you may recall the privatisation of the Yanusk Oil Company in June 1993. It was one of the biggest state privatisations under Yeltsin's new economic reforms. Yanusk urgently needed capital investment to update its ageing infrastructure and increase production. Yanusk was a flagship sale which was expected to lead to improved oil production and increased tax revenues."

Zotkin paused as the Grey Cardinal lit a filterless Prima papirosa, crimping the cardboard holder between his fingers, his face set hard. The gritty fumes of cheap tobacco crept outward and Zotkin's pace quickened. Grozky sensed his anxiety. The persona which might have given Zotkin presence in the Prosecutor-General's office did not carry to GRU headquarters. Grozky might have been sitting next to a 1930s lothario.

"Initially, Tomarov was as good as his word, bringing in new management and improving efficiency. However, we now know within nine months of privatisation, large quantities of oil began to be traded privately, at Yanusk's expense. Put simply, Tomarov manipulated Yanusk's production and stock figures and made significant profits by selling the oil through a Swiss entity, Capri Trading, a legitimate oil trader he controlled in the secondary market. Is that clear?"

If it wasn't, no one at the table was prepared to look stupid in front of the Grey Cardinal. Grozky saw the muscles in Metzov's jaw clench.

"When experienced staff at Yanusk became suspicious," Zotkin continued, "Tomarov ensured their concerns were either barracked or dismissed. We have since discovered the deaths of three senior managers during 1993 were highly suspicious and several other staff were either intimidated or bought off."

Silver or lead, Grozky thought as he listened. Natassja had been right, Tomarov's corruption was the worst kind.

Zotkin reached for the carafe, poured a glass of water and took two careful sips before continuing.

"Tomarov also put up the shares he owned in Yanusk as collateral to replace the commercial assets he had originally used to negotiate the loan. Perhaps an unusual decision, though certainly not illegal. Tomarov's fraud might well have continued had he not defaulted on his loan which resulted in Lensky Bank calling in the collateral and taking ownership of the stock in December 1994. Tomarov's management structure at Yanusk broke down and the external auditors picked up the trail of misstatements and uncovered the scale of the fraud. That was more than a year ago..."

Metzov's voice barked out.

"If you think this is bad, the situation has become a lot worse after what Ilia discovered in Washington."

"I draw your attention to the first page in the file," Ekomov said.

Everyone in the room turned to their folders, except Metzov who drew on his papirosa. Grozky saw a neatly typed sheet entitled 'US Senate Permanent Subcommittee on Investigations – February 1996: Target List', underneath which was a list of names.

"This Subcommittee is the pre-eminent investigative body of the American Senate. It is chaired by an ambitious Republican, Senator Bradley Gravell. Since the GRU identified the threat this subcommittee hearing represents, we have been very fortunate regarding a key witness, Zach Brown, haven't we, Grigori?" Ekomov said.

Grozky saw Grigori Zotkin's index finger absently tapping against the name.

"Indeed," Zotkin said, his tone as fastidious as his appearance. "Zach Brown was formally requested to testify before the Subcommittee because he worked with Archipelago Oil in its dealings with Yanusk. Brown specialises in assisting foreign companies to invest in Russia and, by all accounts, he's very good. The Deputy Head of the Ministry of Fuel and Energy considers him a close friend," Zotkin said, as though that was a clinching factor.

"It's somewhat ironic," Ekomov said, "that Brown is ex-CIA. His profile is in the file. He first came to our notice when he served with the American Embassy in Moscow. He was a commercial attaché, although there is nothing notable during that period. He evidently saw the commercial opportunities and left Moscow in early 1992. We're still filling in the gaps since then, but he's very well placed to play both sides of the border," Ekomov said.

Zotkin nodded. "Brown understands he's in a sensitive position because his testimony could damage the Russian connections he relies upon. Brown called his friends at the Ministry to ensure they understood his situation. He described himself as 'a reluctant witness.'"

Ekomov retrieved another sheet of paper from the file and held it up to the room. Grozky found his copy and saw a small table of rows and numbers entitled 'Commission Payments – US Dollar Equivalent: Yuri Tomarov'.

"This single page," said Ekomov, "represents the biggest risk to the Russian Federation. Conscious his Russian Ministry connections might be in jeopardy, as a gesture of goodwill, Brown passed on this page given to him by the Subcommittee Chairman, Bradley Gravell. Brown knows that this will all come out over the next few weeks," Zotkin added.

At the head of the table, a small flame appeared as Metzov lit another papirosa, his first still smoking in the ashtray. Grozky sensed the quicksand of Tomarov's criminality spreading. Something very dark was happening for the Grey Cardinal to be holding court at GRU headquarters.

"Based on Brown's discussion with Senator Gravell," Zotkin continued, "Tomarov would not have been able to purchase Yanusk's stock without the loans provided by Lensky Bank. In return for the bank facilitating the original loans, Tomarov showed his gratitude by paying a series of substantial 'commission' payments amounting to US$6 million following the purchase of Yanusk."

A growl from Metzov cut Zotkin short.

"In light of this evidence, Tomarov's transfer of his shares in Yanusk as collateral for the original loans can no longer be considered a coincidence. Tomarov made millions in his oil scam, while Lensky Bank has ended up owning a valuable oil company. If we can draw that conclusion, how long do you think it's going to be before the Senate investigation works it out?" Metzov said.

"No one could have foreseen how central Yanusk would be to the Senate's investigation," Zotkin said, his face flushing.

"Have you established how the Americans got hold of their information?" Metzov asked, stubbing out his new papirosa and retrieving the original from the ashtray.

"We're still trying to find out how Gravell came by it. The Permanent Subcommittee on Investigations is very thorough. According to the Ministry, Gravell told Brown the information was purchased in St Petersburg. Someone had good information to sell," Ekomov said, his lean features no longer confident.

Grozky looked at the list of names appearing before the Senate Subcommittee, the first two which had been picked out in bold and underlined: Zach Brown – Managing Director and Founding Partner, Spectrum Consulting, and Arnold Lennister – Chief Executive Officer, Archipelago Oil Company. Below them, he noted an assortment of directors from the CIA, FBI and Department of Justice. Given the chance, the US agencies would not hold back from turning the knife on the extent of Russian lawlessness since the demise of the USSR.

"As you can see," Zotkin said, "the evidence which will be presented to the Subcommittee shows a total of US$6 million paid in 200 separate instalments. They were made to look like normal business transactions," Zotkin said.

"When is the Subcommittee expected to publish its findings?" Grozky asked.

"The investigation started in early February. It will publish its findings by mid-May at the latest. With the first round of presidential elections in June, you can appreciate how this could sink Yeltsin's re-election prospects," Ekomov said.

Grozky saw the perfect storm gathering. Yeltsin's record in delivering economic reform was as unconvincing as his record on organised crime, his policies of 'shock therapy' denounced as economic genocide by his own Vice-President, Rutskoy. Yeltsin had barely survived his impeachment by the Duma in 1993, restoring his power with demonstrators' blood. The revelations of the scale of corruption at Yanusk would be his downfall. Grozky understood the intent behind this meeting: Aleksandr Metzov was on a personal crusade to save Boris Yeltsin.

"We're fortunate to be forewarned of the information the Senate Subcommittee will disclose. We have a chance…"

Zotkin's steady tone stalled as the Grey Cardinal jumped from his seat, sending his chair crashing backwards onto the floor. Metzov stabbed his finger into the file, showering it with embers from his cigarette, and glared around the table, his suit struggling to contain his irate torso.

"What happened at Yanusk was a disgrace. Tomarov may have escaped punishment, but bastards like Kochenko and his accomplices will not," Metzov said.

Koshygin hurried to retrieve the fallen chair. Metzov ignored his assistance and continued his tirade.

"I can tell you one thing, Boris Yeltsin won't be brought down by some damn American Senate investigation. Those responsible for Yanusk are to be crucified. Do you hear me? Yevgeny Kochenko is just another gangster dressed up as a businessman. This charade will stop now. The Russian government is going to demonstrate its leadership in dealing with this scandal."

Metzov's fist hammered onto the table, the force upsetting his glass, sending the water snaking towards his copy of the dossier. Zotkin stared at the spill as Koshygin stumbled towards the table, but it was Grozky's sleeve that deftly absorbed the flow before it could reach the paper. Metzov restored his self-control as quickly as he had lost it. Grozky was surprised by the Grey Cardinal's outburst. Aside from Boris Yeltsin he was one of the most powerful men in Russia.

"Anatoli, take us through your plan," Metzov said, glaring at Koshygin before he stubbed out what was left of his papirosa in the ashtray.

Koshygin nodded and remained standing as he spoke.

"Of course. We work in parallel. Ilia will be returning to Washington tonight. He will do whatever he can to sabotage the Senate hearing."

"I have mobilised every operative. We are looking into the backgrounds of all those involved in this Senate hearing," Ekomov said.

"Grigori is in charge of the prosecution of Yevgeny Kochenko and will be supported by the FSB. We need to find those payments," Koshygin said.

Zotkin cleared his throat and half raised a hand before speaking. He turned to Grozky.

"The Prosecutor-General's office has requested all Yanusk's bank accounts and the personal accounts of Kochenko and Tomarov. We're looking for payments made by Tomarov to Lensky Bank or Yevgeny Kochenko. We don't know when these payments started or finished. In light of the seriousness of what we face, I have requested a further six months of history from 1 June to 30 November 1993 from Lensky Bank when Yanusk was a joint stock company. The details are in the file. If you could chase those up?"

"Certainly," Grozky said, as Zotkin passed him a sheet of paper with account numbers.

"Now you understand what's at stake, I want Kochenko placed under full surveillance while we locate those payments. What resources will you require?" Koshygin asked.

Grozky put the paper on top of the file and closed the cover as he considered his requirements for what would be a twenty-four-hour operation.

"I would want a dozen men for the surveillance shifts. I'd use local FSB men who know their way around St Petersburg. I'd need six for telephone surveillance and another six to review what we find. For a dedicated operations room my office would be sufficient," Grozky said.

"I want to review the field records of the FSB team you propose to use before I approve them," said Koshygin. "You are to avoid any mention of this operation. Say only that you have been assigned to a task force targeting high-profile criminals. I have already approved several FAPSI personnel to assist in telephone surveillance. They are at your disposal."

"Certainly. Thank you, General," Grozky said and paused for a moment. There was an aspect which troubled him.

"General, as the FSB is still getting up to speed, please could you clarify who is following up on the murder of Yuri Tomarov?" Grozky kept his expression to one of mild puzzlement while his open-ended barb of a question required an answer beyond a simple 'yes' or 'no'.

Initially, there was no response. Then came the authoritative voice of the Grey Cardinal.

"Would that Tomarov was alive, but I can't charge a dead man. It is the connection between Tomarov and Kochenko which is now *the* priority. Your knowledge of St Petersburg organised crime is why you're here. You are to assist Grigori in finding the evidence linking Kochenko to Tomarov. Is that clear?"

"Thank you for the clarification," Grozky said. He now understood the selection of General Anatoli Koshygin. With the demise of Yuri Tomarov, Metzov's new target for a show trial was Yevgeny Kochenko. The Russian government was no longer the perpetrator of a fiasco of privatisation, it was as much a victim of a massive fraud. In a country struggling to apply the new rules of capitalism, Metzov was the self-appointed authoritarian who would bring the guilty to justice.

"General, from the file you supplied, I understand Kochenko once served under you. What sort of man are we dealing with?" Grozky inquired in his best deadpan tone.

Next to him, Grozky sensed Borzoi stiffen. From across the table the GRU colonels stared at him. Koshygin paused before answering.

"Yes, I knew him in Afghanistan. An effective officer, although prone to instability. He allowed his emotions to get the better of him. That was eight years ago and since then I've had no contact. His record speaks to his true character, a man who has exploited his military background for personal gain."

Grozky nodded as he saw Koshygin glance at Metzov. Koshygin's response was polished, yet he had omitted his personal confrontation with Kochenko.

Metzov's voice cut through the room.

"Major Grozky, with you leading the operation in St Petersburg, I want Senior Lieutenant Borzoi to remain in Moscow as FSB liaison officer to coordinate your findings with Grigori and the broader GRU operation,'" Metzov said.

"Yes, sir," Grozky replied. The request was dressed up by Metzov, yet he sensed Koshygin's brinkmanship, a GRU hand dividing the FSB.

"Everything will be coordinated and consolidated by Arkady's operations team here in Moscow. That will enable us to review every aspect of what we find. There will be a daily report to me and I will keep you personally informed," Koshygin said.

"Excellent," Metzov said.

Silently calibrating his new partners, Grozky saw now the omission of the Foreign Intelligence Service and the MVD's Main Directorate for Combating Organised Crime. It was MVD Interior Troops who had screwed up the recapture of Budyonnovsk hospital from Chechen rebels in June 1995. Ivan Palutkin would not have made that mistake which was why Koshygin had recalled a battle-hardened veteran. This was a dark operation, prioritised at short notice and accountable to Yeltsin's most trusted adviser. He and Borzoi were late guests at the Grey Cardinal's private court.

Metzov glanced at his watch as he spoke.

"Time is now critical. The American Senate will report by mid-May. The guilt of Kochenko and his associates is *the* priority. The Russian government must make it clear such practices will never be tolerated. Kochenko stands for everything rotten in this country. His arrest and conviction will show President Yeltsin's resolve to tackle corruption."

Metzov paused to look each man individually in the eye, grinning like a smiling executioner. Grozky noticed the clock on the wall read 2.45 p.m. They had been in the room for almost an hour.

Metzov stood up.

"Gentlemen, you now understand the importance of the task entrusted to you. Everything you have heard is strictly confidential. You each have your orders. We shall meet again in two weeks' time. You are here for one reason: to stop the stain of Yanusk spreading. Do not fail me."

*

The return journey to Sheremetyevo airport took less than thirty minutes, their driver reduced to a disinterested GRU corporal. They travelled in silence, the landscape outside as foreboding as the revelations from their audience with the Grey Cardinal. Moscow hadn't changed. Grozky hadn't expected it would. He had once visited the suburban headquarters of the KGB's blue-blooded First Chief Directorate at Yasenevo, south-west of Moscow, memorable only because their *naglost*, or arrogance, had enforced upon him that he was an intellectually average country cousin. If the First Chief Directorate had been brazen in their superiority, they fell short of the GRU's outlook. He was in a league well above his fighting weight.

At the airport, waiting for their return flight to St Petersburg, Grozky and Borzoi found a pair of seats outside their boarding gate where they could talk in private.

"Jesus, this *is* big," Borzoi said, his excitement tempered by his concern.

"It's more than big, Dmitri, it's very dangerous. Did you notice there were no minutes taken? No record of the discussion. Metzov might as well never have been there. If he feels this threatened, you can imagine how much pressure he's putting on Koshygin. The GRU will do whatever it takes to sabotage the American Senate hearing and they're getting ready to lynch Kochenko. None of us are in a good position on this one, including Metzov. Koshygin must contain the situation, which is why he's got Palutkin as his trigger man. That's a lethal combination."

Borzoi swallowed hard.

"What should I do while you're in St Petersburg?"

"We work together, Dmitri. You stick to being professional and thorough. Make yourself useful to Arkady Dratshev, which should keep Koshygin off your back, and stay close to Zotkin, he looks like someone who could use a friend. That should give us a reasonable handle of what's going on. Who knows what Ekomov will get up to in Washington. You'll discuss with me before you report anything to Koshygin."

Borzoi nodded.

"There's one more thing. See what you can dig up on Kochenko's business partner, you mentioned he was called Sergei Malievich. The more we can understand about Kochenko's operation, the better," Grozky said.

"Sure."

Grozky did not elaborate on his concerns. Yeltsin's policies were as much a sham as Gorbachev's. Russians grew tired of the chaos, while Yeltsin paraded the success of his economic reforms. Unless it could be stopped, the American Senate's report would reveal that a Russian flagship privatisation was little more than a fraud. It would be the end of the shaman from the provinces. Metzov had convened a secret tribunal to absolve Yeltsin from any blame. The Russian government had a slim chance to prove itself capable of bringing those responsible for the Yanusk fraud to justice. What surprised Grozky was his inclusion in a state operation run by a GRU cabal. He was one of eight men who would determine the outcome of the Russian election. With a man as fanatical in his loyalty as the Grey Cardinal, Yeltsin might yet escape from the scandal, but if the political situation became any more unstable the Russian Federation could implode.

8

Removed from his normal duties at the Big House, while Borzoi remained in Moscow, Grozky's colleagues took his silence over the specifics of his new reassignment to be a sign of his predicament. A transfer was interpreted as a prelude to either a promotion or a demotion. They had his measure; if it was a step up he'd still have been in Moscow with Borzoi. A few tried to be congratulatory, the rest did not comment. Grozky did not dwell on their ambivalence, for with General Koshygin's daily demands, he felt time was stealing from its very self. Although he read every surveillance report and wiretap summary, he preferred to participate in the shifts to validate the information. He was not one to rely on the opinions of others.

Waiting in the oily damp of the Big House's garage, Grozky heard a laboured engine yearning for its driver to change gear. Grozky left the shelter of a pillar and walked towards the source, his wallet case under one arm. He would have preferred casual clothes except his uniform played its part for this errand. From around a corner, the wing of an unmarked, grey Volvo saloon appeared. Grozky saw the driver give a weary wave through the windscreen before the car stopped beside him. There was a short scuffle as the driver fought to open his door. A smiling head underneath a Ushanka fur hat greeted Grozky.

"A very good morning to you, Valeri," Sergeant Bogdan Pavlova said.

"Good morning, Bogdan," Grozky said as he got into the passenger seat.

"You know the way to the Lensky Bank?"

"Of course. Depending on the traffic I would think we'll be there in about fifteen to twenty minutes, unless you prefer I use the siren?" Pavlova said, hopefully.

"No siren."

"Then twenty minutes it is."

Pavlova's conviction was not matched by the exclamation of the engine as his foot rode the accelerator. Pavlova was a veteran of forty years' service as a 'Niner' in the KGB's Ninth Directorate, the protection service for Communist Party leaders and their families. He had known Khrushchev. In Soviet times Pavlova could have retired on a good pension, now he was as much an orphan as Grozky.

Grozky smelt the scent of stale vodka and saw the pallor in Pavlova's face.

"You haven't started drinking on duty, have you, Bogdan?"

"Valeri, you know I never drink on duty," Pavlova replied, hurt at the inference until he saw Grozky grinning. Pavlova smiled.

"What were you up to last night, Bogdan?"

"Playing cards."

"You lose much?"

"Far from it. I kept winning which is why they kept me

playing. I didn't get to bed until after 3 a.m.," Pavlova said, brightening.

"I'm glad. Consider yourself excused." Grozky hoped Pavlova was legal to drive.

"Thanks, Valeri. You should know there's a lot of talk about Kochenko."

"What have you heard?"

"He's in trouble. The word is the local gangs sense an opportunity."

"Where did you hear this?"

"Around. It came up again at cards last night."

"You didn't let on about the surveillance operation, did you?"

"Valeri, *please*," Pavlova said. He shifted into second gear, forcing the stick and ignoring the gear box's outcry. Grozky punched him lightly in the bicep and Pavlova's pained expression subsided. His sense of duty came from a lifetime of Soviet service. It was a shame his experience hadn't kept pace with modern cars.

"They'd be mad to try anything. Kochenko controls a small army," Grozky said.

"Sure. They're in no hurry. They'll just wait it out."

Grozky frowned at the news. By the time such street gossip filtered up to private card games it was a well-shared titbit. Strength was the cardinal quality the Russian gangs respected. If Kochenko had started out as a member of the *vory v zakone*, his success was envied and there were those who would argue he was too commercial to be a criminal. The spoils from his empire would be significant. Kochenko could be in more firing lines than he realised.

They arrived at the garage's entrance and Pavlova indicated, turning right into Zakharyev Street.

"Let's take it steady, Bogdan, we're in no rush," Grozky said as Pavlova approached Foundry Avenue.

"I'm not drunk."

"No one said you were."

Grozky could have sent someone to the bank to collect Zotkin's request for the additional records except he saw how he could benefit. His skill was in assessing people's habits and their motivations, not financial expertise, which had been the preserve of economic counterintelligence under the KGB's Sixth Directorate. The closest he had come to financial records was the security training he had received on information technology and the threat posed by increasing computerisation. The risk of the illicit removal of data from naval computers concerned him far more than the threat of ideological sabotage from the West. A trip to the bank was an opportunity to learn.

In the absence of a siren, Pavlova drove with a careful respect for the traffic. Grozky unzipped his case and took out the two faxes Borzoi had sent him earlier that morning. The first was the GRU background material on Sergei Malievich. The second was the bonus, a transcript from the previous day's Senate hearing. Ilia Ekomov's Washington operatives had been busy.

Grozky started on the statement which Arnold Lennister, the CEO of Archipelago Oil, had made to the Subcommittee. Reading it, Grozky sensed Lennister's frustration at the American intelligence agencies' claim that the fall of communism was a success. While Lennister recognised Yanusk had been hard to deal with during the communist era, Archipelago's perseverance had enabled it to purchase oil with regularity. Compared to the post-privatisation period, his Soviet experience was framed in nostalgia. Under Tomarov the oil supply dried up. The contracts Archipelago should have been able to purchase through Capri Trading were impossible to secure. Lennister favoured the phrase 'unable to secure the right relationship' which was why Archipelago had resorted to buying the consultancy services of Zach Brown, going as far as trying to make an investment in Yanusk, all to no avail. Lennister erred towards desperation in his summation, 'where one rogue privateer can sabotage the free market, others will follow'. The spectre of Russian oil supply failure was real and growing for Archipelago.

Staring at the page, Grozky understood Metzov's fear; the tunnelling under the walls of the Russian government's reputation was moving apace. As each witness publicly recounted their experience, their statements would accumulate to reveal the foul underbelly of Yeltsin's economic reforms. Once the tunnels converged and the Senate report was published, the presidency of a man complicit in corruption would collapse. To shore up the damage, Tomarov and Kochenko's grand larceny must be exposed.

At the sudden cacophony of car horns, Grozky heard Pavlova sigh and the glare of the Volvo's horn joined the din. Grozky looked up to see they had left Nevsky Avenue and were stuck in a queue over the Griboedov Canal, adjacent to what might have been a replica of Saint Peter's Basilica. From the shoulder of Kazan Cathedral, a monument to Napoleon's defeat, a curved arm of colonnades reached ahead of them, threatening their flank.

"That's bloody typical. Every time there's a hold-up, it's always on a damn bridge. It would be the bloody Kazan Bridge," Pavlova said, slapping the steering wheel in frustration.

"Don't worry. We're almost there," Grozky said, putting the faxes back in his case. St Petersburg was as beautiful to strangers as it was impractical to residents. Tsar Peter the Great had realised his vision of Amsterdam, his 'city on the sea', plumbing together a myriad of rivers and canals and matched in complexity by the connecting bridges. Kazan Bridge was the shortest and widest of the twenty-one crossings over the Griboedov Canal.

As the traffic started to move, Grozky checked his watch, an involuntary habit because he could not be late for a meeting for which he did not have an appointment. However, he wanted to be back at the Big House when, at 2 p.m., Yevgeny Kochenko would present himself with his lawyer, Taras Lugin. The meeting was at the behest of the Russian Ministry of Fuel and Energy, and Andrei Simonov had flown in from Moscow. Grozky felt the meeting was premature, but he had been overruled. There was no time.

Their progress improved along the Griboedov Canal Embankment and a few minutes later Pavlova slowed the car and pulled up at the kerb outside the bank.

"I shouldn't be long," Grozky said.

"I'll stay here then?" Pavlova asked.

"Yes. Do that. Grab lunch if you like," Grozky said and got out of the car.

Inside the bank, Grozky's unexpected arrival was intercepted by the bank manager's executive assistant.

"How can I be of service?" she asked, as steely as she was pretty, a firm smile asserting her experience.

Grozky spotted the door marked 'Manager' behind her.

"Stay right where you are and don't move," Grozky replied and swept past, leaving her to fume.

Without knocking, Grozky marched into the office, the door becoming a casualty as it thumped against the skirting board.

At the far end of the room a middle-aged man in a white shirt and dark tie took another bite of a hovering sandwich, ignoring the interruption to his lunch break. Striding forward, Grozky reached his desk and stood so close as almost to touch it, his proximity as intimidating as his uniform.

The bank manager realised his error and struggled to gnaw through the ham and pickle obstructing his palate. He was still chewing animatedly when Grozky addressed him.

"You are in charge?"

"Y-es," the manager stammered, his speech impeded by partially dissolved food.

"I am here on a matter of state security."

"Please, sit down, Major err…"

"Grozky, Major Valeri Grozky. I don't expect to be here long enough to sit down and, for your sake, let us both hope I don't need to."

Grozky betrayed no satisfaction as the bank manager's face paled and finally he managed to swallow uncomfortably, restoring a small piece of composure at the expense of his indigestion. The bank manager, lacking in rank, drew on a lifetime's experience in customer services and spoke softly.

"Of course, Major Grozky. Luka Peterkof at your service. I totally understand. How can I assist you?"

"You received a request to supply data to the Moscow Prosecutor-General's office. It was supposed to have been ready last week. It is now Monday afternoon," Grozky said.

"You're here to collect the data?"

"I am."

Peterkof held up a conciliatory hand.

"Major Grozky, please accept my apologies for the slight overrun. It took more time than we expected to analyse and extract all the records requested. I have everything ready." He stood up as Grozky watched him coldly.

"Please take a seat. I will arrange everything for you," Peterkof said, walking from behind his desk, an outstretched hand indicating the chairs available either side of Grozky. He hurried from the room while Grozky remained standing.

The bank manager was away for a few minutes. When he returned, Grozky was sitting in a chair, his officer's hat on the desk and writing in a small notebook on his lap. Grozky did not look up as he waved the bank manager to sit down.

"The records are just coming," Peterkof said, sitting down and gesturing towards the open door.

Grozky remained immersed in his notebook.

There was a knock at the door and two clerks entered, each burdened by a large cardboard box. They deposited the weighty cargo inside the door and then returned to deliver another two boxes, grunting in relief as they departed.

Peterkof leapt from his chair and ran after them. Grozky glanced across at the stacked cube of boxes. It was more than he was expecting.

The bank manager returned with a stapled set of papers in each hand, sat down and handed a set to Grozky.

"It's all there, Major Grozky, everything which was requested. You have the additional records from 1 June to 30 November 1993. They are laid out in chronological order and by the type of transaction, for instance whether it was a cheque or a wire transfer. You have the full list of all incoming and outgoing payments for the accounts listed. This shows all movements from the Yanusk Oil Company to the Lensky group of companies and any payments made by Mr Tomarov and any received by Mr Kochenko. The accounts are all listed here…" He paused as he turned the first page.

"You have hard copy printouts and, of course, we have included the data on floppy disks, so they can be reviewed on a computer. An index and an inventory of the filenames is also included."

Peterkof held out his sheets once more, turning to a page where neat rows of typed information ran like regiments down the paper.

Grozky nodded. The bank manager responded well to intimidation. It was time to change tack.

"For six months, it looks like a lot of data," Grozky said.

"Well, there are thousands of transactions."

"From this information, I am able to identify who originated the payment?"

"Absolutely. You can see who originated the payment, the recipient or beneficiary and their account number."

Grozky nodded again. The process of financial give and take seemed reasonably straightforward.

"Let me ask you a question. If I wanted to transfer a large amount of money, say more than 150 million roubles, what would be the easiest way?"

The bank manager barely considered the question before he answered.

"Well, a cheque is the easiest way. If you were making a payment to a regular customer, then a wire transfer from bank to bank would be the simplest. I specify your bank account details and a bank identification code, or BIC, and then my bank makes the transfer. It's an electronic transfer of funds which could be via proprietary bank-to-bank software or, if it's a commercial transfer, via the SWIFT network."

"SWIFT?"

"The Society for Worldwide Interbank Financial Telecommunication."

"And let's say I wanted to be more discreet about how I transferred the money, how might I do that?"

"Well, you could send the funds to what is called an intermediary bank. That would be a two-step process where I send the funds to the intermediary bank and then, separately, that bank sends the funds to the beneficiary's account. The full amount would still show up on your account, except the originating entity would now be from the account used by the intermediary bank."

Grozky saw Peterkof hold up a finger of reassurance.

"You have to remember any transfer of funds requires a bank account at both ends of the transaction. You'll appreciate the administrative overhead involved. The person opening the account must provide documentation substantiating who they are and the purpose of the account. In turn, the bank must be satisfied their potential customer is a reputable individual or company. It's an official due diligence check referred to as 'Know Your Customer'. Does that make sense?"

"Yes, so far."

"Good. I'm glad," Peterkof said. Encouraged, he quickly continued.

"Let's say I use an intermediary bank; the chances are the person transferring the money is going to use the same account at the intermediary bank because of the overhead plus the administration required to keep the account adequately funded. In reviewing the transactions, it's often about what you're not looking for. For example, if I'm searching for a payment originating from you, I look through the data, but I see nothing from a Major Grozky. However, I know I'm looking for a sizeable amount of approximately 150 million roubles. I might find three payments of fifty million roubles originating from a small intermediary bank in the Crimea. There's nothing to connect you directly, yet the transactions to stand out are the ones originating from the bank in the Crimea. You can still find the trail."

Grozky nodded. In the absence of precise information, it was about spotting a pattern which might reveal an anomaly.

"Indeed. I have a car waiting downstairs. I'll detain you no longer. Thank you for your assistance," Grozky said.

"Of course. I'll have the boxes brought down now," the bank manager said with an air of relief.

Grozky arrived back at the car invigorated and unremorseful. Watching the boxes being loaded into the boot of the Volvo, he wondered at the level of refinement Grigori Zotkin was using to search through the financial records in Moscow.

"Shall we stop for lunch? We could grab a sandwich on the way back?" Pavlova asked as they set off.

Grozky checked his watch. Kochenko was due to appear at the Big House at 2 p.m. It was almost 1.30 p.m. A thought occurred to him.

"Where's Kochenko now?"

"The last report I had was while you were at the bank. He was meeting someone for lunch at some flash restaurant near the Kryukov Canal."

"Let's see what he's up to. You can grab lunch when we get back to headquarters," Grozky said.

"Of course," Pavlova said, without sounding disappointed. He kept one hand on the steering wheel, using the other to check in with the FSB surveillance team on the car's radio handset.

Criss-crossing the streets and canals of the Admiralty District, Pavlova drove with the purpose of a man late for his lunch. Grozky retrieved Borzoi's other fax from his wallet case and started reading.

The paragraphs on Sergei Malievich confirmed he had served in Afghanistan for four years, the last three as a full lieutenant under Kochenko's command. They had been stationed at the garrison town of Charikar, protecting the Bagram air base to the south and the Salang tunnel to the north, the only overland supply route from Northern Afghanistan into the Soviet Union. Charikar also provided a base to attack the hotbed of Mujahideen resistance in the Panjshir Valley to the north-east of the garrison. Malievich had been wounded twice and decorated three times. Kochenko was the counterinsurgency strategist while Malievich was the executor, leading the patrols against the enemy and supported by heavily armoured helicopters. This was a battlefield partnership of high stakes where each man relied on the other. Malievich was still serving when Kochenko was dismissed. Whatever had transpired in Afghanistan had not jeopardised their friendship. Malievich had left Afghanistan on 15 February 1989, the same day General Boris Gromov and the last of the Soviet units had crossed back over the Amu Darya river.

Grozky looked up as he heard Pavlova on the radio handset.

"We've just joined Zagorodny Avenue. What's your position?" Pavlova asked.

"We're approaching Vitesbk station. You can't miss the three black Mercedes saloons. They're cruising," came the response.

Ahead, an electric trolleybus clung to the gridwork of cables suspended above the street like Christmas lights. Pavlova accelerated, overtaking the bus on its captive route and driving fast along the wide avenue. The gothic Art Nouveau of Vitebsk railway station flashed by before Grozky spotted the rear of a Mercedes, burnished in black, its armour as thick as a tank's. Grozky touched Pavlova lightly on his shoulder.

"Slow down, Bogdan. There they are. Tuck in and follow them," Grozky said.

The oligarch's security detail impressed Grozky. Kochenko was shadowed by four security guards headed by a blond-haired ex-commando identified as 'Marko' Markovsky who was also his driver. Kochenko's routes through the city were carefully varied, avoiding a pattern which could be anticipated and used against him. Grozky's surveillance details had already identified two other apartments Kochenko made use of in the city.

They passed Prince Vladimir Cathedral marking the merger of Zagorodny Avenue with Vladimir Avenue. Atop the cathedral, five onion domes jostled for dominance while adjacent, the detached belfry tower stood as defiant as a sentry. Resplendent in their ochre and white façades, the pair of buildings lauded over the square beneath like benevolent royalty.

Watching the block of cars ahead it struck Grozky that, without the American Senate's investigation, the business indiscretions of a man like Kochenko would have gone overlooked. In Russia the rise of the entrepreneur was inescapable even among the Internal Security services. Some members of the ex-KGB's Third Directorate had set up 'Santa', a foreign economic association to sell military goods abroad, if that qualified as enterprise. Yet capitalism had been banished since the Bolshevik revolution and it was wishful to think the privatisation of state assets could occur without mishap. Scratch beneath any of the other major joint stock company transitions and there would be irregularities.

The traffic lights were red at the junction with Nevsky Avenue. Pavlova pulled up several cars behind the last black Mercedes. Ahead stood the neat classical lines of the late-eighteenth-century terraced development for which Nevsky Avenue was famous, clouded by the spider's web of cables suspended across the street.

As the traffic pulled away, instead of continuing ahead on Foundry Avenue towards the Big House, the lead black Mercedes turned left into Nevsky Avenue, shadowed by its two outriders. Pavlova sighed at the delay to his lunch. Watching the heavy-set cars in formation, Grozky thought Kochenko's crew would already have picked up the surveillance. If they had, it was a masterclass in pretence, their even pace so nonchalant it was immune from suspicion. The Big House was less than half a mile away and he sensed the drivers taking satisfaction in their charade of feinting left. Kochenko understood the stakes of bluff and double bluff. It could make the difference between life and death.

Their game of follow-the-leader crossed the Fontanka river, the southern border of the city's Central District, and then Anichkov Bridge. Grozky glanced at a great bronze horse which reared up, one of the four *Horse Tamers* by Peter Clodt von Jürgensburg demarcating the corners of the bridge. As a smooth metal flank of hind leg flashed by, Grozky found himself thinking of Natassja. He dispelled the image and focused on the fleet of Mercedes as they turned right down Sadovya Street.

A few hundred yards later the cars turned right again onto Engineering Street, cutting back towards the Fontanka river. Grozky sat up and stared ahead. He had been idly watching a dirty blue Fiat for the last few turns and now the significance dawned on him. He had first noticed the dowdy little car several minutes ago when they had passed the Prince Vladimir Cathedral. Despite the crispness of the afternoon, Grozky wound the window down a half-inch, an arctic freshness penetrating the warm interior. Pavlova knew better than to comment, instead freeing a hand from the steering wheel to turn up the collar of his overcoat. His action further marred the harmony inside the car, the whining pitch of the Volvo's engine appealing for the gear to be changed.

"How long has that Fiat been there?" Grozky asked.

"What Fiat?" Pavlova asked absently, his eyes tracking the gear stick as he moved it and the engine relaxed.

"That *blue* Fiat," Grozky said, flicking a finger towards the only small blue car in the traffic ahead.

"I've no idea, Valeri. I've been keeping back to follow Kochenko on his extended tour to the Big House."

Grozky decided now was not the time to lecture Pavlova there was more to surveillance than keeping a rigid distance behind a target vehicle.

"Let me ask," Pavlova said, quickly reaching for the radio handset.

Pavlova looked both relieved and disappointed when the FSB tail car reported they were unaware of the Fiat, a car inconspicuous in all but its route.

Grozky made his decision.

"Bogdan, we know where Kochenko's going. I want to know what the driver of that Fiat is up to. Let's find out, shall we?"

Pavlova nodded, checking his mirror and pulled out. Vigour replaced fatigue as he locked his arms either side of the steering wheel. Amidst the traffic, the Volvo bore down steadily on the dawdling Fiat.

Grozky squinted in an effort to make sense of the registration number against a plate so filthy the grime obscured the characters.

They were crossing the apex of the Belinsky Bridge, the gap to the Fiat less than ten yards, when the Fiat's driver suddenly accelerated on the descent. Pavlova surprised Grozky by masterfully pursuing the little blue car against the heated rebukes of other vehicles who were forced to make way.

The Fiat raced down Belinsky Street using the tram lines in the centre of the road to squeeze between the traffic and tore past Kochenko's convoy. Grozky swore as he watched the little car pull away. Pavlova punished the Volvo's engine and they shot by the line of black Mercedes whose tinted windows were impervious to the chase. Grozky leant forward and turned on the siren, their pursuit now official. The Fiat's driver took a risk, jumping a red light and turned into Foundry Avenue. Comforted by the roaring siren, Pavlova doggedly followed, narrowly missing a bus.

"Shit!" Pavlova swore, holding his nerve and reimmersing himself in the hunt.

On the wide expanse of Foundry Avenue and the lanes of cruising cars, they began to close on the Fiat and their target became reckless, straying across the central tram lines towards the oncoming traffic. Pavlova, fists clenched against the wheel, hared after the little car until it suddenly veered right and disappeared. Pavlova followed, braking hard to avoid a car on his inside and the Volvo's tyres squealed as they chased their quarry.

The three domes of the Transfiguration Cathedral rose in front of them and Pavlova exploited the Volvo's power to get back into the chase. The Fiat remained in sight, dwarfed by the cathedral, until it skirted down the side of Transfiguration Square. Pavlova followed, struggling against his speed to hold the curve of the road. Trees rushed alongside, while the grand apartments opposite looked down on the pursuit.

The Fiat's brake lights blinked red as the driver tried and failed to pass a van hogging the street. Pavlova closed the gap, only for the Fiat to scurry left and disappear again. Pavlova matched the turn with a smooth double declutch that surprised Grozky. He saw the Fiat was stuck behind a car at the junction ahead. The Fiat angrily turned right as the car impeding it turned left.

"Take him, Bogdan," Grozky said, praying the traffic was light as Pavlova blindly followed the little car around the corner. The Fiat was some twenty yards ahead and, on the long straight of Church Street, the Volvo had the edge, catching it up as they reached Tauride Park, the street's tall lamp posts dwarfed amongst the jungle of trees.

The Fiat kept wildly to the outside lane, while Pavlova kept the Volvo within yards of the jerky blue car and edged to pass it. The north-western State Medical University and the Suvorov Museum flew past and, as the Volvo drew alongside the car, Grozky caught a glimpse of a thin-faced man, his face braced against the windscreen. The Fiat's driver responded to Pavlova's challenge and the blue car found the reserves to push ahead. Pavlova matched the Fiat, but as he accelerated again the Fiat braked suddenly, tyres screaming, and slewed down a side street. Pavlova's reaction was instant, the Volvo skidding past the turning to throw them both against their safety belts. Glancing behind him, Pavlova began to reverse only to receive irate hoots from the oncoming cars. Grozky realised the futility of the manoeuvre.

"Christ. Just take the next right," Grozky said.

Pavlova drove, his urgency desperate and the Volvo's gear box grated in protest. The Volvo's horn attacked anything threatening their progress while Grozky searched for a glimpse of the Fiat. For several minutes they continued their quest until Pavlova slowed the Volvo and sighed.

"Damn." Grozky's hand slammed down on the top of the moulded dashboard. He could not fault Pavlova's efforts.

"Well, Bogdan, at least you know what to look for next time. *That* Fiat. Get an alert out with the description of the driver and the car. Any vehicle matching the description is to be stopped and the driver apprehended."

"Yes, sir. I'll get that distributed. Don't worry, if I see him again, I'll definitely get him next time," Pavlova said.

Grozky cursed at the missed opportunity.

"You can keep the siren on," Grozky said, conscious he was now late for the meeting with Kochenko.

9

Grozky arrived at the Big House to find the scheduled room on the first floor was empty. Confused, he walked down to the reception desk on the ground floor where all visitors were registered. He was irritated to discover the meeting room had been moved to one of the interrogation cells downstairs.

"Really? Who authorised the change of room?" Grozky asked.

The guard checked the register.

"A Colonel Palutkin."

Palutkin. Grozky was dismayed at his inclusion.

"When was the change made?" Grozky asked.

"Almost an hour ago. Colonel Palutkin requested it when he arrived with General Koshygin."

Grozky frowned at the unannounced insertion of the GRU into his sphere of operation.

"Which room?"

"Interrogation Room C."

Grozky thanked him and hurried downstairs.

Interrogation Room C was no better than a police cell with a separate anteroom from where proceedings could be observed. Already late, Grozky decided against disturbing the meeting.

Entering the anteroom, Grozky found Anatoli Koshygin dressed in a suit, standing cross-armed in front of the two-way mirror. Koshygin grinned at Grozky.

"You're late. It's no matter. You've arrived in time to watch the show," Koshygin said.

Next to Koshygin a man in overalls was bent over a video camera mounted on a tripod. The man did not look up from the eyepiece as he filmed the room. Grozky stood next to him and saw the viewfinder on top of the camera displaying the scene in miniature, the tiny characters gathered around the table.

Grozky was surprised to see the room contained five occupants. At the far end of the table, facing the mirror, Ivan Palutkin sat as if he was holding court, dressed in his uniform, his chair tilted against a wall, a glossy boot resting across his knee. Either side of Palutkin sat Taras Lugin, Kochenko's lawyer, and Andrei Simonov. Closest to the mirror, Yevgeny Kochenko faced an unfamiliar runt of a man, his head bent forward and squinting through thick bifocal lenses. More scalp than hair, his liberal use of gel merely slickened his baldness.

"Who's that?" Grozky asked, pointing to the unfamiliar face.

"That is Piotr Petrovitch. He's a special investigator. He'll ask questions Simonov won't even have considered," Koshygin said.

Grozky saw the room's seating was deliberate with Petrovitch and Kochenko placed adjacent to the camera. The hard set of Kochenko's lean profile registered his displeasure, and his lawyer, Lugin, watched over by Palutkin, looked ill at ease. The reduced contrast through the glass hid the room's décor and belied its real intent. The primitive metal chairs would not break when kicked over during an interrogation and the aluminium-topped table failed to show dents and scratches. Under the unshielded bulb obtruding from the ceiling, the industrial dark brown paint gave up no signs of the dried blood on the walls.

Petrovitch sat forward, his elbows resting on top of the table. Through the mirror the special investigator's thick glasses appeared oddly translucent as if he were bug-eyed. Kochenko sat at a disadvantage to Palutkin, who gazed at the oligarch as though he was prey.

The audio was good, picking up the faintest of noises, each transfer accompanied by a faintly tinny twang. Listening to Petrovitch, Grozky heard his vowels take on a nasal echo.

"Of course, you can *claim* you had nothing more than an arm's-length relationship with Yuri Tomarov. Yet, despite Tomarov having no previous record with Lensky Bank, in his first commercial transaction he was able to acquire significant funding which he used to purchase Yanusk Oil."

Kochenko shook his head, dismissing the association.

"Mr Petrovitch, as I am sure you are aware, lending is central to any bank's activities. Tomarov's request for finance was considered like any other. There are obviously risks when money is lent, which is why collateral is required to support a loan. Tomarov provided collateral in the form of property investments and Lensky Bank had the rights to that collateral," Kochenko said.

"If that is true, then why did Tomarov choose Lensky Bank, an organisation with which he had no prior relationship?

Why did he not select one of the other banks which he had previously used? Did that not concern you? He was seeking a fresh source of finance for a very significant transaction. Surely that should have raised concerns about why his current lenders wouldn't put up the finance?" Petrovitch asked.

"All markets are competitive. In the private protection market, companies approach Lensky Security who have no prior experience of using us because they find they get a good service at a fair price – it's a good deal for everyone. The same principle applies in finance," Kochenko replied.

"Ah. 'A good deal,'" Petrovitch said, seizing on the words. "I like your summary, Mr Kochenko. Yes, I agree it was certainly a 'good deal' for Mr Tomarov, wasn't it? He was able to find a source of finance when no one else would lend him such a sum and was then able to organise one of the worst frauds this country has seen."

"What's your point?" Kochenko asked.

"Precisely that, Mr Kochenko. I am seeking to establish the connection. Don't you find it interesting that, after purchasing Yanusk stock, Tomarov switched the original collateral from property holdings and replaced it with the Yanusk stock he now owns? An unusual switch, wouldn't you say, given what subsequently occurred?"

"I don't see the relevance. Like any bank, Lensky is reasonably flexible about collateral, providing its value covers the outstanding debt. Why would that be a problem?" Kochenko replied.

"Because when Tomarov defaulted on the loan, you called in the collateral. His default meant Lensky Bank automatically acquired the majority holding in Yanusk Oil. Tomarov had, during his tenure, established a hugely lucrative scam allowing millions of dollars to be skimmed off privately. The switch of collateral meant you ended up owning an oil company which, in today's market, is worth significantly more than the value of the original loan. Tomarov made a lot of money and so have you. What was that, Mr Kochenko? An underhand payback for putting up the funds for a new client?"

Kochenko's lawyer leant forward to protest too late. The oligarch's fist hammered against the metal table, the percussion captured as a weird whine by the microphone.

"Go to hell. Lensky Bank entered into the loan in good faith. We were duped as much as anyone else. You accuse me when you should start with why the government didn't check Yuri Tomarov's background more carefully when they ratified his purchase of Yanusk," Kochenko said.

The game of cat and mouse was captured on film, Kochenko indignant while Petrovitch exuded the self-control of the diligent official. It was a smug performance from a man keen to please the camera he knew watched him.

"How can you deny the coincidence? You assisted a new client to buy a company and Tomarov sets up a major fraud. The company subsequently passes to you. You made money from your original loan and you've ended up owning an oil company. You seem to have done rather well from your relationship with Yuri Tomarov."

"Yevgeny, these accusations are groundless. We are leaving," Lugin said, his voice unsteady.

"Walk away from the truth, by all means. It is only a matter of time," Petrovitch said.

"That is a *lie*. There is no evidence Lensky Bank or I sought to benefit from what Tomarov did at Yanusk," Kochenko said.

"That is an aspect the Russian government is obliged to consider," Petrovitch said.

"Mr Petrovitch, the only wrongdoing on our part was Lensky Bank's due diligence checks on Mr Tomarov could have been better. My organisation has acknowledged that and been collaborating fully with the Ministry of Fuel and Energy for several months. As soon as we became aware of the fraud we reported it to the authorities," Kochenko said.

The oligarch looked across at Andrei Simonov.

"Andrei, we've been meeting monthly in Moscow ever since we reported the fraud. I've employed professional consultants to establish a proper governance structure. The controls those consultants have put in place were all documented in the detailed report I submitted to the Ministry at the start of January. As I recall, at our last meeting in February, you stated, 'The Minister has asked me to communicate that provided the remaining work is completed as planned, then he is satisfied with the actions taken'. That conversation is a matter of official record," Kochenko said.

Andrei Simonov looked embarrassed. In the short silence that followed, Grozky heard Koshygin chortle to himself. Simonov swallowed, his face growing red, but before he could respond, Petrovitch attacked again.

"That is what you would have us believe, Mr Kochenko, and yet I read it took you another five months before you disclosed the fraud in May 1995. What was that? Another slip in your procedures?"

"I would hope you also know damn well how difficult it is to detect carefully organised frauds. No one could have conceived the scale of what Tomarov was up to. Once the huge breakdown in the internal controls at Yanusk became apparent, Lensky Bank has done everything in its power to address the situation," Kochenko said.

"Mr Kochenko, you continue to protest your innocence. However, I make my living investigating financial crimes. Your bank funded a businessman who set up a massive fraud. The same bank which financed him subsequently takes over the company. Surely you can understand why questions must be answered as to how you both ended up considerably richer as a result?" Petrovitch said.

"You accuse Lensky Bank of making money when we were victims of the fraud as much as the other shareholders!"

Kochenko's fury was evident, although from behind the glass, Grozky wondered at the vehemence of the denial.

Taras Lugin shook his head and stood up to leave, encouraging Kochenko to do the same. Unperturbed, Petrovitch's nasal whine ground on.

"Oh come, Mr Kochenko, look at the facts. Yanusk was privatised at a fraction of its real value, the sweetener to encourage investment. On paper, you can claim you are making a loss on your loan, while the reality is Yanusk is worth millions more than Tomarov paid and you are the majority shareholder in Lensky Bank. I might almost believe you as the outraged victim until I see how you've benefited from your relationship with Yuri Tomarov," Petrovitch said.

The special investigator finished his summation by waving the file in front of Kochenko's face and then threw it down on the table like a gauntlet. Petrovitch's performance was masterful, a man convinced of the infallibility of his case. Grozky glanced at the video's viewfinder, the camera panning in on Kochenko's face, now a study of cold rage.

Through the mirror Grozky saw Palutkin grinning like a voyeur for whom the show was exceeding his expectations. Kochenko's lawyer stood up to intercede, but the oligarch raised his hand and Lugin sat down, shaking his head in disbelief.

Kochenko's voice was a vicious rasp as he glared at his accuser.

"Mr Petrovitch, I think you will find Lensky Bank has been more than diligent in our efforts to address the fraud. We invested heavily to identify how the fraud was implemented and how the internal controls were manipulated. We have spent the last nine months ensuring those controls are re-established and improved," Kochenko said.

"You couldn't really do much else, could you? The real question, which you have yet to convince me on, is the *extent* to which you knew about Tomarov's intentions. Of all Tomarov's business associates, you are the one who has benefited the most," Petrovitch said.

"You're wasting your time. My only relationship to Yuri Tomarov is my bank lent him money for a commercial business transaction. That's it," Kochenko said.

"Which is why your relationship with Yuri Tomarov is being revisited. Whatever you've told the Ministry is an entirely separate matter to the *underlying substance* of your relationship with Tomarov," Petrovitch said, placing his barb with the skill of a picador.

Grozky saw Palutkin's enjoyment at the baiting, his teeth bared in an animal snarl. Ivan Palutkin had fought in the shadow of death for so long he was transforming into one of its demons.

"How often do I need to repeat myself? I have no idea why Tomarov chose to switch the collateral. Perhaps he had cashflow problems or he decided to use the stock to self-fund his investment and free up his property to secure another venture," Kochenko said.

"Self-funding? Indeed. That's a complex arrangement for Tomarov to have been entering into. You say you offered him no advice on this matter?" Petrovitch queried.

"Absolutely not. Lensky Bank only secured his loans. We were his banker. Why don't you ask his accountant? Tomarov made his own decisions," Kochenko said, his shoulders flexing. He looked like he wanted to punch Petrovitch.

"Believe me I would, Mr Kochenko, except unfortunately the Chief Financial Officer, Stanislav Rusnak, was killed. Where was it…?" Petrovitch asked, musing on his own question.

"Grozny," Palutkin said, making the Chechen capital sound like a cursed place.

"Thank you. Well, Mr Kochenko, you see how convenient it is for you those who could answer my questions are no longer able to," Petrovitch said.

The inference Kochenko might somehow be involved was not lost on Grozky. Kochenko's face could not escape the close-up from the camera zooming in. Looking at the viewfinder Grozky recalled the mastery of Nazi film propaganda and the victories secured by the perseverance of the morally righteous. In the confinement of his sullied surroundings, Kochenko would be under no illusion over the clenched fists of power opposing him. The conviction of Petrovitch's blows left Kochenko caught on film against the ropes, his replies those of a guilty man struggling to rebut what he knows to be true.

"Mr Petrovitch, Lensky Bank's work in addressing the weaknesses at Yanusk Oil is also a matter of record at the Ministry. Until today, there has never been any suggestion from either the Ministry or the Prosecutor-General's office that Lensky Bank acted improperly. Unless there are formal charges to be faced, I don't think there is anything further to discuss," Kochenko said.

For the first time in the exchange Petrovitch pointed an accusatory finger at Kochenko.

"This is a man who you claim not to know, yet only three months ago you met with him in St Petersburg. What was the purpose of the meeting?" Petrovitch asked.

"Tomarov needed money," Kochenko said.

"And how much did you give him?"

"I gave him nothing."

"It sounds like your business partner had become something of an embarrassment to you," Petrovitch said, his theatrical chuckle sounding like a giggle. He stared at Kochenko, his mouth fixed in a leer.

"Tomarov was *not* my business partner," Kochenko said.

Grozky listened to another denial. Kochenko couldn't know the information the GRU had obtained from the American Subcommittee, yet with the millions of dollars in commission Kochenko had been paid, Tomarov would have felt justified in approaching him for money.

The confrontation suddenly ended as Kochenko stood up. He strode towards the door, followed by his lawyer. Grozky half expected they would find the door locked, the ultimate humiliation captured on film. Instead, the pair hurried from the room, leaving Petrovitch, Palutkin and Simonov to stare at the empty chairs.

In the small anteroom, Anatoli Koshygin raised a clenched fist in triumph. His cameraman stood up, smiling as he stretched. Grozky was relieved he had been spared from being in the cell during the GRU's staged inquisition.

"Good work. As soon as we are back in Moscow you are to make five copies of the tape and send them and the original to me," Koshygin said to the cameraman.

"Yes, sir," the cameraman replied. He picked up the tripod and left the anteroom.

Koshygin clapped Grozky on the shoulder, the folds of his face warm with success.

"We could not have hoped for more. The Prosecutor-General's office have been dragging their feet. They don't understand the man they're dealing with. Aleksandr Metzov has been very clear on what he wants regarding Kochenko: evidence, arrest, charge, trial. I have some discretion when it comes to the order of those events. This film will set the scene very well at his trial," Koshygin said.

"I'm sure Aleksandr Metzov appreciates your initiative, General," Grozky said.

"You see, we have taken the battle to Kochenko. We've got him right where we want him. He knows that now," Koshygin said.

The door opened, and Ivan Palutkin strode in. He glanced at Grozky as if he was an irrelevance. Grozky felt his status as a co-conspirator vanish.

"Ah, Ivan, there you are. Great work. Kochenko understands the measure of what awaits him," Koshygin said, grasping Palutkin's hand and shaking it vigorously.

"Well done, Ivan," Grozky said, receiving a hyena's grin from the GRU trespasser.

A thought occurred to Grozky.

"General, my driver and I intercepted a small blue Fiat this afternoon which was following Kochenko's vehicles. I don't suppose Petrovitch or anyone else has Kochenko under observation?"

Koshygin looked surprised, his eyes deferring to Palutkin.

Palutkin grinned with the authority of a man beyond reproach.

"No one else on this operation is following Kochenko

because that task is assigned to the FSB," Palutkin replied, addressing Koshygin.

The news seemed to dampen Koshygin's enjoyment of his moment. A look of small alarm stalled the jovial flesh.

"Valeri, Yevgeny Kochenko is not a man to be trusted. If he's got other problems, I expect you to find them. Do you understand? You'll be ready to brief Metzov next Tuesday?" Koshygin asked.

"Of course, sir. You'll receive a full report in advance."

"It had better be good," Koshygin said.

"You'll excuse me, General, I've got a few leads to chase down. I'll see you both in Moscow next week," Grozky said, feeling like a man press-ganged into service.

"Of course, of course. We'll not detain you," Koshygin said, beaming at Palutkin once more before leading him out of the room, his arm clasped around the shoulder of his favoured subordinate.

Alone in the room, Grozky was relieved to be free of Palutkin's presence. As he stood looking at the empty interrogation cell through the glass, Grozky wished he could endorse Koshygin's optimism, but the dark face of Yevgeny Kochenko confirmed the oligarch now knew what to expect. The gloves were off.

*

Grozky returned to his office, conscious he was losing ground to the GRU. He disliked being wrong-footed. They must have been operating unseen in St Petersburg for several weeks, otherwise how could Petrovitch have known Kochenko and Tomarov had met recently? Natassja had been seeking Tomarov, unaware he had broken cover. Metzov had tasked Grozky with finding the link between Kochenko and Tomarov and he could not come up short. Irrespective of Koshygin's disregard for his involvement, how Grozky found the evidence was his affair. He picked up the phone and called Borzoi in Moscow.

"Dmitri, let Zotkin know I've collected the bank data. Could you do me a favour? What were Tomarov's domestic arrangements, by which I mean who's really going to miss him? Parents, wives, lovers?"

"Sure, Valeri. Let me check. The GRU has files on everything and everyone. It shouldn't take long," Borzoi said.

Grozky turned to the day's surveillance reports on his desk, scanning the detailed logs and photographic evidence. He searched until he found the entry for Kochenko's lunch appointment. Outside the restaurant, shaking hands with Kochenko was a grinning, well-fed man in a bold pinstripe suit. Grozky read the report: almost two hours in the restaurant and the reservation had been made in Kochenko's name so it was likely the oligarch had asked for the meeting. When he saw the absence of a name he turned the photograph over, seeing only a handwritten annotation of the date and time. As Grozky cursed, a thought occurred to him. He picked up the phone and dialled a number. It rang three times and then he heard the familiar voice.

"Natassja Petrovskaya."

"Natassja. It's Valeri Grozky. I appreciate this is short notice, but I wondered if we might meet briefly later? It'll be quick."

There was a slight pause.

"The earliest I can do is this Wednesday. Would 9 p.m. be okay if that's not too late?" Natassja said.

"9 p.m. on Wednesday would be perfect."

"Do you know the Novy Arbat bar on Michael's Street? It's not far from where I live."

"I'll find it," Grozky said.

"I'll see you later."

Grozky hung up, his hand still on the receiver when the phone started to ring.

"Grozky," he said.

"Valeri, it's Dmitri. I have the information you asked for. It's a short list. Tomarov's parents are both deceased. He was married to an Irina Tomarov, but no children are listed. She lives in south-west Moscow."

Grozky saw his opportunity.

"Dmitri, now I've collected the bank data, I'd like to fly up to Moscow this Thursday and meet with Zotkin. Perhaps you could be discreet and arrange a short meeting with Tomarov's wife? I won't need more than thirty minutes. If you hit any problems, this is my idea, not yours."

"Certainly, Valeri. Leave it with me," Borzoi replied and hung up.

Grozky returned to the papers on his desk. He started typing his report, stabbing at every keystroke as he sought to make sense of his material. With the GRU's thoroughness Koshygin would have his reasons to feel self-congratulatory, yet Grozky felt anything but assured. He filled a page, paused and then his fingertips stamped out another. Petrovitch's partisan picture of collusion was convincing and while Kochenko was determined to discount his connection to Tomarov, they had met three months ago. Now Tomarov was dead and also his Chief Financial Officer. Those who knew the intricacies of Yanusk's financing would tell no tales. Where Yanusk was concerned, the coincidences were growing. He needed to find out why.

10

Sitting in the passenger seat of the second tail car, Colonel Ilia Ekomov could not see Senator Bradley Gravell's black Cadillac sedan several lengths ahead. That responsibility lay with the first team in front of him, Vasili Gorev and Valentina Leskova. Posing as a couple in their thirties, 'team one' was driving an early model light grey Plymouth Reliant station wagon with a small roof rack, a classic family car.

Ekomov and his driver, Lyov, were well back in a tan Dodge Aries coupé. Both cars had Chrysler's plain, square lines with wide grills and recessed headlights, but where the older Plymouth had the Chrysler pentagon riding atop the bonnet, Ekomov's Dodge had the ornament embedded into the grill. Same manufacturer. Similar styling. Bland colours. Most importantly, a similar profile from the front. Ekomov had balanced out the small differences: enough similarity in a rear-view mirror made it harder to be sure when the cars had switched over while blatant breaks in continuity attracted attention. It was about defusing interest from a vehicle. Deception was about reducing complexity to simplicity –

envision the effect required and establish the mould of its construction. Ekomov had turned the discipline of reshaping detail into the skill of an artisan. A master craftsman of deceit, Ekomov's true artistry was killing.

Since his return to Washington four days previously, Ekomov had scrabbled to get his operation up and running. With the Senate Subcommittee due to publish its findings by mid-May at the latest, Koshygin expected him to have his plan in place and executed by Friday 26 April. Less than five weeks. At least he had a free hand on how he sabotaged the Subcommittee. He had teams checking the backgrounds of all those testifying at the Dirksen building for anything he could use against them, but that was unreliable in the time available. The way he looked at it, what he really needed was something which would shake the Subcommittee to the core. It was *how* to cut the head off the snake which is why he had made Senator Bradley Gravell his prime focus.

Gravell's Cadillac had pulled away from the Dirksen building a few minutes previously, heading east on Maryland Avenue away from Capitol Hill. In the forty-eight hours since he'd made the senator his target, Ekomov was still building a pattern of behaviour, yet what had caught his attention was that Gravell's driver had just driven around Stanton Park in a grand U-turn. He was now heading north-west on Massachusetts Avenue, towards Union Station, when the logical route would have been to turn earlier on Second Avenue. The silver-tongued Chairman of the Senate's Permanent Subcommittee on Investigations was the epitome of everything Ekomov despised about America: privileged, wealthy and as deluded as his government that Soviet power had been defeated with the break-up of the USSR. Russia was the master of deceit. In the Great Patriotic War, thousands of miles of worthless steppes were conceded to Nazi panzer columns while Soviet armaments factories were dismantled and reassembled in the East. Now the Cold War had shifted to a new front, *myagkaya sila* or 'soft force' when, in one of its last official acts, the Central Committee of the Communist Party had overseen the capital flight of billions of roubles from the Russian government's coffers to the West. Russia's financial reserves had purchased foreign currency and infiltrated the Western financial system. In a dollar-hungry country, America's power would be subverted by the very instrument of capitalism. It would take time, but when the victory came, Russia would rise stronger than ever.

The radio handset crackled.

"It's the station. He's not using the front entrance, we're now on the slip road going around the back," Valentina said.

Ekomov looked at the map. If it was Union Station, where could Gravell be going at 3.15 p.m. on a Tuesday afternoon?

Ekomov was six cars behind the Plymouth. He should have been using a three-car tail on Gravell, except every day was a fire drill of how to deploy his resources. Conceding a car had been a question of reprioritisation. Koshygin knew he needed more operatives.

A panicked voice spoke over the handset.

"Shit. He's not turned into the parking. He's going straight around the back of the station. He'll spot us if we stay on him."

Ekomov grabbed the radio handset.

"Okay. Use the parking. We'll pick him up. You can catch us up."

"Acknowledged. We'll take off the roof rack and switch drivers."

Ekomov did not respond. Improvisation was not something he should have to rely on, not for this operation. He turned to Lyov.

"Pull up in front of the station. We'll watch for him as he comes out," Ekomov said.

Ahead, Union Square station dominated the skyline. Semi-circular arches ran like hoops down either side of the building before being absorbed by a vast blockhouse of an entrance at the centre where three cavernous arches were separated by outsized Corinthian columns.

Lyov kept clear of the taxi rank in front of the station and followed the signs for the 'Pick Up/Drop Off' lane. He dawdled past the entrance and pulled up in front of a traffic island at the end of the station, exploiting a dead space and obstructing no one.

"There," Ekomov said as the glossy black Cadillac appeared from the side of the building and cruised into the traffic.

Lyov eased the Dodge back onto Columbus Circle. By the time he'd followed the Cadillac back towards Capitol Hill, the black sedan was three cars ahead, keeping a pedestrian pace in the inner lane.

"What's he up to?" Lyov asked the question both of them were thinking.

"Right now, he's checking for the Plymouth and anything else he thinks he's seen before. Stay back," Ekomov said.

First a U-turn, now a deliberate loop of the station. Why would Gravell's driver be taking the time to read the traffic behind him? Gravell was a busy man. If he was sensitive about his route, he had cause to be. He was married with two teenage daughters. It was possible he was screwing around.

The Cadillac's pace remained patient in the inner lane. Beside them the trees in the Lower Senate Park gave way to the manicured lawns bordering Capitol Hill.

"We're back to where we started. Gravell's up to something," Lyov said.

"That's what we're going to find out," Ekomov said, conscious he was now short of vehicles for the task ahead.

The Cadillac continued to cruise along Pennsylvania Avenue, drifting with a nonchalance foreign to Washington traffic. Ekomov relayed his position on the handset as he looked at the map in front of him. Gravell had feinted east and was now heading north-west. The landmarks of Washington DC idled by: the sprawling National Museum of Art, the square symmetry of the Justice Department and the condensed windows of the FBI building. The black car did not deviate until the White House blocked its path and then it turned north on 15th Street, skirting the President's residence. They passed the gargantuan Department of the US Treasury before the Cadillac turned. Ekomov's finger traced I Street.

"We've turned west onto I Street," Ekomov said into the handset.

The Cadillac had turned west at the first opportunity. If Gravell kept this up, Georgetown was next and beyond the suburbs of Foxhall Village and Berkley. If he turned south and crossed the Potomac river, Arlington seemed likely.

For the first time, the Cadillac picked up speed, now pushing down the outer lane.

"Gravell's driver is good. If he was watching for cars in the slow lane, he'll be checking who's keeping up with him in the fast lane," Lyov said.

Ekomov nodded. This was precisely why he should have been using a three-car tail. Grozky now had a team of two dozen dedicated to surveil Kochenko while Ekomov was having to poach operatives from the handful of Russian consulates in the United States and make do with less than forty to cover the entire Senate investigation. He'd barely slept in the last twenty-four hours.

As they turned to rejoin the broad span of Pennsylvania Avenue, Lyov reached across to take the radio handset from him.

"He favours the big avenues. Straight roads where he can check what's behind him," Lyov said, handing back the handset.

Ekomov was thinking the same thing. In a few hundred yards they would reach Washington Circle, where a plethora of roads intersected like the points of a compass. Gravell's driver knew exactly what he was doing. Ekomov didn't think the spider's web of choice was an accident.

Ekomov spoke into the handset.

"We're approaching Washington Circle. Where are you?"

"We see it. We're a hundred yards behind you and closing fast."

Ekomov's Dodge was two cars behind the Cadillac as it paused to join Washington Circle. Lyov allowed another car on the roundabout to pass before following. The Cadillac clung to the outside lane, its plodding pace highlighting its intent to turn early, except it didn't. It ignored the first turn and then the second. As it passed Whitehurst Freeway, Ekomov sensed the trickery Gravell's driver was using.

"Turn right now," Ekomov said, his hand grasping for the steering wheel.

Lyov responded as Ekomov's hand yanked the wheel and the Dodge made the turn, just.

Ekomov spoke quickly into the handset.

"The bastard. I think he's going all the way round. We've had to turn onto Whitehurst Freeway to avoid being spotted. Where are you now?"

"We're a car away from the junction. We're watching the traffic."

There was a few seconds' pause.

"You're right. Gravell's car has just passed us. He's going around again."

"Tell us where he turns," Ekomov said.

The Dodge dawdled on the freeway, the non-committal pace of a driver who lacks confidence in his route.

"I should have seen that coming," Lyov said.

"No reason to. There's all sorts of ways he could have gone."

The handset crackled.

"Gravell's turned onto Whitehurst Freeway. You'll see him shortly."

"Good. Keep well back. We'll call you if we need you," Ekomov said and turned to Lyov.

"We're still heading west. Stay ahead of him. This road is as straight as it gets. He'll be watching for what's behind him, not what's in front."

"Yes, sir," Lyov said and accelerated.

Ekomov studied the geography of roads on the map. Running parallel to the Potomac river, the freeway was the thoroughfare to Georgetown if that was Gravell's destination. There were no turnings until the Canal Road junction where the Francis Scott Key Bridge provided a last opportunity to cross the river and south to Arlington.

"Where's Gravell now?" Ekomov asked.

"About 400 yards back. Three cars behind us," Lyov said.

"Pull forward a little."

Lyov indicated and overtook an old truck weighed down with scaffolding poles. He stayed in the outer lane for another fifty yards and then pulled over again.

"Where do you think he's heading?" Lyov asked.

Ekomov glanced at his watch. It was almost thirty minutes since they'd left the Dirksen building.

"Are you a betting man, Lyov?"

"Always."

"Twenty bucks on Georgetown."

"You sound sure."

"There are no certainties. You know that. Even though he tries to make it look like he's switching direction, he keeps heading west and there are no turnings off the freeway until we get to Canal Road. My read is he will either go south over the bridge to Arlington or stay in Georgetown. It's 3.45 p.m. If he's got a 4 p.m. appointment, my twenty bucks is on Georgetown."

"Double it. He's taken an awful lot of trouble to only go as far as Georgetown."

"Taken."

The wager made Ekomov wonder. He had driven through Georgetown a few times, a neat suburb favoured by the wealthy and university intellectuals. What was it Gravell wanted to keep so private? Alongside them, a yacht glided on the river, white sails tight against the breeze, sun glinting from the cabin glass. The scene was alien to Ekomov, a bourgeois hobby for those with money to indulge.

"The Cadillac's just moved to the outside lane. He's coming up on our left, fast," Lyov said.

Ekomov felt the hunter's thrill when the prey takes the bait. Gravell's chauffeur would be scanning his rear-view mirror for vehicles responding to his acceleration.

The Cadillac passed them, hurrying without true urgency. Lyov kept to the slow lane and let the Cadillac make another fifty yards before he gently accelerated, playing out the line to allow the Cadillac to slowly gain on them.

"How far are we from the end of the freeway?" Lyov asked.

"Less than a mile."

"We should be okay. He's spent thirty minutes checking he's not being followed. He thinks he's got a clear road," Lyov said.

Ekomov nodded. As they rounded a curve in the road, ahead of them the vista of the river was broken up by the span of a bridge. Ekomov studied the map in front of him. West or south.

"Which lane is Gravell's car in?" Ekomov asked.

"Outside... No, he's switching to the inside lane."

Arlington or Georgetown? Ekomov wondered, as the traffic slowed to begin queuing at the junction. This part of Georgetown resembled a village: a church at the centre surrounded by a gridwork of streets. Why had Gravell's chauffeur taken such care to disguise his route? An extramarital liaison was possible, yet the numerous hotels in central Washington would have been sufficient to cover his tracks for a few hours.

Proceeding down the main street, for a moment Ekomov wondered if the Cadillac would still turn and head over the bridge to Arlington, the ultimate twist to stall anyone who might be following. He relaxed as the black car passed the bridge turn and then, a hundred yards later, the profile of the Cadillac crossed their vision as it turned left.

"Careful, Lyov. We're about to become exposed," Ekomov said, conscious the crosshatch of small streets provided no cover. He reached for the handset.

"Understood."

"We're just turning off M Street onto 33rd Street. When you get to 33rd Street, park up and wait for instructions," Ekomov said into the handset.

"Acknowledged."

By the time they made the turn, the Cadillac was already cresting the short rise in front of them. Lyov accelerated and when they reached the top the Cadillac was two blocks ahead. Lyov kept his distance until, a few seconds later, the sedan turned left and disappeared from view.

"Close up and hold just before that street. It's O Street," Ekomov said.

Seconds later the Dodge stopped yards from the corner and Ekomov got out. He strode to the corner and surveyed the street. Tall trees bordered the houses either side and he saw the black Cadillac some fifty yards away standing amidst the cobbles, its brake lights bright. Then the red lights faded and were replaced by pinpoints of white and the sedan began to slowly reverse. Ekomov watched as the car eased off the street, defusing its presence amongst the parked vehicles.

Ekomov walked back to the Dodge and got in.

"Gravell's parked up fifty yards on the right," Ekomov said, reaching for the map. He studied it intently. He noted the regimented grid of small streets, the church three blocks to the west and the Georgetown University campus beyond. He saw how he would make his approach.

From the glove compartment he picked out a pair of heavy-rimmed glasses with clear lenses and put them on. He made a final check of the map, orientating his approach against how a man unfamiliar to the area might get lost. He handed the map to Lyov.

"I'll get my overcoat from the boot. Stay here and wait for me. Tell Team One to meet us here."

"Yes, sir."

Ekomov got out of the car. Cold as it was, this was no Moscow winter. He retrieved his coat from the boot. From one pocket he took out a hat and scarf, wrapping the scarf around his neck and chin and pulling the hat down. From another, he withdrew a pair of brown suede gloves and put them on. Wrapped up against the season, he could pass as a university academic.

He started walking, reducing his pace to the unhurried steps of a man out for a stroll. Turning the corner, he took a moment to take in the grand houses wedged against each other with expensive cars parked in front. This was a district where neighbours lacked for nothing and made for generous friends.

He crossed the road towards Gravell's Cadillac. A pair of men stood at the rear of the sedan, talking together. Gravell's driver was dressed in a black suit and the other man was in uniform. The scattered trees could not mask the house behind them. From the cream-painted walls extruded conical towers and gothic turrets, transforming the regal construction into a fairytale residence.

Ekomov walked towards the pair, seeing the guarded cigarette the soldier held, cupped between thumb and forefinger, almost hidden by his hand. Ekomov saw the olive drab sedan with the military 'D' plate parked behind Gravell's Cadillac. He memorised the licence number as he passed. He stopped in front of the men, noting the twin chevrons on the corporal's sleeve.

"Gentlemen, good afternoon. Please excuse me for interrupting you. I wondered whether either of you could direct me to the Holy Trinity Church and the Chapel of St Ignatius? I was just visiting a friend at the university and I seem to have missed it."

Ekomov inserted hope into his question. It was the corporal who answered, pointing in the opposite direction from where Ekomov had come from.

"Sure. You've come too far. If you carry on for another two blocks and turn left on 36th Street. It's about a hundred yards down on the left."

"Well, thank you. I've been wandering around for twenty minutes, though these are great streets to be walking through. I have to say, you're standing outside one hell of a house."

Ekomov was a man lost, enjoying his small adventure. It was a house his companions could only aspire to.

"It is, isn't it," the soldier said. "This is Charles Cowan's house, the Washington lobbyist. He owns all three. He couldn't change the exteriors, but inside it's all one house."

"My, my, that must have been some renovation project," Ekomov said, looking up at the three-storey building, populated with generous windows. He allowed himself a few seconds to admire the scale of the property.

"Well, excuse me for interrupting you and thank you for the directions," Ekomov said, gave a half-wave with a gloved hand and strolled away. The corporal was familiar with the area and the property, which inferred he had been here before. Who was Gravell meeting with? Ekomov kept his pace steady as his irritation grew at his limited resources.

Walking down the quiet street, Ekomov noted all the cars facing towards him. If this was a one-way street, then Gravell's driver had turned into it the wrong way, another trick to catch out surveillance.

When under pressure, the best approach was to strip a target down and look for opportunity, like taking apart a faulty weapon to find the miscreant part. A person's life was little more than the components which made it: livelihood, habits, hobbies, family and possessions. Gravell held a most trusted position as Chairman of the Senate Subcommittee and operated in privileged circles. His wealth came with a respectability which matched his status. Atop Capitol Hill, Gravell depended upon a network of people: his own senatorial staff and the personnel administering the Permanent Subcommittee on Investigations in the Dirksen building.

Walking back to his car amidst the rich houses of Georgetown, as he thought about what he knew of Gravell, Ekomov saw how the senator's daily interactions could be used against him. If something sordid was discovered, his standing could be dealt a blow which could derail his hearing. It was about the touchpoints he would need to find and how to manipulate them. Gravell was holding court and pointing the finger at Russia, demonising a country on its knees. The irony was the evil would be revealed to be nesting in Gravell's backyard. The elegance of the solution appealed to him. Executed in the right way, he could bring Gravell down.

As Ekomov rejoined O Street, he saw the Plymouth station wagon parked behind the Dodge coupé and Lyov sitting in the back seat. Ekomov joined him, removing his hat and scarf.

"I've briefed Vasili and Valentina," Lyov said, passing Ekomov the map.

"Good. Gravell is in the grandest house on the street, owned by someone called Charles Cowan. There's a military car with a staff driver parked in front waiting for whoever else is in the house. I want to know who that is."

Ekomov studied the map. Above O Street, P Street ran one way in the opposite direction. Ekomov turned the map around and displayed it to the couple in front.

"You drive around the block and come back on O Street. Cowan's house is here. You can park on the opposite side of the street. Don't get too close. You're to take pictures of whoever leaves that house."

"Yes, sir."

"We've a new target. Find out who's in that military car," Ekomov said.

11

As he exited the Lenin Square Metro station and strode north up Lebedeva Academy Street, Grozky doubted Koshygin would approve of his evening's extracurricular assignment.

After passing through some unfamiliar side streets in the Vyborg District, Grozky found the Novy Arbat bar a few minutes later. For a beerhouse, the small *pivnaya* was crowded, a haze of cigarette smoke and steady conversation from groups of men who sought drinking companions. Grozky was surprised by Natassja's choice for there were much better places a few minutes away on Sampson's Avenue.

He manoeuvred himself between the small groups until he reached the bar. He was early, yet he glimpsed Natassja sitting at a table towards the back by a window. Grozky saw she was with a young couple when he'd expected it would only be the two of them.

Natassja saw him approach and stood up to greet him. Grozky smelt her rich scent as they exchanged a light peck on the cheek. The young man next to her rose to his feet.

"Valeri, let me introduce you to Abram," Natassja said.

"Good to meet you, Abram," Grozky said, extending his hand and receiving a firm shake.

"You too, Valeri," Abram replied. "This is my wife, Galina."

Galina stayed sitting, smiled at Grozky and gave him a little wave.

"Can I get you a drink?" Grozky asked.

"That's very kind, except Galina and I are going out for dinner. We've got to go," Abram said, taking a final gulp of his beer.

"Another time," Grozky said.

"For sure, Valeri. It was great to meet you," Abram said and shook Grozky's hand again.

"Enjoy your dinner. I'll see you tomorrow, Abram," Natassja said.

The couple gathered their coats from the wooden bench where they had been sitting, embraced Natassja in turn, and departed.

"Abram is one of the photographers the *Kommersant* uses. They live nearby," Natassja said.

Grozky sat opposite her, glad they were alone but conscious he did not have a good view of the room.

"Valeri, I was so sorry to read about the deaths of your men on that raid. It was awful," Natassja said.

"Thank you, Natassja. It was a bad situation. There was no way of knowing it would turn out like that."

She made no further comment and Grozky was grateful for her silence. He noticed her half-empty glass.

"What are you drinking?" Grozky asked.

"I'm fine, Valeri, thank you. I need to go soon. You wanted to meet? That's a first. What's so urgent?" Natassja asked.

"I'm intrigued to know what you've found out about Yuri Tomarov," Grozky asked.

"As I recall, the last time we met you were trying to disinterest me in the Tomarov story. Now, you're asking me about Tomarov. What's changed?"

Natassja was parrying his enquiry as he anticipated she would.

"It's professional interest," Grozky said.

"Which sounds like you're asking me to assist the FSB in an investigation?" Natassja probed.

Grozky felt the intensity of her green eyes and sensed the cusp of an argument. His eyes did not waver from hers as he reinforced his half-lie.

"All I would appreciate is whatever background information you feel would be worthwhile sharing. It struck me you've more history on him than I have, and it would save me some time."

She nodded and capitulated.

"Well, Yuri Tomarov was fortunate to have model Soviet citizens as parents. He received a good education and completed a degree in geology before getting his Master of Science at Moscow University. That secured him a future in the oil industry and Tomarov found his calling in oil exploration. He worked hard doing shitty jobs in North East Russia in places no one has ever heard of. He learnt fast and became a general manager at thirty, a role which would have taken most until forty to reach. He got results and he knew the oil business. He was promoted to work at the Soviet Ministry of Oil and Gas in Moscow, which was probably the best and worst thing that could have happened to him," Natassja said.

"How so?"

"He was young, connected and capable and, as a good communist, he progressed rapidly through the ranks. A bright career in government awaited him, until in early 1992 in a post-Soviet world, the opportunity of privatisation raised its head. One of the first companies Yeltsin privatised was the Yanusk Oil Company, a lacklustre performer that had seen better days. Yanusk was converted into a joint stock company as a prelude to privatisation. As a favoured son in the Ministry, Tomarov was appointed as General Manager of the Yanusk Oil Company."

"Do you have any idea how he got the job? Who would he have needed to impress in particular?" Grozky asked.

Natassja took a long sip of her drink as she considered his request.

"It's a good question. Being a member of the *nomenklatura*, the Communist Party ruling class, Tomarov had an advantage over the Ministry's career bureaucrats. Being a party poster boy would have been a big help, but Tomarov would still need to have impressed the senior managers at the Russian Federation's Ministry of Fuel and Energy with his plans. He had the ability and the ambition. Undoubtedly the Ministry would have been a key sponsor in his nomination."

"What role would Tomarov have played in the privatisation?"

"As General Manager he was integral to the process. Yanusk was converted from a state enterprise into a joint stock company where all the new company shares were initially owned by the government. Yanusk's valuation would have been overseen by the government's State Property Committee, but every privatisation relied heavily on the company's management. Yanusk was no different. Tomarov would have a hand in every stage of the process."

"How was he able to take control of Yanusk?"

"Not as difficult as you'd think." By now Natassja seemed to be enjoying relating the depth of her background knowledge. "Remember, most of the privatisations used a model which ensured ownership of the company stayed with the existing employees and managers. That meant fifty-one per cent of the stock was sold to them. You've got to remember every state company was valued at a discount to incentivise ownership. Tomarov would have known everyone's stockholdings. A good cash offer would have secured him a lot of shares. Another twenty-nine per cent of the stock could be purchased publicly in the auctions," Natassja said.

"The auctions?"

"The voucher auctions. Even you would have received a voucher."

"Yes." It had never occurred to Grozky to try bidding at any of the privatisation auctions. Fleetingly he wondered if he had missed a major opportunity.

"Anyone who had accumulated vouchers could use them to buy shares at the auction of Yanusk's stock. Tomarov had access to funds and acquired large quantities of vouchers. All totally legal. He knew Yanusk was undervalued. Provided he could borrow money, he'd have known he was onto a winner."

Natassja's knowledge impressed Grozky. Lensky Bank's loans to Tomarov took on a darker significance. The man entrusted with the privatisation of Yanusk had seen a way to maximise his winnings. Tomarov had known what he was doing when he had plundered Yanusk. Kochenko's bet began to look very one-sided.

"Yet it sounds like Yanusk should have been a great opportunity for him?"

"It was, at least initially. Yanusk was privatised in November 1993 and about six months later the rumours began to surface. The deaths of a couple of Yanusk's managers were initially seen as a coincidence. Then the talk was that Tomarov had begun to exploit the company. With his experience, he was certainly bright enough to take the opportunity. Just over a year after Yanusk was privatised, Tomarov lost control of the ownership to Lensky Bank. Shortly afterwards Tomarov disappeared. No one knows why. He vanished for almost a year and then two months ago he turned up dead in Yekaterinburg."

Grozky nodded. Natassja had yet to mention Yevgeny Kochenko directly. This was the time to bring the oligarch into the conversation. Grozky reached inside his jacket for the photograph of the man who had met Kochenko for lunch as Natassja said,

"Tomarov is the second high-profile death from the Yanusk Oil Company in as many months. Stanislav Rusnak, the ex-Chief Financial Officer, turned up dead in January."

"Really. How did he die?" Grozky asked, his intrigue casual as his arm returned empty-handed from inside his jacket.

"Rusnak was staying with an aunt in Grozny. Her apartment was broken into while Rusnak was out, and she was beaten unconscious. Rusnak was found two days later or at least what was left of him. Part of him was a frozen strip on the ground. He'd been run over by what was likely a half-track or a tank track. That doesn't sound like an accident, does it?"

"The Chechen capital isn't exactly the best place to be staying right now," Grozky said. "The Russian military doesn't make much distinction between the separatists and the civilians, while the Chechen guerrillas hate the Russians.

Rusnak could just have been in the wrong place at the wrong time."

"Exactly. Why on earth would a man like Rusnak have chosen to visit Chechnya? Yuri Tomarov lived in Moscow. You'd think he could afford to live anywhere he wanted to. What was he doing hiding in a city like Yekaterinburg?"

"They were laying low," Grozky said.

"That's my sense too. They were keeping out of the way, except they're both dead. Both run over. Why?" Natassja asked.

Grozky wondered.

"What's your view on why Tomarov met his death? A former business associate? Someone from Yanusk who had a personal vendetta to settle?"

"With a man like Tomarov, who knows," said Natassja, finishing her drink. "He was ambitious and capable. Tomarov was also greedy. It's likely he had a falling-out with someone. I think he knew he was in danger. Whoever was after Tomarov caught up with him in Yekaterinburg."

"It's certainly possible," Grozky said, thinking about what Kochenko had said about his meeting with Tomarov in St Petersburg: that Tomarov had asked him for money.

"Yet, despite what's happened, there have never been any investigations into Tomarov or Yanusk and no one has been charged with anything," Natassja said, toying with her empty glass.

Until now, thought Grozky. Yanusk had suddenly become a priority of national interest to both the American and Russian governments. It struck him that if Tomarov had fallen out with Kochenko, could he have been pressuring the oligarch? Tomarov had the evidence the Kremlin would now kill for, except it was Tomarov who was dead. Rusnak too.

From his jacket, Grozky extracted the photograph of the man who Kochenko had met for lunch and placed it on the table in front of her.

"Any idea who this is?"

Natassja looked at the photograph and smiled.

"What's it worth?"

"You know him?"

"I know of him. That's Vadik Prigoda, why do you ask?"

"Something I've been asked to check. What does Prigoda do?"

"He is a lawyer. These days he spends most of his time advising on mergers and acquisitions. If you're interested in buying or selling a company, Vadik can advise you," Natassja said.

"Anyone he represents in particular? Regular clients, for example?" Grozky asked.

Natassja considered the question briefly.

"Prigoda's well connected and discreet. I know his client list is high profile and private. I have heard he represents foreign investors. With the boom in privatisation, there's a lot of overseas interest in acquiring stakes in Russian companies. There are also a lot of rich Russians looking to get their money out."

Grozky nodded. What was Prigoda doing for Kochenko? he wondered. He saw Natassja glance at her watch.

"Natassja, you are a mine of information. Thank you for the background. That's all I was after," Grozky said.

They left the bar a few minutes later. Outside it was dim and damp, the sheen of rain coating the street in a fresh veneer.

"I'll see you home," Grozky said absently, feeling more relaxed than he had reason to.

"That's kind of you, Valeri, but there's no need. It's not far."

They wandered away from the bar, squinting through the wet haze.

"I'll try and remember an umbrella next time," Grozky said.

"Me too. Bye!" Natassja gave him a peck on the cheek and walked away.

Grozky watched her go, collar up and braced against the cold. He knew now that it would be the combination of events which would do for Yeltsin: the debacle of the Chechen war, the rampant crime, and now the revelation that a flagship privatisation overseen by the government was little more than a scam.

He intended to turn and walk to Lenin Square Metro station and yet, watching Natassja walking alone in the dimly lit street, he found himself following in her path. For the sake of a few minutes, he could take a small gratification in knowing she would be safe.

The street lighting, like the locality, was poor and the small pockets of illumination were little better than those of a makeshift airstrip. Grozky kept fifty yards back, a shadow absorbed by the lines of the buildings, his pace economic and aware of the movements around them. Away from the main avenues, the traffic was light and the few pedestrians, hurrying on their journeys, were focused on their destinations.

It was in the no man's land of their journey that Grozky sighted a pair of men some ten yards ahead who appeared from a side road on the opposite side of the street. Initially, his assessment was neutral until they quickened their pace, crossed the road and took up position behind Natassja.

Grozky did not think they could have followed her from the bar, he would have known. His footsteps quickened.

"Fucking journalist," said one of the men.

Grozky was surprised by the vehemence in the voice.

Natassja ignored the slight and kept walking.

"We're talking to you, you bitch," the man said, his voice louder this time.

Grozky reached behind him, his left hand closing around the grip of the polyurethane handle of his P-9 Gyurza pistol, an upgrade from his old 8-clip Makarov in every way except its bulk. It came with eighteen rounds of heavy-hitting 9x21mm ammunition in a side-by-side clip. Grozky wore the loop holster on the inside of his belt to keep it fitted firmly into the small of his back under his jacket.

"Hey," Grozky said.

His opponents barely paused; one man continued walking, while the other wheeled sharply towards him. Grozky could barely make out the features on the man's face.

"It's time you were gone," Grozky said.

"Fuck off," said Natassja's inquisitor.

Grozky's pistol appeared in his hand. The man glowered at the weapon.

"Oh look, she's found a friend with a gun," the man said with a confidence that concerned Grozky. The man's partner stopped and walked back. Ahead, Grozky saw Natassja turn to observe the confrontation.

"You don't want to get involved in this, friend," the inquisitor said as his silent partner appeared at his side.

"I can always arrest you," Grozky said.

It was the second man who saw sense.

"Just leave it," he said quietly.

There was a pause while the first man considered the situation. He stood there and Grozky sensed his resentment. The man half turned away and then turned back to confront Grozky.

"Next time we won't be so accommodating," he said.

His bravado surprised Grozky and he sensed a new presence to his left too late. Something hard struck down on his wrist, his hand lost control and he dropped the pistol. It clattered across the tarmac.

Instinct took hold. Grozky's right forearm snapped up in defence as he stepped forward and swung his left horizontally in a cross-elbow strike at a shadow's outline. The flat of his forearm drove hard into a body, throwing his opponent off balance. Grozky lashed out with a foot, catching the man in the leg. His assailant lost his footing and fell. Grozky looked for his pistol. He saw one of the men squatting to retrieve the Gyurza. The man's hand was almost on the gun's grip and Grozky knew he would not reach him in time.

A small shot snapped out in the gloom, so close Grozky struggled to gauge its origin. The man reaching for Grozky's pistol yelped, clutching his hand as he spun away, running from the fight. Grozky made out Natassja's figure several yards ahead, arms extended in a double-handed grip. Grozky's peripheral vision caught a sudden movement; he turned to see the man who he had knocked down scamper away across the street. Natassja pivoted, a second shot chasing his retreat as the remaining attacker fled, haring after his wounded colleague.

Grozky ran forward to retrieve his Gyurza. By the time it was in his hand, the attackers were lost amongst the shadows. A few yards away he saw Natassja's handbag on the ground, the contents partially scattered across the damp ground.

Grozky stooped down and helped to recover her possessions. He saw the last item she replaced in her bag was a small .22 calibre pistol that looked like a Baikal 'Margo', the shorter-barrelled version of the MCM target pistol. He wondered where she had acquired it. He tucked his pistol back into its holster, realising his hand was shaking. His anger grew at his own weakness. He was as guilty of allowing his opponents to better him as he was in failing to prevent the deaths of his men outside the Red Star Bar. His opportunity to hurt these men had gone. He looked at Natassja, his mind stumbling through images of flames.

"Come on, I'll see you home," Grozky said.

"Why were you following me?" Natassja asked.

Grozky did not need to see her expression to hear her annoyance.

"Why do you care?" Grozky asked.

As soon as he heard his frustration, he wished he'd said something different. She walked up to him and addressed him like a stranger.

"I don't. I'm quite capable of taking care of myself because journalists like me are targeted all the time. Half the threats I and everyone else at the newspaper get are from the security services. If people like you did your job, I wouldn't have to carry a gun, would I?"

He heard her fear through the anger and then she was gone, striding away and leaving Grozky alone to despair at his dismissal.

12

As Washington DC slept, Colonel Ilya Ekomov lay on the bed in his small studio apartment, the room in darkness except for a thin beam from the bedside spotlight which illuminated the black and white photo Ekomov was studying. He preferred the dark; the absence of distraction focused his mind.

The photo showed a tall one-star general caught standing in front of the open rear door of his car in O Street, Georgetown. He sported the short back and sides favoured by marines of all ranks and the craggy face of a combatant. Ekomov's team had been busy cross-checking the information, and finally he had a name and some sparse background. General Peter Keefe.

The meeting at Charles Cowan's house in Georgetown had lasted an hour and the tail of the military car had taken less than fifteen minutes. It had driven over the Francis Scott Memorial Bridge to North Arlington and then taken Route 29 to Lyon Village. Keefe's driver had dropped him outside a neat house on North Hartford Street.

The preliminary background material handed to Ekomov an hour ago was thin: a typed page, two photocopies of press clippings and a paperback book, *The Boundaries of Anarchy*, which Keefe had published six years ago. The book, which Ekomov had been skimming, sat splayed, face down on the blanket. Keefe was fifty-four and a veteran of the Cold War. For his age and experience, his rank was lacking. The press articles, published shortly after the release of the book, were careful not to go beyond labelling him a dark maverick.

Ekomov dropped the photo onto the bed and returned to the book. *The Boundaries of Anarchy* was not a typical publication for a military author, more a reflection of Keefe's personal philosophy of the world. Keefe's premise was that each nation state could only expand its influence at the expense of others and so state killing was inevitable. Governments proclaimed the sanctity of life while killing with impunity. Keefe cited the killing of the Bulgarian dissident, Georgi Markov, in London in September 1978. Markov's murder was a condemned and then forgotten death, no more than 'a casualty on the boundaries of anarchy'.

The book helped to explain Keefe's lack of career progression over the last few years. With his record he should have been a three-star general by now. Keefe's assertions were extreme by American standards. No US government wanted attention drawn to the darker choices it made as part of its global dominance. Keefe was a casualty of his own philosophy.

The question still unresolved in Ekomov's mind was why had Gravell taken such care to hide his presence at Cowan's house? Cowan owned his own lobbying firm and played any side for money, a hired gun who would fight any cause for the right price. Keefe's presence at the house raised its own questions. Was Cowan hosting a meeting connected to Gravell's Senate investigation, and if so, why had Keefe been chosen? There were far more reputable military experts Gravell could be consulting in public than a rogue general in secret. Ekomov wondered what Gravell was hiding.

Aside from the burden of adding Cowan and Keefe to the surveillance of his badly stretched team, Ekomov began to see how he might trip Gravell up, not fatally, but long enough to slow him down. Whether or not Keefe was being consulted as part of the Senate investigation, the clandestine meeting could be used to infer he was. On its own, it was minor, but if Ekomov could link it with some major financial impropriety it would damage Gravell's credibility, even his position as Chairman of the Permanent Subcommittee on Investigations.

In a dollar-hungry country, money greased the wheels of government. The millions of dollars of foreign currency spirited out of the USSR by the KGB before its breakup had been put to good use. Small amounts had been paid into many senators' accounts, all from legitimate investment sources seeded by Russian government money the GRU controlled. Some were one-off donations, others regular monthly payments. With the funds washing through the American political system, the amounts were small enough to stay unnoticed, while they remained a matter of record. In Gravell's case, the previous month's amount had been increased from US$2,500 to US$5,000. Greed would be Gravell's undoing: the revelation his office was in receipt of donations whose source would be revealed as originating from one of the KGB's final operations would damage his standing as a patriot. It was the circumstances of their exposure which would be key. Ekomov needed to make sure a bad situation became unsalvageable. To ensure the mud would stick, the blood of a victim was required.

Ekomov put the book down, swung his legs off the bed and stood up. He stretched and walked to the window in his Cardozo apartment. Opposite him, the features of Meridian Hill Park remained hidden, the linear pattern of lights betraying the walkways. Enough evidence would be needed to be found on the victim to light the trail to the true source of the donations paid to Gravell. That person required irrefutable links to Gravell. The easiest candidate would be one of Gravell's Senate office staff at the Dirksen building. It was how the body would be found which required care. If it appeared the victim was being blackmailed to prevent the disclosure of the Russian funds, that would reinforce Gravell's guilt. While Gravell could proclaim his innocence, he could not deny the funds or his connection to the body. The aura of guilt would do more than slow Gravell down, it would strike at the heart of his credibility to chair the Senate Subcommittee. It would be enough.

In six hours, three miles to the south-east, Gravell would chair another day's hearing in the Dirksen building. Time was a commodity of which the Russian government was very short.

Ekomov walked back to the bed and picked up the phone from the bedside table. He dialled a number. His call was answered after a few seconds.

"I need to meet tomorrow. I may have to liquidate an investment at short notice," Ekomov said.

"Is it a sizeable investment?"

"No, but it may impact the portfolio."

"I understand. I await your instructions."

Ekomov hung up. Sacrificing a stream of funds could put others in jeopardy. The American backlash would inevitably drill into the sources of political donations. With what was at stake, it was necessary. Murder and money were the base ingredients of conviction. He would need Koshygin's approval for the operation he had in mind. Some very precise killing was required. He could think of no one more efficient than Ivan Palutkin.

13

Grozky arose earlier than he wanted to. Standing barefoot in his kitchen just before 6 a.m. he listened to the ring tone in the telephone receiver. He'd called Natassja when he got home and then thirty minutes later. Nothing. He'd gone to bed irritated and slept badly. Intimidating a journalist did not require the excess of a three-man team. Somehow she had crossed a line. He could think of only one story worthy of such a response. Yuri Tomarov. She had been raking over the life of a man with a past now under guard. The threat to the Russian presidency was now a state vendetta and the security perimeter was being sealed until Yevgeny Kochenko was brought to account. Anyone caught within the corral was at risk.

He let the phone ring, cursing her failure to pick up his third call. By now she must know who was calling. She thought a .22 pistol would protect her. Natassja did not appreciate the danger she was in. He hung up, infuriated at her silence, turned on the electric kettle and walked to the bathroom to shower.

His apartment was at the north end of 11th Line Street on Basil's Island, one of twenty-six such *Liniya* streets running north from the Great Neva river until they reached the Smolenka river which bisected the island. A serviceable two-bedroom affair, he'd purchased it on his KGB salary. That was when he and Marisha had a future. Other than her clothes, she had not taken anything with her when she left, leaving him with the detritus of their lives together. It was as if Marisha had wanted nothing to remind her of their union.

He showered, shaved and went to his bedroom to dress. No longer the working clothes of surveillance, but the formality of his olive-green FSB uniform, dark green tie and white shirt. He had a flight to catch to Moscow and would have driven straight to Pulkovo airport, but for the threat to Natassja.

Returning to the kitchen, he made himself a cup of coffee and stood looking out on the street below where flecks of snow were falling. He wore his uniform so rarely it seemed strange to see a cold man of authority reflected against the glass. His father had always been at ease in uniforms, but then Keto had been a soldier first and from a generation who had lived with the sacrifices made in the Great Patriotic War. His father would have admired Grozky's appearance, for he considered a uniform was the foundation of the soldier's code – 'the eye into a soldier's soul' as he put it. You had to earn the right to wear a uniform, while the medals marked a soldier's service and his achievements. Grozky had never felt comfortable in his. It was not the expectation which went with the uniform, it was the display of formality he was uneasy with. He had never been a man for show.

He finished the coffee and ran the cup under the tap. Walking to his front door, he put on his FSB overcoat and peaked service cap as he considered his route to Natassja's flat: either take the direct route and cut through the centre of Petrograd Island or use the wide embankment avenues and skirt alongside the Neva river. At this time of the morning he'd take his chance with the traffic and choose the shorter route.

Outside, he discovered it was not snow now, but sleet. Crystals of freezing rain grazed his cheeks as he walked to his car. Grozky's twenty-year-old Volga 24 was unremarkable to the point of being down at heel. Marisha hated the archaic car because of its age. Grozky coveted it for the same reason, for his tired, four-door sedan was a Volga 24-24 model, the plain successor to the original 'Chaser' cherished by the KGB's Ninth Directorate. Used as outriders for escorting parades, the worn bonnet hid a V8 ZMZ-2424 engine whose brutal torque handled best on straight roads. Somewhere, on a state asset inventory, his Chaser would be listed as missing, though with the passage of time, Grozky was more proprietor than caretaker.

Driving over the Tuchkov Bridge the traffic was lighter than he'd expected. By the time he'd crossed the Little Neva river and turned onto the one-way Great Pushkar Street the full beam of his headlights picked out no vehicles ahead. Grozky accelerated, enjoying the urgency of the V8's power as the Chaser coursed along the straight road.

Since the start of the Moscow operation his opportunities to think had been stolen from him, his daily regime so compressed his brain struggled to breathe. The residue of his days accumulated in his mind, tormenting his sleep as the dark thoughts resurrected themselves into his consciousness like demons.

He didn't want to admit it, but his frustration with Natassja was a symptom of his own situation, the fragility of his future. The Soviet regime which had given Grozky's life structure and stability was gone. Whatever Russians said about change what they really wanted was *poryatok* or order – a roof over their heads and food on the table. The promised benefits from the economic restructuring of *perestroika* had been a disaster – hyperinflation and the plundering of Russia's assets for the benefit of the few. Russia had lost the order its people craved. Yeltsin was a stumbling President whose reforms benefited only those who had enriched themselves. Unless the spectre of Yanusk could be contained, the political chaos it would unleash would change Russia's course. Yeltsin would succumb to Gennady Zyuganov, the die-hard communist whose National-Patriotic Alliance promised to resurrect the shackles of the Soviet model and the renationalisation of industry. Grozky was into the ninth day of his new assignment with its highest of high stakes. He'd have to step up his game if he was to restore General Donitsyn's faith in him and gain selection to the special unit to fight the drug gangs in St Petersburg. He owed it to Timur.

Crossing the Grenadier's Bridge, he put aside his predicament and considered what he would say to Natassja. Her reaction to his intercession had surprised him. By now she should have calmed down and be more willing to listen.

Grozky drove up Forest Avenue, following the railway line until he could cross under the bridge and cut back on the other side of the tracks onto Cast Iron Street. The railway line was the boundary where the residential collided with the industrial. Natassja's claim that she lived 'by the river' rivalled the most optimistic of estate agents. Grozky had given her a lift home after their meeting at the Imperial Hotel. While she was only half a mile from the Grenadier's Bridge, her apartment block on Mendeleev Street was squeezed against the Vyborg Metro station on the wrong side of the tracks.

He passed the entrance to the city's old Tram-Mechanical Factory, a squat, red brick building hemmed in by an avenue of trees. Half a mile later he pulled up in front of the junction with Mendeleev Street, out of view from her block. Her apartment building was a five-storey *khrushchyovka*, a prefabricated construction of concrete panels and the Soviet answer to mass housing. Swathes of *khrushchyovki* were scattered across the city. She lived on the top floor. He had watched the lights go on after he'd dropped her off.

He got out of the car, leaving his peaked service cap with its gleaming Russian double-headed eagle badge on the passenger seat. Under the USSR the outsize crown marked the omnipotence of the KGB. Now it looked a caricature of authority. Locking the car, he walked round the corner to her door.

There was no one about. The only light came from a solitary lamp behind a twelve-foot wall on the opposite side of the street. Under the illumination the roofs of light industry peered over the top of the wall. Beyond was an army of machine-tooling shops and metal fabricators encamped outside the St Petersburg-Finland freight station and the locomotive and wagon depots.

Grozky walked up to the door. Trying to pick the lock at this hour was not his preferred option, the building would have locks as solid as its construction. He looked at the rows of metal buttons above the intercom. The *khrushchyovka* was a long, narrow block so likely it had two apartments per floor. That meant one of the top two buttons. He could imagine Natassja's surprise at the hour. He pressed the top button. There was no response. He pressed the second button. The steel grill of the intercom made no sound. He waited a few seconds and then repeated the selection, holding the buttons down firmly. After a short pause, he heard her voice on the intercom.

"Who is it?"

"Natassja, it's Valeri Grozky."

Silence. Other than the fire escape stairs running down the side of the building where he was parked, this would be the only entrance to the block. She could not avoid him.

The buzzer sounded. He pushed the door and entered the building. A *khrushchyovka* was not required to have lifts provided it did not exceed five floors. St Petersburg was littered with such blocks. Ahead of him was a set of narrow concrete stairs protected by metal railings which passed for a banister. Grozky jogged up the steps, forcing his right leg to accept his pace, his footfall accentuated in the confined space. At the first landing two apartment doors sat opposite each other.

On the fifth floor the light was escaping from an apartment door left ajar. Grozky would have knocked, except the door swung open and Natassja stood before him, dressed in a tan overcoat and with a long umbrella wrapped over one arm.

"I'd invite you in, except I've got to get to work," Natassja said, as she pulled the door shut and locked it.

"I'll give you a lift."

"There's no need."

She didn't wait for his response, walking past him to start down the stairs. The stage-managed absence of a greeting was a side to Natassja he hadn't seen before. She didn't question his arrival, nor showed any signs of trauma from the previous night's struggle. Grozky could still feel the bruise on his forearm.

He followed her down the stairs. Natassja was not in a conciliatory mood and the cramped stairwell was not the place to strike up a conversation, not when last night's confrontation was still raw.

Leaving the building, she paused to pull up the collar of her coat and extend her umbrella. The sleet was steady, the slush rotting on the ground. Grozky used the moment.

"Natassja, I'm driving to the airport. I can drop you at Uprising Square in fifteen minutes. My car's warm and it will save you waiting for the train," Grozky said.

"Okay, thank you."

They walked to his car. Grozky unlocked the passenger door and tossed his service cap into the back seat. Natassja got in and Grozky closed the door. That gave him fifteen minutes to warn her off. In her mood, he needed to avoid another argument. At least she'd accepted his offer of a lift.

Grozky retraced his route while Natassja sat in the passenger seat, tight-lipped and aloof. Detached resilience had replaced her contempt. Her willingness to accept a lift did not extend to conversation. Since their chance encounter at his brother's funeral, their collaboration was based on the exchange of information. He had no illusions he was anything more to her than a good source, just as she was a means to publish information in a way he could not. Despite their collaboration, he represented the dark side of modern Russia. Last night was their first argument.

As he turned under the railway bridge to rejoin Forest Avenue, Natassja said,

"I didn't expect to see you. It must be something important."

"I was concerned about your welfare."

"Ha. We meet once a month and suddenly it's twice in

two days. Why are you suddenly so concerned about my welfare? Is that why you were following me last night?"

He hadn't expected her suspicion, but he saw how he could use it.

"It was late and dark and, after we parted, I thought I'd see you home. It was a snap decision, that's all. I was as surprised as you by what happened. I came over to see if you're okay."

"Do I not look okay?"

"No, you look fine."

"There you are. That's because I wasn't shocked by what happened last night. When I start getting threatened, it's because I'm doing my job properly."

"Why do you think you were targeted?" Grozky asked.

"Something I wrote."

Vehicle lights now decorated both sides of the broad road, the traffic heavier heading into the city. They passed an ancient tram carrying a clutch of passengers, its fatigued red paint with aged cream trim brightened by the Volga's headlights. Grozky accelerated and the V8's growl became a snarl as they sped by Sampson's Park.

"Listen, Natassja. You're a good journalist, but I get the sense you like to spice everything up. Does every story have to be presented as a conspiracy?"

"It sounds like you're defending what happened last night."

"I didn't say that."

"So, why do you think I was targeted last night?" Natassja asked.

Already she'd turned the question back to him. She would sieve everything he said, looking for that chink of truth. Natassja was more resilient than he'd expected. Towards the end of Forest Avenue the city's grander, late-nineteenth-century tenement buildings, *dokhodny doma*, now bordered their route. Grozky went with a lie baked in truth.

"Think about it. We're two months from voting in a free election and political tensions are running very high. There's never been more at stake."

"After what the country has been through over the last few years, don't you think Russians have the *right* to be kept informed so they can make up their mind who to vote for?" she said, defying him to contradict her.

Grozky was not going to disagree. For the first time in Russia's history the people would choose their head of state; the challenge was choice and that didn't sit well with an electorate used to having their leaders decided for them. They were being offered a poor selection. Yeltsin behaved with the impunity of a delusional tsar, while Zyuganov would return Russia to the Soviet dark ages. Grozky favoured Zyuganov over Yeltsin though neither gave confidence they could find a compromise in the no man's land between communism and capitalism.

When he did not respond, she reinforced her point.

"After decades of failed five-year plans, don't you think we owe it to our people to make the country the way it should be, instead of the way it is? To do that, you *must* pick a side," she said.

He heard the conviction in her voice. Until now, he'd thought of her as a pretty journalist who was good at stoking a story. Now he realised she saw herself as a crusader, that demanding change was the people's right to improve their lives. She saw hope where he did not. He let her question hang, forcing a pause in the verbal fencing as he waited to ask the question.

"Whose side do you think you'll pick?" Grozky asked.

"I won't be voting for Zyuganov. His politics belong to the past."

"Yeltsin needs all the votes he can get."

"And whose side are you on?"

"It's not going to make a lot of difference. I think the election is too close to call. Therein lies your problem," Grozky said.

"Knowing you as I do, that sounds like you're giving me a warning."

"If someone gives you some advice, it's usually with good reason."

"That depends on who's giving the advice."

"All I'm suggesting is you stick to constructive criticism and rein back your aggressive style until after the election."

"Unless someone makes a stand, nothing changes."

He heard her defiance. She was an idealist who accepted the risks of her circumstances, while he understood the danger she was running into. Ahead of them, at the end of Lesnoy Avenue, the view was interrupted by a brutal eleven-storey block housing the Russian Federation Defence Ministry on Lebedeva Academy Street.

"You don't have to take my advice, but if you notice anything out of the ordinary or get any more threats, you should call me," Grozky said as he turned right at the junction.

Half a mile from Foundry Bridge, the buildings became municipal in character; the grand Kirov Military Medical Academy, set back from the street behind a lawn, was guarded on either side by solid, neoclassical buildings bordering the street and looked more like barracks than surgical schools. The campus of clinics and hospitals stretched to the river.

"Why would you stick your neck out for me?" Natassja asked as they crossed the bridge.

That was a question he'd anticipated.

"Because if you carry on the way you've been going, you may get into trouble. If you do, I'd feel better knowing you'll call me."

She did not respond. She didn't need to. He'd done more than warn her off. No member of the Internal Security Services in his right mind would be sharing information with a journalist, let alone offering to keep an eye on her. He had crossed a line he should not have done and she knew it. His answer implied he cared. Perhaps he did, in his way.

Grozky turned east onto Zhukov Street and accelerated along the straight road.

"You watch everything, don't you?" Natassja said.

"What do you expect? You know what I do. You are what you become, isn't that what they say?"

"It's not that. You're a lot smarter than you pretend to be."

Grozky didn't answer. The KGB specialised in breaking someone down and using their weaknesses against them. He knew how to find those levers and exploit them. He'd joined the KGB as one person and left as another, a master manipulator. He was the product of his training, more aware, more ruthless.

Ahead, at the junction with Ligovsky Avenue, the Baroque vista of residential buildings was broken by the industrial glass and concrete of the Grand October Concert Hall which dominated Greek Square.

"Where shall I drop you?" Grozky asked.

"Uprising Square is fine."

Grozky turned south onto Ligovsky Avenue. Above them the sky was lighter now and though the sun was still hidden to the east, the tops of the buildings lining the street were no longer in shadow.

As Grozky pulled up outside the Uprising Square Metro station, Natassja turned to him.

"If it makes you feel any better my editor, Liliya, has asked me to cover a trade fair for the next two weeks."

Grozky was about to reply, but she did not give him a chance, opening her door and stepping out.

"As for your advice, I'll think about it."

Then the door slammed and she was gone. He was not expecting to be thanked for pointing out the fragility of her situation. While she hadn't spurned his offer, he took neutral as a negative. Despite her exposure, something convinced her she could prevail.

As he headed for Pulkovo airport, it occurred to Grozky that Natassja was proud of what she did in a way he had never been.

14

As he left Moscow's Sheremetyevo airport in the back of a taxi, Grozky was grateful a GRU escort was no longer required. It was still below freezing, yet the early morning sun was irrepressible, the spectacular light almost dispelling Grozky's unease. In his wallet case on his lap were the computer floppy disks he would give to Grigori Zotkin, the Prosecutor-General's expert tasked with finding the financial connection between Yuri Tomarov and Yevgeny Kochenko.

To Borzoi's credit, he had managed to arrange thirty minutes with Irina Tomarov. Grozky unzipped the case and withdrew the fax Borzoi had sent him. Ignoring the cover details, he turned to the second page:

Interview with Mrs Irina Tomarov
Time of meeting: Thursday 21 March. 11.30 a.m.
(confirmed)
Place of meeting: 35 Kirov Park (her apartment is Apartment H, 25th floor), off Vernandsky Avenue, Moscow.

Background: Subject has been interviewed by Grigori Zotkin, Prosecutor-General's office (minimal records on file). There is little to indicate the extent of her knowledge of her husband's business dealings.

Subject's lawyer, Viktor Baranov, was contacted to explain the reason for the interview – to follow up on a few minor points. Thirty minutes only has been agreed. Offer made to the lawyer to be present – Baranov declined. Baranov stated he hopes this will be the final meeting for what has been a very unpleasant episode for Irina.

Other details: Born 25 May 1956 (Moscow). Aged thirty-nine. Irina was married to Yuri Tomarov for almost two years. According to local realtors, apartments in the building start from US$1 million.

Irina Tomarov lived in an exclusive area near the Southwest Forest Park, almost ten miles from central Moscow. Grozky had considered dispensing with his uniform. He decided to wear it on the basis she was likely to respond better to authority. His official presence also allowed him to hide in plain sight and, if the GRU chanced upon his request for the meeting, it would appear to be an oversight rather than deceit on his part. Grozky refolded the paper and replaced it in his case.

Amidst the chaotic events of the last week, he welcomed the respite to think. His investigative instincts were to throw the net wide and see what came up. From inside his jacket, he took out a small notebook. Aside from his official reports, he kept a record of names and events for reference. Grozky coveted his lists not because he doubted his memory. His notes were markers. Once on paper a note became a checkmark, ticking over in his subconscious. Each record remained discrete, waiting to see where it might fit. Surveillance work was about turning over the available information and seeing how the pieces might join together.

In the nine days since he had started working for the GRU, normally Grozky would have been satisfied with his progress, but this was not an ordinary operation. The premise of intelligence work was to find what your opponent had hidden and exploit it to your advantage. The revelation that the Americans had already uncovered Tomarov and Kochenko's collusion had caught the Russian government off guard. The irony was, while the Senate Subcommittee's discovery had saved Metzov's operation a lot of time in what to look for, the Russian security agencies were on the backfoot as they raced to find the payments Kochenko had received and which could prove the oligarch's guilt.

Grozky would leave Zotkin and his team to sift the financial transactions; he was trying to unravel the threads of information and understand the network of Kochenko's business associates and their purpose. On reflection, there could only be so many people connected directly or indirectly to Kochenko who would have been in a position to make the US$6 million commission payments. It was identifying who had that capability. Grozky only needed to find out how one commission payment had been made to prise open the connection.

Aside from Tomarov's killing, what intrigued Grozky was why someone had taken the care to rub out Stanislav Rusnak, Yanusk's Chief Financial Officer. Grozky would not have connected his death in Grozny had Natassja not highlighted Yanusk as the common denominator. There was something very rotten to be unearthed and the US Senate was following the stench.

The man in everyone's crosshairs was Kochenko. The oligarch was not a man to show mercy to those who crossed him. He had made his fortune through hands-on investment and taking calculated risks. Yanusk was a deal too far, contaminating his reputation beyond salvage. Piotr Petrovitch, Koshygin's special investigator, had implied Kochenko's hand was behind the deaths of Tomarov and Rusnak. If Kochenko had realised he was exposed, had he removed them before they could be used as witnesses? Someone else was taking a close interest in Kochenko's affairs and Grozky was no closer to understanding why the man in the blue Fiat had been following the oligarch. He ringed 'blue Fiat' as he worked his way down the page, more from frustration as he was no closer to establishing its significance.

The new face of interest was Vadik Prigoda, the broker between sellers and buyers. A man like Kochenko would not have made time for a two-hour lunch with Prigoda without good reason. What was Prigoda offering or being offered? That was a question Grozky had for the St Petersburg lawyer. Grozky's challenge was that the partial information he held was bringing him no closer to establishing Kochenko's guilt. He had a lot of ground to cover and speculation was not a commodity Aleksandr Metzov traded in.

As they passed Moscow's outer limits, the factories gave way to barbarous tower blocks the Soviet planners had provided for the industrial workforce. This was an area unchanged by the lofty ideals of *glasnost* and *perestroika*. The sun seemed determined to break through the concrete structures, the edges of the buildings lost in a back glow so bright it darkened the endless rows of mean windows, hazing them until they were consigned to darkness.

A horn blared loudly from behind as the Lada made a right turn, rebuking the taxi driver for some slight caused by his manoeuvre, and Grozky heard him swear at the accusation. Grozky glanced behind him while the taxi driver sighed as if he were blameless.

The taxi slowed and Grozky replaced the notebook inside his jacket pocket. The driver's attention on the road wavered, his head pressed forward against the windscreen as he scanned a street dominated by towers of stone, glass and steel. Seconds later, the driver pulled up alongside a parked row of expensive cars and pointed. Grozky saw the number '35' emblazoned in stainless steel the size of a man atop a base of rusticated granite. Grozky paid the driver, stepped out of the cab and made his way in between a Toyota Land Cruiser and a Mercedes towards the statuesque numbers.

The building's entrance was a pair of sheet glass doors bordered by more stainless steel. The transparent panes slid open automatically and, a yard into the spotless lobby, Grozky's nostrils were refreshed by a rich perfume and the glass doors closed smoothly behind him. A few yards further and the reeking scent so dominated the enormous foyer he could only think of how to escape its unpleasant intensity. Distracted, Grozky almost walked into one of the dark, marble-clad pillars blending into the floor. Even amongst such louche grandeur Grozky thought that US$1 million for an apartment was a ridiculous sum. Under communism a high-ranking Soviet official could have worked a lifetime and never been close to affording such a property.

At the far end of the lobby, almost thirty yards away, stood a bank of four lifts guarded by a solitary concierge on parade behind an ornate desk. He showed no discomfort at his immersion in the cloying cologne. At the faint percussion of Grozky's shoes against the polished stone floor, the gold braid on the concierge's shoulders and cuffs twitched. A greying head turned, and his authoritative gaze announced that visitors were expected to present themselves. Grozky, conscious his uniform was as discreet as a clown's suit, paced himself into a march.

Ten yards from the lifts and keeping his head firmly in profile, Grozky hailed the people-watcher with an officious 'Good morning!' His greeting was reciprocated and Grozky made it to the elevator unscathed. The concierge disappeared from view and Grozky hit the button to the thirtieth floor. The doors closed promptly and Grozky's relief was cut short as he gagged on the concentration of scent pooled in the lift.

When he arrived on the thirtieth floor, he found the fire exit and walked down five flights, a ruse of habit. Even the empty stairwell felt luxurious, a hybrid of metal steps in satin black and a polished steel banister never needing fresh paint. On the twenty-fifth floor he made his way to apartment 'H' and rang the bell, hearing faint chimes announce him.

Thirty seconds later, Grozky wondered whether he should ring again. His hand hovered over the buzzer and then the door opened, and she stood before him. Irina Tomarov was not what he expected. Almost forty, she looked much younger than her age. Her peroxide blond hair, cut in a short bob, was a little too aggressive and she wore a low-cut red dress which was both very expensive and left her cleavage overexposed. Slim and attractive, her natural beauty was offset by heavy make-up, professionally applied, making her look like an exotic dancer. Grozky favoured restraint against overfamiliarity, removing his officer's hat with the deftness of a career diplomat. He gave a courteous bow of his head before he introduced himself.

"Mrs Tomarov, I am Major Valeri Grozky of the Federal Security Bureau. Please excuse my intrusion at what I appreciate must be a difficult time for you."

If Irina Tomarov was still in mourning, she did not show it. To the contrary, her readiness to make his acquaintance caught him off guard; the broadest of smiles parted the heavily rouged lips to show the most translucent white teeth Grozky had ever seen. She dispensed with the verbal greeting, emphasising the bulbous red eroticism of her mouth and the arousing green eyes, bewitching in dark mascara.

Grozky was equally as surprised by her apartment. He found himself in a wall-to-wall blond arena. There could be no contrasting colour collision in the large room, the furniture and accessories blending against a spotless carpet which merged with the white walls. Wherever he looked, his gaze was drawn to the woman in red. He tried to focus on the windows at the far end of the room. They ran floor to ceiling, the walls fading into the sky and an uninterrupted view across the Moscow skyline. He sat down on a white leather armchair and placed his wallet case on the armrest.

Opposite him, Irina Tomarov sat back on a taut white sofa and crossed her legs, her dress parting to reveal a pair of tanned, well-toned thighs. She did not adjust the dress and her eyes watched him with amusement, her rich smile intimating he could let his gaze drop. Grozky kept his eyes on hers as he retrieved his notebook and a clutch pencil from inside his jacket. She was alluring, in her way, just not a woman he was attracted to. He thought about the fresh beauty of Natassja, a spontaneous desire, whereas the woman in front of him represented an entirely different proposition.

"Mrs Tomarov…"

"Iiireeeena, please."

They were her first words and she drawled her Christian name as if it was pure sexual innuendo.

"Irina, I'm looking to establish whether you think Yuri was in any kind of trouble and whether he shared any of his problems with you."

He held his pencil, relaxed, in one hand, the other balancing his notebook on his knee. Used in the right way, a notebook could be invaluable in developing a rapport and energising a chat. His considered questions became a conversation over an open page, impressing upon the listener he was sharing something important and there was quicksilver in what he imparted. He never lost interest in a response, his gentle attentiveness expectant and encouraging people to think of the things they might not otherwise have mentioned.

"Why do you ask?" She seemed surprised by the question. Grozky persevered, his voice measured.

"The reasons for your husband's disappearance remain a mystery. I'm hoping to establish the events leading up to his death, his state of mind."

"The last pig who was here was only interested in his documents and papers," Irina replied, inferring Grozky's question should have been asked by the previous inquisitor.

"Who was that?" Grozky asked, his tone more conversational than curious.

"A pig of a man. A colonel."

Grozky thought 'pig' was a compliment if it was the man he was thinking of. Palutkin's visit was absent from Irina's file. Palutkin had been familiar with where Stanislav Rusnak, Yanusk's Chief Financial Officer, had been killed and now he was questioning Tomarov's widow. If Palutkin had extended his hobbies to Irina Tomarov, he would have a reason.

"That might have been a Colonel... Palutkin?" Grozky offered. "He has a scar on his cheek – here."

He used an index finger to circle his right cheek.

She thought for a moment.

"Yes."

While Grozky could imagine the GRU's special investigator, Piotr Petrovitch, sitting here with his endless assertions, Ivan Palutkin was a different proposition. Palutkin's preferred interrogation technique was at the end of something blunt. He wondered what the GRU colonel might have found.

"What were you able to give Colonel Palutkin?"

"Nothing to give. I took him to Yuri's desk, but there was nothing in it. I didn't know Yuri had cleared it out. There was nothing I could show him."

Irina Tomarov didn't strike Grozky as the sort who was interested in business provided the money kept coming in. Nor did she seem the type for whom loyalty was a virtue when the cash ran out.

"Do you know why Yuri felt he needed to run?"

She paused before answering and then shrugged. He was half expecting her to say "nothing to tell".

"He was frightened. That's why he ran."

"Frightened? Of what?" Grozky asked.

"That's what I thought you'd tell me. Yuri could be a devious son of a bitch, but he treated me well. He felt as if he could do no wrong. He was so sure of himself," Irina replied.

"When did that change?"

"I don't recall exactly. He would wake up at night, sweating. He woke me up too, the sod. I know he was having some business difficulties. I assumed he would sort them out. He'd always managed to before. Then he disappeared."

"When was that?"

"The end of February last year."

"And you reported this?"

"No, he just sent me a note and said he'd be back when things quietened down."

She looked soulful.

"And then he was killed in Yekaterinburg. We never got to live in Geneva," Irina said.

Geneva. Grozky understood the appeal to a man like Yuri Tomarov. With its expertise in private banking and a seventy-five-year jail sentence for anyone defaulting on the draconian Swiss privacy laws, Geneva represented a rule of law which could not be manipulated. It was a sanctuary, distant and secure, from the writhing corruption Tomarov inhabited. Tomarov would have revelled in his triumph of being welcomed by the discreet banking fraternity who sought to manage his wealth.

"Tell me about Geneva, Irina," Grozky said softly.

She smiled as he repeated her Christian name.

"Yuri dreamed of living in Geneva. We made several visits before he found out there was some sort of problem with his residency. I couldn't understand it, with all his money it should have been easy. For some reason, the Swiss banks wouldn't let him open an account. He was furious. Yes, it was about that time his problems started."

"I see," said Grozky. He saw the irony, for Tomarov's problem *was* his money. Tomarov was too hot for the Swiss banks. Even with the secrecy surrounding the bastions of private banking the question of 'Know Your Customer' would have become a problem. The Swiss banks' background checks would have been as rigorous as their reputation. Even if they could guarantee anonymity to Tomarov, they could not reconcile the risk his Russian funds posed, even if transferred piecemeal to disguise the true value. In the genteel surroundings of undisclosed wealth, the monies would have been attractive, except for the blood attached to them. Money should have been Tomarov's salvation, except he was too great a risk to the Swiss financiers.

"Did you discuss this with Colonel Palutkin?"

"No, he never asked."

"Out of interest, did Yuri have any dealings with any foreigners?" Grozky asked.

Irina looked blank.

"Foreigners? What sort of foreigners?"

"Any Europeans or Americans, for example?" Grozky asked.

"I don't think so, not unless he met them in Geneva," Irina replied.

"May I ask when you last spoke to Yuri?"

"About two weeks before he was killed."

"Really?" Grozky made his interest sound casual.

"Yes, Yuri contacted me. He phoned me. He sounded desperate. It was a short call and he said he would contact me again in twenty-four hours."

Grozky's face betrayed no interest in the revelation while an outline of Tomarov's last hours began to form in his mind.

"And did he contact you again?"

"No. That was the last I heard from him."

"I see. I'm very sorry," Grozky said.

He held her eyes and then stood up to gaze at the Moscow skyline. If the surveillance Grozky had established to watch Kochenko was anything comparable to those who sought Tomarov, his phone call had been his undoing. Grozky turned back to the jaded blonde who lived in a world of her own and wanted for nothing.

"And you, Irina, are you still hoping to live in Geneva?"

"Without Yuri, what would I do?"

Her indifference seemed genuine. Sitting in a white lair looking out over the Moscow skyline, Irina Tomarov was, on the face of it, one of the winners of the new order. Her artificial world was so at odds with everything in the Russia he stood for, Grozky could not countenance ever wanting to live as she did. He thanked her for her time and let himself out of the decadent apartment.

On his walk back to the thirtieth floor Grozky paused to check the morning's events in his notebook. Irina Tomarov struck him as ignorant of her husband's business dealings. Grozky was beginning to appreciate that whatever Yuri Tomarov was into had become bigger than he could handle. Tomarov had assumed his wealth would open the doors to wherever he wanted to go. The Swiss authorities had denied him his escape route before he could make alternative arrangements.

He left the elevator and was relieved to see the greying concierge had been replaced with a much younger doorman, his head stuck into a newspaper, a sandwich in his hand. Grozky didn't give him a look as he marched out of the building, keen to be free of the synthetic environment and its inhabitants. He walked to the end of the street, grateful the cold air was tainted by nothing except damp, and hailed a cab.

On the way to GRU headquarters Grozky saw several more brash residential developments set back from the road in lush, landscaped grounds, their gated security proclaiming their place at the forefront of the country's renaissance. His ex-wife, Marisha, was living with some young architect who churned out such designs. Grozky did not blame her for wanting a change. The days when the KGB held a certain dark kudos had died with its dissolution in November 1991. Grozky would never compare Marisha with Irina Tomarov, they were very different people, except they had one thing in common: they had moved with the times and forged new lives while he remained a relic of the Soviet state.

15

On the second floor of GRU headquarters, his wallet folder under an arm, Grozky walked alongside Dmitri Borzoi whose outstretched arm gestured to the far end of the corridor.

"Every room serves at least one purpose: Yanusk Fraud, Senate Hearing, Personnel Background, American Media and a central Operations room coordinating everything. There's a start- and end-of-day meeting in Arkady Dratshev's office to go over the key priorities and daily developments," Borzoi said.

"You have your own office?" Grozky asked.

Borzoi grinned.

"Of course. As FSB liaison officer I'm three doors down from Dratshev," Borzoi replied.

Grozky reassessed his view of the GRU's effort; he had not been prepared for the scale of the Military Intelligence operation.

"You're getting daily reports from Washington?" Grozky asked.

"Of course. What do you want to know?"

"What's been publicly reported so far?"

"That would be American Media. Let me show you," Borzoi said.

They walked past several open doorways and Grozky saw the fully staffed rooms. Borzoi stopped in front of a closed door and knocked before entering. Grozky followed him into the room and closed the door. A low barrage of noise came from a half-dozen televisions mounted against the opposite wall. The bright frames competed for his attention while the dialogue and sound from a mixture of cartoons, westerns, cooking shows and motor racing cut over each other and merged into gibberish. In front of the screens, two men in green fatigues paced back and forth, patrolling the media chaos.

"The main news channels are monitored and any reference to the subcommittee hearing is recorded, before it's translated over here," Borzoi said, turning to lead the way to the other end of the room. Grozky saw a soldier, his back to him, watching a monitor under which sat a video recorder. The soldier frequently stopped to pause the tape and type.

As the screen went blank the soldier finished typing. Borzoi leant forward and spoke quietly in his ear. The soldier extracted the paper from his typewriter and handed it to Borzoi.

"Here, Valeri, watch this," Borzoi said, passing the sheet to Grozky.

The soldier rewound the tape and Grozky looked at the screen as an image appeared again: a pair of men standing at the top of some steps in front of a huge stone column. The camera zoomed in on a man in glasses who held a microphone, the interrogator in the question-and-answer session.

Grozky read the transcript title, "CNN: Interview with 'Chuck' Cowan of Charles Cowan Associates".

Glancing at the footage, Grozky could not recall the name.

"Who is Cowan?" Grozky asked.

"He's a political lobbyist," Borzoi said.

"Thank you, Dmitri."

Grozky scanned the transcript as he caught Cowan's voice. Listening to a language he had only a basic grasp of, he heard Cowan's tone was measured and calm, a man in command of his subject and earnest in his reassurance. He read the words and found Cowan's pitch was convincing:

'Where oil is concerned, the Republicans and Democrats are united. That doesn't happen often except Russian organised crime is one of the biggest threats to domestic oil imports today. The fraud at Yanusk is an example of how the supply can dry up overnight…'

Grozky heard the translator's voice talking over Cowan's.

"This thirty-second clip went out on CNN last night at 11 p.m., Eastern. Over breakfast, several million Americans probably discussed when their oil will run out."

Grozky smiled. If there was one thing to unify the American political establishment, it was their Cold War enemy, even with Russia on its knees.

"Thank you for the context," Grozky said, returning the transcript to the translator.

They walked back towards the doorway.

"What about the Senate Subcommittee itself?" Grozky asked.

"Ekomov has an operative in the audience who takes notes in shorthand. Those are sent directly to the Operations room. Any televised footage from the Subcommittee is classified as media and translated here. The Chairman, Bradley Gravell, is fond of making statements. I'll show you the one from yesterday," Borzoi said.

Grozky followed him to a table next to the door which held another video recorder with a small screen above it. Next to the recorder was a stack of videotapes. Borzoi took the top tape, placed it into the recorder and turned on the screen. He pressed play and the screen's fuzzy grey disappeared as a man's face appeared.

"I'll find you the transcript," Borzoi said.

"There's no need, Dmitri," Grozky said. The fresh face of the enemy was different from the one he expected. Gravell looked straight at the camera as he made his statement. The Chairman of the Senate Subcommittee couldn't have been older than his late thirties, his hair thick and dark and swept back in a loose parting. He grinned, the white teeth working his smile with the appeal of a buccaneer, while his rebel eyes toyed with the viewer's gaze. Had Gravell's voice been anything other than soft and low Grozky would have been suspicious, but it added to his credibility. Picking up a few of the phrases, Grozky understood why viewers would trust this man.

"Gravell's dangerous," Grozky said.

"He's convincing, isn't he? The two people Ekomov is focusing on are Gravell and Zach Brown, one of the key Subcommittee witnesses," Borzoi said.

"What's Ekomov found?"

"Ekomov knows Gravell is the prize if he can find something on him. Let me show you Zach Brown," Borzoi said.

They left American Media and Borzoi led the way down a corridor and into another room where neat rows of

A4 paper were stuck like gridwork against every wall, every page starting with a thumbnail face underneath which were varying lengths of text.

Grozky tried to make some sense of the picture presented by the huge jigsaw.

"This is the Personnel Background room," Borzoi said. "These are all the names on the GRU's radar. The ones linked to the Senate Subcommittee in Washington are being tracked by Ekomov, while the non-American ones are covered by Arkady Dratshev's teams."

Borzoi led the way to a wall topped by a small American flag.

"These are updated daily. That's Zach Brown," Borzoi said, scanning the wall until his finger pointed to a page.

Grozky saw a headshot of a man in a T-shirt, a tanned, wideset face, the backdrop the mast of a yacht. He scanned the text: Zach Brown owned properties in Boston and Newport, Rhode Island and enjoyed racing yachts. He sounded affluent, though Grozky noted the humble beginnings, born in October 1953 to Ukrainian immigrants. Brown had worked hard to make something of himself. He'd set up Spectrum Consulting in early 1992.

The second paragraph caught Grozky's attention. After graduation, Brown had served in Vietnam, rising to become an intelligence officer. There were some vague periods in the timeline before Brown had come to the KGB's attention when he served as Commercial Attaché in Moscow until December 1991. There was nothing of note on record prior to his departure from Moscow.

Grozky looked at the tanned face of commercial success. Brown represented more than a savvy entrepreneur, he knew how to operate in Russia. Grozky recalled Ekomov's list of those testifying at the Subcommittee; the majority were FBI and Department of Justice, but there had also been directors from the CIA and an inter-agency task force.

"Who's checked Brown's CIA service?" Grozky asked.

"Ekomov. Brown left intelligence when he left the Moscow Embassy. He's ex-CIA and now a legitimate businessman," Borzoi replied.

"Legitimacy is relative. How legitimate?"

"That's what Ekomov is focusing on. He's convinced Brown must have been making or taking bribes in his Russian business dealings. Ekomov's asked Dratshev to grill the Ministry officials. Andrei Simonov is cooperating, though he's made it clear how valuable an asset he considers Brown to be," Borzoi said.

Grozky nodded. For the Ministry of Fuel and Energy, Brown was bringing in the millions of dollars of investment Russia desperately needed.

"You can see what Ekomov's up against. He's a lot of faces to cover," Borzoi said.

Grozky looked at the rows of pages under the American flag. The task facing Ekomov was daunting. Trying to dig up the dirt on the Senate Subcommittee members and witnesses or find something which could be used against them was challenging enough. That was before it was extended to family members. The catalogue of misdemeanours varied in severity, including criminal records, drug use, even the favoured 'honey trap' where a target would be lured into a sexual liaison with a man, woman or multiple partners.

Another name struck Grozky.

"What do you have on a Vadik Prigoda, a St Petersburg lawyer?"

Borzoi walked over to a list of names on another wall. His finger traced upwards from the bottom.

"Found him. He's over here," Borzoi said and walked to the far corner of the room.

The material on Prigoda was thin, a long-serving lawyer at the Soviet Ministry of Oil and Gas before he had moved into private practice. It was the photograph of Prigoda which caught Grozky's eye, not even an individual headshot, but an older newspaper photostat showing three faces smiling for the camera. Prigoda's head was circled in red and Grozky read the caption *'Ministry officials celebrate Yanusk becoming a joint stock company (Left to right) Vadik Prigoda, Andrei Simonov, Yuri Tomarov'.*

Grozky stared at the meagre information.

"Are you alright, Valeri?"

He heard Borzoi's question and stayed squatting in front of the page. Prigoda had been part of Yanusk's journey to privatisation. How involved was he in the aftermath? The line connecting Tomarov and Kochenko grew into a triangle. Grozky took out his notebook and sketched an inverse triangle, putting Tomarov and Kochenko at the top and Prigoda's name underneath with a box around it. Prigoda was no longer a coincidence, he was a priority with questions to answer. He wrote down the telephone number of Prigoda's law firm against it.

"I'm fine, Dmitri. Our surveillance has just turned up a new name connected to Yanusk and linking Tomarov and Kochenko," Grozky said.

He stood up, pointing at Prigoda's picture.

"More than a coincidence?" Borzoi asked.

"It could be. Kochenko conceded Tomarov asked him for money and we've only Kochenko's word he refused to give him any. What if Prigoda was the middleman? I'll raise this with Zotkin when I give him the disks. Can you get me a GRU car?" Grozky asked.

"You won't need a car," Borzoi said.

"Why not?"

"Zotkin's still based in central Moscow, except he spends three days a week at GRU headquarters. He doesn't want to, but it doesn't make sense to be split across two sites."

Borzoi led the way back to the corridor. As they walked Grozky asked,

"Dmitri, is Dratshev about?"

"He may be. What are you up to?"

"When Koshygin hears I've been to Moscow, I want him to know it was with good reason," Grozky said.

"Of course."

"Leave me with Zotkin. Don't worry if you can't find Dratshev," Grozky said.

They stopped outside another closed door. Borzoi knocked twice, opened it and departed.

In front of Grozky, Grigori Zotkin, head down and pen in hand, sat behind a desk piled so thickly with papers the surface was hidden. Grozky walked into the office, leaving the door open. Ignoring the interruption, Zotkin's nib hovered over a row of numbers from a printed report. His decision made, Zotkin underlined the description next to the numbers and scribbled a phrase in the margin.

"Good morning, Grigori. I won't disturb you, I've brought you the remaining data from Lensky Bank. The printouts and papers are in boxes which are being delivered to the Prosecutor-General's office," Grozky said.

Zotkin studied the page he was working on.

"Ah, thank you," he said, without looking up.

Taking in the mound of pages covered in endless rows of numbers and typeface, Grozky struggled to understand what they represented. Zotkin's bearing was easier to read: his sculpted wedge of hair was intended to make an impression, yet such stubborn individualism was misplaced amidst the functional military pates of GRU HQ.

"You'll have to excuse me. I'm helping my team to review the suspicious payments. We have a lot to do," Zotkin said.

"Of course, Grigori," Grozky said, unzipping his wallet case and extracting the box of disks. As he was about to hand them to Zotkin, Colonel Arkady Dratshev walked into the room, followed by Borzoi.

"Good morning, Valeri. What brings you to Moscow?" Dratshev said, without extending his hand. With his shirtsleeves rolled up, his knuckles on his hips, Dratshev might have been making his morning round.

"Good morning, Arkady. I've brought the additional data for Grigori," Grozky said and gently placed the disks on the piles of paper without disturbing Zotkin's pen strokes.

Dratshev's gaze did not leave Grozky's face.

"Following the FSB surveillance on Kochenko, I've just been discussing with Dmitri that, separate from any payments Tomarov made directly, I believe he may have used an intermediary," Grozky said.

"Who?" Dratshev asked.

"In tracing payments made through Lensky Bank, I'd like the account details of the law firm of Vadik Prigoda added to the search," Grozky said.

Dratshev considered him silently. Grozky sensed it was as much whether he had exceeded his remit as the request itself. Zotkin sighed and Dratshev's gaze turned to glare at the hapless Prosecutor-General's representative.

"We've got too much to do as it is. How much more work will this add?" Zotkin said, preoccupied as his pen circled another set of numbers.

"I can't say. It could be anything from one-off fees to monthly bills. It's what else has been paid which interests me," Grozky said.

"How sure are you?" Zotkin asked.

"It's early days. Prigoda knew Tomarov and he's met with Kochenko. Did either of them make any payments to Prigoda, if so, what for? I can hold off until I'm more certain, but it will take time…"

"Time we don't have," Dratshev said.

"What if… what if…" Zotkin said, "the more we widen the scope the more work we create. Minister Metzov was clear, we're searching for payments made directly to Lensky Bank or Kochenko's accounts. That is my priority. I will request the information on Prigoda and my team will review it," Zotkin said.

"Thank you, Grigori. That's what we need," Grozky said.

"Good. We all recognise there's a lot to do, we just need to get on and do it," Dratshev said, staring at Zotkin who had immersed himself in a fresh page.

Dratshev turned and left the office. Grozky followed him into the corridor.

"You've set up an impressive operation," Grozky said.

"It would be, if we had more resources in Washington. Time is our problem where the Senate Subcommittee is concerned," Dratshev said.

Borzoi left Zotkin's office, closing the door behind him, and joined them.

"I'll be heading to the airport once Dmitri and I have caught up. If there's anything I can do to help, please ask," Grozky said.

"You'll be back next Tuesday?" Dratshev asked.

"Of course."

"Good. Ekomov has plans for Gravell. He's working on laying a blood trail to undermine the subcommittee investigation. Koshygin needs you and Zotkin to deliver the evidence against Kochenko. We attack on both fronts," Dratshev said.

"Ekomov will be back from Washington?" Grozky asked.

"Certainly. Koshygin wants to impress Metzov with how he's managing the situation. What will you have to report?" Dratshev asked.

Grozky considered his position. The GRU were masters at planting a body and fashioning the narrative from the death. His surveillance progress could offer nothing as certain as a victim, no further sighting of the suspicious blue Fiat and Zotkin wasn't going to get to Prigoda's finances by next Tuesday. His best bet was to speak to Prigoda directly.

"I'll make sure I've spoken to Vadik Prigoda on what his connection is to Kochenko and Tomarov. It's too early to know if he is a middleman. I'll have a much better idea of how he fits in after I've met him," Grozky said.

"Good. Metzov must have results," Dratshev said, turned and left them.

Grozky knew. Under-resourced in Washington, Ekomov would have reviewed his options and realised he needed something dramatic. It was about finding a lever to exert pressure. With the lack of time, he had fast-tracked the selection process and found someone to sacrifice. A body required an explanation. The better the evidence of foul play, the stronger the accusation. That was the GRU way. Of the three GRU colonels, Dratshev struck Grozky as the grafter, a capable custodian who lacked the flair of Ekomov or the brutality of Palutkin.

Borzoi led the way to his office. Unlike the other rooms, Borzoi's furnishings were restricted to the essentials: a small table used as a desk, two chairs and a phone. Grozky sat down as Borzoi closed the door and pulled up the other chair.

"Well, Dmitri, a spartan billet is better than no billet at all," Grozky said.

Borzoi grinned.

"Like you said, I work hard and keep my head down," Borzoi replied, removing a square of folded paper from a trouser pocket. He handed it to Grozky as he sat down.

"This may interest you. The death certificate I found in Tomarov's file," Borzoi said.

Grozky read quickly. The mortal wounds sustained by Tomarov were more than severe; even the most careless of drivers would struggle to inflict such damage, the trauma more consistent to being run over by a lorry than a car. Natassja was right, someone had been very thorough. That type of thoroughness required coordination and Kochenko's security company employed hundreds of capable ex-military personnel. He retrieved his notebook from inside his jacket and added the word 'execution capability' against Tomarov's name and saw the phone number for Vadik Prigoda he had written down earlier.

"How did you get on with Irina Tomarov this morning?" Borzoi asked.

"My sense is Yuri Tomarov felt very threatened by someone. He was planning to use Geneva as his escape route. It fell through."

"What did Tomarov know which was worth killing him?

"That, she didn't know. Prigoda might. He knew about this damn oil company," Grozky said. He picked up Borzoi's desk phone and dialled the number.

The phone had barely rung when it was answered.

"Good afternoon, Vadik Prigoda's office," a friendly female voice said.

"Good afternoon. My name is Major Valeri Grozky of the FSB. Vadik doesn't know me, but it's imperative I meet with him tomorrow. It's a matter of state security," Grozky said.

"Certainly, Major Grozky. I have Vadik's diary in front of me. Let me check his availability."

"Thank you."

"May I ask what it is concerning?"

"It's better I tell Vadik when I see him," Grozky said.

"Of course, Major Grozky. It's short notice and Vadik is very busy tomorrow. If it's not too early, the only time available is 7.30 a.m.?"

"Perfect. I'll be round at 7.30. Thank you for your help," Grozky said.

"You're very welcome, Major Grozky. See you tomorrow."

Grozky hung up.

"There's one thing you should know. This morning I heard Koshygin has asked Ivan Palutkin to work on an operational contingency plan," Borzoi said.

"Koshygin's leaving nothing to chance. Metzov knows there's too much at stake," Grozky said, frowning at the development. A contingency plan developed by Koshygin and Palutkin was a conspiracy in itself.

"If you get a chance, Dmitri, see if you can give Zotkin a hand and understand how he checks the payment transactions. The Prosecutor-General's team are swamped, but you could take a look at what Prigoda's been up to?" Grozky said.

"Sure, Valeri."

"Thank you, Dmitri."

Grozky left GRU headquarters twenty minutes later, preoccupied by Borzoi's last revelation. Grozky had to convince Vadik Prigoda of the importance of telling him whatever he knew. However unpleasant Grozky could make life for Prigoda, it was nothing compared to what Ivan Palutkin would do to him if he held out.

16

The dawn was struggling to wake when Grozky drove down 11th Line Street in his aged Chaser, his preference for a crisp thirty-minute walk to the Big House banished by the demands of his surveillance operation. Many FSB officers drove religiously to work in the belief a car offered more protection. Grozky considered the choice redundant; being shot in a car or in the street amounted to the same end.

Grozky was thinking about his appointment with Vadik Prigoda. The lawyer had history with Yanusk before Tomarov had purchased it. At the meeting, Grozky would focus on Tomarov before raising Prigoda's history with Yanusk. He would leave Prigoda's lunch with Kochenko until last and see how the lawyer reacted. Prigoda was sharp enough to know his association with Kochenko carried risk, though he doubted the lawyer knew what was at stake. Preoccupied in his thoughts, Grozky barely registered the words on his radio. He picked up the handset.

"This is Grozky. What was that about the car?"

"Kochenko's surveillance team has reported shots fired at the marina. The suspect escaped in a blue Fiat…"

"When did this come in?"

"It just happened. We're still getting the details."

"Where's the marina?" Grozky asked.

"On the south side of Cross Island, almost opposite the Central Yacht Club. It's on the Southern Route. Do you know your way to the Central Yacht Club?"

"Yes," Grozky said, recalling the blue-blooded club on the western tip of Petrov Island.

"Where are you now?"

"Almost over the Palace Bridge," Grozky said, conscious he was only a hundred yards from the cavernous archway of the wing of the Admiralty building. He manoeuvred into the most central lane, punished for his expediency by irate hoots from the cars in the lanes behind him.

"Just before you reach the Central Yacht Club take the only right turn available at Petrov Square and you'll cross Great Petrov Bridge. After the bridge the road turns west and you'll hit the marina in about half a mile. Depending on the traffic you should be there in twenty minutes."

"Got it, thank you. Tell the surveillance team I'll meet them at the marina," Grozky said.

"Yes, sir."

Grozky considered his options to cross the river again: either circle around the Admiralty building and the Alexandra Gardens or cut along the Palace Embankment and use the Trotsky Bridge. In the end he did neither. As he passed the blond columns flanking the Admiralty arch and joined Palace Avenue, he indicated left and braked, immediately incurring a long horn blast from the car following him. Grozky added to the chaos, his own horn announcing his urgency to the oncoming traffic. The advancing traffic wavered and, to a cacophony of irate hoots, Grozky took his chance to use the three lanes of the avenue to execute his U-turn. The Winter Palace Garden floated by like a panorama and then it was gone, and he was speeding towards Palace Bridge.

The drivers in front of him were unprepared for the determination of his worn car. He accelerated through Exchange Square, skirting the spit at the eastern tip of Basil's Island and across the Exchange Bridge, a steppingstone over the Little Neva river onto Petrograd Island.

Two rivers from the Central District and the traffic thinned. Grozky sped down Dobrolyubov Avenue and a few hundred yards later he passed the Prince Vladimir Cathedral. When he saw the Petrov Stadium across the water, he turned left onto Petrov Island, barely a hop over the Zhdanov river, a wiry snake of land where Petrov Avenue ran like a backbone, a collection of sports stadiums, small parks and ponds spread around its vertebrae.

In the shrouded dawn, a few headlights pottered along the wide road and Grozky realised the Chaser's potential, the racetrack performance no longer masked as a chameleon of urban anonymity. His speed became reckless, the Chaser tearing ever westward towards the Neva Bay, its headlights fighting pockets of fog as they devoured the road.

Just before he reached the Central Yacht Club, Grozky turned north. Within 200 yards he was crossing the Little Nevka river and, through fading strips of mist, he was relieved to catch a glimpse of the pontoons bordering a thickly wooded shore. Spread out like antennae, the berths were peppered with the white hulls of different craft.

Neither island defending the eastern edge of the Neva Bay was large, but Petrov Island was a minor corvette against

Cross Island's sturdy frigate. The smaller island guarded a mongrel of mixed-use development, whereas Cross Island was entrusted with the regimented landscape of the Primorsky Victory Park and the Severny Lakes.

Grozky left the bridge to find his view restricted by the icy bocage of branches surrounding the road. Several hundred yards later he spotted a sign in the undergrowth and turned left.

Pulling off the road, he smiled when he saw the Chaser had made the distance in a little over twelve minutes. He allowed the car to dawdle. Ahead the driveway through the trees widened, expanding along the shore to reveal a pair of broad, wood-panelled buildings surrounded by hardcore. A handful of cars were parked in front, dominated by the trio of black armoured Mercedes parked side by side. Grozky saw the unmarked FSB Volvo resting at the opposite end of the line and parked next to it.

Grozky left the Chaser and walked between the buildings. In the early morning gloom the place seemed deserted except for the lonely masts of boats rearing up along the shore. He reached a slope glazed with frost and fifty yards away, between the pontoons and the wood, Grozky saw Pasha Fett and Kostya Gagolin talking to a man, his head half hidden by a close-fitting watch cap. Walking towards them, Grozky felt the damp air from the Baltic absorbing his heat and turned up the collar of his greatcoat.

Fett spotted him first.

"Someone made very good time," Fett said and Gagolin grinned.

"Good morning, Pasha."

"This is Iosif Dymov, the guard at the marina," Fett said.

"Major Valeri Grozky. I was nearby," Grozky said,

glancing northward. The suburbs of St Petersburg, sprawling around the coastline, included the M10 Federal Highway running from Finland to Moscow.

"Good to meet you, Major Grozky," Dymov said, shaking Grozky's hand.

"What happened, Iosif?" Grozky asked, noting Dymov's well-pressed charcoal grey battledress. His livelihood as a watchman was embossed in black, *Охрана*, against a yellow rectangle, his small badges of purpose adorning his epaulettes and breast pocket.

"We were just going over that," Gagolin said, his pen hovering over an open notepad.

"I was patrolling along the shore. I cover a hundred-yard walk up and back. It's generally quiet here during the week, it gets busy at the weekend. I spotted a man in the woods with a pair of binoculars. I asked him what he was doing and he ignored me. When I approached and asked him again, he fired a shot at me," Dymov said.

"You start early. Where was this man?" Grozky asked.

Dymov pointed towards the trees.

"Right over there, behind that large pine."

Grozky looked across at the thick foliage dominating the shoreline. The undergrowth bordering the pontoons had been cleared, creating a twenty-yard strip of clear ground, yet the iced-crystal branches of bushes and trees grasped outward in denial of the boundary. Several yards away, hidden by the trees, the Southern Route ran parallel to the shore. It was a good observation point. The watcher had either been unlucky or overconfident.

"You said one shot?" Grozky asked.

"Yes. I dived on the ground. I can handle myself, but I don't carry a gun," Dymov said.

Grozky heard the contractor's confidence returning, his shock dispelled by the assurance a shooting at a remote marina was receiving the attention it deserved.

Gagolin turned back to gesture to the buildings beyond.

"Pasha and I were passing. When we got to the clubhouse we heard Iosif shouting for help," Gagolin said.

"Kostya and I drew our guns and identified ourselves as FSB officers," Fett said.

"He started firing at us," Gagolin said.

"We each fired a couple of rounds so he'd understand the score, except he fired back. I started working my way down to the pontoon while Kostya covered me," Fett said.

"It was working, except I was running short of ammunition. I shouted to Pasha I was going to get the sub-machine gun from the car," Gagolin said.

"He heard that and suddenly I came under automatic fire. It was like he'd decided to put an end to it. I buried myself on the ground," Fett said, brushing a hand across his sleeve.

"Automatic fire? You're sure?" Grozky asked.

"Definitely. Two bursts," Dymov said.

Grozky frowned. A gun fight was a far cry from surveillance.

"Then it went quiet. I heard an engine start up and ran towards the trees. I reached the road and got a glimpse of the rear of the car. It was definitely a blue Fiat," Fett said.

"Number plate? You've put an alert out for the car?" Grozky asked.

"No chance on the plate. I put the call out within minutes," Fett said.

"You're sure it was a Fiat? Not a Yugo?" Grozky asked.

"I'm sure. It was one of the old Fiat 127 hatchbacks. Small car, small rear window."

Grozky nodded, recalling the desperate pursuit he and Pavlova had made of a blue Fiat tailing Kochenko the previous week. Amidst the empty roads of Cross Island the driver would have had an easy run to Stone Island and across the Great Nevka river to join the M10 highway. He saw the confusion on Dymov's face.

"The strange thing is last week one of the club's members said they thought they saw a man in the woods with binoculars. I had a look and couldn't find anyone. After today, it looks like they were right. If criminals are targeting the marina, I'm going to need to increase security," Dymov said.

Gagolin's pen scribbled the news.

"When was this?" Grozky said.

"Last Tuesday or Wednesday. I can check," Dymov said.

Grozky thought back to the surveillance schedules from the previous week. Kochenko had not visited the marina.

"Criminals, you say?" Grozky asked.

His tone was so earnest he saw Gagolin exchange a glance with Fett. Gagolin's pen hovered over his pad.

"A man possessing a gun who immediately starts firing when challenged is almost certainly a criminal, no?" Dymov said.

Grozky took a step away from the discussion, gazing towards the horizon of the Neva Bay, Kochenko's yacht lost in the gloom. He appeared to consider Dymov's statement for a few seconds before turning back and addressing the marina guard.

"Iosif, was Kochenko's yacht moored here last week?" Grozky asked.

"Yes. It's almost always moored here unless he's using the yacht," Dymov replied.

"I ask because there's a reason for most things. I don't doubt this man is watching the marina, the question is why?"

"As I said, he may be preparing to rob a yacht," Dymov said.

"I noticed the three armoured Mercedes in the car park. The same morning Kochenko leaves on his yacht you spot a man hiding in the woods. There's not a lot else to see around here and birdwatchers aren't generally the trigger-happy types. It seems a possibility he was watching Kochenko?" Grozky asked.

"I hadn't thought of that. It's possible," Dymov said.

"Out of interest, where is Kochenko going?" Grozky asked.

"He's going to his dacha. He goes there for a week in the spring and a couple of weeks over the summer," Dymov said.

"The three Mercedes, are they going to be collected?" Grozky asked.

"Yes. If he goes for a coastal cruise he leaves security to watch them, otherwise he sends people to pick them up," Dymov said.

Grozky nodded. The discussion was interrupted by an engine being over-revved and Grozky turned to see a set of headlights appear from the side of a building. The engine and the lights died, and a figure got out, followed by a shout from a familiar voice.

"I heard the call about the Fiat," Bogdan Pavlova said.

He walked towards the group, the light from a torch in one hand. As he grew closer Grozky saw he held his Makarov pistol in his other. Compared to the torch, the pistol was modernity itself.

"It sounds like it's our man," Pavlova said. Grozky smiled; the car would have suffered as Pavlova's pride competed with his professional interest.

"The war's over for the moment, Bogdan," Fett said.

"You get him?" Pavlova asked, putting his pistol away in his jacket.

"Too many trees. He came close to getting me. At least I saw the car," Fett said.

"Good for you," Pavlova said.

Grozky saw the marina guard wondering what was afoot. The assistance of a two-man FSB team was appreciated; four surrounding him was cause for comment. Grozky turned to Pavlova.

"Bogdan, our man was over there by that large pine. Take a look and see what you can find."

"Certainly, Valeri," Pavlova said. He hurried away, the beam of his torch bobbing like a bloodhound's head searching for the scent.

Grozky turned to Dymov.

"Iosif, I'm glad you're alright. Any description, however vague, would be of help. I'll leave you to finish up with Kostya. I need a quick word with Pasha. After today's incident, I'm sure the police will step up their patrols. I'll make sure my men keep an eye out," Grozky said.

"Of course. Thank you," Dymov said.

Grozky took Fett to one side.

"Pasha, if Kochenko's gone for the week, we need to know where his dacha is. Talk to Dymov and use satellite coverage, aerial reconnaissance, whatever you need, but stay on top of Kochenko. His range is only restricted by his fuel and he can always refuel," Grozky said.

"Sure. I'll get onto it now," Fett said. He half turned, pointing towards the club buildings. "We were as surprised as Dymov when we were standing there watching the yacht sail away and 'bang', a shot from nowhere. As far as I can tell, Dymov thinks we were driving by and heard the shot."

A thought struck Grozky.

"How close would you say you were to Kochenko's group?" Grozky asked.

"Close enough. We held back until we saw them leave their cars. We watched them board the yacht and depart. We were making our report from the car. It couldn't have been more than two or three minutes later when the first shot was fired."

Grozky nodded.

"It makes me wonder. We know the man in the blue Fiat pulled up on the Southern Route. It sounds like he's been here before. He could have been behind you, pulled over and walked through the trees or was he already waiting?"

"It's a good question. There were a few sets of headlights on the road behind us. I don't know," Fett said.

There was a loud shout from the trees.

"Valeri!"

Grozky turned to see Pavlova's torch waving back and forth like a lamp. His urgency might have been warning of a train accident.

Grozky ran lightly across to where Pavlova stood.

"What is it?" Grozky asked.

Pavlova was chuckling with success. He pointed the torch at the ground, its wavering beam illuminating little gems of light from the myriad of scattered shell casings. Grozky couldn't understand his excitement until the beam steadied and, disguised amidst the dark camouflage of the leaf mould, Grozky saw the black square of a small notebook.

"Well done, Bogdan. Be careful with the evidence. You collect the shell casings and I'll pick up the notebook. You can take them to the Big House," Grozky said.

"Of course."

"And when Pasha and Kostya have finished their shift I want to see all of you," Grozky said.

*

Arriving at Prigoda's office over an hour late, Grozky's annoyance was tempered when he saw the disappointment in his assistant's face.

"Major Grozky? You've missed your appointment with Vadik," she said.

"It's entirely my fault. I was on my way and something completely unexpected came up," Grozky said.

"I understand."

"When will Vadik be back?" Grozky asked.

"Unfortunately, Vadik is out at a client meeting and then he's going straight to the airport. He'll be in Moscow on business until the end of next week," she said, stifling a sigh.

Grozky considered Metzov's reaction to his situation.

"What are my chances of seeing Vadik in Moscow before next Tuesday at 2 p.m.? It's very urgent," Grozky said.

Prigoda's assistant gave him a look that suggested he should have made the 7.30 a.m. appointment. Her finger traced the diary in front of her as she spoke.

"Well… if you can be in Moscow on Monday Vadik is attending a Ministry drinks reception at 7 p.m. I'm sure he can spare fifteen minutes. Would that work for you?"

"Sold," Grozky said.

"Let's say 7.45 p.m. I'll let Vadik know. He's very punctual," she said as if to remind Grozky he wasn't.

"Do you know the Grand Hotel?" she asked.

Grozky didn't.

"It's easy to find. It's on Tverskaya Street. Very close to the centre."

"Thank you. I'll find it."

Grozky departed and returned to the Chaser, conscious his morning was already in disarray. He drove slowly, the intensity of the marina confrontation making him uneasy. He needed to work out the loner's purpose, a man as dogged in his surveillance of Kochenko as the twenty-four-hour FSB teams, yet determined to elude identification. But for the stand-off, there would have been no yield. The shell casings held slim value; the notebook offered possibilities.

17

Grozky sat in his office with Fett and Gagolin, the FSB reunion from the marina completed as Pavlova entered. In one hand Pavlova grasped two polythene bags, one bulging with the metal casings, the other containing the black notebook. His other hand held the thinnest clutch of papers. He dropped the two bags on the desk and then handed out a single sheet of paper to each of them before sitting down. Grozky saw it was a photocopied page, a twelve-digit handwritten number scrawled at an angle.

"Thank you, Bogdan. You've been busy. It was quite a morning. What could Dymov tell you, Kostya?" Grozky asked.

"Not much we don't already know. Dymov's description is weak. He saw the man very briefly. Height indeterminate and appeared balding. The one aspect Dymov is certain of is the man was late middle-aged. That puts him somewhere from his early to late fifties," Gagolin said.

"That's a close enough match to the man who evaded Bogdan and I last week," Grozky said, glancing at Pavlova who nodded.

"The FSB forensics team have been over the notebook and shell casings. Not a fingerprint in sight," Pavlova said.

"What can they tell us about the notebook? What's this number?" Grozky asked.

"Very little. This is the only entry in the whole book. You see the '001'? It's almost certainly a phone number because that's the dialling code for the United States," Pavlova said, holding up the photocopy.

Grozky sat up. Across the spectrum of the suspect's purpose, he'd tagged him as an observer for the local criminal elements. An American phone number was an anomaly. He would not have credited the man in the dowdy little car being part of a different scenario.

"Well done, Bogdan. That's something, isn't it," Grozky said, reaching across to pick up the bag containing the notebook. The cover rested flat against the pages, its body as pristine as its spine. Turning it over, he saw the price tag still stuck to the back.

"Whoever bought this has got as far as putting one phone number in it. Yet we've seen this man twice in the last week. He has plenty he could be writing down, so unless he's carrying two books, he's not using this one for notes, is he? Why do any of us write anything down? Because it's important. He's either unfamiliar with this number or he wants to make sure he has it to hand in case he needs it," Grozky said, dropping the bag onto the desk.

"I've already called one of the FAPSI team assigned to us and told him it was urgent. He'll be here shortly. I'd have used an old friend from the Eighth Directorate. He runs his own telecommunications consultancy and you won't find anyone better, but I know this is sensitive," Pavlova said.

"Excellent, Bogdan. Here, catch," Grozky said, picking up the bag of shell casings and lobbing it across the table.

Pavlova caught it in both hands, the metal tinkling between his palms.

"What's your view on the gun?" Grozky asked.

"I've been discussing these with the forensics team. The casings are not the standard 9x18mm, they're 7.65x17mm calibre. I picked up thirty-four casings, at least the ones I could find," Pavlova said.

"That's a lot of shooting from a man I would have thought would want to avoid confrontation," Grozky said.

"Once you switch to automatic, you start burning ammunition. Based on the calibre and the rate of fire, it's likely our man uses an old Skorpion vz.61. They're easy enough to get hold of," Pavlova said.

"Strictly old school," Fett said.

"Ha ha," Pavlova said.

Grozky saw Pavlova was wearing a dark brown leather jacket with four patch pockets.

"Out of interest, Bogdan, where do you carry your pistol these days?"

Bogdan patted his bottom left pocket.

"I used to keep a holster, but I find the jacket easier. The pistol is all I keep in this pocket."

"The reason I ask is because our suspect is in his fifties. Let's say he favours your set-up. What does that tell us?" Grozky asked.

"All of us carry a pistol. Our man carries a small sub-machine gun which gives him more options and he's more than prepared to use them. The Skorpion is well known across the Eastern bloc, except he's using an old model, not a modern one. Given his age, he could be ex-army or ex-KGB," Pavlova said.

"He could be, couldn't he, and where do you keep your ammunition, Bogdan?" Grozky asked.

"Top left pocket," Pavlova said, patting his upper pocket.

"How many spare clips?" Grozky asked.

"Three."

"Old school," Fett said.

"Less of the old school, thank you," Bogdan said. "Everyone should carry three extra clips. You never know when you might need them."

"Except, you picked up thirty-four casings. How many clips is that, Bogdan?" Grozky asked.

Bogdan reflected, his fingers helping his counting.

"The Skorpion holds a ten- or twenty-round clip. If I was firing on automatic I'd make sure I had a twenty-round clip. I'd say he was carrying two, probably three extra clips," Pavlova replied.

"Four clips for a Skorpion is an arsenal. That's you going to war, Bogdan," Fett said.

"That's very old school. This man is more than prepared for trouble," Pavlova agreed.

"A man has to be that well armed for a reason. If he has to be that self-reliant, he's probably operating on his own. The common denominator is his proximity to Yevgeny Kochenko. That's twice we know of and likely three if we include the marina guard's sighting last week. This man's being paid to watch Kochenko," Grozky said.

"It could be one of the gangs, waiting for an opportunity," Pavlova said.

"That's what I'd thought until you mentioned the telephone number in his notebook is American," Grozky said.

"He'll have seen Kochenko leave on his yacht. It's possible he'll watch the marina waiting until he comes back," Fett said.

"That's a good point. If he's a one-man surveillance team, he'll have reported the sailing and he'll be expected to report in when Kochenko returns. You and Kostya stay close to the marina and make sure the local police know this is a priority. They're to call us the moment they spot a blue Fiat."

"Yes, sir," Fett said.

There was a short tap on the door and a young man in a blue suit entered, carrying what might have been a large suitcase except for its official-looking black square design. FAPSI was little more than a rebranding of the KGB's Eighth Directorate and Grozky was expecting an older man. He thought the man's youth and sharp features affirmed his intelligence.

Pavlova stood up and walked over to him.

"Fadei? Bogdan Pavlova. We spoke earlier," Pavlova said, extending his hand.

"Fadei Filimonov. I'm pleased to meet you," Filimonov said, shaking the veteran's hand.

Pavlova made the introductions and Filimonov pulled up a chair at the side of Grozky's desk, his case out of sight on the floor.

Grozky handed his photocopy to the FAPSI man.

"Fadei, what can you tell me about this number?" Grozky asked.

"You mean separate from the forensic analysis I carry out, you'd like any other insights? Filimonov said.

"Everything and more," Grozky said. He liked Filimonov already.

Filimonov half disappeared down the side of the desk and a quick double tap followed as the locks of his case were unclasped. He reappeared holding a stapled sheaf of papers which he placed on the desk.

"It's a United States phone number. The mobile phone network for national roaming calls within Russia is limited to the big cities. It's possible it could be a mobile phone number, but I would say it's almost certainly a landline in the United States. I'll get that checked," Filimonov said.

"Can you find out where in the United States?" Grozky asked.

"That's what I'm doing," Filimonov said, a thumb and index finger tracking through the pages. Grozky saw the faint movement in the young FAPSI man's jaw, the distracted grinding of his inside lip as he scanned long lists of numbers tabled against words until he finally found what he was looking for.

"A number starting 001-202 would be a Washington DC number," Filimonov said, looking up.

The room went quiet until Grozky spoke.

"Could you find out where this number has been called from in Russia?"

Filimonov stared at the table for several seconds, his lip taking the brunt of his consideration. Grozky saw the telling absence of a nod.

"It's possible, assuming the number is being called directly. The problem comes if the number you found is being given to someone else to use. For instance, I call you in Paris and ask you to call the American number to relay the information. We'd never find that," Filimonov said.

"Yes, I see what you mean," Grozky said. Nothing was ever simple when it came to technology. He checked his watch as a thought occurred to him.

"It's almost 4.45 p.m. in St Petersburg so, unless I'm mistaken, in Washington DC it will be 8.45 a.m. Most people are up and about. Is there any reason why we shouldn't call the number?" Grozky asked.

Filimonov's restlessness relaxed and he grinned, reaching

into his bag to retrieve a small tape recorder and place it next to the phone.

"Please go ahead," Grozky said, picking up the phone from his desk and placing it in front of the FAPSI man. Filimonov's features were calm, his expression one of an adolescent who knows he will impress a parent with his skill.

"Thank you," Filimonov said, one hand pressing the buttons on the tape recorder, while his other dialled the number. He held up both devices, the handset outward, shared between his head and the tape recorder. The room went silent as the FSB men leant forward. There was a brief pause followed by the clicking of the digits being registered. Another pause and the rhythmic pulse of a ring tone started. The sound played out once, twice, three times and then, as the fourth tone started, the call was connected.

"Hi," Filimonov said, his accented English upbeat.

Everyone listened for a response. The silence in the room continued for several seconds until Filimonov spoke again.

"Hello." Filimonov's voice was enthusiastic, a man keen to talk.

The room listened to catch any sign of acknowledgement. Silence. A few seconds later a momentary click followed by the return of the dial tone confirmed the call was over.

Filimonov turned to the room. Grozky thought he looked pleased by the lack of results.

"This tells me more than you might expect. The person on the other end of the line is prepared to answer the call. However, before there is even a greeting, there is most likely some sort of pre-agreed phrase or password to be used before any conversation is initiated. If the caller fails the authentication step, the person receiving the call hangs up. It's good security," Filimonov said.

"Someone is being very discreet in their communications," Pavlova said.

"As soon as you've got more details on the American phone number, please add them to your report and send a copy to Colonel Arkady Dratshev at GRU headquarters in Moscow," Grozky said.

"Of course," Filimonov said.

"I appreciate your help. I don't know what they told you about this assignment, but after you've written your report, unless I or Colonel Dratshev contact you directly, you are to forget about this phone number," Grozky said.

"I understand," Filimonov said, retrieving the tape recorder and returning it to his case.

"Thank you again, Fadei. You can find your own way out?" Grozky asked.

"Yes," Filimonov said.

Grozky stood up from his desk, shook Filimonov's hand and escorted him from the room. Turning to face Fett, Gagolin and Pavlova, Grozky remained standing.

"Something else occurs to me. A man with a Skorpion sub-machine gun could have taken out Kochenko if he'd wanted to, couldn't he? He uses a clip to kill the guards protecting him and the next clip to kill Kochenko. It's not foolproof, but he's got surprise on his side and we're talking a matter of seconds," Grozky said.

"I agree, Valeri. Fifty yards from Kochenko's group would have been close enough," Fett said.

"He's found an opportunity to kill Kochenko and yet he hasn't used it. That makes him a watcher who's prepared to fire thirty-four shots. Why? I think he underestimated the opposition and he's desperate not to be picked up. After what we've just heard, he'd be explaining that Washington DC phone number at the end of a beating. He knows he can't afford to be caught," Grozky said.

There were nods around him.

"I want all the surveillance teams to keep a lookout for the blue Fiat. We need to find what this man is up to," Grozky said.

After Fett and Gagolin had left his office, Pavlova took Grozky aside.

"Valeri, I have a bad feeling about this," Pavlova said.

"I know, Bogdan." Grozky was aware his report to Koshygin would raise more questions than he could answer. The man in the blue Fiat who guarded a Washington DC phone number troubled him. With the Senate Subcommittee hearing taking place on Capitol Hill, it seemed likely someone in Washington DC was receiving a report on Kochenko's movements, yet if that was the case, it was odd for the American government to watch the oligarch when the Subcommittee had already captured the goldmine of evidence it needed. Whichever way he looked at the day's developments, none of them could be considered positive.

18

As the plane descended towards Moscow's Sheremetyevo airport Grozky struggled to dispel his unease at returning to the capital. His concern was not how late he had left it to meet with Vadik Prigoda, it was his contribution to the Kremlin operation. Kochenko had temporarily escaped the cage of his surveillance by sailing to his island, which left Grozky chasing the threads of the oligarch's network in St Petersburg. Grozky could delude himself he was making a difference, while Koshygin kept him at arm's length from GRU headquarters. Being back in Moscow only reinforced how dislocated he was from what was going on. Though he had been handpicked for the team, he was remote from the GRU cabal. That was his worry. Koshygin was his conduit to the Kremlin while the man who would decide the manner of his return to the FSB was the Grey Cardinal.

Grozky had worked late at the Big House on Saturday, using his work to distract him from his self-doubt. It was on Sunday morning when his melancholy had taken hold. Glancing at the calendar on his kitchen wall, he had noticed

Easter was three weeks away. The holy event marked when Georgians made the pilgrimage to remember their dead. He would return to Serafimov Cemetery and pay his respects at Timur's grave. It was the realisation he could not remember when he had last visited the cemetery which had caused his distress. It wasn't that he was holding on too tight, it was what he yearned for was slipping away from him. Almost two weeks since he had handed over his drugs investigation to Major Rastich, he might as well have been lying at the bottom of a canal for the difference he was making to organised crime in St Petersburg. His admission had compounded his weariness. He felt however hard he tried, his efforts were being neutered and his energy diffused by the tasks he no longer had any control over. Despair had seeped into his mind.

He needed Sunday to finish his review of the backlog of surveillance reports, but Grozky drove to the cemetery anyway. Though he craved respite from the haze blurring his thoughts, with Easter three weeks away he should not have gone. His anger had turned inwards; he despised himself for sinking into hopelessness.

At the cemetery he made time to walk alongside the tree-lined avenues interspersed with neat shrubs. It was comforting that the serene green so resembled their favourite childhood place to play, the Batumi Botanical Garden. When he knelt and touched Timur's gravestone, he imagined he could feel the intimacy of his brother's presence. Comforted by the bond of remembrance and feeling protected beneath the canopy of the trees, his memory captured the scene, making it a place he could return to in his mind.

Walking back to the Chaser he stopped to sit on a bench in front of the blue and green painted church of Saint Seraphim of Sarov. Gazing at the simple, wooden lines, he reflected on what his father would make of his situation. Keto was fond of telling his sons, "you can have anything you want, you can't have everything you want". Grozky's turmoil was that he was weighed down by the responsibility of saving Yeltsin's presidency; he was waist-deep in a task he'd been given no choice over nor was it one he wanted. Keto would have berated him: show Moscow what you're made of and make good on your oath to Timur, he would have said.

Before he left the cemetery, Grozky returned to Timur's grave, knelt and repeated the words, "*Your own lives align with the lives of the fallen*". He had needed the space to think. He owed General Donitsyn for trusting him with the Moscow assignment, while all he craved was to get back into the fight against the drug gangs who twisted Soviet values and corrupted them into the worst excesses of free enterprise.

*

Grozky took a taxi from Moscow's Sheremetyevo airport to the small hotel in Khodynka Borzoi had recommended. Dressed in uniform, he was received with the polite welcome reserved for a member of the Internal Security Services arriving from the airport with business at GRU headquarters. Grozky did nothing to correct the impression. He confirmed he would be taking breakfast and required a taxi to drop him at GRU headquarters in the morning when he checked out.

A few minutes later Grozky walked the short distance to Polezhayev Metro station, his uniform now swapped for a tan mackintosh, navy turtleneck sweater and a dark grey woollen hat. In the late afternoon there were few pedestrians on his side of the platform; most of the commuters were returning home from Moscow.

In nineteen hours, Aleksandr Metzov would judge his operation's progress. Even the GRU would be on edge and the pedigree of Grozky's surveillance update wouldn't match the thoroughbred achievements of Ekomov or Dratshev. These were not the circumstances Grozky would have chosen to become an acquaintance of the Grey Cardinal. With the pressure he was under, Metzov's hair-trigger temperament made him even more unpredictable. The consequences of falling from favour with the pitiless Kremlin Kingmaker would be severe.

His journey to rendezvous with Vadik Prigoda was quicker than he expected, the four stops on the Tagansko–Krasnopresnenskaya line taking nineteen minutes. He followed the exit signs from Pushkin Metro station, admiring the rows of thick stone arches, flexed like muscle, which supported the barrel-vaulted roof.

Outside the station he was met by a small park. He did not know this part of Moscow. The tourist map from the airport showed Tversky Street as one of the main arteries to the Kremlin approximately a mile to the south-east. He almost went down Tversky Boulevard until 'Tversky Street' appeared below it on a pair of road signs criss-crossed together. He thought 'street' was too modest a categorisation for the six-lane highway.

Grozky checked his watch. It was almost 7.20 p.m. The Grand Hotel could be no more than a few minutes away and he was not due to meet Prigoda in the reception until 7.45 p.m. It was no matter, he would find a quiet seat in one of the hotel's bars. Away from the frustrations of St Petersburg and the claustrophobia of the GRU enclave at Khodynka, he yearned for a temporary reprieve from the madness of salvaging Yeltsin from his own chaos.

He walked briskly, refreshed by the light breeze and the freedom of his anonymity. Tversky Street was an alien experience compared to St Petersburg's grand avenues, the piecemeal opportunism of modern developments forcibly eroding the old and compressing their legacy into history.

He noticed the flag first. On the opposite side of the street it was the huge tricolour of the Russian Federation whose bands of white, blue and red rustled awkwardly across each other. The banner was dwarfed by the dark granite behind, encasing the hotel save for the small rows of windows pitted against the leviathan's surface like scales. The jostling colours of the flag hinted at an entrance below and Grozky saw the handful of wide steps leading to a pair of rotating doors.

Navigating his way towards the hotel, Grozky saw a man in a bold pinstripe suit appear from the doorway. He registered the suit before he recognised Vadik Prigoda. The lawyer lacked a coat, his hand quickly buttoning his double-breasted jacket before he stopped to light a cigarette. Grozky considered his good fortune at arriving early. Prigoda paced in front of the hotel as he smoked, his free hand sheltering in a trouser pocket.

Grozky was about to start across the street when another figure left the hotel, pausing to tie his scarf and tuck it inside his dark overcoat. Prigoda noticed the man, raised a hand in greeting and strode to meet him. Prigoda's companion smiled as they shook hands.

Gazing at the pair, the familiarity of the second man struck Grozky. It was the same expansive grin he had seen in the photo at GRU headquarters, the tanned face set against a yacht's cockpit. Zach Brown, the American Senate witness, was bigger than Grozky had imagined, close to six foot two, he estimated, the American's physique bulked by his overcoat.

With the Senate Subcommittee underway, Grozky wondered at Brown's presence in Moscow. It could not be chance Brown was at the same hotel. The interaction of the pair marked them as acquaintances, certainly, but how did they know each other? They were strolling together now, talking about something as Prigoda smoked. Intrigued, Grozky followed them, curious about their purpose.

Thirty yards later, the pair paused amidst the pedestrians for a parting shake of hands before Brown continued his journey. Prigoda stood smoking as he watched the American for several yards, and then the St Petersburg lawyer turned and started towards the hotel. Grozky noted the American's nonchalant pace; the man was in no hurry wherever he was going.

Watching Brown's receding image, Grozky was about to cross the street to Prigoda when, forty yards ahead of him, he saw two men step from the pavement in quick succession. The second man was smaller, a nobody, except Grozky's gaze was drawn to the double-folded newspaper he clasped, gripped with a readiness alarming to small insects. Barely three yards separated the two men, the bigger man in front, wrapped in a fur hat and heavy overcoat. Grozky sensed their shared purpose, the first man providing a respectable cover to his forgettable accomplice whose tightly wrapped newspaper was as unremarkable as its owner except when used to sheath a stiletto blade.

Grozky stepped back onto the pavement, Prigoda fading from his thoughts as he watched the path of the two men track ahead of Zach Brown. Three yards became four as the smaller man allowed a car to pass in front of him. Grozky realised his own quandary and overrode his instinct to act. He cursed his training, hating himself for accepting the coward's choice.

The men reached the other side of the street. Grozky became aware of a second figure hurrying after Brown. There was a flurry of a coat being put on and the canter of a person in haste. Grozky stared more closely for there, clutching a small black bag, was Natassja. Grozky swore as, advancing towards Brown, a buoyant head in a fur hat was closing the distance, his partner now unseen.

Grozky cursed Natassja's presence, his steps lengthening as he gauged the distances on the opposite side of the street. She was now no more than twenty yards behind Brown. The assassins blended with the pedestrians, their footsteps reeling in their target. Grozky damned Natassja's haste. A witness was not a consideration. She would inadvertently assist the assassins, distracting Brown before an expert's blade would do for them both.

As Grozky drew level with the fur hat, he left the pavement and jogged, feeling the warmth rise in his muscles and lungs. Natassja was ten yards from the American's shoulder. Once she reached Brown and they paused to talk, the assailants would be through Brown and onto her.

Halfway across Tversky Street Grozky sprinted, aiming to run behind the car ahead until the driver braked at his passage. A horn blared. The fur hat turned and saw him coming. Grozky shouted a warning.

He was too late. Brown half turned in alarm, spotted Natassja and then looked back. Grozky saw a hint of newspaper peek out from the side of an overcoat and then the fur hat passed gracefully behind Zach Brown, his physique cloaking the strike of a matador's blade.

Grozky struggled to take in the speed of what happened next. For a stout man, Brown moved with remarkable precision. As the newspaper fell, the American spun around, a forearm parrying the assassin's blade, and he pivoted, the heel of his other hand punching into the man's nose. Grozky saw the textbook cartilage kill-strike and heard Natassja scream. Brown ignored her, expertly shifting to confront the man in the fur hat who faced him with what looked to be a slim, metal cudgel with a sharpened spike at the end.

Natassja's shrieking did nothing to stop the showdown. The fur hat saw Brown was at a disadvantage, a thin blade skewered either side of the American's forearm, then the attacker took a step forward, switching his weapon to his other hand. At that moment Grozky hurled himself horizontally at him, the impact sending them both tumbling across the pavement. The weapon cartwheeled across the street like bouncing cutlery.

The man recovered quickly and Grozky found himself facing an opponent likely in his late forties with receding grey hair and a craggy face which would have been handsome, but for the thin, cruel eyes. He circled Grozky with military care, his guard high and his arms as confident as a boxer's.

"What's happened?" queried a bystander from behind Grozky.

"There's a fight," someone responded.

Grozky was conscious of the pedestrian traffic slowing to gawp at the contest. He glared at his opponent as the crowd became a loose amphitheatre around them. He saw the man waver at his exposure in the presence of the spectators. Then he was gone, running through the crowd to make his escape.

Grozky would have followed him, but for Natassja. He turned to find her nursing Zach Brown, resting on his knees and clutching a badly lacerated forearm, the thin dagger now discarded on the pavement. Blood trickled between his fingers, the patter of drops becoming a red pool on the flagstones.

"My God, what the hell just happened?" Natassja asked.

Frowning in pain, Brown nodded at the body of a young man with a crew cut lying a yard away. The only sign of the struggle on the fresh face was a dribble of blood from a nostril. Nearby, the edges of an open newspaper flapped weakly like the reflexive response of a dead fish.

"He looks innocent enough, doesn't he," Zach Brown said, "except he was lining me up, the bastard. I know a Russian State hood when I see one. That's the last ambush he will ever pull."

Rocking gently on his knees, Brown had his hand clamped tight against his bleeding forearm, the knuckles white while his fingers dissolved into red. Consumed by pain, he no longer looked like the victor.

"I'll get help. No, I'll call the police and an ambulance," Natassja said, struggling with her decision.

"After what's just happened? Are you out of your tiny Russian mind?" Brown glared at her, his tone accusatory.

Natassja froze at his rejection. Grozky understood Brown's outburst, his fear verging on paranoia. In the space of a few minutes Brown realised he had become persona very non-grata in an alien country.

"There's a pharmacy. Wait here," Natassja said, sounding tearful.

Grozky glimpsed Natassja darting between the pedestrians and then she was gone. He walked to where the assassin's newspaper lay and picked it up, using the edges to lift the needle-like blade from the pavement without touching it. If it had once been a fishing priest, someone had modified it into a specialist's dagger, the pointed tip honed so finely it could strike as deep as a bullet.

Folding the paper around the blade, Grozky placed it inside a breast pocket and walked over to the dead assassin. He crouched, rolling the corpse on its side as he patted the man's pockets. A set of keys jingled. Grozky put his hand into the trouser pocket and felt a leather wallet which he pulled out and kept hold of. Under the man's jacket Grozky felt the hard outline of an automatic. A gun was too brazen, even a silenced one. A hushed blade avoided the ruckus of a bullet. Yet such a scrupulous choice exposed how unobtrusive Brown's death was to have been. Someone had been forewarned Brown would be in Moscow. He left the gun where it was.

Grozky was ruing the delay to his missed meeting with Prigoda when he heard the shout from a pedestrian too late. He turned to confront the danger, his arms coming up in defence. He glimpsed Brown as a sharp blow struck the side of his neck and felt the wallet fall from his hand before he crumpled to the pavement.

When Grozky came to, neither Natassja nor Zach Brown were to be seen.

19

By now Grozky should have been at his hotel in Khodynka instead of explaining himself to the Moscow City Police. Had Zach Brown been present to confirm Grozky's intercession in the fight that should have been the end of it. Instead, the wounded American had fled and Grozky was left to wonder why Natassja had abandoned him. He had allowed a token emotion to get in the way, a cardinal sin he was now paying for.

It was not until he was escorted from the police car to find himself scrutinised by tall, Athenian temples either side of the vast courtyard he realised what would follow. The headquarters of the Ministry of Internal Affairs reflected its imperial ambition; the eighteenth-century mansion would have been a palace except for its purpose. Number 38 Petrovka Street was reserved for those deserving punishment.

His rank kept him from a cell. Instead, the policemen focused on eroding his resolve, his induction a medical examination from a suspicious doctor on the ground floor, then rapid questions from two uniformed officers on the first.

Somewhere he had mislaid his watch. It must have been in the fight. They used the architecture against him, transferring him up and down stairs between floors without explanation. He was left to make a statement in a cold, windowless room. By the time he was abandoned in a sprawling office on the fourth floor of the Criminal Investigations Department, his disorientation was complete.

In warm, spacious surroundings Major Nikolai Aristov maintained a shrub topiary in a dozen terracotta pots covering a table next to his desk. Aristov had made a point of watering them to varying degrees before departing to find Grozky a coffee.

Trapped in Petrovka Street, Grozky kicked himself for underestimating Brown's capability; his ascendancy to the world of business consultancy had not been at the expense of his CIA training. Brown's assassins had learnt that to their cost. It had taken Brown seconds to realise he was a target. A man that well on his guard must have a reason to be.

The door opened and Aristov returned. Grozky was not surprised he was accompanied by a uniformed colleague nor that each of them held what looked to be a copy of his statement.

"It's late. I managed to find you a sandwich. I hope ham is to your taste," Aristov said, handing across a small roll, tightly wrapped in polythene, with the care reserved for an accident victim.

"Thank you," Grozky said. He doubted his interrogation would end as well as it was starting.

"This was found. It may be yours?" Aristov asked, handing across Grozky's watch.

"It is. Thank you," Grozky said.

He took the watch and put it on, wondering at Aristov's sleight of hand. The Moscow policeman wanted him at ease. Grozky would have to watch that.

"How are you feeling, Valeri?" Aristov asked, sitting down next to Grozky, his smile supportive while his green eyes were lustreless. He made the prelude to Grozky's inquisition sound like empathy for the bereaved.

"I'm fine, thank you," Grozky said.

It was when Aristov interlinked his fingers that Grozky registered his opponent. Aristov's hairless hands were as unremarkable as his clean-shaven face except their demonic rigidity gave them a strength the slim physique under his dark grey uniform could not explain. The concerned Major Aristov was betrayed by hands befitting a hangman.

The second policeman placed a small plastic cup of black coffee on the table in front of Grozky.

"This is Lieutenant Anton Bessonov. He's working on establishing the identity of the murder victim," Aristov said.

"Good evening," Bessonov said.

"Thank you for the coffee," Grozky said and engaged the bright blue eyes too intelligent for the inch-deep crew cut Bessonov sported. Grozky avoided the pitfall of asserting Brown's action was self-defence. Aristov had dangled his statement as a lure. Now was not the time to challenge the policeman, to do so would concede Grozky knew more about the incident than he had admitted to. Aristov would wait until he could provoke an error. Grozky decided to avoid conflict.

Bessonov sat down next to Grozky, corralling him between sombre grey authority at the end of the table.

"This is a very bad business," Bessonov said.

"Yes, it is," Grozky said, meeting the young lieutenant's earnest gaze. Aristov would have assigned one of his best bloodhounds to the short straw, a dead hood minus his wallet.

"I've read your statement. It's very thorough," Bessonov said as if he expected no less from an FSB officer.

Grozky nodded. His statement was a double-edged sword the Moscow police would use to find any omission or lack of clarification. They would play the same mind games he knew, knowing he would anticipate them. Bessonov looked the more intelligent, though Aristov controlled what went on in the room. They knew the game as well as he did. His decision to intercede in the attempt on Zach Brown's life gave him very little margin to deflect and distract. Grozky had taken care where he had peppered his points of emphasis.

"We'll come to your role in this incident. I'm interested in the comment the American, Zach Brown, made," Aristov said.

Grozky nodded again. He wondered when they'd get around to that.

"You state Brown said, 'I know a Russian State hood when I see one'. What do you think he meant?" Bessonov asked.

"Those were his words. He was in shock and in pain from his arm. It sounded like an exclamation. It struck me he was either using a pejorative term because he'd been attacked by men who had the look of government operatives or he genuinely believed they were," Grozky said.

"Yet you yourself spotted these two men, as you put it, 'being up to no good'. You have never seen the two assailants before?" Bessonov asked.

"Never."

"You're very observant. With all the pedestrians on Tversky Street, what was it about these men in particular?" Aristov asked.

"The newspaper caught my attention. If they hadn't been crossing the street a few yards apart and the newspaper had been single-folded, I doubt I would have given them another look," Grozky said.

Aristov stared at him while Bessonov scribbled something on Grozky's statement. It was late for an officer of Aristov's rank to be present. Bessonov struck Grozky as more than capable for his interrogation. Aristov was either a driven officer or someone had made a call to involve him. Being able to read an opponent was something Grozky had learnt in the Chidaoba ring, well before he had joined the KGB. He registered the disparity between Aristov's brutality and Bessonov's intellect. As a tag team their respective strengths complemented each other. Bessonov would challenge and Aristov would disrupt and together they would confuse. This was a pairing to be careful of.

"Vadik Prigoda has confirmed you were due to meet him in the hotel. Instead, you seem to have been waiting on the other side of the street, watching him. What were you up to?" Bessonov asked.

"I haven't been to the Grand Hotel before and I arrived several minutes early. I walked down from the Pushkin Metro station," Grozky said.

"Yes. I read your statement. If you were early and you had already agreed to meet, why didn't you wait for Prigoda in the hotel?" Aristov asked and his eyes glinted like jade.

"I would have done. Prigoda came out of the hotel for a smoke. I was about to cross the road when he started walking away with someone. I paused because I was curious where he was going," Grozky said.

"Curious?" Bessonov inquired.

"It was almost 7.30 p.m. and we were due to meet at 7.45 p.m. I wondered where he was going," Grozky repeated.

"How long did you stand watching?" Bessonov asked.

"Not long. I would think fifteen to twenty seconds. Prigoda started walking back towards the hotel. That's when I saw Natassja Petrovskaya, an acquaintance from St Petersburg, rush from the hotel."

"Seeing Natassja Petrovskaya prevented you from meeting Prigoda?" Aristov asked.

"No, not at all. I was just surprised to see her in Moscow. That was when I saw the two men crossing the road," Grozky said.

"And how long did you watch them?" Bessonov asked.

"Not long. I would think about ten seconds," Grozky said.

"How could you know these men were a threat? Where have you seen them before?" Aristov asked.

"I haven't seen these men before. Natassja has been threatened recently. She was hurrying down the street and I wondered what had happened. Instead of going straight to the hotel, I decided to cross the road to check if she was alright," Grozky said.

"Would that all acquaintances are so fortunate," Aristov said.

Grozky did not rise to the remark. He used the moment to unwrap the sandwich. Only a man preoccupied with being found out would not eat. He took a small bite and chewed slowly.

No good deed goes unpunished, Grozky thought. He was paying for his folly.

"You understand why Lieutenant Bessonov raises the

question? Based on a folded newspaper you decided to start a fight?" Aristov asked.

Grozky paused to consider the implication, taking a sip of coffee and swallowing part of his mouthful before replying.

"I don't consider I started anything. I was assuring myself an acquaintance wasn't at risk," Grozky said.

"Let's say that's true. There's one aspect we're struggling with," Bessonov said.

Grozky sensed the question before it was asked. It was the disconnect he could not hide. Grozky continued chewing slowly. A mouth in motion was the most natural of facial disguises.

"You go to the assistance of an acquaintance, Natassja Petrovskaya. You defend her, and, according to bystanders, you also fight off a man intent on doing harm to Mr Zachary Brown, an American visiting Moscow. After you defend him, Brown assaults you and then your acquaintance leaves you unconscious on the pavement. How do you explain that?" Bessonov asked.

Grozky swallowed, nodding as he did so.

"I'd like to know the answers to both those questions myself. I didn't get a chance to speak to Natassja. I could see she was very shocked by the violence. She may have been hysterical," Grozky said. If there was one consistency he was relying on in the bystanders' statements, it was Natassja's screams.

"Possibly," Bessonov said.

"And why do you think the American struck you?" Aristov asked.

"I don't know. He'd just been attacked and his arm was bleeding badly. In my experience, when people feel threatened, they can behave unpredictably," Grozky said, taking another bite of the sandwich.

"He couldn't have felt that threatened by you," Aristov said. "He let you live."

Grozky heard a knuckle crack as the Frankenstein hands flexed. He sidestepped the trap of speculation by chewing. When he did not answer the two detectives watched him for several seconds, willing him to speak. Eventually Aristov unfurled his barbarous fingers and pointed to Grozky's statement.

"You've been very thorough except in one regard. You make no mention of your relationship to the American."

Grozky swallowed in relief.

"I've never met him before. I saw him talking to Prigoda. I thought that was clear," Grozky said.

"You state you think he stole the wallet?" Bessonov asked.

"It happened very quickly. I'd just searched the body and had the wallet in my hand. After I came to, the wallet was gone," Grozky said.

Bessonov nodded.

"A witness confirms your statement. Would it interest you to know our assessment of the incident?" Aristov asked.

"It would."

"We don't think Natassja Petrovskaya was the target. We suspect the American was the target," Aristov said.

He waited for Grozky's reaction.

Grozky allowed an eyebrow to rise.

"Really?" he said, taking a sip of coffee.

"We've established Brown was a guest at the reception being held by the Ministry of Fuel and Energy. Ms Petrovskaya was invited to the same event. The hotel reception has confirmed Brown dropped off his room key and left the hotel shortly before the attack. Our working presumption is Ms Petrovskaya became caught up in the attack on Brown. It's possible he was the reason she was hurrying from the hotel," Aristov said.

"I see. I consider my actions were justified," Grozky said.

"I can see why you would," Bessonov said. He didn't sound as if he shared Grozky's conviction.

"What is Natassja Petrovskaya's relationship to Zach Brown?" Bessonov asked.

"I don't know. You'd have to ask her," Grozky said.

His face betrayed no interest at the comment. It was the very question he would be asking when he caught up with her. She must have realised by now her journalistic instincts had almost got her killed.

"You can understand why we want to talk to both Natassja Petrovskaya and Zach Brown as soon as possible. In reality, Brown is our priority," Aristov said.

"What contact details do you have for Natassja Petrovskaya?" Bessonov asked.

"I have her number at the *Kommersant*. Let me write that down," Grozky said.

"Thank you," Bessonov said, passing Grozky a pen and the copy of his statement. Grozky wrote the details on the back of the last page and returned the pen and paper to Bessonov.

"I will share that the Ministry of Fuel and Energy are cooperating closely with us. They are outraged one of their overseas guests was attacked in Moscow," Aristov said.

"I understand. I appreciate you sharing your progress."

"I used the term murder earlier. What puzzles me is, if this American was defending himself, why would he flee the scene? Until we can resolve that, we're treating this as a murder inquiry because it makes finding him a priority," Aristov said.

"I understand."

"I see you're staying at Khodynka. Why are you in Moscow?" Bessonov asked.

"I'm in Moscow on FSB business."

"Who could verify that? Is there someone who can vouch for you at GRU headquarters? Aristov asked.

Grozky thought about it.

"General Donitsyn. St Petersburg FSB," Grozky said.

Bessonov wrote down the name as Aristov eyed Grozky.

They kept at it for another thirty minutes. Grozky kept his answers concise, only for them to start over in a different order. Their capacity to listen for variation in his responses seemed endless. Grozky answered a question only to find himself back at the same point minutes later. In their game of snakes and ladders, they kept him from the rungs.

"When do you expect to be back in Moscow?" Bessonov asked, starting a fresh angle.

"I don't know," Grozky said.

Aristov looked at his watch. Grozky glanced at his, seeing the time was almost 11 p.m.

"We thank you for your cooperation in this matter, Major Grozky. You understand we have to corroborate and cross-check the statements of those present," Aristov said.

"Of course," Grozky said, doubtful any of the other bystanders had endured such forensic scrutiny.

"We still need to contact Natassja Petrovskaya and locate Brown. Both have some explaining to do, would you agree?" Aristov said.

"I would."

"You couldn't really say otherwise, could you?"

"If you need anything else from me, you'll let me know?" Grozky said.

"I will. We've kept you long enough. I'll have a car drop you back," Aristov said. He made eighty minutes of interrogation sound like light conversation.

"Thank you," Grozky said.

On his arrival at the small hotel in Khodynka, he left a message for Borzoi to meet him at 8 a.m. at GRU headquarters, showered and went to bed, too exhausted to wonder why Natassja had abandoned him.

20

Grozky arrived at the gates to GRU headquarters at 7.45 a.m, conscious his uniform did not hide his exhaustion. He had yearned for sleep only to be denied by his mind, each effort to rest becoming more fatigued than the last. He had slumbered, replaying his interrogators' questions until they were interrupted by ones he could not recall. In his struggle to distinguish real from imaginary, his responses had become as abstract as the untruths in his statement. He realised now his error with Natassja. In using her for background, he might have well told her where to keep looking. He should have known she could not leave the story alone. She'd met Zach Brown at the Ministry reception and found something worth chasing him in the street for. Had she found out about Yanusk? He prayed not.

Getting out of the taxi, the greeting from the GRU sentry alerted him to his notoriety.

"Major G-r-o-z-k-y."

The sentry relished his name as if he was arriving late for latrine duty.

"Please follow me, sir," the sentry said and escorted him through the door next to the double gate.

Inside the perimeter, a highly polished grey Lada Zighuli waited. The engine was idling and two lean NCOs, immaculately uniformed, stood by the car, their AK-47 assault rifles shouldered. They snapped to attention and one opened a rear door.

"General Koshygin's compliments, sir," the sentry said and left him.

Grozky got into the back seat, one guard joining him, while the other rode shotgun with the driver.

"It's not far," the driver said, "you should feel privileged. Not everyone gets this attention."

The driver laughed and the two guards smirked.

Grozky's escort, as smart as an honour-guard, had the presence of prison warders. The merest misdemeanour and he'd answer to the GRU personnel. Looking out at the empty ground between the wall and the building, Grozky was in the securest of the capital's stockades.

The journey bordered on the ridiculous. Grozky estimated the Lada drove 800 yards before pulling up outside a tall brick tower at the centre of the glass-clad building.

"I told you it wasn't far," the driver said.

Grozky was escorted inside by the pair of NCOs. After two flights of stairs they entered a carpeted corridor resembling a comfortable hotel and stopped outside a room marked '7'. One of the NCOs knocked on the door and opened it. The pair remained outside, on duty either side of the doorway.

"Thank you," Grozky said.

He entered and found himself in an L-shaped room where a small kitchenette became a compact living room containing a sofa, tub chair and a glass coffee table. On the sofa was an open briefcase and several scattered papers.

A door opened to Grozky's right and General Anatoli Koshygin walked into the room in a state of undress. Koshygin's bulk was bound together by the cord on his black dressing gown, his neck obscured by the white towel wrapped around it. Barefoot and clad in his general's trousers, Koshygin ran a hand over his damp scalp as he perched himself on the arm of the sofa. He did not offer Grozky a seat.

"You look tired, Major Grozky. I'm not surprised. Up late explaining yourself to the Moscow police. Am I correct?"

"Yes, sir."

"Vadik Prigoda confirmed your meeting, yet you never met. Instead, you get involved in a street fight. Of all the people you could come across in Moscow, you expect me to believe you chance upon Zach Brown? What the hell are you playing at?"

There was nothing jovial amidst the folds of Koshygin's face, the rubber flesh frozen in a hunter's poise.

"My only involvement was to help an acquaintance in danger," Grozky said, his head bowing in contrition.

"This journalist, Petrovskaya. How do you know her?"

"She knew my brother."

"Would you have interceded in the fight had it not been for your journalist friend?" Koshygin asked, leaning back on the sofa.

"No, sir. I accept full responsibility for my actions," Grozky said.

"You're an FSB officer. Listen to yourself," Koshygin said. He was toying with Grozky's discomfort, like the bully who knows his victim won't fight back.

"You know Brown has disappeared? There's a full description out and the police have been watching the American Embassy. Not a sign of him," Koshygin said.

"Yes, sir. The Moscow police said as much."

"Prigoda's based in St Petersburg. You arrange a meeting with him in Moscow? That's something the Moscow police failed to ask you," Koshygin said.

"Operational delays, sir. I had a meeting with him in St Petersburg. Unfortunately, that was the morning there was a shooting at the marina after Kochenko's yacht left for his island," Grozky said.

"You're wasting time we can't spare. Would it interest you to know the Moscow police don't believe you? Neither do I," Koshygin said. He stood up suddenly, used the towel from his neck to wipe his scalp, and discarded it on the sofa.

Grozky remained silent.

"What is this journalist to you?"

"An acquaintance, sir."

"She must be good skirt. You know she is scheduled to fly back to St Petersburg this morning? The Moscow police will pick her up. She seems to have been the last person to have seen Zach Brown. You can understand why these events trouble me. Why was she *running* after Zach Brown?" Koshygin asked.

"I don't know, sir."

Koshygin faced Grozky, glowering.

"No? Well, it's time you did. You know her, so you should know what she's up to. As of now I'm making you personally responsible for Natassja Petrovskaya. I want to know what she's working on and who she's talking to."

"Yes, sir."

Grozky rued his situation. He could tell himself he

hadn't put Natassja at risk, except all he had achieved was to encourage her. She had kept on scratching at the surface of the story without realising she was digging her own grave. If Grozky had been a tricky shape in a troublesome jigsaw, Koshygin no longer struggled to see where he fitted. Koshygin had simply extended the puzzle and it was Grozky who must complete it. Whether Grozky warranted any credit in its completion hung on how he assembled the extra pieces.

"I've got enough problems without having to check on an FSB officer recommended to me by General Donitsyn. Do you know what I was doing before Metzov selected me to lead this operation?" Koshygin asked.

Grozky didn't.

"I was fighting the Chechen war. Correction – I was trying to fight the war. No one saw fit to establish a combined joint headquarters to coordinate the campaign. I spent most of my time resolving squabbles between the Defence Ministry, the Interior Ministry and the FSB. Can you believe the incompetence? How can Russia not be beating *Chechnya?*"

In his despair, Koshygin slowly made a fist and then shook it in front of Grozky as if he could crush the grubby little country he despised in the palm of his hand.

Grozky knew. The Chechens were settling a vendetta started by Stalin in 1944 when the entire Chechen and Ingush populations had been deported across Soviet Central Asia and nearly a third had perished. By declaring independence, the Chechens had done more than secede from the Russian Federation. Yeltsin could not recognise the Republic of Ichkeria without igniting the fuse of nationalism across every minority in the Commonwealth of Independent States which had been created after the dissolution of the USSR. Russia's ill-equipped sons were being sacrificed as Yeltsin fought to restore constitutional order to the North Caucasus.

"Chechnya... Yanusk. What a mess. The elections are twelve weeks away. Twelve weeks..." Koshygin said. He roused himself from the spectre of despair, turning on Grozky.

"You've had your last chance, Major," Koshygin said and stabbed him in the chest with a stubby index finger. Grozky swayed, caught out by the sudden ire of Koshygin's exasperation.

"You'd better not screw up any more orders. You know where you stand. Get out," Koshygin said.

"Yes, sir," Grozky said. He saluted, turned and left the room.

Sitting in the back of the Lada with his three-man escort, Grozky's mind was in turmoil. He'd expected a dressing-down, not to be beaten into a corner. It was the first time he had experienced the new pecking order of the Russian Federation. The FSB intimidated the population on behalf of the Russian government and was, in turn, menaced by the GRU. Koshygin had just reminded him he was in the lower, not the upper, security echelon of the state hierarchy. Whatever illusion Grozky might have had that he was a member of the GRU team, the selfless actions of a passed-over major from St Petersburg had condemned him as the imposter in the ranks. Grozky had deserved the rebuke, it was the malevolence which surprised him. It was as if the man who had selected him had suddenly lost faith in his choice. The practised routine of finding fault with a subordinate had left him at Koshygin's mercy. The GRU general, riding on Metzov's coat tails, was as copper-bottomed as they came and now had a marker on him which he could call in at a whim. Grozky would not know who watched him and unless he could contain Natassja, she would do for them both. A bad report from Koshygin would put an end to his ambition of joining Donitsyn's new URPO team. He could forget any chance of his rehabilitation into the FSB. It would be an inglorious end to an unremarkable career.

Outside the main GRU building Borzoi was waiting for him, pacing outside the entrance.

"I got here early. From your message you had some trouble in Moscow last night?" Borzoi asked.

"Is there somewhere we can talk?"

"Here is probably as good a place as any," Borzoi said.

They walked away from the building and then strolled in a small circle.

"What happened?" Borzoi asked.

Grozky told him, including his run-in with Koshygin.

"Who the hell would go after someone like Zach Brown?" Borzoi asked.

"Who indeed. It would have meant one less witness for the American Senate investigation," Grozky replied.

"With the evidence and testimonies the American Senate has already gathered, that sounds desperate."

"Exactly, but he was close to Yanusk. Someone saw an opportunity to get rid of him," Grozky said.

They continued to pace slowly, watched through the glass doors by a guard.

"So how much progress has Zotkin made?" Grozky asked.

"They're still going through the data. There are certainly unexplained payments, though that doesn't mean they were illegal," Borzoi said.

"If the payments were made in US dollars, wouldn't they stand out?" Grozky asked.

"In theory, yes, if Lensky Bank held a US dollar account. Apparently, it doesn't. If the payments were made in US dollars, they would need to have been converted into roubles before the transfer. Zotkin is checking for any foreign exchange broker transactions that transferred roubles to Lensky Bank," Borzoi said.

"It doesn't sound like Zotkin has found what he needs?" Grozky asked.

"It's a work in progress. Zotkin has started tracing Tomarov's assets. Although Tomarov had some cashflow problems, he owned several properties. He could have used one as part of the pay-off to Kochenko. It's an easy way to transfer a large amount of money," Borzoi replied.

"How long is that going to take?" Grozky asked.

"That's the problem. Zotkin has a huge task. Last week, he went behind Koshygin's back and told Metzov he didn't have enough resources. Koshygin's been forced to reassign GRU operatives. Dratshev told me Koshygin feels he's been screwed into giving up some of his best people."

Grozky understood. The GRU's priority was to reveal *kompromat*, 'compromising information', on Senate witnesses, and monitor the Subcommittee's progress. Koshygin would not have diverted his specialists voluntarily.

"What have you managed to find on Vadik Prigoda?" Grozky asked.

"It's early days. Zotkin's team have yet to find any payments between Tomarov and Prigoda. The one thing which stands out is that Kochenko's been paying Prigoda a regular sum every month for the last six months. There are invoices for 'consultancy services'," Borzoi said.

"At least the theory's working. How's Ekomov getting on?"

"All I know is he and Palutkin arrived back from

Washington last night. Did you see the report from your FAPSI guy, Filimonov?" Borzoi asked.

"No."

"Your Washington DC number is a landline in Arlington, Virginia. He's trying to find the street."

Grozky registered the significance of the location. Of all the American government sites which had sprung to mind, he hadn't imagined it could be the Pentagon, headquarters of the US Defence Department. He checked his watch. It was 8.15 a.m. The briefing would start at 8.30 a.m.

"Metzov is expecting solutions, not problems. Let's hope we can find some. We should get ready, Dmitri," Grozky said, conscious the problem was now as much Ekomov's headache as his own.

*

"Do you realise what would have happened if Zach Brown had been murdered in Russia?" Metzov asked.

On the opposite side of the table, Grozky saw Colonel Arkady Dratshev wince. Next to Grozky, Grigori Zotkin's hands absently fiddled with the corner of the manila folder.

"Brown's death would only have reinforced his testimony – *'The last will and testimony of Zach Brown points a finger at corruption in Russian Oil industry… before the Russians had him killed,'*" Metzov said, mimicking his headline in heavily accented American.

No one in the room had the courage to join in with the Grey Cardinal, except Ivan Palutkin, who chuckled.

"As it is, we have a missing person and, of course, we are doing everything we can to find the American, aren't we?" Metzov asked.

"Of course," Dratshev said. "I spoke to the Moscow police this morning and they are handing out leaflets across central Moscow with a photograph and description. The search continues."

"Find Brown. What about those who attacked him?"

"One dead. No identification on the body. The other attacker escaped. Valeri gave a good description. The Moscow police are keeping us informed," Dratshev said.

"Highly unsatisfactory," Metzov said and turned to face Grozky. "Valeri, I believe we have you to thank. Russia owes you a debt."

Grozky saw Koshygin freeze as he heard the compliment.

Before Grozky could respond, Metzov glared at Dratshev.

"Arkady, but for Valeri, it would have been Zach Brown lying in the morgue instead of one of his assailants. Why were the GRU not watching him?"

Dratshev blanched at the implication.

"He was only in Moscow for two days and he was a guest of the Russian Ministry of Fuel and Energy. He was not considered to be at risk," Dratshev said.

"Yet less than a mile from the Kremlin, the American Senate witness becomes a target?"

Koshygin might have come to his subordinate's rescue until Metzov gave his verdict.

"You must be simple."

Suddenly, Metzov's hand came down, the percussion of flesh against wood ringing out like a mallet striking the table. Dratshev struggled for an answer. Grigori Zotkin's state of mind was betrayed as his fingers inadvertently tore off a large corner of the manila folder.

"Enough. Let us dispense with how Zach Brown has been able to disappear in Moscow. I have heard enough excuses,"

Metzov said. He scowled and turned to face Grozky's side of the table.

"Where is the proof of Kochenko's collusion with Tomarov?" Metzov asked.

Grozky saw a tear of sweat slide from beneath Grigori Zotkin's ear until it touched his collar and vanished. Zotkin's hairline glistened as he started speaking.

"We have been focusing on the financial transactions. So far, the loan agreements are genuine. Lensky Bank was the biggest lender and syndicated some of the loans by bringing in other banks to help with the funding. That is normal practice. Lensky Bank still carried the greatest risk. We have re-examined the default on the loan by Tomarov and there was nothing unusual in the triggering of the collateral call..."

"How can you be sure?" Metzov demanded.

"No one could have foreseen the scale of Tomarov's criminality at Yanusk. When the loan was set up, Tomarov..."

Grigori Zotkin did not get to finish his sentence before the Grey Cardinal cut him off.

"You just said it, 'set up' is exactly what it was. Tomarov makes millions before allowing his accomplice to take over an oil company that was privatised well below its true value?"

Metzov dismissed the opinion of the Prosecutor-General's representative with a wave of his hand.

"Don't you see? Kochenko *knew*. He was in it from the start. He conspired with Tomarov. Kochenko's just as guilty," Metzov said.

"So far, we've yet to find that evidence," Zotkin said.

'*So far*'. Grozky heard those words again, the hope something would present itself to prove Kochenko's complicity in the scandal. Zotkin was struggling in the quicksand of absent proof.

There was the shot of a slap as Metzov's open palm hit the table.

"Well, find it. I need results. Damn it, use Petrovitch. That's why Anatoli brought in a special investigator," Metzov said.

"Yes. I will," Zotkin stuttered, his cheeks flushing.

"Follow the money. You have all the data. Get it double-checked and find me that evidence."

"I will do whatever you require. This is time-consuming work, we need more resources," Zotkin said.

"You've been given the extra resources you asked for. You must do whatever you have to do, but I *must* have results…"

Metzov paused as Grozky raised a hand. Koshygin glared at the interruption.

"You can add something Grigori cannot?" Koshygin said.

Metzov was staring at Grozky who was still playing the pieces of information over in his mind. Zach Brown was a foreign troubleshooter for American businessmen. Prigoda was a lawyer who represented Russians seeking investment. Had Prigoda known Brown would be in Moscow beforehand? It was quite possible.

"We know the American Subcommittee is very well organised. You've read my reports. We know someone in St Petersburg is passing information on Kochenko's movements and we've just had confirmation from FAPSI it's a landline in Arlington, Virginia. When you consider what the Senate Subcommittee has been able to find, the American intelligence on Yanusk almost seems too good. How have they been able to find out so much?" Grozky said.

"American Intelligence purchased it," Koshygin said.

"Precisely. How do we know that?" Grozky asked.

"Because Senator Bradley Gravell, the Subcommittee Chairman, has the information," Koshygin said.

"He certainly does. We know he has it because Zach Brown shared the page of commission payments with the Ministry of Fuel and Energy."

"We know all this," Koshygin said.

Sitting next to Koshygin, Ivan Palutkin scowled at Grozky as he persevered.

"Yes, we do, but where did this payment information originate from?"

Koshygin would have answered, but Metzov cut him off.

"Where do you think the information came from?" Metzov asked.

"We believe Gravell was the recipient of the information because that's what the Ministry was told. Who told the Ministry? Zach Brown. What if the information didn't originally come from Bradley Gravell, but Zach Brown was the one with the information and he gave it to Gravell?" Grozky said.

"Why would you think that?" Koshygin asked.

"Grigori is checking thousands of transactions, yet there can only be a handful of people who could have known about Tomarov's payments to Kochenko."

"You suspect Brown purchased this information?" Metzov asked.

"Someone did. We know Brown represented Archipelago Oil in its dealings with Yanusk after privatisation. Brown knew Tomarov and Tomarov needed money. Until Brown killed a man with the ease of a professional yesterday, he had put himself above suspicion. He's a businessman who has brought millions of dollars of investment into Russia, allowing him to ingratiate himself with the Ministry of Fuel and Energy in a way no other foreigner could. By sharing the commission payments with the Ministry and disclosing he had been called to testify at the Subcommittee, what better way to protect himself and buy a lifetime's goodwill? He's almost too good to be true and I'd say he is."

"You're implying Zach Brown is still working for American Intelligence?" Dratshev asked.

"I'm not saying he is, but he has the perfect cover to be hiding in plain sight. He's a man very well placed to be playing both sides, isn't he?" Grozky said.

"What are you proposing?" Metzov asked, his hands very still on the meeting's folder.

"To find the trail of financial transactions between Tomarov and Kochenko, we're not just following the money, Grigori is already focused on that. I'm suggesting we need to look for the person who *knew* where to find the transactions in the first place," Grozky said.

Metzov's finger pointed across the table and hovered at Dratshev's head.

"I want Brown found, immediately. I don't care where he is in the world, I want the American found and interrogated," Metzov said.

"Yes, sir," Dratshev said, scribbling down the order.

"Ivan will find him," Koshygin said.

"Valeri, an excellent insight," Metzov said.

Grozky nodded. He had speculated enough.

Metzov turned to Colonel Ilya Ekomov.

"Ilya, I'm told you have a plan to share with us?"

Ekomov acknowledged his audience with a gracious nod.

"With twelve weeks before the Russian elections, we're expecting Gravell will publish his Subcommittee's report by early May at the latest. That would mean the Yanusk scandal would hit the press six weeks before the election. Worse, it will fuel Zyuganov's election pledge that Russian industry must be renationalised," Ekomov said.

"What is your plan?" Metzov asked.

"In the time available, the most effective way would be to lay a blood trail to Gravell which he cannot refute. Since early 1992, Gravell's Senate Office has been in receipt of a monthly donation from an Estonian Investment Fund which is an ex-KGB front. Those funds are a matter of record with William Danvers, Gravell's office manager. Documents which prove the true origin of the funds will be found on the body of a dead Russian prostitute. It will look as if she had been blackmailing Danvers who will not deny it because he will be dead. A murder-suicide in a Washington motel room," Ekomov said.

"Timing?" Koshygin asked without emotion.

"Saturday 20 April is the preferred date. That gives us two weeks before Gravell publishes his report. Once our story breaks in late April, Gravell will be fighting a very personal scandal of his own."

"Will it be enough?" Koshygin asked.

"This is bait American journalists cannot refuse. They will be more interested in Gravell's receipt of historic KGB money than anything his Subcommittee is investigating. Not only will it delay Gravell's report, he will have to explain why his office accepted such funds. The murder-suicide confirms Danvers must have known about them, and Gravell is close to Danvers. Blood sticks. Gravell appears guilty by association. He will be explaining himself to the FBI for weeks."

Grozky listened to Ekomov's matter-of-fact assessment of what it would take to derail the Senate Subcommittee. Money. Sex. Blackmail. Murder. Suicide. It was as brilliant as it was cruel. Ekomov had layered his dark ingredients with care, rearranging fact with fiction until he had reshaped primitive subterfuge into a masterpiece. The most genial GRU officer in the room was no less a sociopath once human sacrifice became necessary. Amongst the fragmented tribes the Russian security agencies now represented, no one challenged the GRU for supremacy for they were unmatched in their savagery. No other clan craved the right to kill.

There was a sharp knock at the door and a uniformed GRU man strode into the room. He handed Koshygin an envelope before excusing himself and leaving. Koshygin glanced at it, seemingly in a quandary as to whether to put it down or open it.

"May I, Aleksandr?" Koshygin asked, using Metzov to resolve his dilemma.

Metzov nodded.

Koshygin tore open the envelope and read the single sheet inside. Grozky watched Koshygin slump, his face ashen.

"General?"

Metzov's prompt caused Koshygin to recover his posture, not his composure. He turned to address Metzov, his voice a croak.

"According to this report, Kochenko has just been killed at his dacha in the Gulf of Finland. He was shot this morning."

Christ, thought Grozky, *that's all we bloody need.*

21

Kochenko's killing shocked everyone in Metzov's operation and left the Grey Cardinal suddenly lacking the star defendant he was relying on for the Kremlin's show trial. If the near miss on Zach Brown's life had enraged Metzov, the unsanctioned hit on Yevgeny Kochenko tipped him into a frenzy. Grozky feared he would be the first to suffer from the fallout. Though the oligarch had been shot on his island in Finnish national waters, the boundary was so close to the Russian Federation the distinction was academic. While Grozky's operational reports had highlighted the opportunity to kill Kochenko at the Cross Island marina, it remained a loose thread in the fabric of his surveillance assessment. He was sure Koshygin would use the oversight against him only for the Grey Cardinal's fury to find the culprit in Colonel Arkady Dratshev. Incensed at the second security slip-up in as many days, Metzov banished Dratshev from the operation. He replaced him with Ivan Palutkin, demanding the Chechen veteran redouble his efforts to find the wounded Zach Brown.

Grozky knew Koshygin would not have selected him to collect Kochenko's body, he was Metzov's choice for the errand. Grozky would have asked for Dmitri Borzoi to accompany him to Finland, except the decision was not his to make. Instead, he arrived at Helsinki's Vantaa airport wearing a dark grey suit and paired with a pathologist and a translator assigned by Koshygin. While his new chaperones would watch him and report on his activities, he doubted they knew his predicament. They didn't need to, it was enough for Koshygin to monitor him.

With the oligarch dead, Grozky could see his value to Koshygin was fading. As the pieces of the puzzle were being removed the GRU's priorities were shifting, Koshygin's attention focused on Washington and the salvation Ekomov's kill strategy would deliver. Once Gravell's report was defused, Grozky's usefulness would have run its course. It would be the deaths of William Danvers and a high-class whore in Washington DC on Saturday 20 April which would mark the end for Grozky. Twenty-two days.

On the aeroplane Grozky was seated apart from his companions. At Helsinki airport, well before they reached passport control, the little group was intercepted by three plainclothes officers, whisked through a private door and fast-tracked through customs. In an anteroom an older man with close-cropped grey hair and wearing a dark blue mackintosh awaited them.

"Good afternoon, I am Detective Chief Inspector Matthias Lasola. Welcome to Finland. I hope you had a good flight." Lasola smiled as he spoke slowly in passable Russian, the syllables faintly distorted by his lilting accent.

"A good flight, thank you, Chief Inspector," Grozky said.

"Please, call me Matthias," Lasola said, giving Grozky a handshake which gripped like warm leather, and Grozky felt the scrutiny of Lasola's eyes, a fusion of grey-green. Without the warmth of the hand, his stare would have been cold and diffident.

"Major Valeri Grozky. Valeri," Grozky said.

The Finn would already know who they were, nevertheless the detective took the time to apprise himself of each of them with the clasp of his hand and his cool gaze.

Grozky was still acquainting himself with his new companions. Dr Katerina Kozhevnikova was not what he would have expected from a GRU-sourced pathologist. Slim and more good looking than pretty, she had warm brown eyes and the toned physique of an athlete. She had not offered him her military rank. If she was a civilian, she would have to be very competent indeed. His translator was Lieutenant Pavel Ikkonnen, the cross-pollination of a Finnish father and a Russian mother, who, after a Soviet upbringing, was Finnish in name only. He had lank, untidy blond hair and pinched, pimply cheeks on an otherwise plain face. His skinny body was one he could take better care of and marked him out as a linguist, not a fighter. During the flight Gozky had seen his overlong, expectant stares at the attractive pathologist being ignored.

"Where did you learn your Finnish?" Lasola asked in Russian, his tone friendly.

"I'm from Karelia originally," Ikkonnen replied.

"Ah, like myself," Lasola said, patting Ikkonnen's shoulder as if he were a fellow national.

"Where did you learn your Russian?" Ikkonnen asked the detective.

"Oh, here and there."

At Ikkonnen's peeved expression, the Finn headed off further questioning with a quiet statement.

"Young man, before the Winter War my family were farmers. After the war, they were left with nothing."

Grozky heard no anger in Lasola's voice. During the Second World War the Finns had lost the Karelian Isthmus to the Soviet Union. Forced to side with Germany, they had failed to win it back. To them, the Russians were a race to distrust.

Lasola turned to address the group, his tone relaxed.

"I am very pleased to meet you all. I am sure we will work well together."

"Likewise, Matthias," Grozky said, already wary of the detective's disarming manner. Lasola's thinning grey hair and slight stoop put the Finn in his early fifties. If he had stayed in the same line of work, he had almost three decades of experience.

Within minutes, they were chauffeured from the airport in an unmarked white people-carrier escorted by a single police car. Sitting in the front of the foreign vehicle with Lasola and watching the official outrider keep them in tow reminded Grozky that, by now, Major Nikolai Aristov would have picked up Natassja in Moscow. Aristov had the benefit of Grozky's statement. He would cross-check her answers against his and pick over why she had left the scene. Zach Brown was their focus, the American now the object of a national manhunt. Natassja was a curiosity unless she gave them cause to think otherwise. She was sharp, with a distrust of authority. He could only hope she would keep her head under interrogation.

Behind them, Dr Katerina Kozhevnikova and Pavel Ikkonnen sat together in quiet conversation. Grozky noted their uniformed driver bore no evidence of carrying a pistol. He reflected that, but for the surprise killing of Yevgeny Kochenko, Finland was a country lacking the lawlessness which scarred the Russian Federation.

"Our journey will be quick. It's a straight run down Highway 45 to Helsinki," Lasola said.

"Where is Kochenko's body now?" Grozky asked. He saw the police car ahead keeping a steady pace; Lasola favoured discretion to speed where his Russian visitors were concerned.

"In the morgue at Koskela Hospital. It's our first stop," Lasola replied.

"How was he killed?" Grozky asked, seeing a silent burst of blue strobe from the police vehicle blitz a slow-moving car in its path.

"He was betrayed by one of his bodyguards and shot by a sniper. Someone put a lot of planning into his killing. I have signed statements from his security detail," Lasola said.

"Do you have anyone in custody?"

"Not yet. The sniper was pursued by Kochenko's guards, but escaped from the island by boat. The bodyguard who betrayed Kochenko was trying to join the sniper and was shot before he could get away. After the autopsy, I'll take you through in detail what I have on the killing ground. I am hoping, with your knowledge, you may be able to help me when it comes to suspects?"

Lasola's grey-green eyes gauged him for a reaction. Grozky was developing a respect for the detective whose honest confidence was refreshing compared to the dark world he knew.

"As you say, someone went to a great deal of trouble to work out how to get to Kochenko. For the St Petersburg gangs, for example the Tambovs, this seems too clinical. To have compromised his security detail is an achievement. Until I've seen the evidence you've found, it's difficult to be more specific," Grozky said.

The detective nodded.

"We can discuss it after the autopsy," Lasola said.

Grozky recalled Bogdan Pavlova's warning. Perhaps the St Petersburg gangs had organised themselves to finesse Kochenko's downfall.

"We're almost here," Lasola said, pointing to a modern tower block breaking over the tree line ahead. The two-vehicle convoy turned into a driveway where smaller residential apartments nestled amidst the landscaped campus. Moments later the van pulled to a halt.

As they disembarked, Grozky wondered what Lasola made of the Russian entourage. The inclusion of a pathologist was a novelty in itself.

Their visit was expected. A doctor in a white coat stood waiting at the reception desk while a mixture of the ill, the fearful and the medically qualified criss-crossed a chessboard floor of black and white tiles. Grozky watched him move from his preassigned mark, a hint of cardigan peeking from his open coat. He was older than Lasola, early sixties, with fine, silvery hair lightly slicked back from the widow's peak, small ringlets curling at the sides of his head.

"Dr Oskar Markus, I am the Head of Pathology," he said as Ikkonnen quickly translated.

Markus looked gaunt, not from ill-health, but from the tireless purpose of his vocation. He wore round glasses with thin, wire rims, adding to his image as a sage of anatomy. Dr Markus seemed completely unfazed by the Russian delegation as he shook hands. He took longer with Dr

Katerina Kozhevnikova, an unexpected bonus in what was probably going to be a long morning for everyone.

The introductions complete, Markus led his visitors past reception, along a corridor and down a stairway to the lower ground floor. Here the overhead neon blasted everything with an artificial brightness. They continued walking, the selection of names on the overhead signs decreasing until only one remained. They descended another set of stairs to the basement. It was quiet, the resting place of utility cabinets and mechanical and electrical equipment. It seemed to Grozky, in an institution designed to fight for life, the department of the dead was kept at a distance. They stopped outside a pair of white wooden doors with square portholes at head height. Markus paused and made a short comment.

"Welcome to my world," Ikkonnen said, his translation struggling to echo Markus's enthusiasm.

Markus pulled a door towards him and gestured the group through.

"Ah, changing rooms," Lasola said and pointed to the rows of benches and lockers opposite. Markus followed the group and spoke briefly. Ikkonnen translated, his voice dour.

"Everything you need is laid out for you. You can leave your clothes in the lockers. They all have keys. Your belongings will be safe."

Several minutes later the entire party assembled in the autopsy room, the dress code broadly matching the clinical hierarchy. The pathologists were both dressed for the surgery of the dead in long blue scrub gowns and surgical latex gloves. Markus's silver locks were scraped back under his pale blue scrub hat. Grozky and Ikkonnen wore long white aprons over their clothes. Only Lasola remained unchanged, choosing to retain his mackintosh.

The long room felt like it had been designed to respect the deceased, the white tiled floors and walls so ceramic in character they might have been porcelain. Laid out across the floor were five steel tables, waist high and broad as slabs, dominating their white tiled bases. Each table was accompanied by a tall metal stand holding a pair of steel trays, one above the other. On the first two tables lay a pair of naked corpses while two trolleys were parked flush against a wall, draped with sheets so white they might have been shrouds awaiting their cargo for the journey to Hades.

A series of outsize stainless-steel sinks ran along the far wall, their proportions more suited to an abattoir. The air in the windowless room smelt as preserved as the bodies, while from the ceiling, large bulbs hung like fertile stamens, their illumination pollinating the tiles with light.

Dr Markus ignored the first corpse and led the way to the second. The two pathologists took their positions of natural authority either side of the head. Markus fussed over the position of a small tray holding a tape recorder, moving the metal stand out of the way to rest behind the head at the top of the table. He pulled another stand closer and checked the tray holding his instruments was secure. Satisfied with his preparations, he smiled at Katerina Kozhevnikova and selected a small scalpel.

Amidst the solemn coolness, Grozky felt like an unwelcome voyeur, intruding upon the privacy of the cadavers. Under the sharp light, Kochenko's nudity looked foreign in death. His skin was dulled, a dirty grey corpse sullying the pristine metal against which it rested. Grozky glanced briefly at the second corpse on the table next to him, a smaller man whose torso was pockmarked by bullet wounds, the death of a Judas shot down as he tried to escape.

Despite their language barrier, the two doctors had already established a working bond, their profession rising above their cultural differences. Dr Markus clearly relished the chance to demonstrate his experience to his attractive Russian observer. He compensated for his absence of Russian by visually guiding her with the courtesy of worldly gestures from his scalpel, illustrating each step before making the cut. As he recorded his commentary for the tape, he might have been talking to himself.

Standing next to Katerina Kozhevnikova the translator, Pavel Ikkonnen, seemed distracted by the pathologist's wandering scalpel, his translation becoming more stutter than statement as the incisions grew. Ikkonnen took a step back, distancing himself from the immediacy of the cutting to find himself overlooking the shrivelled genitalia of Kochenko's corpse. He retreated to stand by the feet. Grozky saw the GRU boy's discomfort. Watching the laborious task of dismembering the human body was not a scene for the uninitiated.

Ikkonnen fumbled for a packet of cigarettes. He had the packet almost open when Lasola caught his eye.

"I'm afraid it's no smoking in here," Lasola said, pointing to a sign at the far end of the room so small as to be invisible against the sea of white.

Grozky was about to argue the point when Dr Markus spoke quietly. It was Lasola who translated.

"He says a cigarette won't help you. Both bodies are fresh, with minimal decomposition. If you feel faint, just turn away, go outside and get some fresh air in the corridor."

Ikkonnen nodded and returned the packet to his pocket.

In the cool calm of the chamber the two pathologists worked patiently together, absorbed in their clinical butchery. Markus was unhurried, carefully cutting away and allowing time for his descriptions to be translated. Katerina Kozhevnikova watched, her silence affirming her satisfaction with what she was seeing.

Markus paused at the head. The face was ghoulish, Kochenko's visage now horribly disfigured. The left-hand side had been torn apart by the blast of a weapon. Markus spoke as he held out a cupped hand behind which he made a pistol shape with his other thumb and forefinger.

"Shotgun… blast… at… point blank range…" Ikkonnen said, speaking slowly. He separated the words as if, by doing so, he could isolate himself from the horrific image. Ashen-faced, his gaze was fixated on the bald feet.

Grozky listened to the faltering description while he took in the scale of destruction to the face. The blast had decimated the skin, bone and tissue into a bloody pulp, glossy against the light. The jaw was indeterminate on half the face. He had never seen gunshot wounds to rival this.

The features looked more demon than human, the symmetry of the face destroyed, one side inflamed and contorted while the other was reduced to a red mush. Markus severed what was left of the muscles in the jaw and carefully removed the shattered lower mandible. The Finnish pathologist flicked his bloodied gloves across the swollen side of the face and a rash of red pellets flecked the skin like varnish. Ikkonnen's translation ceased.

"It's the velocity of the pellets," Katerina Kozhevnikova said. "At this range the shotgun destroyed the bone, the teeth, the tissue – everything."

At the end of the table, Grozky saw a mute Ikkonnen sway.

"What happened, Matthias?" Grozky asked.

Lasola pointed to the smaller body on the adjacent slab.

"The witness statements are consistent. Kochenko was hit by the sniper and the second killer, a bodyguard, who was close by, used a shotgun to finish him. The sniper was covering the escape of the bodyguard who used a 125cc trial bike for his getaway. He almost made it before he was gunned down," Lasola said.

"What was his name?"

"Milosz Klepin. He'd been with Kochenko for almost two years."

Grozky looked at the corpse. From what he knew of Kochenko's security arrangements, someone had to have been paid a very significant bounty to betray the oligarch.

Markus took a thin torch from the tray, his bloody hands smearing the metal tube as he pointed the light into the shattered mouth. Grozky glanced up to see Lasola watching him. Their eyes met briefly and then Grozky returned to the gruesome spectacle.

The two pathologists peered into the disfigured orifice. Katerina Kozhevnikova bent forward, holding her breath, as if the air might carry some evil stench. In contrast, Markus might have been preparing food. His soothing tones remained uninterrupted and only occasionally did he shake his head from side to side, seeming to despair at Kochenko's fate. Lasola translated the Finnish pathologist's observation.

"Markus is highlighting that dental records are out. You'd be lucky to get a third of the teeth with what's left of the jaws."

"There's also huge damage to the soft tissue at the back of the palate," Katerina Kozhevnikova said.

Markus turned off the torch and carefully returned it to the tray. The two pathologists looked at each other in silent recognition of their trade.

There was a small choking noise from the far end of the table. Grozky turned to see Pavel Ikkonnen clutching the sides of the steel table as he struggled to support himself. He stumbled forward to grasp at the nearest sink and retched heavily into it. He stayed above the basin, turned on the tap and proceeded to clear his nose and throat. He turned back to the table.

"I'm sorry. I feel awful," Ikkonnen said.

"Don't worry. We can manage," Lasola said. His matter-of-fact tone gave no hint of empathy for the young translator.

"Dr Markus is doing a fine job. We can certainly manage, really. Thank you," Kozhevnikova said, confirming Ikkonnen could consider himself dismissed.

Despite his wan complexion, Ikkonnen gave a sickly smile, encouraging a thread of sickly saliva to drop from the side of his mouth. He raised a hand to wipe his lips, mumbled an apology and stumbled from the theatre of the hideous.

With the loss of the interpreter, Markus's pace became more business-like, his phrases shorter and more frequent while his careful gestures remained unchecked.

He used a scalpel to make the broad sweep of the Y incision, a neat alphabetical slash across the body to expose the chest and abdomen. As he pulled the flesh back, a telltale bullet hole was visible on the bared chest plate below. Like a macabre magician, Markus's bloodied gloves began to bring out the internal organs. He held each item out so Kozhevnikova could inspect it, his commentary capturing his assessment.

It's like two people talking in a language of the dead, thought Grozky.

There were short pauses in the excavation of body parts as a darkened organ became a point of brief pathological prodding between the two physicians.

Only the arms and legs gave an indication the corpse had once been complete, yet the medical plunder continued. Markus returned to the chest to examine the small hole. He took a very thin metal probe from his tray and used it to feel into the hole. Once it had taken purchase he released his grip, leaving it standing against the bone. He looked across at Kozhevnikova, inviting her opinion.

"If this man was standing, then the trajectory of the shot was well above him. You can see by the angle made between the metal and the bone," Kozhevnikova said, as she placed her hand in line with the probe, illustrating her point.

"The bullet was fired downwards relative to his position," she said, completing her assessment.

Lasola translated into Finnish and Markus beamed at her, bringing his bloodied gloves gently together in a series of small, silent claps.

Markus removed the metal probe and brought out a stubby handsaw sporting a serrated square blade. He started to cut through the chest bone as if it were a log. He made short, quick strokes, the teeth of the saw crusting with bone dust until the chest was severed in two.

Unhindered, Markus explored the chest cavity. He removed the bulbous distraction of the heart and then the lungs. He checked each lung carefully, pointing to the torn tissue at the base of the second. He held it out and uttered a word.

"Bullet," Lasola said.

Markus deposited the lung alongside the growing collection of organs at the side of the table. He stooped to peer carefully into the cavity, his bloodied fingers feeling gently across the surface as if he might read the bone like Braille. Momentarily, he stopped to retrieve a small pair of medical pliers before reaching back into the hole that was once a chest. Grozky wondered where the medical trail was leading.

Markus gripped onto something and pulled, his other hand braced against the neck of the corpse. It looked to Grozky as if the pathologist was intent on one final act of burglary. The prize gave up the fight and Markus held up his pliers for inspection. Between the tip was a small, deformed piece of metal still recognisable as a bullet.

"It was embedded in the spine," Kozhevnikova said.

Markus took a small kidney-shaped bowl from the instrument tray. He dropped the bullet in and passed it to Grozky. The bullet had been badly twisted on impact.

Kozhevnikova leant across to pick up the bullet between a thumb and index finger.

"Look at the damage. The bullet would have been travelling very fast when it hit him. Almost certainly high velocity and you can ask Chief Inspector Lasola once the exact calibre is confirmed by the ballistics department. I would say the shock alone would probably have been enough to kill him," Kozhevnikova said.

Grozky saw the thoroughness of the assassination. Two killers in play in case one failed.

There was a drill-like sound as Markus started a small rotary saw. He stood over Kochenko's head before he saw he had interrupted their conversation. He smiled and turned the saw off.

"I've seen enough, Katerina. I'll leave you to it," Grozky said.

"If anything else of note shows up, I'll let you know," she said.

"Thank you," Grozky said and began to remove his apron.

Markus restarted the saw, the high-pitch whine deepening as metal ground into bone.

Grozky paused in front of Lasola before he left the room.

"As thorough a kill as I've seen," Grozky said.

"Not the sort of killers we're used to in Finland," Lasola said.

Grozky left the room. Even as the sound of metal grating against resistance receded, he realised a new problem: Sergei Malievich and the hundreds of Lensky mercenaries would not leave Kochenko's murder unavenged.

*

On the way back to Lasola's office in Pasila, the Finnish detective insisted they get a breath of fresh air. In the cool, spring sunshine Grozky stood in the Senate Square looking up at the bleached white cathedral which dominated the skyline.

"That is the *Tuomiokirkko*, the Lutheran Cathedral. It was originally known as the Church of Saint Nicholas because Helsinki owes much to the Tsars. Nicholas I was also the Grand Duke of Finland. If it looks familiar, it's because it is modelled on St Petersburg's Kazan Cathedral," Lasola said, sweeping his arm towards the chalk-white colonnades topped by a huge copper dome, its chloride bloom blanched to a pale turquoise. Standing in the square, Grozky might have been in St Petersburg.

"Despite your schedule, I felt it would be a shame for you to come to Helsinki without seeing this. I'm afraid where I work is far less grand," Lasola said and turned to walk slowly across the square.

A few yards ahead of him, Lasola paused to turn back and gestured up at the cathedral behind them.

"Helsinki can never rival St Petersburg as the 'Venice of the North', though this is why our capital is known as the 'White City of the North,'" Lasola said.

Grozky nodded, now conscious of the reason for the impromptu tour. After watching the autopsy together, Lasola sought him as a partner.

"This isn't on your itinerary, but if you have time, I'd like to show you the island. It will help you understand what happened," Lasola said.

"I can make time."

Another offer. Lasola's regal patience was borne from years of graft and his reserved air belied a rapier intellect. But for his situation, Grozky would not have considered sharing information with the Finnish detective. Trust was a quality alien to everything in his training.

22

They'd been flying for more than an hour, the morning bright with sun, initially hugging the coast south-east from Helsinki before heading across the Gulf of Finland. The helicopter was compact, the McDonnell Douglas MD-500 resembling a sphere impaled by a stick. Compared to the Mil models Grozky knew, it felt like a toy. Lasola hadn't disclosed its origin and the two pilots, clad in olive drab jumpsuits, exuded military nonchalance. The small side window limited Grozky's view, the sliver of sea below resembling navy glass scattered with pistachio crumbs – the tiny islands of the vast archipelago of the Finnish National Park. Looking at the little flecks of land, they might have been puffs of surf thrown up by a skimming stone. As children, he and Timur had skimmed pebbles on the banks of the Chorokhi river outside Batumi. Next to Grozky, his headphones discarded around his neck, the Finnish detective sat, dozing.

Despite his fatigue, Grozky did not sleep. The offer to visit the island was as unexpected as it was revealing. He returned to study the file Lasola had given to him on boarding. The Finnish words were redundant for the photographs told their own story, a multitude of aerial black and white shots with the ground-level pictures in colour. The aerial snapshots were a case study in reconnaissance, taken at varying levels of magnification and at a very high shutter speed to prevent blurring.

Grozky returned to a wide-angle panorama of the dacha, taken from a few hundred feet above the ground. It showed a walled compound bisected by a building whose visible windows were deeply recessed, almost slits, to provide maximum protection. At the rear of the building two wings ran along the compound's walls, bordering a garden. Grozky saw the regularity of darker shadow at the edge of the garden, the row of arched colonnades a cloister providing both shade and protection. At the centre of the dacha, emphasised by its shadow, stood a four-storey tower that could have been an airport observation post, the final floor clad in sheer glass panels. It provided a perfect vantage point.

The helicopter was buffeted by a downdraft and Grozky leant forward, reassured by a pilot's grin. Looking at the relentless watery landscape pockmarked by the pimples of land the thought struck him. The remoteness of the island *was* the factor discriminating against the Russian gangs as the primary suspects in Kochenko's killing. The image of a lone marksman in a high-powered boat formed in his mind, his rifle secured in a camouflaged scabbard as he navigated across the water. This was precision and finesse when a Russian gang would have sent a helicopter gunship to the island or amphibious assault teams to board Kochenko's yacht.

Grozky saw Lasola stir and the detective glanced at the photo in his hand.

"You'll see for yourself shortly," Lasola said, "my understanding is that the design and scale of a Russian summer house or *dacha* can vary considerably – small and simple to the grand and ornate, yet even by Russian standards this is a very defensive building. My men refer to it as 'the fort'; it's what you would call an *ostrog*."

Grozky nodded. An *ostrog*, derived from the Russian *strogat* or 'shave the wood', was a small military construction surrounded by a wooden fence of four to six metres and usually built to defend remote areas. Kochenko's summer house resembled a fortified stockade. Looking at the photo, the building was indeed a redoubt and not a dacha.

The co-pilot turned to face them. He pointed downwards with an index finger several times, the universal cockpit language to indicate their descent. The helicopter banked gently and, from between the pilots' seats, Grozky saw the wide tower against the backdrop of a steep, wooded hill.

Grozky expected they would land either in the courtyard or just outside the compound. Instead, the MD-500 circled the fort once and touched down on a small plateau jammed against the side of the hill like a buttress. The rotors subsided and Grozky disembarked into the fresh, spring air and found himself facing Lasola in a meadow roughly 400 metres square. On one side the plateau fell away steeply, the shore below hidden by trees, while on the other it formed a promontory overlooking the cleared ground in front of the fort, several hundred metres below. Behind the fort, rising another half-mile to the summit of the island, a forest of pine trees obscured the slope to the skyline. But for its location as the killing ground of Yevgeny Kochenko, it would have been idyllic.

The conviction of bright sun could not disguise the chill in the gentle breeze. Grozky saw Lasola had the stem of a pipe between his teeth. The detective reached into his pocket to retrieve a small pouch of tobacco. He took the pipe from his mouth and held it between his thumb and forefinger while the rest of his hand cupped the pouch. He toyed with some sinewy wisps of tobacco and lined the bowl. He did not test the draw by sucking on the pipe, instead relying on the experience of his fingertips to gently press down on the soft leaves until he was satisfied with the compression. A match flared, the first faint embers glowing as Lasola drew carefully. The surface of the tobacco ignited, the tiny flames dissolving into the first signals of smoke.

"Let me show you why I brought you here," Lasola said and led the way to the edge of the ridge overlooking the fort.

"What is the first thing you notice?" Lasola asked, gesturing vaguely in the air with his pipe, before returning it to his mouth and sucking on it thoughtfully.

Grozky took in the densely wooded hill; his gaze worked down from the summit to where the trees had been cleared and then traversed the slope of scrubby grass to the fort. One item dominated the landscape.

"The tower," Grozky replied.

"Indeed. You have an unspoilt 360-degree view. It is also central to the fort's defence. It's built around a reinforced concrete core. The glass windows at the top are bulletproof."

Pursued by the GRU and conscious he could become a target for the larger gangs in St Petersburg, Grozky understood why Kochenko would have felt unassailable on his private island. Somehow, someone had breached his defences.

"Now look down at your feet," Lasola said.

Grozky saw they were standing in front of the carcass of a large, fallen pine tree at the crest of the promontory, devoid of its bark, and its fractured branches long since denuded by time. He saw first the fresh chips of wood scattered down the slope and that the tree itself was grossly splintered where chunks had been forcibly gouged out, the ground resembling the floor of a sawmill.

"This ridge is something of a blind spot. The sniper had a good field of view up here, protected by the edge of the ridge. He saw his shot and may have seen the bodyguard use the shotgun. He would have been prepared for small-arms fire from the dacha, I doubt he was prepared for the machine gun. Here, take another look at the tower," Lasola said, reaching inside his jacket to retrieve a sniper scope and hand it to Grozky.

Grozky lay down on the grass and looked through the eyepiece. From the top of the log, the features of the fort became sharp and close.

"A marksman firing from this position would be almost unassailable. It's a killing ground," Grozky said.

"Take a look at the tower. What do you see?"

Grozky scanned the construction through the scope. He saw the thin slits of windows rising to the glass panels at the top of the tower. Beneath the observation floor at the top, the building was clad with metallic-looking panels before it tapered to concrete.

"A solid defensive construction," Grozky said.

"That's what you're supposed to think. What you don't see is those metal panels are on recessed hinges and can be dropped instantly. There's a very lethal rotary cannon mounted on rails around the steel core providing a 360-degree field of fire. It's controlled from the observation post above it," Lasola said.

Grozky studied the tower again and saw the cleverness of the design. The tower's offensive capability was hidden from view. He moved from his prone position to squat as he studied the shredded chips of wood scattered in front of the branch. The planning would have anticipated small-arms fire from the fort, not the firepower Kochenko kept in reserve. Once the rotary gun started firing, the sniper would have been pinned down.

"After the initial shot, the sniper turns his fire on the compound to cover the bodyguard, except the tower's machine gun opened up within seconds," Lasola said.

"It's a game-changer. A professional would have known that. He can't provide cover fire because he's pinned down and the rest of the guards will be heading straight for him. He would have had to make a run for it while he still could," Grozky said.

"That is what happened. The second killer used a 125cc trial bike to get away. They're ideal for patrolling the island. With sniper cover, in the confusion he would have had a reasonable chance, except for the rotary gun," Lasola said.

Looking down at the fort, Grozky took in the scene. The sniper could hit the target, but one shot couldn't guarantee the kill and he might not get a second shot. The second killer would have made sure he was close to Kochenko and had the trial bike nearby.

"Someone has spent a lot of money putting this together," Grozky said, standing up and returning the scope to Lasola. The Finn replaced it inside his jacket.

"This may interest you," Lasola said, retrieving a small plastic bag from a coat pocket and handing it to Grozky. In it were three shell casings.

Grozky opened the bag and extracted a cartridge. He felt its weight and, upon examination, saw the neat lettering 'R-P 308' milled into the headstamp. He checked the other two casings through the plastic and saw the same markings. He returned the casing to the bag and handed it back to Lasola.

"It's a .308 calibre, favoured by marksmen and hunters because of the accuracy it provides over longer distances. These cartridges are made by Remington," Grozky said.

Lasola nodded as if an FSB major should know such details.

"You are correct. We found these by this log. Once the tower gun started nailing him, the sniper didn't have a chance to collect all his casings," Lasola said.

Grozky glanced back down the slope at the compound and the commanding tower. A picture began to form in his mind.

"The .308 calibre is widely used for hunting, though smaller than the standard Russian 0.311 calibre. There are some civilian-based .308 rifles available in Russia, like the Tigr-308, but in Russia the preferred sniper ammunition would be the 0.311 calibre round. It's possible this was fired from a Russian weapon, though given the circumstances, I'd say more likely a Finnish rifle."

Lasola nodded again.

"We're in agreement so far. Anything else?" Lasola asked.

Grozky realised the anomaly almost instantly.

"If these weren't fired from a Russian rifle, then why use an American round?" Grozky said.

"That is exactly what I have been thinking. Why indeed? They're not Russian and yet for a Finn, why not from a Finnish manufacturer like Sapo or Lapua? Those cartridges are readily available to the local hunting community. The origin of these cartridges becomes interesting, does it not?" Lasola asked.

"It does. The cartridge itself is telling, not conclusive. It was either fired by a Finnish national who wanted to make it look like it was fired by an American or it's conceivable the marksman favours Remington .308 ammunition which would widen the search."

"Which do you think?" Lasola asked and Grozky saw the warmth in the detective's eyes fade to cold steel, waiting for what Grozky would share.

"It could be either," Grozky said, recalling the single telephone number for Arlington, Virginia he had found at the marina on Cross Island.

"Go on."

"The shooter has done his reconnaissance and knows he can make the shot. The thing is, it *must* be on this island. A foreigner would stand out in St Petersburg, so the sniper is either Finnish or a tourist in Finland," Grozky said.

"A view I agree with," Lasola said and a thin swirl of grey smoke rose, oblivious to the small pieces of information starting to disentangle the shooter's origin.

Lasola gestured to the trees scaling the hill and strolled towards them.

"The killer either hired or purchased a fast boat. You can find rigid inflatable boats, RIBs, in every harbour. They are light and strong. There is no better coastal transport. A couple of 360-brake-horsepower engines on a RIB could give you fifty to sixty knots," Lasola said.

"So, if the sniper isn't Finnish, how does he keep out of sight in Finland? He's having to wait until Kochenko arrives on the island," Grozky said.

"It's not as difficult as you might think. Hunting is very popular in Finland. In a gaming district like Kymi Karhula, licences for hunting roe deer are good until mid-June. The sniper could masquerade as a hunter. A foreign marksman would blend in as well as a local."

"If that's true, it emphasises the level of planning involved. This would have taken weeks if not months of preparation. A sports tourist would need to provide details of his gun licence and receive approval before entering Finland?" Grozky asked.

"Most certainly."

Hiding in plain sight, Grozky thought as he nodded. This man's identity would match his passport and his rifle would match the paperwork. The rifle *was* his credibility. He would be accepted, even welcomed, in Finland when he could not have camouflaged himself in Russia.

"So, if this man is using Remington .308 ammunition, you could start by checking all licences with a Remington-700 rifle, possibly even an M40-A1, which is a military model and looks very similar. They're popular with hunters. This man wouldn't make mistakes with his paperwork," Grozky said.

"Thank you for the suggestion," Lasola said, raising his pipe in salute, while his eyes did not leave Grozky's face. Lasola's intensity was wearing. The Finn seemed to shadow his every thought.

"Where would you check first?" Grozky asked.

"My own sense is Kotka or Kamina. Both are fair-sized coastal towns, popular with tourists and have sizeable harbours. They are easy places to find a suitable boat," Lasola said.

Grozky nodded. The hypothesis made sense.

"I'm glad we have both come to the same conclusion," Lasola said. "The Finnish police have already begun checking the licences of both local and foreign owners of .308 calibre rifles. Despite it being late in the season, I discovered there are a surprising number of Europeans who fit the profile. Germans and Norwegians, in particular, enjoy their hunting."

Grozky did not allow his irritation to show. Lasola had not needed his observations, it had been a test of partnership.

"Do you have a lead yet?" Grozky asked, wary of the Finn's doggedness.

"We're working through the list. I'll keep you posted on what we find," Lasola said.

"Thank you, Matthias."

"Perhaps you could enlighten me on one item. With the small entourage you arrived with, what exactly is the FSB's interest in Kochenko?" Lasola asked.

The Finnish detective had made his question seem like an afterthought and he let it hang as he retrieved a box of matches from his pocket. He ignited a flame and used it to reawaken the dark embers in his pipe bowl.

"Kochenko is of interest because of his business affairs and possible links to organised crime. The lengths to which someone has gone to kill him are not something I can explain," Grozky replied.

A haze of smoke drifted as Lasola drew on his pipe and studied him.

"It does indeed seem to be a complicated situation. If I can assist you in any way, you have only to ask," Lasola said and led the way back to the helicopter.

As he boarded the MD-500, Grozky was preoccupied by the finesse used to disguise the killing. The presumption was Kochenko had been killed by a Russian gang settling an old score because they had the most to gain, except the list of suspects was now broader. That worried him because, until there was evidence to the contrary, Sergei Malievich would sift through the St Petersburg gangs for evidence of their guilt.

Grozky knew the gangs wouldn't support such a challenge for long. A wrong word and Malievich might decide he'd found those responsible, his retaliation swift. The St Petersburg gangs' uneasy status quo could tip into civil war.

23

It was late afternoon by the time Grozky landed at Pulkovo airport. He took a taxi straight to the Big House, conscious Koshygin would be awaiting his report.

There were several new papers in his in-tray, including the one-page report from Fadei Filimonov confirming the landline in Arlington, Virginia. Sitting at his desk, Grozky sorted through them, prioritising their urgency. Top of his list was a solitary message from Natassja who had left her number. Next was a request from Vadik Prigoda for a meeting on Monday at midday; no response was required unless the time was inconvenient. Third was the fax from Major Nikolai Aristov containing the statements Vadik Prigoda and Natassja had made to the Moscow City Police. Lastly, Grozky was surprised to find that Major Emile Rastich of the OMON had left two messages and, clipped to them, was a scribbled note in Bogdan Pavlova's spidery hand which puzzled him; Rastich had called in person at the end of Friday afternoon requesting Grozky to get in touch as soon as possible. Grozky frowned at the OMON major's sudden urgency for contact with him when General Donitsyn was available. He made a note to speak to Rastich on Monday.

Grozky was about to ring Natassja when, glancing over Aristov's fax, he saw what the Moscow policeman wanted and the artistry of his request. Aristov was appointing him the arbiter of the content in Natassja's statement. Grozky could not refuse without condemning himself. In turn, Aristov would use Grozky's own responses to reassess the consistency of both their statements. Koshygin was reminding him he was in the kingdom of the GRU, watched from the high castle in Khodynka. Protecting the Russian presidency was a GRU operation and to the victor would go the spoils. The Moscow brothel of politics was descending into a bare-knuckle fight and Koshygin would keep Grozky pinned against the ropes.

Reading Natassja's statement, Grozky noted Aristov's steady questions, repeated in a different sequence. It was only at the end Aristov had asked why she had fled the scene. Scanning her phrases, her denials were consistent: '*I didn't see Brown assault Major Grozky. I was looking for a chemist's shop…*','*Zach Brown insisted on walking to the Metro station…*', '*I was binding Zach Brown's arm…*'. He could visualise her trying to help, her shock disassociating her from her actions. Brown would have spotted that and exploited her goodwill. The American was one of many new people she had met at the party. She had spoken with him only briefly, mainly about investing in Russia and sailing in Newport. Andrei Simonov, the Deputy Minister of Fuel and Energy, had been privy to the conversation. Grozky could believe her assertion she had missed the opportunity to give Brown her business card except, by seeking him out, Brown moved from being an acquaintance to someone she wanted to contact. Simonov's presence had been fortuitous this time, but Natassja was still wandering through a lethal game she did not understand with an impunity that could not last. Whatever her motives for abandoning him on the pavement in Moscow, she owed him an apology and an explanation, in that order.

The bell on his phone rang, interrupting his thoughts. He picked up the receiver.

"Grozky," he said.

"Valeri?"

Grozky heard the lilting tone of Matthias Lasola.

"Matthias? You're calling late," Grozky said.

"I was going to leave it until Monday and then I thought I might catch you tonight," Lasola said.

"It's good of you. You have something for me?"

"Our efforts are paying off. In cross-referencing foreign tourists owning a .308 rifle with hunting licences, several names came up. However, only two hired a rigid inflatable boat and only one was using a RIB that day. He was staying in a hotel in Kotka and he checked out on the morning of the shooting. His passport is listed as Steven Robert Williams from Richmond, Virginia," Lasola said.

Grozky recalled the single phone number recovered from the Cross Island marina. The sniper had been primed.

"That's impressive work, Matthias."

"We've interviewed the hotel staff. They remember Williams as a polite, private man who spent very little time in the hotel. His clothes matched his accent and he gave them no reason to think he was anything other than American. If he's not, he can certainly pass himself off as one. We've checked his flights. He flew into Finland from London and prior to that from New York JFK. He spent a week in the UK where he had a permit for the rifle," Lasola replied.

"Do you know where he stayed in England?"

"We know he flew to Scotland. He had the rifle with him. It seems likely he may have done some shooting there. The British police are checking."

Hiding in plain sight, thought Grozky.

"He's good at tradecraft. By taking two shooting trips, he hides his origin and strengthens his cover as a sports tourist. Once he's got the rifle through British customs, why should the Finns doubt him?" Grozky said.

"Indeed. The challenge I have is there is no record of Williams leaving Finland. If he is our man, it seems inconceivable he would still be in the country. We've put an alert out with Interpol and the US State Department," Lasola said.

"The Americans have no record of him arriving back in the United States?" Grozky asked.

"Not yet. The US State Department has confirmed the passport number and name belong to Steven Robert Williams. We're still waiting to confirm whether the physical description is also a match. If this man is as professional as I think he is, it's more than likely he was using Williams as an identity," Lasola said.

As a section of the jigsaw came together, the disparate pieces joined parts of a picture Grozky would not have considered. His worry was not that the American connection had eluded him, but the implications.

"This is where I am hoping the FSB's knowledge of Kochenko can help us. Who would have hired such a man and why was Kochenko shot? If we can find the first, we can get to the second," Lasola said.

"Matthias, thank you for the call. This is very useful. For me to speculate wouldn't be helpful. What concerns me is this no longer feels like a Russian hit," Grozky said.

"It looks like that, doesn't it," Lasola said.

"I'll call you when I have something," Grozky said.

"I appreciate it, Valeri. Let's stay in touch."

Grozky hung up and glanced at his watch. It was already 8 p.m. He called the number Natassja had left. He heard the ring tone and then the familiar voice answered.

"Natassja."

"Natassja, it's Valeri Grozky."

"Valeri, how are you?" Natassja asked.

"I'd like to say all the better for hearing you, but I won't."

"Valeri, don't be angry. We need to meet," Natassja said.

"When?"

"Have you eaten?"

"No."

"What time?"

Grozky considered the necessities. Natassja was now secondary to the information from Lasola.

"I have something I need to do. How about 9.30 p.m.?"

"I'll book a restaurant. Do you know the Gondola? It's fairly new."

"I'll find it," Grozky said.

"See you there."

Grozky hung up and stood up from his desk. He stretched as he looked at the name scribbled on his blotter. Steven Robert Williams. The dogged Finnish detective had sieved the information with the care of a prospector and found the match with an ease that belied the complexity of the task.

He walked to the filing cabinet next to his desk and skimmed through the small pile of books stacked on top until he found the atlas. He looked up Richmond in the index and located it, some hundred miles south of Washington DC. He checked the index again and returned to the page, his finger tracing along the peninsulas jutting out into Chesapeake Bay until he found Quantico, tucked along the shore of the Potomac river. Sitting between Arlington and Richmond was the US Marine scout sniper school at Quantico. Zach Brown had worked for the CIA. Grozky drew a circle around Washington DC to include the Pentagon and CIA headquarters at Langley, Virginia. He could already see the shape the different locations formed, but he took a pencil and joined the dots to form a short arc reaching along the coast.

Returning to his desk, Grozky reconsidered his findings. A master sniper able to travel through two countries with a legitimate identity required organisational skills beyond the Russian gangs. They could afford the fee, but why use an American when there were countless Russian snipers who could have made the shot? Without the care of Lasola's cross-referencing and the chance find of the phone number, the sniper's nationality would have remained in the shadows. To bribe a member of Kochenko's security detail would have required a careful approach and a very significant payoff. The finesse required to breach Kochenko's security and the likelihood the killer was an American pointed the finger towards the involvement of a US agency. The killing of Yevgeny Kochenko contorted an already complex picture. Next to a Russian triangle joining Tomarov, Kochenko and Prigoda, the arc of the American conspiracy could no longer be camouflaged and Prigoda knew Zach Brown.

Grozky reached for Aristov's fax. He read Prigoda's short statement and then read it again before the omission struck him. The lawyer's summation of events was accurate so far as it went, it was what he had left out. Prigoda mentioned greeting Brown and having a brief conversation about the Ministry reception they were both attending. There was nothing about walking with him on Tversky Street. But for Grozky, Prigoda would have been the last person to see Brown alive. Grozky stared at the page. Prigoda was distancing himself from Zach Brown.

Inserting a fresh sheet into his typewriter, Grozky's fingers rapidly distilled the new information. With every answer came more questions. He took care before typing the final page, conscious of its impact. If he was right, Metzov's rearguard was already being outflanked. Grozky removed the final page from his typewriter and reviewed the last paragraph.

Status

As the current owner of Yanusk, Kochenko's killing will inevitably receive attention at the Senate Subcommittee and, with his background, continued speculation as to his killer(s). The Russian government cannot control the media agencies operating in Finland. The disappearance of Zach Brown in Moscow is an increasing embarrassment to the Russian government.

With Yanusk so central to the Subcommittee's focus, the timing of both these incidents is favourable to the American Senate's agenda: Kochenko was deliberately killed outside Russia and Brown has disappeared inside Russia. Even if the coincidence is discounted, it is too convenient when both events can be used to inflame the Senate's conclusion that the reach of Russian organised crime represents a threat to America's oil imports.

In the absence of an agreed explanation, the evidence suggests another agency is working to further the Senate's agenda by linking these events to Yanusk and attributing them to Russian organised crime. If an American counterintelligence operation is active, then

*the Russian government is facing an even greater threat
to their efforts to counter the political fallout.*

Satisfied with his summation, Grozky added it to his other pages and checked them a final time. He included an appendix, a translation of the autopsy report from Dr Oskar Markus which Lasola had handed him on the way to the airport. Katerina Kozhevnikova was a day ahead of him. If her debriefing to Koshygin was as forensic as her performance at Koskela Hospital, his appendix would be redundant.

Grozky faxed three copies of his report to GRU headquarters: Koshygin, Zotkin and Borzoi. Koshygin would welcome the information, not the upstart of a messenger sending it. Well hidden as they were, the footprints creeping across the puzzle were American. Metzov had a bigger challenge than he realised.

*

Grozky arrived first at the restaurant, a few minutes late. The Gondola was new, glistening with fresh paint and bright varnish. For a Sunday evening, the rows of red and white cross-hatched tablecloths were as redundant as bunting for only two other tables were occupied. Grozky selected one in the corner, grateful for the privacy.

The smell of fresh tomato and basil heightened his appetite and made him realise how tired he was. Collecting Kochenko's body had turned into a reconstruction of the minutiae of his killing. For forty-eight hours he had done nothing except focus on what each piece meant and then to consider their significance in aggregate. Trying to make sense of it all was exhausting.

He was sure of one thing: where the Russian government had been countering a political threat, there was now the spectre of a full-blown conspiracy. Yet the more he sifted the specifics in his mind, the more the incongruity of the geography began to rankle. Surely it would have been easier to kill Zach Brown in the United States and exploit the reaction of the American press? Whoever had killed Kochenko had taken extraordinary care, banking on the oligarch making use of the island. A foreign sniper reeked of a special operation whereas Zach Brown's assassins were Russian and adept with blade or bullet. A knife carried more conviction than a pistol if you wanted to make his death look like a street robbery gone wrong, a very discreet killing compared to the island. Brown was familiar with Moscow and his lack of a bodyguard showed he hadn't felt under threat. Brown had business history on both sides of the Atlantic. Someone in Russia wanted Brown dead or it had been set up to make it appear that was the case.

The coincidences of both incidents were their timing and their connection to Yanusk. Yet if they were linked, he was no closer to understanding why. He scribbled 'attention to detail' against both events, exasperated by what eluded him. It was more than frustration, he was trying to solve a puzzle with no support. Isolated from Moscow, his reports flowed one way to GRU headquarters while Koshygin and his colonels shared nothing. Without Borzoi he would have been completely in the dark.

In twenty days, Ekomov was primed to derail Gravell in Washington DC. Grozky's report from Finland had exposed a new intrigue. His insights would remind Metzov of his usefulness, though the Grey Cardinal would demand certainties he could exploit. Any lever which could be used against the Senate Subcommittee hearing would be seized.

One of the mantras of Grozky's KGB training was success was as much adjusting to circumstances as it was to ability. It echoed his experience of Chidaoba: a lifetime of mastering the different grips, takedowns and ways to pinion your opponent got you so far, it was the mindset to overcome difficulties which won victories. The wrestling bouts he should have won rankled most. He could not trust Koshygin, he would stay afloat at the Grey Cardinal's pleasure and to do that he had to keep Metzov's interest. If he was to prevail, every day was now a bout he must win. Grozky was going to have to punch above his weight. To stay on the right side of the Grey Cardinal, the one thing he could not afford was Natassja Petrovskaya turning over any more stones. In chancing upon Zach Brown, she had realised he meant something. Her interrogation by the Moscow police would only have reinforced his importance. Grozky had learnt his lesson when it came to misjudging her perseverance.

"Someone looks like they're in a foul mood," Natassja said, interrupting his thoughts.

Grozky looked up to find himself facing Natassja wearing one of the littlest black dresses he had ever seen. She smiled and he could see she was in celebratory mood. Her choice of couture was not by chance. She'd been back in St Petersburg long enough to get over the shock of the Moscow police interrogation and convince herself of her abilities. Her self-belief triumphed over adversity.

"What are we drinking?" Natassja asked.

Grozky thought for a moment. On his own, he'd have been tempted to get quietly drunk. With Natassja, he needed to stay sharp.

"Let's have a bottle of red."

"Perfect."

Here she was, ready to make an evening of it. No apology, no mention of Moscow. Aristov had done enough to test her, make her think she was believed and cast her back, waiting to see what she would do next. Her folly was she could not gauge their cunning.

They ordered, dispensing with the starter and going for the main course. Grozky chose *linguine al vongole* and she selected *tortellini alla panna*. The waiter returned with what Grozky considered to be a very overpriced bottle of imported Montepulciano, uncorked it and poured a small glass for Grozky to taste.

"I'm sure it will be fine," Grozky said.

The waiter filled both their glasses and departed.

Natassja smiled, her lips channelling victory.

"*Nastrovje*," Natassja said.

"*Nastrovje.*"

"So, the Moscow police were satisfied with your story?" Grozky asked.

"Why wouldn't they be?"

"You're knee-deep in trouble and you don't even know it," Grozky said.

"How would you know?"

Grozky tired of the duelling. She seemed to have decided she was above explaining herself. He decided to end the swordfight. From a trouser pocket he produced Aristov's fax and placed it on the table in front of her.

"The Moscow police feel your proximity to Zach Brown at the time of the attack is too much of a coincidence. They believe you about as much as I do. You don't need to thank me for stopping you getting hurt, but they've asked me to find out what you were up to," Grozky said.

"Oh God, I'm sorry."

He took no satisfaction from her alarm, reminding himself that whatever vulnerability she projected was encased in steel.

"What were you talking to Zach Brown about?" Grozky asked.

"My statement is true. I was introduced to Brown at the Ministry drinks party. We talked about various things: how he got started in business, his passion for sailing. He mentioned the work he'd done at Archipelago Oil. They wanted to buy a stake in Yanusk. Tomarov was asking too much. The sale never happened," Natassja said.

Grozky recalled Arnold Lennister had said as much in his statement to the Senate Subcommittee.

"Why did you run off after Brown knocked me out?" Grozky asked.

"I didn't run off. I mean I didn't intend to run off. I swear I had no idea Brown had hit you. Brown asked me to help him wrap his tie around his arm. He refused to wait for an ambulance and I was trying to stem the bleeding while he was walking. He was in a bad way," Natassja said.

"Where did you leave him?"

"At the Hunters' Row Metro station on Tversky Street. It only took us five minutes to walk there. He was very angry at what had happened."

Grozky nodded. A bleeding man boarding a train, particularly an angry foreigner, would have attracted attention. Where else would Brown have gone? As alien as the image might be to Aristov, he himself could imagine Natassja nursing Brown's injury. He envied her selflessness.

"Did you see him go into the station?"

"No, I left him at the entrance. He said he was going to take the train," Natassja said.

Grozky wondered at Brown's resilience. The GRU's manhunt had now turned to interrogating members of the Russian Ministry of Fuel and Energy, enraging Andrei Simonov that any civil servant could be suspected of being complicit in Zach Brown's disappearance. Quite how the wounded American had managed to elude the GRU was a mystery. To Grozky's way of thinking it only proved the significance of what the American had to hide.

"Do you believe me now?" Natassja asked.

Grozky sensed a thaw in her attitude, yet embraced by the warmth of the room and the wine, he struggled to fight his exhaustion. If she was lying, her performance was masterful.

"What you need to understand, Natassja, is that those men would have killed you. You were in the way."

He felt her fingertips brush his and stay there, the faintest of touches. There was a sincerity in the gesture, a departure from their previous encounters. Perhaps he had moved up from being an official to be pandered to.

The food arrived. Grozky couldn't recall when he had last eaten Italy's national dish. His meal tasted pleasant enough, spoilt because he would never see pasta as amounting to anything beyond cooking wheat flour and water. He was paying restaurant prices for street food and a small ransom for the wine. At least the Montepulciano was warm and mellow; Grozky poured another glass. He seemed to be doing all the drinking.

"You've told me to stay clear of Tomarov. Are you also going to tell me to stay clear of Yanusk?" Natassja asked.

"Yanusk?" Grozky said, parrying her new thrust, his question hiding his surprise.

"The oil company where people keep turning up dead. It's almost as if the company is cursed," Natassja said.

Grozky listened as he drank his wine. This was what he had feared.

"Why do you say that?"

"I have it on good authority Yevgeny Kochenko was approached to sell a stake in Yanusk," Natassja said.

"How?"

"When Andrei Simonov heard me talking to Zach Brown about Tomarov he got seriously pissed off and led Brown away. That's when I met Vadik Prigoda…"

The waiter hovered, holding up an empty bottle of wine. Distracted, Grozky dismissed him with a hand.

"… foreign companies are lined up trying to get a share in Russia's natural resources. Oil is a commodity everyone wants," Natassja said.

"You're saying Prigoda was brokering a deal to sell a stake in Yanusk to a foreign investor?" Grozky asked.

"You'd have to ask him," Natassja replied, picking up her glass.

Grozky nodded, watching her take a sip of wine as a darker possibility struck him. Only a few people in St Petersburg could have known Tomarov was paying off Kochenko. If Prigoda had been the source of that information had Zach Brown told Prigoda what it was to be used for? Private leverage was one thing, but public disclosure to the American Senate was a very different proposition. Had Prigoda seen a chance to remove the threat Brown represented? It was one of many questions Grozky had for Vadik Prigoda. Nothing was straightforward in this damned affair.

"What's wrong, Valeri?"

Grozky's thoughts were interrupted. He saw Natassja's concern and realised their conversation had died. He held her gaze to counter his fatigue, hoping it did not show. The burden of what Koshygin would throw at him next was wearing him down.

"You found all this out at a Moscow drinks reception?" Grozky asked, stalling as he tried to shrug off his malaise.

She did not meet his gaze. Was it guilt at her actions or something else?

"Let's go, Valeri."

Grozky paid the bill and tried not to think what he could have bought for the money. They left the Gondola. Outside in the cold, he felt her arm entwine with his.

"We could share a cab," she said.

Grozky was momentarily thrown because he was short on cash and the restaurant was nowhere near his apartment. A passing *chastnik*, a motorist prepared to take a passenger for a small fee, saw them waiting and stopped. Relieved, Grozky was haggling for the fare until Natassja dismissed the chastnik and hailed a taxi she saw approaching.

Natassja gave the driver the name of her street and Grozky opened a rear door. He stood for a moment in the chill air remembering the cab he had boarded outside the Red Star Bar. The images of men burning coursed through his mind. It wasn't until he became aware of the gaze of the taxi driver wondering at the man who would keep such a beauty waiting that Grozky broke from his reverie.

Despondent, he sat down next to her, surprised he was doing so. The warmth of the interior came with a false hint of fresh pine, its source a miniature green fir tree hanging from the rear-view mirror. Grozky was glad when the smell was dispelled by the rich, deep scent next to him. Her perfume attracted him like a lure. In moments, his lips were on hers, her sweet taste a narcotic delight. A fresh kiss was something genuine he had not felt in a long time. Natassja responded to his probing tongue, heightening his urge for her. It was a silent trip as they revelled in their mutual desire, oblivious to the lights of St Petersburg.

Grozky could not assuage his yearning for her even if he had a mind to. Within minutes of their arrival at her apartment, they were lost in each other in the large bed that filled her small room.

24

Vadik Prigoda was standing by the side of his desk when Grozky was shown into his office. Grozky smelt resin, traced with citrus, and Prigoda beamed, his smile as prepared as his position in the room.

"Major Grozky, I'm glad we finally manage to meet," Prigoda said, a pinstriped arm broadcasting the surroundings before he extended it in greeting.

Grozky walked towards him, feeling the depth of carpet underfoot, and took in the walls peppered in a montage of framed photographs. The pedigree of Prigoda's connections extended to Soviet Politburo members and Ministry officials. In one picture, the lawyer was in a group shot including Yeltsin. In Grozky's experience, people kept a photo as much as a memento to showcase their achievements. Prigoda didn't just want a reminder of the occasions, he wanted others to acknowledge them.

"I heard you had some trouble in Moscow," Prigoda said as they shook hands.

"You know I had trouble. You were required to confirm our meeting to the Moscow police."

"Please, take a seat," Prigoda said, escorting Grozky to his desk and offering him an armchair.

As Grozky sat down, amongst a cluster of smaller frames standing on the desk, he spied a snapshot of Prigoda leaning against a sea wall, his face obscured by sunglasses, and with a man standing next to him. The coastal geography was indeterminate, but the second man was familiar: Zach Brown. A lie only became a lie when it could be proven to be untrue. Prigoda's keepsakes were a weakness.

"To save us both time, let me come to the point. What is your relationship to Zach Brown?" Grozky asked, reaching across the desk to retrieve the photograph and place it in front of the lawyer.

Prigoda looked at the picture before he answered.

"You're observant. I've done some business with him," Prigoda said.

"Business? Selling information to him, for example?"

"No. I put buyers in touch with sellers. I know Russians, Zach knows Americans. It's a good mix," Prigoda said.

"Did you know Zach Brown was testifying on his dealings with the Yanusk Oil Company at the Senate Subcommittee on Russian organised crime?"

"Yes, he told me," Prigoda said.

"Did he tell you the Subcommittee Chairman has information that Yuri Tomarov paid Yevgeny Kochenko US$6 million as a backhander for providing the loans which enabled him to buy Yanusk?"

"No, he didn't," Prigoda said, frowning.

From a pocket, Grozky retrieved the page showing the commission payments made to Yevgeny Kochenko.

"How do you think this information found its way into the hands of the American intelligence services?" Grozky asked.

Prigoda studied the page.

"Where did you get this?" Prigoda asked.

"I thought you might tell me?"

"I've no idea. Yuri's affairs were his own. He was always a deal ahead of himself, borrowing money from the wrong people or struggling to pay them back on time. Where would he have found US$6 million? Why would a man with Yevgeny Kochenko's wealth have agreed to it?" Prigoda asked.

"You knew both men. Don't you think it's something of a coincidence the Senate Subcommittee has been able to acquire this information?" Grozky asked.

Prigoda considered the question.

"I am still shocked Yevgeny is dead, but in light of what you've shown me it cannot be a coincidence. If someone wanted it to look like Yuri was paying Yevgeny, what better way to cover their tracks than rub out the other end of the deal? With them both dead, their guilt becomes proven by association," Prigoda said.

Grozky listened to the plausibility of the logic. Prigoda would be wondering how much he knew about the lawyer's dealings with both men. If what Prigoda said was true, the deception was brilliant, yet the lawyer had deflected attention to the Subcommittee without exposing his own role. He was a master at staying submerged while he released flotsam to the surface. Tomarov and now Kochenko had been killed and Zach Brown would have been dead, but for Grozky's intercession. Prigoda knew them all.

"Are you surprised at Tomarov's and Kochenko's deaths?" Grozky asked.

"Yuri? No. Yevgeny? Very," Prigoda replied.

"What was your relationship with Kochenko?"

"What do you mean?"

"You were seen meeting with him. Your firm has billed him for the last six months."

Prigoda sat back before answering.

"How do you know that?" Prigoda asked.

"You deny it?"

"No, but I don't see what my private client affairs have to do with matters of state security."

Grozky listened to the bluster of entitlement as he met the lawyer's glare. Prigoda was a man for whom the switch from Soviet values to unprincipled capitalism had not been hard.

"I heard you were representing Kochenko to sell a stake in Yanusk."

"That, I categorically deny," Prigoda said.

Grozky took out his Gyurza pistol. He cocked it and pointed the barrel at Prigoda's head.

"Vadik, I want you to understand how unpleasant your life is going to become unless you start telling me the truth," Grozky said, resting his hand on top of the desk, the pistol levelled at Prigoda's chest.

"What was your business with Zach Brown?" Grozky asked.

Facing a loaded gun brought clarity to Prigoda's predicament. He stared at the barrel and carefully half raised a hand, trying to calm the situation. His confidence retreated.

"I helped him arrange investments, that's all, I swear. It's difficult for foreign companies to make investments in Russia, there are restrictions. I helped set up some nominee companies for him when Archipelago Oil was trying to buy a stake in Yanusk from Yuri. Legally, they're Russian, but the ownership isn't as Russian as it looks," Prigoda said.

"What about Kochenko?"

"If you tell me Yevgeny Kochenko was selling a stake in Yanusk, I believe you, but it's the first I've heard of it. As I was his adviser, I find that odd," Prigoda said.

"You're lying."

The lawyer stood up slowly and leant forward, his fists on his desk.

"Trust me when I tell you I know where I've crossed the line, as far as anyone can draw the line in this country anymore. You come into my office asserting I know something about the source of some American subcommittee evidence I've never seen and I don't. Now, you accuse me of another falsehood. I know nothing of Yevgeny trying to sell a stake in Yanusk. Shoot me if you don't believe me."

The lawyer's fear was masked in righteousness. Whatever half-truths he had been telling, Prigoda defied him, his groin inches away from the primed pistol. Grozky tasted the salt under his tongue before the bile grasped his throat. The memory of Natassja's flesh sullied in his thoughts as he recalled her words 'I have it on good authority Yevgeny Kochenko was approached to sell a stake...' If Prigoda was prepared to take a bullet for his ignorance, how could Natassja have known Kochenko had been approached? What else was she hiding?

*

The OMON police station on the Griboedov Canal Embankment was on the way to the *Kommersant*'s offices. Grozky would drive until he found Natassja.

Seeking to avoid the compressed traffic at the city centre, Grozky sought out the long-limbed avenues bordering the Admiralty District. He headed south on Foundry Avenue and turned onto Zagorodny Avenue, following the Fontanka river. In a matter of minutes, he cut north on Ascension Avenue before turning onto the Griboedov Canal Embankment. The canal had once been the Krivusha river until Tsar Peter the Great had neatly plumbed it in between the Fontanka and Moyka rivers.

Even if Grozky had been unsure of his destination, he could not have missed the OMON police station, for the historic façade was all that remained of the building's legacy. A huge tricolour flag hung at a brazen angle from the roof and beneath it squads of mixed blue and white vehicles were parked against the embankment's railings, overlooking the canal below. Along the waterfront, navy blue paramilitary figures patrolled, the presence of dogs reinforcing their authority.

Grozky parked the Chaser in a free bay between a pair of blue and white saloons. He had barely left his car when a shout called him back.

"Hey, you can't park there!"

Grozky's ID was already in his hand as he strode towards the OMON militiaman.

"I can. I'm here to see Major Emile Rastich," Grozky said.

"Says who?" the militiaman asked.

"Says Major Valeri Grozky of the FSB. I will be a few minutes or less," Grozky replied and held out his ID card.

The militiaman eyed the card without examining it. Grozky expected a further challenge which did not materialise. The militiaman shrugged and turned away to resume his patrol.

Inside the police station, a young paramilitary at the reception desk checked his ID and purpose and then made a phone call. After a short conversation he hung up and turned to Grozky.

"Well, Major Rastich has not been in this morning and his whereabouts are not known. Would you care to leave a message?"

"No message. This can wait until tomorrow," Grozky said.

"I'll tell Major Rastich you called by if I see him. There's no guarantee, but being lunchtime, it's quite possible he may be at the 777 Bar on Great Naval Street," the paramilitary said.

"Where's that?"

"Very close. Three blocks down Ascension Avenue, cross over Siny Bridge and it's about 800 yards on the right."

"Thanks. I'll try that. I appreciate your help. If I find Emile, I'll pass that on. And your name is?" Grozky asked.

"Borya Solokov."

Grozky extended his hand.

"Thank you, Borya. Valeri Grozky. You can dispense with the Major," Grozky said. They shook hands.

Outside, Grozky considered whether to go to the *Kommersant*'s offices on Ligovsky Avenue. It took him less than five minutes to cross the Moyka river and find the bar. Above the entrance a little flag of triple black sevens rested against a green background that might have been baize.

He parked the Chaser opposite the bar and walked across the street.

Entering the bar, he discovered the entrance was only a frontage and a set of worn wooden steps led to the basement. The sounds of foreign rock music drifted upwards.

He descended and entered a smoky room with a juke box next to the doorway. There were several men sitting at the bar with tumblers of spirits and tall glasses holding beer chasers. As soon as Grozky walked in he saw the men turn to watch him. They eyed him coldly before returning to their conversation. Behind them, men in black/blue combat fatigues stood around, drinking and smoking. A few scrawny girls stood at the edge of the group, wearing too much mascara. Grozky thought most of the girls couldn't be more than teenagers.

There was a pause in the music as the juke box fell silent. One of the girls detached herself from the group and walked towards him. Her pace was so delicate she might have been dreaming. Her gaunt looks were as much hallmarks of her substance dependency as her detachment.

"Go, Katya!" shouted one of the standing men.

The girl paused in front of the juke box, barely seeming to study the music she selected. As the opening riff of the new song started, her stance became more of a squat and her hips began to gyrate slowly, rhythmic and sensual.

"Kat-eey-a, Kat-eey-a," chanted her group.

Katya turned and Grozky saw her vacant grin at their attention. Grozky used the distraction to approach the bar. He saw the black flag draped behind the bar with the letters printed in red:

'THE HONOUR OF THE DIVISION STANDS ABOVE ALL ELSE'

The militiamen occupying the stools were older, with the salty presence of NCOs. Whatever the bar was, the state of the girls was as telling as the exclusively OMON gathering.

Grozky tried to catch the barman's eye, but the man expertly avoided him and the first militiaman sitting in front of Grozky ignored him. It was the man behind who initiated the ritual welcome. He stood up from his stool, revealing himself to be the same height as Grozky and as stocky.

"We haven't seen you in here before," the self-appointed OMON spokesman said.

"That's because I've not been here before."

"We don't serve lunch," the barman said.

Grozky thought that came as close to a welcome as he would receive from his host.

"I came in looking for a friend. I was told he might be here," Grozky said.

"I'm not sure you'll find many friends here because we have a lot of history together. We're careful who we call a friend," the spokesman said.

There was a conspiratorial set of whoops from the OMON tribe seated at the bar and Grozky felt the pack being readied.

The spokesman took his cue and reached forward, draping an arm around the shoulder of the militiaman who sat in front of Grozky.

"You don't want to piss off Oleg. He's been to all the shitholes," the spokesman said. He used his fingers to count out the man's pedigree on one hand.

"Afghanistan... Karabakh... North Ossetia... Chechnya... and... he'll outlive us all!"

The spokesman laughed, and the tribe cheered their champion.

Grozky met Oleg's gaze, hair-trigger eyes undimmed by the glaze of booze.

"Oh, I think you've upset Oleg," the spokesman said, priming the gunfighter.

Grozky felt the mood shift against him as he knew it would. To pass into the OMON, every recruit had to don a pair of boxing gloves and fight off three serving members by hand. Fewer than one in five applicants passed. The prospect of a beating receded as Natassja's betrayal stoked his anger. He'd go down, but not before he'd set an example to the exploited girls.

"Excuse me, Oleg," Grozky said to the gunfighter.

Grozky's left hand shot out and gripped the spokesman's shirt by the neck, twisting it and pulling the man to him, leaving Oleg pinioned against the bar.

"Friend, we can take this anywhere you want. Before we do, I suggest you check with Emile first. I'm here because Borya told me, not ten minutes ago, there was a chance Emile would be here. It would be a shame if he found out you were about to screw up his arrangements."

Grozky's familiarity with Rastich was registered. The hint of doubt in his inquisitor's eyes was enough.

"I'm sure Emile would appreciate you letting him know Valeri Grozky is looking for him," Grozky said, staring at his opponent for a full three seconds before he released his shirt.

The spokesman chose not to contest Grozky's assertion. The pack, including Oleg, saw their fun was over and returned to drinking and reaching for the girls.

Grozky left. The OMON were trained to follow orders at any cost. Major Emile Rastich's authority carried more weight than he had anticipated.

By the time he returned to the Chaser he was trembling – the cocktail of adrenaline from the confrontation and the accumulation of cortisol. Triggered by constant stress, cortisol polluted his brain just as heroin poisoned the bodies of the girls in the bar. Oleg the gunfighter was no different; alcohol gave only the illusion of respite from the constant tension.

He drove the short distance to Nevsky Avenue and up to Uprising Square. Skirting the square, a few hundred yards later he parked. His hands were still shaking as he entered the ground floor of the *Kommersant*'s offices.

Ahead of him, sitting behind a desk was a watchful, coiffured lady protected by the unsmiling security guard standing next to her.

Grozky walked up to her, his FSB ID card hidden in the palm of his hand.

"Good morning. I'm here to see Natassja Petrovskaya, one of your journalists. She knows me. If you could let her know Major Valeri Grozky of the FSB is here," Grozky said, providing a glimpse of the authority in his hand.

Within a minute of announcing himself, Grozky was shown to a small meeting room on the second floor. Four modern office chairs surrounded a circular wooden table with a phone at its centre. Moments later a tall, graceful woman entered.

"I'm Liliya, Liliya Usova. I'm Natassja's editor," she said.

Grozky received the briefest of handshakes from a warm hand that left him feeling he'd been clasped by a spring trap.

"Major Valeri Grozky. Valeri."

"I know who you are, Valeri," Usova said, greeting him with a brusque familiarity he did not expect.

Usova had a slim, elegant face, her hair pulled back and tied in a loose knot. Grozky liked the authority in her manner. He could imagine she would be less accommodating when it came to deadlines. He wondered whether Usova knew Natassja carried a .22 Marjo.

"You came to see Natassja?" Usova asked.

"I've been away for the last couple of days. I was passing," Grozky said, wondering why Usova had intercepted him. Her fingers rapidly wound a rubber band around the end of a pencil.

"You've not heard?"

"Heard what?"

"There was an unpleasant incident yesterday. Natassja and one of our photographers, Abram, were assaulted. She's fine, although shaken up a bit," Usova said.

"Where did this happen?"

"It was close to the Russian National Library, opposite the Moscow Victory Park on Moscow Avenue. Natassja insisted on coming to work this morning. I sent a taxi for her..."

Her voice trailed off, momentarily, and Grozky saw the sheen of tears in her eyes.

"... except she didn't answer the door. One of her neighbours has a key. When they went into her flat there were signs of a struggle. I'm afraid we've no idea where she is," Usova said, restoring her composure.

"You've already reported this?"

"Of course. Not that the police are going to make a missing journalist much of a priority, are they?"

Grozky stared at Liliya Usova until she looked away, concerned by the numbness of his glare. His worst fears had been realised.

25

Grozky cursed the source of his awakening. The ringing of the telephone intruded into the no man's land of his semiconsciousness, dragging him from sleep. He sat up, the sheet falling from his chest as the bell ceased. Looking at the fluorescent dial of his watch, he saw it was 5.40 a.m. Grozky fell back on the bed, his mind retreating until the phone calls he had made in the early hours pierced his consciousness. His memory's rearguard reminded him he must find Natassja.

The phone rang again. Furious, Grozky stumbled from his bed in his underclothes. He was halfway across the floor before he realised it was the doorbell. He left his bedroom and turned on the hallway light. Oblivious to his state of undress he walked to the door and squinted through the keyhole. Contorted into a sphere by the fisheye lens was the outsize profile of Dmitri Borzoi who should have been in Moscow. Grozky opened the door. Borzoi was dressed for business, a large green parka over his dark fatigues while the open jacket failed to conceal the stock of a pistol butt under a shoulder.

"I thought you were in Moscow?" Grozky said.

"I flew in this morning. All very sudden. A private military transport courtesy of Ivan Palutkin."

Grozky grimaced at Borzoi's mention of Koshygin's trigger man. Nothing good would come of this.

"I'll get dressed, then you can tell me what's going on. Help yourself to coffee and make me one," Grozky said and walked down the hallway to the kitchen. He turned on the kettle and then returned to his bedroom to find some clothes. He heard the popping of cupboard doors as Borzoi acquainted himself with the kitchen.

From a bedroom cupboard Grozky grabbed a pair of lightweight khaki trousers in need of a belt, and a green jersey, then disappeared into the bathroom. He considered whether to shave, dropped the idea, dressed and then turned on the cold tap in his basin. He stuck his head under the water, his temples raging at the shock.

He returned to the kitchen refreshed, his hair plastered back and droplets of water running from his cheeks, gathering on the jersey's collar like dew. Of a shirt there was no sign. Around his waist his belt holster was strapped over the jersey. He carried a pair of black boots in one hand and a fresh pair of socks in the other. Grozky dropped the boots onto the floor, sat down on a stool next to his kitchen table and pulled on the socks. He saw Borzoi had found the coffee, an open jar sat next to two mugs. The kettle began to shake, the water jostling against itself as the wisps of steam grew.

"You can tell me what's going on while I finish dressing," Grozky said.

"Sure, Valeri," Borzoi said, retrieving a folded map from inside his parka and placing it on the table next to Grozky. He unfolded it as the steam from the kettle puckered into a low whistle.

Borzoi pointed to the section covering north-east St Petersburg. Grozky, pulling on his boots, glanced across to see a small 'x' marked at the fringes of the city on Piskarev Avenue.

"The GRU are raiding one of Kochenko's warehouses this morning," Borzoi said with an alertness that belied the hour. The edge to his voice worried Grozky.

Borzoi turned the kettle off, poured the steaming water into the mugs and placed one on the table.

"Thank you. You're part of this raid?" Grozky said, lacing up a boot.

"I was pulled in at the last minute. On the plane Palutkin told me you'd want to be involved. You think he doesn't know I hadn't thought of that? His goons are already doing the heavy lifting. I'm on my way there. I came to pick you up."

"You drove here?" Grozky asked, his face grim at the GRU's plotting. Palutkin would not be loose in St Petersburg unless Koshygin had ordered it.

"I did."

"We'll take my car. It will be quicker," Grozky said as he finished knotting the lace on his other boot. He picked up the mug and blew on the liquid, feeling the heat from the surface.

"You're going to shave?" Borzoi asked.

"I could, but I'd hate the GRU to think I'd put shaving in front of their appointment. I want to know what they're up to," Grozky replied.

They departed a few minutes later, leaving Borzoi's AZLK Moskvitch 2141 parked on 11th Line Street. The 'Aleko', as it was known, was a mid-range hatchback and superior to Grozky's ageing Volga in every category, except the Chaser's insane horsepower.

The traffic was still light as they headed east, crossing over Tuckhov Bridge onto Petrograd Island. Grozky turned onto Dobrolyubov Avenue and within a mile they were back on the waterfront skirting the strip of the Rampart Sound. Fifty yards away, on the tiny Hare Island, the Peter and Paul Fortress was hidden by a high brick wall, above which sprouted the tops of stone turrets and the tall spire of the Peter and Paul Cathedral, burial ground of the Russian tsars. Along the road a line of mounted modern cannons greeted them until they were past the Artillery Museum, hiding the crescent moon of Alexander Park behind it.

"What is Palutkin after?" Grozky asked as they left the river frontage, crossing Stone Island Avenue to join Kuybyshev Street. He accelerated and the Chaser surged past a tram holding a straggle of commuters.

"Palutkin has intelligence Kochenko was using the warehouse to distribute drugs. Koshygin is desperate for anything he can use against him. He gave Palutkin the green light."

"Where did Palutkin get his information from?" Grozky asked.

Ahead, the grand buildings on the far side of Sampson's Bridge came into view.

"I know it was a local tip-off. The GRU hasn't shared the source. I guess they'll either find something or they won't," Borzoi said.

They crossed the Great Neva river to the south, where the distributary flowed from the Neva; the three funnels of the cruiser *Aurora* stood tall against the embankment. The ship, now a museum, was moored by the Nakhimov Naval Academy. During the Nazi blockade, her guns had been stripped from her decks and used in the city's defence.

Shadowing the river's path, Grozky exploited the wide roads of the Arsenal Embankment and the Chaser's reckless speed. The buildings here were cast-offs compared to the grandeur of the Palace Embankment opposite. They bordered each other in a hotchpotch of purpose: the robust Mikhaylov Artillery Academy, a statue of Lenin holding court dropped into a large square dedicated to his memory and then the squat colonnades of the Concert Hall. As they sped past the regimented blocks of the Kresty Prison complex, it seemed to Grozky that the thousands of mean red bricks lining its claustrophobic construction were as incarcerated as the prisoners behind them.

Overhead the light fought to break through the grey clouds, while the character of the city darkened into the sprawl of the industrial plants or *Zavods*, interspersed with hard-looking apartment blocks. Grozky drove, the thought of dealing with Palutkin making the morning feel more oppressive.

"What progress has Zotkin been making?" Grozky asked.

"Limited. He still can't find anything conclusive," Borzoi said.

"I can think of a reason why Palutkin's been let off the leash. When I challenged Vadik Prigoda yesterday, he discounted Tomarov making any payments to Kochenko. I'm not saying Prigoda's right, but if he is, Zotkin could be on a fool's errand."

"My God, all that effort for nothing."

"It's cunning counterintelligence. Create the illusion of something where nothing exists, yet how does the Russian government disprove the ruse? Let's hope that's not the case. Look at it from Koshygin's perspective, he's running out of options," Grozky said.

On Sverdlovsk Embankment the Neva bent sharply south and on the opposite bank the giant towers of Smolny Cathedral rose from the Smolnin District. Grozky turned north-east onto Piskarev Avenue, a long artery of a road taking them away from the river. Here the long lines of trees and shrubs bordering the road hid the industrial-scale residential apartment blocks.

Borzoi kept his eye on the map and called out their progress. Grozky, conscious they were within minutes of their destination, avoided the excess of his earlier speed. As they passed over the railway line, he caught a glimpse of Piskarev station. Several hundred yards away was the Piskarev Memorial Cemetery, where Grozky's grandfather lay alongside the half a million Russians who had died during the Nazi blockade. Forced to survive on little more than a daily ration of 125 grams of bread made from sawdust, Leningrad had refused to yield while it starved.

Your own lives align with the lives of the fallen, thought Grozky and gripped the Chaser's wheel more tightly.

"The warehouse is up ahead. Less than a mile," Borzoi said.

Grozky nodded, accelerating past a lorry, its polythene tarpaulin unable to hide the lustre of bright red bricks beneath.

It was Grozky who spotted their destination amidst the factories and industry lining the avenue. In front of a light blue fence two men stood, dressed in grey/blue combat fatigues and cradling assault rifles, their faces hidden behind black balaclavas. As Grozky braked one of the men waved him on repeatedly. Grozky ignored him and reduced the Chaser's speed further until a guard stood in front of the car, his hand outstretched in warning.

"Identity cards would be in order, Dmitri," Grozky said, bracing himself against the footwell and retrieving his ID card from a trouser pocket. He noticed the fence which hid the warehouse from view was made from corrugated metal, the painted blue sheets providing a periphery of privacy.

Grozky wound down the window as the other guard reached the car.

"You can't stop here," the GRU guard declared impatiently.

"We're expected," Grozky said, with irritation. He handed over his FSB identity card and then passed across Borzoi's.

The GRU guard looked briefly at the cards.

"Wait here," he said before walking briskly away and disappearing into the warehouse entrance.

"The GRU are edgy this morning," Grozky said.

"There's a lot at stake," Borzoi said.

The GRU guard returned, ID cards in hand.

"You're cleared. When you park inside, stay close to the gate and keep out of the way."

The ID cards were handed back.

"Thank you," Grozky said, putting the three-speed automatic transmission into drive once more and slowly moving the Chaser forward. Turning into the entrance he saw the pair of black gates twisted in defeat. One pair of hinges had given way completely, the gate lying on the ground, while the other hung limply, its rails bent by dents.

Grozky drove through the gap and past a pair of prefabricated huts either side of the entrance. Another camouflaged figure suddenly appeared from inside one of the gatehouses. He repeatedly gestured to them to park next to a black Niva 4x4 jeep standing a few yards away at the end of the yard.

Moments later, Grozky and Borzoi were out of the Chaser and looking at the spectre of a ghetto. The rectangle of a yard in front of the warehouse, some hundred yards by fifty, now resembled a ghastly compound; Grozky counted fifteen men, standing a yard apart, who were lined up against the blue metal fence. A few feet away several masked GRU men pointed AK-47 assault rifles at them, the parade evoking the spectacle of a firing squad.

The warehouse ran down the opposite side of the yard, a tall, single-storey building typical of those used for storage and distribution. The floor of the loading bay was raised to be flush with the tailgates of lorries, while the high ceilings would not impede the movement of pallets and forklift trucks. A short wall ran like a quayside in front of the building where, at regular points, small sets of concrete steps led down to the yard.

With the warehouse staff corralled by guns, swarms of heavily armed GRU men clad in grey/blue camouflage combat uniforms moved like driven ants up and down the steps, their tasks seemingly random. Some worked in pairs to carry wooden packing cases and deposit them at the centre of the courtyard, others checked manifests as they examined the contents. Grozky thought charred vehicles would not have been out of place amidst the mayhem.

"Let's try the office first," Grozky said and Borzoi nodded glumly.

They walked towards the building and were suddenly assailed by a shout from the centre of the yard. They turned to see Colonel Ivan Palutkin, arms held aloft in triumph, his grin more of a sneer. He was flanked by a pair of masked men holding AK-47 assault rifles. Palutkin turned to meet his new arrivals. He shouted, drawing everyone's attention:

317

"Look, the FSB have made it. Welcome."

Palutkin's greeting had the sincerity of a butcher at slaughter. Around him, the small army of GRU men in the courtyard watched their master hold court. Palutkin was revelling in the intimidation his squad was causing.

"Over here," he said, gesturing for them to join him as his men looked on, then he walked to an open crate at the edge of the pile. At the urging of a small group of masked soldiers, he paused to join a 'victory' photograph in front of the crates. Palutkin stood like a champion at the centre of his paramilitaries, while around him, their AK-47s pointed skywards, his men cheered their success. The photograph over, the men strode towards the obscene line-up of frightened men at the side of the courtyard for more trophy photographs. Palutkin shook his head in mock despair at their behaviour.

"An impressive operation, Ivan. You've been successful?" Grozky asked, careful to avoid baiting the predator.

"Successful? Absolutely. There was never any doubt."

Palutkin's attention returned to the crate.

"What have we here?" Palutkin said, pinching his chin between a thumb and forefinger in an affected gesture of enquiry.

Grozky saw the splintered edges where a jemmy had been used to force open the lid. Inside, fine strands of multicoloured paper lay like confetti. Palutkin reached into the packaging, his arm disappearing to the elbow, and rummaged briefly.

"Ta-da," he announced and withdrew his arm. In his hand he clutched a classic Russian nesting doll, a *matryoshka*, with plain painted features and red roundels for cheeks.

For a moment he stood displaying the doll in one hand and then his other suddenly clasped the head and twisted it as if he was snapping the neck of a chicken. The painted wooden face remained doleful as it broke from the torso, the plaster splintering like flakes of bone. Palutkin discarded the head and it bounced briefly on the yard before rolling in a small circle, its jagged neck the fulcrum. He dipped his fingers into the top of the hollow body like a pincer and extracted a thick polythene sachet containing a white powder.

"Heroin, to be exact. These crates are full of them. Well hidden too. The first layer contains legitimate dolls you can unscrew all the way," Palutkin said, savouring the image by running his tongue around his lips, "but underneath they are all like these."

"You have done well. What do you estimate the haul to be?" Grozky asked.

"We've yet to weigh it. I am hopeful it will be close to thirty kilos of heroin."

"Your intelligence was certainly good. How did you establish the drugs would be here?"

Palutkin momentarily considered the question. Grozky sensed his reluctance to answer and then Palutkin relented. He leant forward and spoke in a low voice.

"A tip-off was made locally to the OMON who, aware of the interest in Yevgeny Kochenko, passed on the information to the GRU. This is part of the Lensky Group's freight operation. We can add drug trafficking to Kochenko's list of crimes."

Grozky nodded. He wondered whether that was the reason Major Emile Rastich was so keen to speak to him.

"We'll leave you to it, Ivan. Your men are doing an exemplary job," Grozky said.

At what he interpreted as a professional accolade, the twisted smile returned to Palutkin's face.

"It's been a good morning. General Koshygin is waiting to hear the news. You will have to excuse me while I call him to confirm our success," Palutkin said and tossed the empty shell of the doll back into the crate. He strode off towards the warehouse, then stopped and turned to face Grozky.

"You know Stalin's saying: 'If there's a person, you can always find a charge'. Well, listen to how I've improved on that: 'If there's a reputation, you can always find a charge'. I think General Koshygin will be impressed," Palutkin said, laughing at his joke as he walked away.

Grozky's poker face concealed his relief at Palutkin's departure.

"Stay close, Dmitri," Grozky said and Borzoi fell in beside him.

Grozky led the way towards the line of warehousemen held at gunpoint against the fence. As they approached, a burly GRU sergeant stepped forward to challenge them. Grozky was in no mood for an argument with an NCO. Before the sergeant could protest, Grozky barked an order.

"Sergeant, I've told Ivan how impressed I am with your operation. I will have a quick word with some of the prisoners."

Grozky did not wait to be acknowledged and behind him, he heard Borzoi following his lead.

"It's an impressive haul. What are the plans for the warehouse staff?" Borzoi inquired.

Grozky did not hear the sergeant's response for he was already swaggering towards the first of the prisoners. His gait was for the benefit of the GRU onlookers. He saw the fear on the faces of the warehouse staff, intimidated by the guns, yet also their discipline as they stood upright and faced their adversaries.

He reached the first man whose thin, hard face regarded him with defiance.

"Would you have a cigarette on you?" Grozky asked.

The man said nothing as he fumbled in a trouser pocket and produced a packet of cigarettes. He offered it to Grozky who took one. The man thought better of taking one himself, returning the packet to his pocket and exchanging it for his lighter. He lit Grozky's cigarette and received a curt nod for his trouble.

Grozky stared into the man's eyes.

"Who can tell me when these crates were delivered?" Grozky asked, his voice low enough so that the GRU henchmen could not hear his question.

"The warehouse manager, Kirill Blotski, except he's off sick today."

"When was the last time he was sick?"

"He's never missed a day since I've been here. That's more than three years ago."

Grozky nodded. He felt the stirrings of a suspicious coincidence.

"So where would I find Kirill Blotski?

"He lives somewhere near Deviatkino."

"Where exactly?"

"I don't know."

"Who *would* know?" Grozky persevered.

A short pause.

"I'm not sure. You could ask Buzhkov."

"Where do I find Buzhkov?"

The man thought for a moment and then let out an indifferent sigh. His head didn't turn as he spoke quietly.

"Third from the end."

Grozky leant forward.

"Thank you. In case anyone asks, I gave you the third degree, understand? I asked you what you knew about Kochenko's smuggling operation. You told me you knew nothing and I repeated my question. I said I'd make sure you get ten years in prison. You gave me the same response. I called you a liar and you swore you knew nothing. Got it?"

There was now mild confusion on the prisoner's face. He gave a barely perceptible nod.

"To show we've not been having a cosy chat, I'm going to slap you across the mouth. Of course, if you want to repeat any of this, no one will believe you anyway," Grozky said.

Grozky turned and took a small step down the line. He suddenly swung around and brought his right hand sharply across the face of the prisoner. The theatrical strike clipped the cheek and nose of his target. The man stayed upright, wincing at the blow and a large bead of blood spilled from a nostril. There were sniggers from the GRU guards.

"Liar!" Grozky shouted.

He went to the next man, careful to avoid going straight to the end of the line. He paused to make decoys of two more men, berating their involvement in smuggling heroin into the city.

By the time Grozky reached the man named Buzhkov, the GRU were enjoying his show.

Buzhkov had the same dour, angry expression as the rest of the prisoners. His scalp was covered by a thick woollen cap and his face half hidden by a scrubby beard. Grozky changed tack again, his voice quick and earnest.

"You've no reason to trust me. I urgently need to speak with Kirill Blotski. I could go inside and try and find out from whatever personnel records you keep here, except I can't afford to while these goons are watching me. I'm told he lives in Deviatkino, do you know where?"

Buzhkov's stern presence watched Grozky sullenly, his silence affirming he was not interested in cooperating.

Grozky hid his disappointment. He winked at Buzhkov as he stubbed the cigarette out underfoot. From his holster, Grozky drew his Gyurza pistol and raised it until it touched Buzhkov's temple. There were jeers from the GRU men. Grozky winked again before he made his voice loud and theatrical so the GRU men could hear his threat.

"When they've finished with you, I'll get them to drop you off at the Big House. We can talk in the basement where it's more comfortable."

The GRU audience chuckled. Grozky left his pistol where it was and leant in close to Buzhkov.

"If this was a set-up how the hell can I help you unless I can speak to Blotski? Do I look like I'm related to those GRU animals?" Grozky said.

Buzhkov stared back, his beard giving him the skill of a ventriloquist as he quietly relayed the address of Kirill Blotski.

"It's less than twenty minutes from here," Buzhkov added.

Grozky acknowledged the message by stabbing the barrel of his pistol into Buzhkov's chest before holstering it. As he walked away, Grozky spat on the ground, his phlegm grazing Buzhkov's boots. Grozky addressed Borzoi and the GRU sergeant with exasperation.

"Lying – all of them. They claim ignorance of any heroin, yet the evidence is right there in plain sight."

The GRU sergeant nodded and Grozky saw nothing that would indicate his suspicions were aroused. Palutkin would no doubt hear of Grozky's performance.

The FSB pair walked back to the Chaser. The Niva jeep was no longer there. They waited until they were in the privacy of the car before speaking.

"What was that little charade all about?" Borzoi asked.

"I'm playing a hunch," Grozky said and told him about the absent warehouse manager.

"Dmitri, do me a favour and find the quickest route to Deviatkino," Grozky said.

He reversed the Chaser slowly, the idling engine giving no evidence of its true power. They drove slowly through the gates, leaving behind the warehouse scene which could have come straight out of Kafka.

The mid-morning traffic on Rustaveli Street was heavier than that on Piskarev Avenue. Grozky took his opportunity to weave in and out of the traffic.

"There's something you should know. Palutkin approached me with the offer of a transfer to the GRU," Borzoi said.

Grozky should not have been as surprised as he was.

"You're a good candidate. Military background, you follow orders and you're good at punching people. I doubt, though, that's why he asked you," Grozky said.

"The catch was he wants to know what you're up to. He doesn't trust you," Borzoi said.

"I can't imagine he does. Palutkin isn't the trusting type. What did you tell him?"

"I pretended I was interested in his offer."

"You did the right thing, Dmitri."

"I would have told you before we got to the warehouse. I was worried about your reaction," Borzoi said.

Grozky nodded. With only eighteen days until Ekomov killed William Danvers, Gravell's office manager, in Washington, the GRU were closing the circle on his isolation from Moscow. Koshygin was not a forgiving patron. Palutkin's success at the warehouse would only strengthen their resolve.

26

ST PETERSBURG, RUSSIA
TUESDAY 2 APRIL 1996

Leaving the outer limits of St Petersburg and driving fast, they crossed the boundary into the Murino District. In the passenger seat, his map folded out across his lap, Borzoi's finger traced their route.

"Once we're in Deviatkino look for signs to the railway station. It will be on the left," Borzoi said.

"Understood, thanks," Grozky replied without decreasing his speed.

Deviatkino was a suburb at the end of the Kirov-Vyborg Metro line, an afterthought when it came to the investment at the heart of St Petersburg. The station was a squat, functional, fifties design, ubiquitously favoured by Soviet architects for municipal transport buildings. The unremarkable single storey was a conning tower of concrete painted a sandy pastel to resemble stone. It rode above the multicoloured waves of scrappy graffiti swimming along the station's perimeter wall.

"Where to?" Grozky asked.

"It should be just over that rise," replied Borzoi, pointing to where the road forked right and ahead, where the road rose, Grozky saw the tops of five apartment blocks. Even from a distance their scale was imposing: massive, inverted rectangles of concrete, their surface indented by rows of tiny windows.

Grozky accelerated gently, the V8 barely engaged, and the Chaser cantered up the gradient, the tower blocks rising into view. The Metro station was imagination itself compared to these Brezhnev-era masterpieces, each block a replica, isolated from its neighbour by the great hardcore desert on which they were laid. Where there had once been full employment, Deviatkino was as much a victim of the post-Soviet order and crippling hyperinflation of the early 1990s as the rest of the city. With the rise of petty crime and drugs, Deviatkino was another working suburb struggling with the memory of better days.

The five-block estate overlooked the Metro line to the east and regimented arrays of smaller developments to the west. No inhabitant had been disadvantaged by the egalitarian Soviet planners; each apartment was assured of either a sunrise or a sunset.

Grozky could not remember when he had been this far outside the city. They passed a signpost so faded that the red background almost blended with the white Cyrillic lettering marking 'Block-1'. The concrete colossus overshadowing them seemed just as aged, a distant reminder of a different society. So much had changed.

"Next right," Borzoi said as several hundred yards ahead a similarly worn signpost announced the location of Block-2.

Grozky turned off the street into a weary road where fifty yards of scrubby trees and struggling foliage marked the final approach. The token greenery seemed luxurious compared to the sight which greeted them: the line of towers stood on a barren, grey wasteland, devoid of people but with a hotchpotch of vehicles clustered at the base of each block.

Driving across the depressing vista, the Chaser's suspension countered the uneven surface, and Grozky took a meandering line to avoid the depressions where the hardcore had cracked and been left to fester. They passed a forlorn shopping trolley lying on its side next to a blackened residue of what looked like the remains of a bonfire. A small movement caught Grozky's attention and he turned to see three ragged boys pedalling on small bicycles some seventy yards away. Unhindered by any traffic, Grozky continued swerving to avoid the worst of the pitted ground until they reached Block-2.

Grozky parked the Chaser thirty yards from the entrance, the car blending in between a grubby white Lada and a rusty brown sedan. Neither he nor Borzoi looked up at the twenty-storey monstrosity. From the rows of windows stacked above each other, it felt like hundreds of faces were peering down. Grozky wondered whether Kirill Blotski was watching their arrival.

It was Borzoi who spotted the black Mercedes, the shiny anomaly of success amidst the mediocrity of older vehicles. The tinted windows emphasised the expensive import and deflected attention from the heavy armour of the custom bodywork.

"This is the type of car Kochenko's security people favour?" Borzoi said as he tried to peer through the driver's side window.

"It is."

Grozky stood in front of the bonnet, admiring the car. A Mercedes was outside the reach of this part of Deviatkino. He leant forward, his body hiding his actions from the block

327

behind, and felt the bonnet with the back of his hand. It was not cold to the touch, neither was it warm.

"I'd say this was used no more than thirty to forty minutes ago," Grozky said as they turned away from the Mercedes and made their way towards the building, their movements unhurried and relaxed, like two friends who've been admiring a car they could only dream of owning.

The building's entrance was a master class of Soviet architecture. The doorway was dominated by the vast concrete motif above it, reminding the entrants of the value of the proletariat: huge Soviet workmen, stylised by chiselled jaws and the physiques of gymnasts, hammered and crafted tirelessly to make unseen goods. The altar of communism preached a religion where only through selfless commitment to the collective could a true Soviet succeed. Passing underneath the symbolic headstone into the dim hallway beyond, Grozky could imagine a communist anthem piping out a welcome home; the rousing 'Workers are Marching' by Basnev or Dunaevsky's 'Enthusiasts March' would have been appropriate. Now, there was only stillness and silence.

To live here now, thought Grozky, *must seem as hollow as the dream once promised by Soviet propaganda.*

The faint lighting inside was the only sign of occupation. On the way to the lifts, they passed a long bank of mailboxes which looked like a miniature replica of the building itself, each metal box embedded into the fabric of the frame. Borzoi cursorily checked the boxes for the sixth floor and Blotski's name, only to find rows of anonymous apartment numbers.

The lifts, although dated, were built with the industrial reliability of a prouder era and still painted with the favoured Soviet dark grey. Their ascent to the sixth floor was smooth. Upon arrival, the motorised stop of the heavy car resonated around them, the echoes spreading as if they were surrounded by some enormous unseen atrium.

They entered a long, empty corridor. In contrast to the entrance, the illumination was brash, dominated by the brutal neon bars running along the ceiling, the natural light feebly peering in from the windows at either end.

Grozky estimated there were some fourteen or fifteen apartments on each side of the floor. The neat lines of doorways tailed away, their rigidity and silence making the corridor a soulless place. To live suspended in this honeycomb of apartments was to be compressed into solitude.

The first door they knocked on yielded no response. Two doors down they were more fortunate. The face of an elderly babushka appeared, framed by a bright shawl draped over her head and shoulders, the door's security chain drawn tight across the gap. She seemed to distrust their inquiry, before finally confirming that Kirill Blotski lived at number 6-08.

Blotski's apartment was near the middle of the corridor. Grozky put his ear against the door and listened for the sound of voices. He heard nothing except a faint mechanical hum he attributed to the lifts.

Grozky unholstered his Gyurza pistol as Borzoi drew his own Makarov PMM. Very carefully, Grozky tried the handle, turning it fractionally and applying slow pressure against the door. He was surprised to feel a slight movement of success. The door edged away from the frame and Grozky gently pushed it open. He saw the back of a faded brown cloth sofa and, against one wall, a rack of laminate shelves holding books, ornaments and housing a small television set. They stayed either side of the doorway, shielded by the doorframe, their pistols covering the living area, watching for any movement.

The space was not as grim as the apartments appeared from the outside, natural light shining in from a long strip of window at the far end of the room. By Soviet standards the living room was generous. Grozky left the safety of the doorway, moving forward while Borzoi covered him. A small island of rug with abstract shapes in shades of purple gave a touch of colour against the harsh zigzag of dark parquet tiles. Amidst the worn furniture a chunky wooden coffee table, perforated with bright metal studs, looked like a new purchase. The room exuded a tired homeliness bordering on comfort.

They listened for any sound. Kirill Blotski did not appear to be at home. Grozky started his sweep of the apartment. In the next room, a bedroom by the front door, he found the body. Lying on his back, fully clothed in blue slacks and a white shirt and with the expensive black loafers still on his feet, was Sergei Malievich. There was colour in his face while his eyes stared blankly at the ceiling. A pair of small tears in the shirt, tainted by a damp red stain, marked where the bullets had burrowed through his chest.

Leaving Malievich's body where it was, Grozky checked the rest of the bedroom, finding only a partially filled wardrobe and a pair of dusty suitcases under the bed. He returned to the living room and inched along the wall towards an open doorway adjacent to the window, Borzoi covering him. He found a small, square kitchen, not unlike his own. It was clean, the telltale odour of cooking absent and the aged stove cold to the touch. When Grozky looked from the kitchen window, he saw the black Mercedes below had not moved.

Outside the kitchen, on the other side of the living area was a half-open door. Grozky silently signalled Borzoi, who left the corridor and took up a position by the doorway. Grozky squatted low as he walked, his pistol held ready, conscious if anyone was lying in wait, it would be here. He crouched on the balls of his feet and gently nudged the door. Borzoi braced himself by the doorway, his Makarov ready.

The door swung slowly ajar, revealing a tiled floor in tired cream supporting a squat bathtub and a lavatory in the same tones. The tiles stopped halfway up the wall, handing over to faded grey paint. Against the bland pastel, an incongruous note was struck by a thick yellow towel in front of the bath on which a naked corpse rested, its back to Grozky, the head nearest to him. The flesh was an anaemic grey, an unnatural hole at the base of the skull the product of an assassin's bullet tearing through the brainstem.

Grozky pushed back the door until it touched the wall, revealing a white towel on a rail that obscured a small sink. Grozky stood up, satisfied the only occupants of the apartment were not a threat. He gestured back to the bedroom with his pistol.

"There's another body in the bedroom. Sergei Malievich. Shot in the chest, left on the bed."

Grozky approached the corpse on the bathroom floor, its cheek resting against the towel. He peered into the empty bath. By the sinkhole, against the faded enamel, a small rivulet of discoloured, dirty brown water rested. Grozky squatted down again and now saw the bloodless cuts running the length of the corpse's inner forearms. The edges of the wound were as dull as the flesh surrounding it, hiding the knife's incision. He used the barrel of his pistol to raise the corpse's chin, exposing the neck. Another deep slash had severed the artery. Someone had taken care to bleed the body out before it was moved.

"This one has been dead for considerably longer. Most likely it's Kirill Blotski."

"What do you think?" Borzoi asked.

Grozky considered the black Mercedes in the car park.

"I think Sergei Malievich had the same idea we did. He probably got a call as the GRU were breaking down the gates. Everyone at the warehouse is panicking and the warehouse manager is nowhere to be found. Malievich wonders what the hell is going on, so he drives here looking for Kirill Blotski. He knocks on the door, alerting whoever's inside and bang, end of Malievich," Grozky replied.

"The coincidence continues?"

"Continues? This confirms it. What does Blotski know worth killing him for? He's only a warehouse manager, except someone had to have known those crates of dolls would be on the delivery manifests. I think we'll find Kirill Blotski was the man who signed them in. He was the perfect conduit," Grozky said.

"The GRU have still netted themselves a major drugs haul."

"Exactly. It's too convenient. It's possible Palutkin came up with this on his own, but I think it's more likely this is the start of Koshygin's contingency plan. Take a look at the body. Tell me what you think."

Grozky straightened up and stepped back into the living area, leaving Borzoi to inspect the corpse beside the bath.

Grozky was considering how the GRU could have found such a large heroin haul when a movement caught his eye. He turned to see a man in scruffy overalls at the entrance to the apartment. He looked like a janitor until Grozky saw the cold malice in his eyes and registered the pistol in the man's hand. Instinctively Grozky fired, his snap shot hitting the wall by the door. Its percussion was followed by the suck of a silenced round and Grozky felt something tear through his upper left arm. He cried out at the stabbing pain, at the same time sensing the bullet had missed bone. The Gyurza dropped from his hand, while his opponent supported himself against the doorway and took aim. Grozky ducked and scrabbled on the floor for his pistol, his gun hand now useless.

Behind him there was a succession of small explosions as Borzoi fired rapidly from the bathroom, the Makarov's bullets smacking into the wall above the gunman. There was a loud crack as the top of the doorframe splintered. Their attacker, caught out by the revised combat equation, darted from the doorway, frantic footfall sounding his retreat.

"Get after him," Grozky said, grimacing at his injured arm. He watched Borzoi's hulking frame tear across the apartment and out of the door. Grozky stumbled after him, his pursuit hindered by his bleeding arm.

In the corridor Grozky glimpsed Borzoi disappearing through the fire exit by the lifts and followed. He entered the stairwell to hear heavy footsteps reverberating down the metal steps. Grozky persevered, keeping his left arm tight against his side. He tried to ignore his pain, but each jolting step sent a stabbing reminder of the damage to his upper arm. He cursed as he staggered downwards, conscious he could no longer hear the footsteps. He was still on the first floor when he heard an exchange of shots outside.

As Grozky reached the bottom of the stairs he felt chill air. He turned to see the emergency exit doors flapping at the end of the corridor. In the silence Grozky paused. Outside, an assassin's gun could be waiting. He steadied his pistol in his good hand and edged towards the light.

Grozky pushed one of the doors open with his foot and waited for a shot that did not come. Instead, he was relieved to hear the familiar voice.

"Valeri, it's okay. It's safe."

Grozky walked outside and saw Borzoi less than fifty yards away, his pistol now holstered and a broad grin on his face. Of their assailant, there was no sign. Borzoi walked towards him.

"It looks like you'll live," Borzoi shouted.

"Let's hope so. What happened?" Grozky's reply was pained as he clutched his arm.

"I got to the bottom of the stairwell and he fired at me from outside. I couldn't see where from. By the time I got outside he was already at his car. I fired several shots at him as he drove off," Borzoi said.

"Could you identify him if you saw him again?"

"I didn't get a good look at him," Borzoi said. "It's not all bad news though."

He held up a scrap of paper.

"I got the registration."

"Good work, Dmitri."

They walked back to the building as the distant screech of sirens began encroaching on the silence.

27

On Middle Avenue, half a mile from his apartment, Grozky sat in the corner of the *Kanonersk Kabak*, the 'Gunboat Tavern', watching while Borzoi carried a pair of beer glasses to the table. He felt more comfortable than he had cause to, the opioids prescribed by Feliks Fedorov leaving him with a sense of diffused lethargy. They succeeded in partially numbing the rumblings from his damaged nerves even if they didn't take away the pain. Feliks would have told him if he wasn't to drink and Feliks hadn't. Even if he had, Grozky doubted he would have followed his advice. His wounded arm immobilised in a black sling, his low mood was in need of lifting. That justified a drink and he couldn't see how it would affect his ability to think any more than the painkillers.

Borzoi put the glasses of dark beer on the table.

"Have you tried Baltika porter before?" Grozky asked.

"No."

"It's thick, rich and cold."

Grozky took a long swallow of the porter. When it was very cold, a Baltika porter chaser with his vodka was his combination of choice. Even without the vodka, the porter was glorious, a dense liquorice of a drink which reassured him.

"How's the arm?" Borzoi asked.

"Very sore, not that Fedorov was concerned. In medical terms, a bad graze. I'll have a groove in my upper arm to remind me I was lucky. His only worry is infection. He's signed me off and wants to see me again in four days' time."

"You look as if you need it."

"I evidently feel better than my appearance would suggest. You managed to write up the report as we discussed?"

"Yes. I was following your orders. You proposed going to Deviatkino to find and arrest the missing warehouse manager, Kirill Blotski. It was your idea to search the apartment after we found the bodies," Borzoi said.

"Good work. A backhanded compliment does enough to hint at you being the dissatisfied subordinate," Grozky said.

They had discussed what the report should say in the Chaser on their return to the Big House. Borzoi drove and Grozky told him what to write. While Feliks Fedorov saw to Grozky's wound, Borzoi authored their report which would read as an uninhibited account of events. The circumstances required Borzoi to put some distance in their relationship.

"And where is Palutkin now?" Grozky asked.

"Reported to be having dinner with General Donitsyn."

Grozky felt his fragile hold on his return to the FSB slipping. On the face of it, the GRU had secured a coup against the drug gangs of St Petersburg. One agency was being congratulated by another for its assistance.

"I'll be on the same military transport plane with Palutkin and his men tomorrow morning," Borzoi said.

"I expect you will. Palutkin needs to think you've bought

his recruitment pitch," Grozky said, taking another swallow of porter.

Borzoi leant forward.

"I managed to find the owner of the car. It's registered to a Maksim Popov, a native of St Petersburg. Popov spent ten years with the MVD before transferring to the OMON where he lasted less than three months. He left the OMON in April 1995," Borzoi said.

"Interesting."

"If it was Popov in Deviatkino, he's certainly got the history for that type of work."

"Either way, he needs to explain what his car was doing there. You left his name out of your report?" Grozky said.

"Of course."

"Good. I'm in no state to go after Popov on my own. After what we found in Deviatkino, Maksim Popov will be safest in anonymity."

Grozky sat back. Popov would understand what might happen to him if his name became public. The threat of exposure might pressure him into yielding what he knew about how the GRU had found millions of dollars of heroin planted in crates of *matryoshki*. Popov was a name to keep in reserve. What concerned Grozky was that whoever had tried to kill him in Blotski's flat would not have known he was FSB, which signalled the importance of removing any witnesses to Blotski's murder. Sergei Malievich had paid the price.

"My report is going to be lightweight against Palutkin's. I wasn't expecting the GRU to find so much heroin. Thirty kilos is unheard of," Borzoi said.

"That's the question, isn't it? We've been working on tracking down heroin for months and we've never got this close. Rastich only took over three weeks ago and yet the GRU find a huge haul."

"I've heard no mention in Moscow of the GRU investigating Kochenko for drugs. Dratshev never shared details of what Koshygin's contingency plan was," Borzoi said.

"Remind me, when did you first hear about the contingency plan?"

"Thursday 21 March."

Grozky considered the timeline. Ekomov had picked up on the American Senate investigation in early February. Even if the GRU had been covering this since then, at best they had had a month. The maths of their haul didn't hint at Kochenko's involvement in drugs, a coup like this carried the conviction of numbers.

"Think about it, Dmitri. A one-kilo bag is worth around US$50,000. By the time that's been cut down for street sales in America, it would make 76,000 two-grain bags at US$8 each. That's a retail value of US$18 million," Grozky said.

"Palutkin said a tip-off was made to the OMON."

Grozky leant forward, a darting pain from his wound reminding him of his vulnerability.

"Palutkin's going to be interested in your report; show some interest in his and see if you can share notes. His report might have a name in it. I can give Rastich a call. He must be cock of the roost if Palutkin's credited the OMON as the source," Grozky said.

"I will. Another stout? It's been a hell of a day," Borzoi said.

Grozky looked at his half-empty glass of Baltika. He felt more relaxed than he had a right to since his brutal wake-up call in the early hours. It was the first chance he'd had to properly sit back and analyse the sudden turn of events.

"Why not. Thank you, Dmitri."

Grozky took a slug of Baltika, savouring the rich flavour. Around him small groups sat at tables in quiet conversation, enjoying each other's company and unencumbered by the mind games of the Russian state. Though he appeared to be one of them, he served their master. He didn't defend the rights of the people, he protected the tyranny of the state. Since Timur's death his purpose had become more honest as he sought to rid St Petersburg of the drug gangs. Now he had been sucked back into the depths of what the Grey Cardinal would do to save Yeltsin, a no-holds-barred fight to the finish. Even if his role had been reduced to little more than an onlooker in the GRU's operation, he lived a life at odds with ordinary people. It was an existence Natassja would call duplicitous.

Natassja. The realisation he had all but forgotten her disappearance cut through his reverie. The torrid events of his day had denied her presence in his thoughts. Whatever annoyance he had felt about her lying to him had been replaced by fear for her safety. In the morning, he would go out in search of her, that much he could control. Grozky finished his first Baltika as Borzoi returned with two fresh glasses of porter.

"*Nastrovje,*" Borzoi said, taking a gulp from his glass.

"*Nastrovje.*"

Grozky took a sip of his second porter, conscious the vigilance of his mind was beginning to slip. Perhaps he should not have been drinking, but now he was in the mood for it, the alcohol clarifying the significance of what they had found. The pieces were settling to reveal the ugliness of what he had suspected about the GRU's raid.

"Something else occurred to me," Borzoi said. "The way the *matryoshki* were moulded around the heroin. To disguise thirty kilos to that standard took care and time. Wherever that heroin came from, it's part of a sophisticated operation."

"You think Kochenko was involved?" Grozky asked.

"I thought he was. Kochenko had the organisation and distribution capability to be a major player in the drugs trade, didn't he? Then I thought about what we saw at the warehouse. None of the Lensky men had any guns. If I was guarding thirty kilos of heroin, I'd be armed. They weren't."

"I trust you left that observation out of your report?"

"I did."

"You'll go far, Dmitri. Initiative *and* discretion. I could almost believe in Kochenko's involvement except for one thing."

"Which is?"

"The bodies in Deviatkino," Grozky said and took another sip of his porter.

Borzoi nodded.

Grozky might have been of a mind to believe Kochenko was involved in the drugs trade until he and Borzoi had searched Kirill Blotski's apartment in Deviatkino. As Grozky had struggled to stem the blood seeping through the tea towel Borzoi had applied to the bullet wound, he had found a small holdall bag, the canvas cloth old, but the US$15,000 inside were very fresh, too new to have been carefully amassed savings. Blotski had been well paid for his betrayal. He knew how the raid had been fabricated and Malievich must have suspected as much.

"Why kill Blotski? Because he knew," Grozky said. "With Blotski dead, there's no one who can challenge the GRU's version of events. The GRU didn't have a choice. They needed a way to end this and an US$18 million haul gives them that credibility. The size of the evidence can't be ignored. It fits the Kremlin's narrative. Kochenko's wealth is no longer a sign of success, it's a source of shame. With Kochenko dead and a huge drugs haul, the Lensky Group becomes no more than a criminal's empire. The Russian government can hold up the man who lived by the gun, dying by the gun. Yanusk becomes a byline of his corruption," Grozky said.

Borzoi's brow furrowed as he nodded.

"If the heroin wasn't Kochenko's, then the question is how did the GRU source their coup?" Borzoi asked.

"That's my question, and you won't find the answer in Palutkin's report."

"I'll see what I can find out."

"Be careful, Dmitri. Koshygin is playing for the highest stakes and Palutkin is a very dangerous individual. His offer could be a ruse. This isn't what you signed up for."

"I owe you, remember? You're not the type to call in a marker. I'm not one to forget."

"You take care of yourself," Grozky said and took another sip of his porter. He could feel the sloth of the alcohol now embracing him.

"You look tired, Valeri. Let me drive you home."

"Thank you. While I'd welcome a walk, getting some sleep appeals even more."

They finished their drinks and left the tavern.

As the sharp cold of Middle Avenue struck Grozky, the dull pain in his arm was not what preoccupied him. Even if his performance in the warehouse yard had been convincing, he doubted Koshygin would believe his motives. His concern was that he was not supposed to have discovered the bodies in Deviatkino. He was now in the unenviable position of having found what the GRU had tried very hard to keep hidden.

28

ST PETERSBURG, RUSSIA

WEDNESDAY 3 APRIL 1996

Grozky awoke, shrouded in nausea and paying the price for his cocktail of opioids and porter. He despised the weakness of his senses, wishing he could suspend time and feel nothing until it passed. It was as much his mood as his throbbing wound; the way in which Koshygin had marginalised him from the GRU operation festered in his mind. Palutkin would be credited for reducing Kochenko to a plain criminal, while Metzov would not be interested in how the drugs got into the warehouse; what mattered was that the GRU had found them. Koshygin would impress upon the Grey Cardinal it was the GRU's perseverance which had found the flaw in the oligarch's business dealings. The Kremlin's desperation was making the GRU general more ruthless. In seventeen days Ekomov would strike in Washington DC. Koshygin would not be generous in victory when it came to the FSB's contribution, it was not in his nature.

Cursing his fragility, Grozky forced himself to repeat *Your own lives align with the lives of the fallen* in his mind until

342

the backflow of bile in his throat subsided. When he felt he could get up without vomiting, he roused himself.

It was after 11 a.m. when Grozky left his apartment. The prescription painkillers he'd washed down with black coffee added a wooziness to his malaise. Taking coffee with everything was a habit he promised himself he'd stop. At least he hadn't given in to vodka. He walked slowly, feeling his sensibilities succumb and welcoming the sloth of the opioids. After cleaning and suturing his wound, Feliks Fedorov had signed him off sick on the basis rest would aid his recuperation. He was not to exert himself.

Outside, his overcoat draped across his shoulders and his left arm in a black sling, Grozky became aware of the grey chill. The cold air seeped through his jersey and shirt, reached his chest and then chided his back. Although his wound hurt like hell, Grozky was grateful for the opportunity his injury presented. He needed to find Natassja and why she had lied to him about Vadik Prigoda. He thought she'd finally realised the danger she was in. She must have known he'd speak to Prigoda so what was it she felt was so important to conceal? In the restaurant she had been convincing, which meant she was comfortable withholding whatever she knew. For someone as moral as Natassja, he wished she could have been honest with him. He didn't know what he would find at her apartment.

As he tried to focus on what might have happened to her, his mind drifted and instead resurrected the image of his bloodied arm and the corpses in Deviatkino. He tried to dispel the memory only to succeed in replacing it with the forlorn plaster head of a *matryoshka*, torn from its body, and rolling on the fulcrum of its neck. Blotski had been well paid for his betrayal, and Malievich had suspected as much. It had taken Grozky's wound to make him realise he was as complicit as Palutkin in the lie which the Kremlin would endorse.

It took him five minutes to reach Basil's Island Metro station. Walking down the steps he felt the heated metronome of pain in his arm step up its beat. He could have driven to Natassja's apartment, but he welcomed the crisp air. If challenged, he would claim it was recuperative exercise, although he saw no signs he was being followed.

The platform was busier than he expected, populated by robustly dressed ladies in late middle age. They clasped empty bags and were preoccupied with the gossip of their acquaintances. Only a mother with a young child in a pushchair studied him. Marked out by his incapacitated arm, Grozky was unconcerned by her glances.

By the time the train reached Merchants' Court station it had passed under both the rivers Neva and Moyka, and the Griboedov Canal. The Great Merchants' Court shopping arcade straddled both Nevsky Avenue and Garden Street. At the station the ladies in Grozky's carriage disembarked en masse and he was left alone in a corner seat, his arm shielded by the carriage side. His peace was interrupted as a pair of students, clasping books, jumped aboard and collided with the doors as they were closing. They laughed at their achievement and leant against the doors, breathless with bravado.

At the next stop, Mayakov station, Grozky disembarked. The angry pulse in his wound felt calmer now. He walked down Nevsky Avenue, grateful to be outside again. A few hundred yards away, dominating Uprising Square, the Obelisk of Leningrad rose like a giant lance, 118 feet of grey granite. Grozky never tired of the great pillar. Leningrad had been the first recipient of the Soviet 'Hero Cities' monument, a reminder of the privations the city had endured and the sacrifice his grandfather and hundreds of thousands of others had made to hold out.

Your own lives align with the lives of the fallen, Grozky thought, feeling the flush of adrenaline.

A wailing siren interrupted his thoughts. Its urgency grew in intensity and Grozky arrived in the square to see an ambulance pull up beneath the clock tower of Moscow railway station. An elderly man in a wheelchair, his head bowed, was carefully wheeled into the back of the vehicle. The ambulance departed sedately down Ligovsky Avenue, its urgency reduced to that of a hearse. Grozky gave it no thought as he descended into the Uprising Square Metro.

At midday the wide hallways of the station dwarfed the few passengers who meandered along the concourse. On the platform Grozky noted a four-minute wait for the next train north. Feeling fragile after his walk, he sat on a bench and retrieved his small notebook from inside his overcoat and reviewed his list of events. Natassja's lie that Prigoda was trying to sell Kochenko's stake in Yanusk gnawed at his psyche. Everything seemed to connect, directly or indirectly, to that damned oil company. He had many of the pieces and she had found one he was missing. Perhaps it unlocked the puzzle of how the deaths of Yuri Tomarov, Stanislav Rusnak, Yanusk's Chief Financial Officer, and Yevgeny Kochenko were connected. The killings of Tomarov and Rusnak were made to look like accidents, whereas Kochenko had been executed with the greatest skill. He could not, though, rule out Kochenko's involvement in Tomarov's demise. What had these people known about Yanusk which warranted their execution? Even Metzov had been shocked by Kochenko's killing. If American Intelligence had arranged that shooting, it seemed too far-fetched they could also be responsible for the termination of Tomarov and Rusnak. Yet, as he thought about the planning involved in Kochenko's death, it was well within the Americans' capability to hire local assassins to mask their involvement.

His index finger traced the list again. As Kochenko's right-hand man, Sergei Malievich would also have known about Yanusk, though he discounted the connection. The spontaneity of his killing in Deviatkino most likely lay at the hands of Maksim Popov. Had Grozky not found the bodies in Deviatkino, he might have believed the new evidence against Kochenko; he had the money and the fleet. Popov was a card he would save for General Donitsyn when he tried to salvage his return to the FSB. A tip like that would buy him some badly needed goodwill.

Grozky's thoughts were interrupted by the train's arrival. There was standing room only, forcing him to exploit the carriage's configuration, wedging himself against the partition by the door to protect his injured arm. He braced himself for the acceleration, his good arm gripping the rail above him, while the hand of his damaged arm gingerly held the open notebook. The train departed with a sharp surge and seconds later the light outside disappeared and they entered a tunnel.

"Hey."

Grozky looked across at the middle-aged man sitting opposite him. He had previously been ignoring everyone while he read his paper. He wore a dark, knee-length leather coat and his thick grey hair was moistened down with oil. His paper now lay folded on his lap.

"I think you need this more than I do," the man said, his expression questioning the cause of Grozky's condition. He stood up and indicated the vacant seat.

"I appreciate it, thank you," Grozky said, sitting down with relief.

He rested his notebook on his lap, grateful his left arm was now protected by a partition. He studied what Natassja had said about Prigoda selling Kochenko's stake in Yanusk, aware the passengers wondered at his injury and what preoccupied him so. Natassja did not know about the Kremlin's operation. For her to have found something she felt unable to share, she was likely worried he would react to it. Her performance had been masterful. As he recalled her expression, her conviction struck him again. What if she *had* shared the information?

He held the thought, forcing it to a conclusion. If Kochenko had been approached to sell a share in Yanusk and Vadik Prigoda was not the source, Natassja had caught herself in her own half-truth. Who could have told her? Looking at the names on the page, Grozky settled on Zach Brown. The ex-CIA man's success as a businessman and his network of contacts on both sides of the border made him the logical candidate. He'd impressed upon the Russian Ministry of Fuel and Energy that he was a reluctant Senate witness. He was, though, trained in deception. That the wounded American could go to ground and still evade discovery hinted he was playing a very secretive game. Dark forces were at work and Natassja had become enmeshed in the maelstrom. A sudden jolt on the track made Grozky wince as his wounded arm struck the partition. Natassja's image faded, while around him, people with ordinary lives now avoided looking in his direction.

Grozky sat back carefully, protecting his bad arm. Something on the list niggled at him. The roar of a passing train disturbed his focus. He stared at the page, unable to see what eluded him.

At Chernyshev Metro station, the last stop in the Admiralty District before the Neva river, a surge of new passengers boarded, barely acknowledging each other. A squat woman with a bulging mesh bag fought for the seat next to him. He noted her coarse hands and the worn coat whose cuffs and elbows were expertly patched. On her lap, small parcels wrapped in newspaper poked through the worn string. He suspected she had boarded at Avtovo station several stops south on the Kirov-Vyborg line and come direct from the Juno Fair rather than the Great Merchants' Court shopping arcade. Juno Fair on the east side of Strike Avenue was the biggest bootleg market in the city. There was good money to be made from reselling Soviet junk to tourists. In the daily challenge to make ends meet, every little helped.

A few minutes later, passing under the Neva river once more, the train shuddered and the carriage lights flickered again. The page vanished and then reappeared. When he looked again at the last entry, Grozky realised what had been bothering him.

'2nd April – Lensky warehouse – Kirill Blotski & Sergei Malievich killed at Deviatkino > MVD (OMON)?'

He saw he had written 'MVD (OMON)' when he should have written 'Ex-MVD (OMON)'. He wondered at his inadvertent lapse and put it down to the opioid in his painkillers when he made the notes.

Arriving at Vyborg station, the metallic doors were mechanically punched apart, once more allowing the egress of passengers. Grozky left the train and kept to the edge of the station concourse, his damaged arm protected by the regimented stone columns.

Outside, he walked the few hundred yards to Natassja's *khrushchyovka* on Mendeleev Street. He rang every bell until one answered.

"I'm Major Valeri Grozky of the FSB. I'm here to follow up on your missing neighbour, Natassja Petrovskaya, on the top floor."

"Okay," a man's voice said and the buzzer on the door sounded.

Grozky was not sure what he expected to find, but the fresh smear of dried blood on the wall by her front door caught him off guard. He was not expecting evidence of violence. Grozky was examining the stain when strong arms seized him from behind and twisted him into a crouch. He felt a damp cloth clamped over his nose and mouth. He writhed to escape and tried not to breathe, but the hands that held him were unyielding. There was a faintly sweet smell he could not place. He sought to recall the drug and instead found himself yearning for the narcotic scent of Natassja. Moments later he was unconscious.

29

Grozky awoke in gloom, fully clothed and lying on something soft. His second awakening of the morning was a repeat of his first except less pleasant. The nausea from his chemically induced unconsciousness was nothing against the pain in his left arm which was throbbing badly to its own beat.

Although in deep shadow, he could make out the features of his captivity. Several yards away, thin lines of light were sketched beneath the slats of a shutter. He studied his watch until the tiny luminescent markers told him it was almost 4 p.m. If that was accurate, he had been unconscious for more than ninety minutes. He carefully touched his wounded arm to find someone had expertly redressed it, the bandage firm without being overly tight.

He smelt leather. Raising himself on his good elbow, he found he was resting on a sofa, his comfortable pillow a suede cushion. Feeling groggy, he carefully swung his legs onto the floor, sat up and braced himself for the next wave of nausea. He felt the expected pulse start to tick across his temple. His feet found a thick carpet and his knees brushed the unfamiliar edge of a coffee table. Grozky was relieved to find another round of wooziness seemed to be the extent of his malaise. He thought he was alone until he looked across his shoulder and saw the silent silhouette of a man guarding the door.

His stirring must somehow have been reported for shortly afterwards the light in the room grew as the bulbs in the ceiling were turned up and another sturdy guard entered and deposited a cup of steaming black coffee on the table in front of him. Grozky heard discreet voices from outside the room. A man dressed in dark jeans and a black polo-neck jersey entered and sat in one of the leather armchairs opposite him.

Grozky thought he must be hallucinating because he was staring at a ghost. It took him several more seconds before he realised he was looking at the unmarked features of Yevgeny Kochenko, resurrected from the dead.

"Well, Major Grozky, we finally meet," Kochenko said.

The oligarch's tone was polite, yet Grozky sensed menace behind his still features. Grozky's hand grazed his trouser pocket to find his notebook was missing. He wondered when the questioning would start. He took a sip of his coffee, then said:

"Here I am, Mr Kochenko. How does this work? Do I answer your questions and then you let Natassja loose? You do have her?"

"All in good time, Major Grozky. I'm interested to understand your role in the raid on my warehouse. How did you know it was taking place?"

"I didn't. I only found out because my associate, Dmitri Borzoi, told me about it."

"Of course, Lieutenant Borzoi. I'm informed he spends a lot of time in Moscow these days."

"He doesn't have much choice."

"No, I don't suppose he does."

Kochenko stood up as Grozky took another sip of coffee.

"I hear the drugs haul was substantial?" Kochenko said. He seemed almost distracted as he asked the question.

"It was. The GRU reported thirty kilograms of heroin."

"That much? Lensky may be many things, Major Grozky, but I have never dealt in drugs. I give you my word on that."

Grozky heard the anger in Kochenko's voice.

"Let's say I believe you."

"Why should you want to believe me? I am the pariah the Kremlin must punish."

"Two words. Kirill Blotski," Grozky said and met Kochenko's stare.

"Buzhkov told me your instincts were good. My men were unsure of your motives at the warehouse. It's one of the reasons you and I are still talking. It's a shame you didn't find Blotski earlier. I'm sure a man of your abilities has a view on the circumstances of his death. I don't think the GRU are going to leave any loose ends on this one."

"You have evidence Blotski's killer was GRU?"

Kochenko scowled at Grozky's challenge.

"Spare me. Even you can acknowledge the timing of the GRU raid was a little too convenient. Before we discuss who killed Blotski and my friend, Sergei, there is someone I want you to meet. It will explain some of the things that have been going on recently."

Grozky countered Kochenko's suggestion.

"You expect me to answer your questions? Before I do that, I want to see Natassja and know she is safe."

"More than reasonable. She is in the next room. I'll bring her in," Kochenko said.

The oligarch left the room and Grozky savoured another mouthful of coffee, his nausea dissipating. He did not hear Natassja enter. He caught the trace of her rich scent as Kochenko returned to his armchair.

Natassja sat next to him. When she turned and smiled, Grozky noticed the nasty red welt on her right cheek and the darkly discoloured shadow surrounding her eye.

"You bastard!"

Grozky launched himself at Kochenko.

"Valeri! No!" Natassja pleaded.

Grozky choked as an immovable forearm caught around his neck, dragging him backwards and he was flung onto the sofa. His wound screamed at the exertion.

"I apologise," Kochenko said. "I should have explained. I am not the one responsible for Natassja's condition."

Natassja hugged Grozky and he embraced her as the pain from his arm pulsed through his shoulder and neck.

"I am as unhappy as you are at what happened," Kochenko continued. "Unfortunately, things have got out of hand. I give you my word you can both walk out of here today if you wish. However, there is someone I must introduce you to first."

Grozky looked at Natassja and she nodded tearfully. He had never seen her cry, yet she was beautiful in her vulnerability. He could not repress a savage desire to hurt whoever had assaulted her.

"We can talk later, Valeri. You should go with Yevgeny," Natassja said.

Grozky stood up and looked around the room. From beyond the shutters the sounds of the street were audible, though muted. A large dresser of richly polished wood rested against a wall, well stocked with books. On either side were two large landscape paintings of scenes which might have been Italian. It felt like a private residence. Grozky wasn't sure where he was except he doubted it was Kochenko's grand house on the Griboedov Canal.

"You're still in St Petersburg. This place can't be traced to me. You're safe here," Kochenko said, heading for the door.

Escorted by a guard, Grozky followed him. Through a dim hallway, the oligarch led them towards the back of the house to a door under the stairwell. They descended narrow, wooden stairs, their footfall contained by stone walls. It grew cooler, the closed quarters of the subterranean den embraced by the ground. Despite the overhead lights in the stairwell, the confined space made the atmosphere oppressive. Grozky felt a sense of foreboding about their destination.

The corridor in the cellar was poorly lit but Grozky glimpsed stone flags. Kochenko walked past two doors then stopped at the last. Made of solid metal, it looked more in keeping with a prison than a house. Kochenko knocked twice and entered.

Compared to the cool corridor, the warmth in the room surprised Grozky until he breathed the air, rancid with sweat and fear. A few yards away, a man sat tightly bound to an old wooden armchair, nylon ropes around his exposed torso and spiralling down his arms, pinioning them to the armrests. Several men stood around him, watching an interrogation in progress.

Grozky felt the queasiness he endured at every interrogation, a dark memory from his induction to the KGB. His mock interrogation then still haunted him. It was the hideous fear of not knowing what would happen next. That uncertainty, his tutors had emphasised, was the essence of control. Brutality, for the sake of it, achieved little. An honest response could prevent the pain, or an interrogator could inflict it to reinforce a victim's predicament. It was the subjects' inability to exert any control which destroyed them.

"Do you recognise a colleague?" Kochenko's question snapped Grozky from his thoughts.

Distracted by what was happening, Grozky had not studied the prisoner. Now he looked at the shaven head above a very bloodied face. Without warning a wash of cold water from an unseen bucket hit the prisoner's head, choking him momentarily and dispersing the blood to reveal the bruised and swollen features. Despite the damage, Grozky suddenly recognised the man's identity – Major Emile Rastich. Rastich gasped, coughing away the unwelcome fluid. His bloated features contorted in complaint.

Kochenko's voice cut through the room.

"You were looking for the person who struck Natassja. This is the culprit."

Despite Rastich's pitiful circumstances, Grozky felt the anger mounting in him as he looked down at the venomous OMON man.

"It's an interesting story. With you out of the picture in Finland, your OMON friend decided he would find out what a certain journalist of our acquaintance knew about Yuri Tomarov," Kochenko said.

"Tomarov?"

"When you were at GRU headquarters, you asked about Yuri Tomarov? It was inferred, from your question and your liaison with Natassja, you must have some reason for looking further into Tomarov's death. That was why Rastich was trying to get up close and personal with her," Kochenko said.

Grozky stared at Rastich. He no longer felt the pain in his arm. Who would have sent Rastich on such an errand? Grozky saw the man's little eyes squinting at him in a smirk. Despite his pain, he seemed to enjoy Grozky's discomfort.

"We've since verified with Rastich there was another reason why he was so keen to have Natassja out of the way. He wanted some leverage over you. She was to be a hostage," Kochenko said.

Grozky's ire rose. He tried not to think about Natassja sitting in a cell, bound like Rastich, her face a mass of swollen pink flesh from carefully aimed blows. Then they would have started on her body. He was conscious of Kochenko's steely gaze before the oligarch turned away to speak in a low tone to one of the interrogators.

After a short discussion, Kochenko shared the conversation.

"My men are wondering whether the FSB would like to show us some new interrogation techniques?"

Grozky felt the scrutiny of the men in the room, waiting for him to vent his rage. To not participate now seemed somehow alien, yet he checked himself. An expert at counterintelligence, Kochenko had Natassja at his mercy and could have prepared this spectacle for his own benefit. Grozky's fists were clenched when he responded.

"How did you come to be so conveniently involved in Natassja's rescue?"

In the fetid cellar, Grozky's challenge brought angry stares from the men around him. Kochenko raised his hand to control them.

"It was fortunate. Natassja did not know her attackers except that it was a deliberate assault against the media. They made that much clear. She was not hurt and managed to escape after her cameraman came to her rescue. With you away she called me for help. A car was despatched and fortunately arrived at her apartment to find Major Rastich had been waiting for her. An unpleasant incident," Kochenko said.

Grozky stepped forward. He began to understand Rastich's significance.

"When was the last time you saw Maksim Popov?" Grozky asked.

Kochenko's men exchanged glances at the unfamiliar name. For the first time, Rastich's piggy eyes twitched nervously at the fresh inquisition.

"Come, come. Maksim Popov was a member of the St Petersburg OMON. Surely you can tell me when you saw him last?" Grozky said with mock encouragement.

Rastich stayed silent until the man nearest to him raised a menacing fist.

"Six, maybe seven months ago."

"Really? So, you would have no idea what Popov was doing in Deviatkino yesterday?"

At the mention of the location, the mood in the room darkened. Hard eyes stared at the prisoner.

"What makes you think I know anything about Maksim Popov being in Deviatkino yesterday?" Grozky asked.

Rastich shrugged, his eyes darting back and forth in desperation. Panic had an odour and Rastich stank.

"Because the number plate of his car was taken outside a tower block in Deviatkino," said Grozky. "You met with Maksim Popov six months ago, you say? That was after his dismissal from the OMON, so you and Popov have kept in touch. Perhaps you can tell us what he's up to these days?"

Rastich recoiled from the words that threatened to condemn him. His head shook desperately, twisting on his neck as if the physicality of his denial would convince them of his innocence.

"Maksim Popov was there to silence Kirill Blotski, wasn't he?" Grozky said.

Rastich's head wriggled in fear.

Grozky savoured his final statement, letting the syllables drop into place with the precision of a hangman.

"Maksim Popov killed Sergei Malievich."

Rastich's jerky movements ceased. Amidst the fury of the faces surrounding him, he stared ahead.

"I'm impressed," Kochenko said. "It's a shame you missed his earlier admission. It is not so strange why elements of the OMON and the GRU are co-operating. Despite their different masters, the link is stronger than either of us could have imagined. They have recently been fighting together in Chechnya."

Chechnya. Grozky mentally kicked himself. The war involved regular army, military intelligence and militia forces. The image of Colonel Ivan Palutkin triumphantly brandishing a broken Russian doll took on a new significance. He glared at Rastich.

"You were working with Palutkin. You knew about the drugs raid at the warehouse?"

Rastich shrugged as if the accusation was baseless.

"It was your men in St Petersburg who planted the drugs in those crates, wasn't it?"

A smaller shrug from Rastich could not hide the panic in his eyes.

"Because you knew where you could find that amount of heroin." It was not a question.

Grozky's logic was relentless. Rastich's head remained inert, his eyes dim from exhaustion.

"You knew because you're part of the drug-smuggling operation in St Petersburg."

Grozky stepped back as a new realisation hit him. The ambush at the Red Star Bar. He wondered whether Nedev had been party to the smuggling and immediately discounted the thought. Nedev's contribution put him above suspicion. Kochenko's voice broke into his troubled thoughts.

"Well, Major Grozky, you can now appreciate why I find it hard to believe I am the guilty party in your investigation. The GRU are up to all their old tricks. It's time I settled up," Kochenko said.

"And Rastich?" Grozky asked.

"What Rastich knows may keep him alive a little while longer," Kochenko replied.

As they left the cell, Grozky felt he was sinking into a quagmire. It was as much the shock of Rastich's bare-faced betrayal as the dilemma he was now faced with. How to explain Yevgeny Kochenko was still alive? However he tried to spin it, Koshygin would not believe him. The GRU would string him up like Rastich to get at the truth. He put the thought out of his mind as he was escorted upstairs. Not only was Kochenko alive, he was drawing up battle lines for his survival. The pressures which would have cracked a lesser man were being absorbed by the oligarch. The Kremlin's scapegoat wasn't on the defensive, he was preparing to attack.

30

Confined to Kochenko's house, Grozky resented his incarceration. Even raising a blind was forbidden. While the house represented a temporary sanctuary for him and Natassja, it held no hope for Major Emile Rastich. Grozky could not banish the wretched images from the cellar. The scale of Rastich's duplicity unnerved him. The OMON officer had exploited his position to stay a step ahead of Grozky in St Petersburg, regardless of the cost, and had then gone after Natassja.

When he took the Moscow assignment Grozky could not have foreseen the morass it would become. Discovering the source of the drugs seized at Kochenko's warehouse did little to resolve Grozky's predicament. With sixteen days until Ekomov's strike in Washington DC, the Kremlin's crisis plan now depended upon exploiting Kochenko's death, a disgraced criminal drug lord, whose assets would likely be subject to state seizure. The amended playbook did not include his resurrection. With Kochenko alive and Rastich's confession, Palutkin's evidence would not hold up. Witnesses were a liability the GRU would not entertain. Kochenko and his men were on borrowed time.

If Koshygin might have been prepared to overlook Grozky's discovery of the bodies in Deviatkino, the revelation regarding Kochenko would be his death knell. Koshygin was thorough, he wouldn't leave loose ends like Natassja and Dmitri Borzoi. The GRU would clean house and Grozky would take to his grave what he had found out about Rastich's drugs operation in St Petersburg. Until the last twenty-four hours, he'd thought he might prevail. Now hope failed him.

In the gloom, Natassja sat next to him on the sofa, her hand entwined in his. The warmth of their small embrace was a source of comfort. She knew she was in the firing line. The events of the last few hours had not given him the opportunity to raise Vadik Prigoda with her, trumped by the peril they faced. Sitting opposite, Kochenko's lean features gave no sense of his own worries. The oligarch seemed to come and go with the impunity of a man untroubled he might be discovered.

"I've had Natassja's apartment watched since Rastich tried to abduct her. I wondered who would show up. Other than a policeman who made a cursory inspection, you have been the only visitor. My sense is you are as much in need of protection as she is," Kochenko said.

Grozky felt Natassja squeeze his hand. He didn't want to concede Kochenko was right.

"Someone also needs to look after Natassja. It's the second time she's had to call me," Kochenko said.

"The second time?" Grozky queried and felt Natassja's hand go still.

"Ah, we'll come to that. For now, I think you can both benefit from Natassja's disappearance," Kochenko said.

"That would depend on your point of view," Grozky replied.

"I look at it this way. Rastich was sent to kidnap Natassja. Who has Rastich been helping? Palutkin. Since Natassja has disappeared, it will appear Rastich has succeeded. Palutkin will assume he has Natassja confined somewhere. I would think that gives us seventy-two hours at best before the alarm is raised when Rastich cannot be found. In the meantime, Natassja should remain a house guest here," Kochenko said.

Grozky nodded. He could not offer an alternative.

"My concern is, once Palutkin realises Rastich is missing, he will know something is amiss and he will redouble his efforts to find Natassja. You are an obvious lead. It's fortunate you were in Finland when Rastich tried to snatch her. Your alibi stands up, at least until they send that madman of a colonel to talk to you," Kochenko said.

The thought of being interrogated by Ivan Palutkin was a very unpleasant prospect, Grozky reflected.

"I find myself in the middle of a conspiracy not of my making. I would think you may feel the same way. Might I suggest that we pool our information? That way, we may all survive this mess," Kochenko said.

Grozky did not contest the precariousness of his situation. "Whose body did I bring back from Finland?"

"I was very fortunate. One of my guards, Andrei Androvitch, was too proud to admit he was suffering from the flu. He was shivering badly as we left the yacht in Finland. I lent him my overcoat. The sniper mistook Androvitch for me. He then shot a second guard, Milosz Klepin, as he raised the alarm. For the purposes of the deception, Milosz became the 'traitor' who had shot me at close range. Of course, my men corroborated the ruse. It seems to have withstood scrutiny."

"A clever improvisation."

"I was lucky. As the Russian government is determined to parade me as a pariah, my elimination has proved convenient. What have the Finnish police come up with?"

Grozky shared his discussion with Lasola and the identification of the mysterious Steve Williams of Virginia. Kochenko listened, his face betraying no reaction.

"An American?" Kochenko asked.

"That's what the evidence points to," Grozky said.

Kochenko sat back in his chair, the fingers on his left hand tapping the arm rest.

"Several months ago, I received a direct and very generous offer from an offshore American investment company for a stake in Yanusk. I declined, but the extent of their due diligence and knowledge of the company's problems surprised me at the time. Now you tell me the sniper was an American. I was discussing with Natassja how it's possible the American Subcommittee can know so much about Yanusk. Don't you find it odd?"

"I do," said Grozky. "Even though the Subcommittee has a witness, Zach Brown, with first-hand experience of the problems at Yanusk, my sense is American Intelligence are working to play up the spectre of Russian organised crime. It suits the American political agenda."

"Interesting," Kochenko said.

The oligarch stood up and crossed to a desk on the far side of the room. From a drawer he removed a stapled document. He handed it to Grozky and returned to his armchair.

"That is a sworn statement from Zach Brown which he made without duress in the presence of my lawyer."

"How did you get this?" Grozky asked.

"I am indebted to Natassja. After Brown was attacked in Moscow, she asked me for help. I provided it. Brown may resent being protected by his enemy's enemy, but he knows he is in my debt. I had no appreciation how critical a figure he is to the Senate's investigation," Kochenko said.

Grozky understood the reason for Natassja's reticence. She might sleep with him, but when it came to sheltering Zach Brown she could not risk trusting an FSB officer. Brown had been spirited away. He did not blame her. His arm seemed to react to the revelation, the throb now tinged with a soreness which had not been there before. Grozky released Natassja's hand and stood up, gently covering his wound. He felt it beat in his fingers.

"In his statement, Brown concedes he received a personal 'goodwill' fee of US$100,000 to pass on a file of information to the Russian Ministry of Fuel and Energy. Brown received an anonymous phone call from someone who knew he would be testifying to the American Senate and said it would be 'in Russia's best interests'. Brown had already disclosed to the Russian Ministry he was required to testify before the Senate."

"An anonymous phone call?" Grozky asked.

"Brown had a call scheduled with someone called Barnaby Smith who he thought was a prospective client. Smith sounded American and had an authoritative voice. He seemed to know a lot about Brown and about Yanusk. He told Brown the information in the file had already been submitted to the Senate Subcommittee. For simply passing on a file, it was easy money," Kochenko said.

"Do you think he's telling the truth?" Grozky asked.

"He's no reason to lie. Brown knows how exposed he's become in Russia," Kochenko replied.

"Brown's statement also clarifies the scale of what Yuri Tomarov was up to. Look at page three," Kochenko said.

Grozky turned to the page and read.

'Historically, oil production was controlled through the Soviet oil export monopoly, Soyuznefteexport, before it became a private company in 1991. That change marked the beginnings of the first independent oil trading companies in Russia.

Instead of central state control the big oil producers, including Yanusk, could benefit from these new oil trading companies and sell to the highest bidder. By controlling the supply, Tomarov was illegally syphoning off oil and diverting it to be sold through a Swiss trading company, Capri Trading...'

Grozky looked enquiringly at Kochenko.

"Brown's insights confirm what I have already learnt to my cost," the oligarch said. "Tomarov was screwing the Yanusk shareholders because he was controlling the sale of the oil on the secondary market and the proceeds were going into his personal account," Kochenko said.

"So how did he get caught? It seems like he had it all tied up."

Kochenko's voice was grim. "He didn't. Tomarov's fraud went undetected until he defaulted on the loan repayments to Lensky Bank. He then lost control of Yanusk Oil. I've been having regular meetings with the Ministry of Fuel and Energy to explain how I've spent a small fortune cleaning up this mess. I keep being accused of fraud. I swear I had no knowledge of what Tomarov was up to with the trading company in Geneva."

Geneva. Grozky recalled an exotic widow in a blond apartment in Moscow and how Yuri Tomarov had been trying to move his funds into a private bank in Geneva. Grigori Zotkin was looking for payments between Yanusk and Lensky Bank based on the disclosure from the American Senate Subcommittee. Grozky doubted the same scrutiny was being applied to Tomarov's Geneva operation.

"So, as the owner of Yanusk Oil, if you have a stake in Capri Trading, you could access payment activity records in Geneva?"

"In theory, I could. What exactly are you looking for?"

Grozky told him. The SWIFT transfers, the bank identification codes and the intermediary banks which would help to follow the money. Kochenko made notes.

"You've obtained a lot of information from Zach Brown. Where is he?" Grozky asked.

"Better you don't know. He's my ace in the hole and he came very close to leaving Russia in a coffin. Until this matter is resolved, I'm keeping him safely out of sight."

Grozky nodded.

"My turn. Who's running your operation in Moscow?" Kochenko asked.

"None other than Aleksandr Metzov. He's recruited General Anatoli Koshygin of the GRU Second Directorate. Effectively, it's a military intelligence operation," Grozky replied. He saw Natassja's mouth drop at the names.

"Koshygin!" Kochenko's face turned into a furious scowl.

"The very same," Grozky said.

Kochenko was silent for a moment. When he spoke the quiet fury in his voice was unmistakeable.

"That explains the discovery of drugs in one of my warehouses. It was no coincidence. Even you must have wondered how someone like Rastich could find a haul like that."

"How do you know?" Grozky asked.

Opposite him, the oligarch's face remained a mask of anger.

"You don't know Koshygin. This goes back to the Afghanistan war when I was stationed at Charikar, running counterinsurgency operations into the Panjshir Valley. It was a bad time. The CIA was funding the Mujahideen with those damn Stinger missiles. Our attack helicopters had to fly so high to stay out of missile range, do you know what we began calling the pilots? Cosmonauts. Once we'd lost our air cover it became a war of attrition we couldn't win," Kochenko said.

Grozky saw the oligarch's knuckles were bunched tight.

"Over several weeks, I became aware some of the local drug lords were distributing opium with impunity. During a patrol, Sergei Malievich captured a map case with details of a drugs drop. Using that intelligence, one of my units intercepted a Pashtun courier and his mule. When confronted, the courier claimed he was under 'the colonel's protection'. Back then, Koshygin was our garrison commander. While Soviet soldiers were being killed daily, Koshygin was lining his pockets by dealing drugs with the enemy."

"That's why he had you dishonourably discharged," Grozky said.

"Yes. I misjudged Koshygin's influence. He denied any involvement and ordered me to stop interfering in non-military matters. That was the final straw. You know the rest. Koshygin used his connections to have me dismissed as suffering from battle fatigue. No one believed my accusations after that. Back then there was talk of military transport planes from Kabul being used to fly heroin consignments to the Chkalovsk military airfield near Moscow. Koshygin will have found new routes. He'll be making millions. He sacrificed some heroin because he needed a major score to attack my reputation and give Metzov something concrete to hang around my neck," Kochenko said.

Grozky stood by the window, staring at the light seeping through the shutters. He recalled General Donitsyn's words,

'I put forward several names, but you were selected by General Anatoli Koshygin, GRU Second Directorate'. His shock was the cunning the GRU general had used to play him and divert him from pursuing his St Petersburg drugs operation. Koshygin would betray them all.

"Ever since the American Ambassador started raising Zach Brown's disappearance, Metzov has been on the war path at the lack of progress in finding him. Koshygin has turned his man hunt into a crusade. How much longer do you think you're going to be able to keep him hidden?" Grozky asked.

Natassja beat the oligarch to the answer.

"Valeri, what will never be reported is the significance of the man Zach Brown killed in self-defence. The wallet Brown took identified his attacker as Georgy Kramov. In isolation the name means nothing. However, in the Moscow missing persons' reports a man called Nikita Chirkin failed to attend his mother's birthday and hasn't been heard from since. She reported him missing. The physical description could have been written for Georgy Kramov."

Her next sentence left Grozky cold.

"Chirkin was a captain in the GRU."

"Jesus! Chirkin died under his operational name and there was nothing on his body to identify him. Koshygin can deny any involvement in sanctioning a hit on a Senate witness, but Metzov has to be made to understand the liability he has become," Grozky said as the faint lines of a strategy began to form in his mind.

"Unless you can give Metzov a way out of this, I think you're too late. The inquisition will run its course along with my reputation," Kochenko said.

Reputation, thought Grozky, *is a bloody understatement. Our very lives are at stake.*

Grozky realised Kochenko was grinning at his reaction to the remark.

"Don't worry, Valeri. I can look after myself. Now you understand what I'm up against, what do you propose?" Kochenko asked.

31

Crossing Manezhnaya Square, Grozky's pace slowed before he reached the cobblestones on Kremlin's Passage. Dressed in a black overcoat and scarf with his wallet case under an arm, he could have been anyone. Despite his diligence over his route, he sensed he was being followed. He wondered if he was becoming paranoid, his fear heightened because unless he could convince the Grey Cardinal he was not a traitor, his legacy would be that of a Judas.'Trust no one who hasn't earned it,' Keto had once told him. Kochenko was the last person he should be working with, except Grozky had no one else to rely upon.

Instead of reaching Red Square by walking between the State Historical Museum and the Arsenal Tower, Grozky turned and stopped in front of the museum, pretending to admire the statue of Marshal Zhukov while he surveyed the pedestrians. In the gusting wind, Muscovites and tourists clasped their coats tighter. Grozky ignored the elements. Spotting nothing untoward, he walked to the twin towers of the Resurrection Gate protecting the north-eastern approach to Red Square. Passing under the dense red-brick guardian, the breeze became urgent, funnelling him through the small arches to herald his arrival onto the sea of cobbles.

Ten yards later he avoided the gawping tourists and ducked into the small Kazan Cathedral. The Russian Orthodox interior might have been a religious memorial ground, its walls adorned by ancient wooden panels with painted rows of saints immortalised in beatific portraits. Across the ceiling angelic figures, radiant against skies of dark gold and bronze, gazed down. The light could only creep in from slits carved beneath the dome, insufficient to touch the glow of candles, leaving the sanctuary consigned to contemplation. Grozky was not a man for worship, but he stopped in front of the altar, knelt and took strength by repeating, "Your own lives align with the lives of the fallen". Against a man as merciless as Koshygin, he was outnumbered and outgunned. He was making a stand in his brother's memory. He hoped God would understand it was the only prayer which mattered to him.

Standing up, Grozky scanned the dim interior, admiring the room while his eyes checked the faces. He saw nothing out of the ordinary, though it was small comfort. The short span of the cathedral was easy enough to observe from outside.

Leaving the cathedral, he walked briskly to the *Gosudarstvenny Universalny Magazin*, the GUM communist department store now a brightly lit emporium. He browsed the rich displays, casually strolling back and forth while he searched for signs of surveillance. At the far end of Red Square, the domes of the eight chapels of Saint Basil's Cathedral rose like architectural turbans fighting each other for supremacy.

As satisfied as he could be, Grozky crossed Red Square, forcing his gait to remain at a stroll. In a month's time, on

Victory Day, the square would be packed and Yeltsin would lay a wreath at the tomb of the Unknown Soldier. If Grozky lived that long, he would visit Piskarev Memorial Cemetery and pay his respects to his grandfather. For the first time he would also hold a vigil beside Timur's grave in Serafimov Cemetery. He took strength from their memories.

Ahead, the Kremlin's impenetrable wall ran the length of his view, dominated by the muscular *Spasskaya*, the Saviour's Tower. The bright red brick seemed to scream in warning, the jagged, swallow-tail crenellations at the summit indenting the sky like a serpent's scales.

Grozky passed behind Lenin's Mausoleum and approached the squat Senate Tower, the polygonal hips of its stone tented roof dwarfed by the Spasskaya. The tiny portico at the tower's base, watched by armed guards, was his entrance to the political fortress. He'd considered the Pinery Tower or the squat Kutafya Tower. Although they offered more privacy, they lacked the crowds of Red Square.

The Presidential Security Service processed him with a polite efficiency that belied their professional scrutiny, their search of his bag bordering on deferential. The irony of his preparations was a record of an FSB major arriving for a 5.30 p.m. appointment with Metzov would be available for those who cared to check. In a few minutes it wouldn't matter anymore. He felt his stomach churn at the prospect of the Grey Cardinal. Metzov coerced others as he bent the world to his will, entrusting Koshygin to save Yeltsin which made the GRU general almost untouchable. There was no longer a right or wrong way to resolve the quagmire Grozky had sunk into. He was taking the only course of action he could which might prevent him from being sucked under. Metzov had to be made to understand there was a different path.

The Presidential Security Service assigned him a uniformed escort, more guide than guard. Grozky had never been inside the Kremlin. He found himself walking through a large square, dressed in trees, past a small park, then a miniature city of towers and ancient religious buildings revealed itself: boxlike cathedrals with scalloped gables capped by golden domes and the tall crosses of worship. His chaperone pointed out the sights. The significance of the history and the names were lost on Grozky who could only wonder what Metzov's mood would be and the outcome of his reception.

Entering a large building, Grozky's passage was delayed as they were stopped by two uniformed guards and required to reauthenticate their identities. In the rarefied sanctum of power, Grozky struggled with their curiosity at his purpose. He tried not to sweat. The privilege of his private audience could have been a moment to cherish except for the circumstances. To negotiate you had to propose something someone wanted. It was whether Grozky could persuade the Grey Cardinal that what he was being offered was enough to resolve Yanusk. Grozky had only one hand to play.

His guide kept a steady pace, intruding on Grozky's thoughts with the phrase 'Not far now' which became an irritation. Grozky was led along stone-flagged corridors, his footsteps stifled by a rich stripe of blood red carpet. The cloth, its pigment the emblem of the workers' sacrifice, looked like a woven relic of Soviet failure.

Amidst this hidden city of power, as they took another flight of stairs and walked silently down a corridor, Grozky felt feverish. Despite the absence of security he felt isolated, lost even. His vision closed in, the shifting fabric of the guard's jacket all he could discern. Disoriented by dizziness, he wondered how he would find his way back through the labyrinth. It struck him he should have tied a piece of string at the outset of the journey, unrolling it to mark their passage.

"Hold on a moment. It's getting warm in here," Grozky said and stopped to remove his overcoat, bundling the scarf into a pocket. His hand moved to straighten his tie only to find the flesh of his neck. He recalled he'd decided to ditch the tie and stick with a dark blue suit and white shirt.

"Sure. Not far now," the guard said. He seemed oblivious to Grozky's state.

The weight of his overcoat removed, Grozky felt his sense of stifling confinement ease.

The Lord hates a coward, he told himself.

He glanced behind him and saw an exit sign above a doorway they had just passed. He forced himself to take deep, calm breaths and felt his discipline return.

After a myriad of further turns, they stopped outside an ornate wooden door. Grozky's guide knocked twice, then opened it.

"I'll be back in thirty minutes," he said and, with a curt nod, departed.

Grozky kept his black leather wallet case under an arm and marched into the room, surprised as his heels clipped off burnished wooden floorboards. He halted a respectable distance from the desk and brought himself to attention between a pair of slim wooden armchairs, decorated in a broad, yellow Lille stripe. Metzov sat writing and did not initially acknowledge his presence.

Finishing his sentence, Metzov studied it, his expression bordering on hostility, and then crossed out a word. A thin trail of smoke wove upwards from the papirosa in his hand as if marking the passage of time since Grozky's arrival.

Without looking up, Metzov gestured to a chair with a brusque wave. Grozky sat down and heard the thin frame creak. As he felt a wooden leg waver, he adjusted the placement of his weight. Metzov was an exacting person and the demise of the prize chair, whether reproduction or not, was an affront to be avoided. He put his case on his lap, undid the clasp and took out two A4 envelopes, one much thicker than the other. He braced one leg against the floor and leant forward to place the envelopes on the desk. The chair squeaked as he sat back.

"You asked to see me?" Metzov said, his attention on the sheet of paper in front of him.

"Yes, sir. I appreciate you making the time. There is a matter I must discuss with you."

The fountain pen hovered and Metzov looked up, his dark eyes suspicious.

"This is a matter you felt unable to resolve with General Koshygin?" Metzov asked.

"Correct, sir."

"Go on," Metzov said, replacing the lid on the pen and tucking it inside his jacket pocket. He extinguished his cigarette and immediately extracted another from a silver box on his desk. He did not offer one to Grozky.

"Several things have come to light recently which have a critical bearing regarding the outcome for President Yeltsin," Grozky said.

Metzov looked at him while, with a practised flick of his thumb, he ignited his gold lighter and lit the cigarette. He exhaled, watching Grozky as the fumes encircled him.

"This had better be good," Metzov said, his sharp eyes boring into Grozky's.

"I'll be brief. You won't thank me for what I have to tell you, but you will understand why when you have heard my report. Let me start with the fact that Yevgeny Kochenko is alive. We were all duped by his death. He narrowly missed being killed and used the situation to disappear."

Metzov sighed and his voice became hostile.

"And why is it you felt unable to discuss this with General Koshygin?"

Grozky told him, relaying the dead assassin, Nikita Chirkin, who served in the GRU, the murders of Kirill Blotski and Sergei Malievich in Deviatkino and the history of Koshygin's heroin smuggling. Only after the last revelation did Metzov react.

"Enough!"

Metzov's hand swept across his desk, the envelopes tumbling to the floor with a slap. Grozky met Metzov's glare calmly.

"My reason for coming to you directly is to suggest how these recent events may help the President in how he deals with Yanusk," Grozky said and retrieved the envelopes from the floor, the chair quietly growling at his efforts.

Metzov glared at Grozky, the muscles in his jaw clenching until his teeth cracked. Grozky persevered.

"Kochenko holds Zach Brown and Major Rastich. He has signed testimony from Brown who has disclosed he received a payment of US$100,000 from an offshore account in Nauru to pass information to the Russian Ministry of Fuel and Energy. Under the circumstances, such a payment would alert the FBI's Inter-Agency Task Force…"

He did not finish as Metzov interrupted him.

"That means we can add kidnapping to Kochenko's list of crimes? Why haven't you arrested Kochenko and recovered the witness? If what you say about Major Rastich is true, he will be dealt with," Metzov said.

"By anyone's standards Koshygin's behaviour borders on

delusional. His actions at best show a cavalier attitude which threatens to destabilise a fragile situation. You have heard the evidence. If Kochenko were to release this material, it would be even more damaging."

"He would not *dare*."

Grozky heard the anguish in Metzov's exclamation and knew the political fire he was playing with. Unless he could broker a solution, they would all succumb to the blaze of the scandal. Even Metzov was being drawn into the heat of the flames, the rising temperature making him more dangerous than ever. The only way to defuse his aggression was to convince him, otherwise the retribution would start. Death would follow death. Grozky avoided thinking of the atrocities Ivan Palutkin was capable of.

"Kochenko has good reason to feel threatened: the attempt on his life in Finland, the killing of Sergei Malievich and Koshygin's vendetta against him. In his letter, he makes it clear he sees himself caught up in a conspiracy he holds General Koshygin responsible for," Grozky said.

"A conspiracy? He's a fine one to talk. All you're giving me is more problems. I need solutions. What are you offering?" Metzov asked.

Grozky heard the doubt in the Grey Cardinal's challenge. It was now or never. He leant forward.

"A way for the Senate investigation to discredit itself. Zach Brown's integrity will be questioned once it's revealed he assisted Archipelago Oil's attempt to buy a stake in Yanusk through suspect nominee companies. The companies which Vadik Prigoda set up are a matter of record. More importantly, Brown, Nikita Chirkin, Anatoli Koshygin are all linked by recent events. What if there was another reason to connect them, separate from Yanusk?"

Grozky let the suggestion hang while Metzov's face remained furrowed in anger.

"Brown is an American businessman who travels frequently to Russia and acknowledges he has recently received a substantial payment from an offshore bank in Nauru. That payment becomes a matter of public record. General Koshygin is linked to a narco-military crime syndicate shipping substantial amounts of heroin to the United States. While on a visit to Russia, Brown narrowly escapes being killed by Chirkin, a man linked to General Koshygin. Follow that thread and heroin becomes the reason for their falling out. Brown cannot disprove the individual facts; taken together they destroy his credibility as a Senate witness."

Grozky paused. Amidst the half-truths and lies of counterintelligence, the trick was where to stoke the fire beneath the smoke. One version of events could be turned into another.

"Go on," Metzov said. He took a fresh cigarette from the silver box. This time he pushed the box in Grozky's direction.

"Thank you, sir."

Grozky accepted the offer, conscious of the smallest of bonds with the man who held his life in his hands. Metzov's arm stretched across the desk and Grozky leant forward to accept the flame from the gold lighter. There was a conspiratorial pull on their cigarettes. Grozky prayed silently as he struggled with the harsh smoke from the filterless cigarette. The Grey Cardinal would either listen or else he would be thrown to the GRU pack.

Grozky replaced the bulkiest envelope face up on the desk.

"These are audited reports from external consultants on how internal controls and management accountability have significantly improved at Yanusk. These can be submitted as evidence to the Senate Subcommittee. No one is challenging Tomarov's guilt, yet the Russian Ministry of Fuel and Energy can take credit for its oversight in resolving the corruption at Yanusk," Grozky said. He made no mention of Geneva, optimism was not a commodity for this discussion.

Metzov withdrew his hands from the desk as if the envelope was tainted with toxin. He sat back and took a drag from his cigarette before replying.

"There is one aspect you have not answered. Where does that leave us with Kochenko? What does he expect to get from this?"

"He wants an end to the state witch hunt against him. He is asking for détente," Grozky replied.

"D-é-t-e-n-t-e?"

Metzov chewed the word over and then leant forward to study Grozky, his elbow on the table. The smoke from his cigarette scurried upwards into the gloom.

"Why would I choose détente instead of scorched earth? Napoleon rued the day he crossed Russia. He invaded with half a million men and left with less than 100,000. If there's nothing left to burn, then there is no longer any scandal?" Metzov asked, his voice dark with intent.

"You could indeed, except a sensitive situation sometimes requires a subtle solution. If you pursue Kochenko, he could present the evidence in a very different way from the one I have outlined. Such revelations would be hugely damaging. If we stand down, Kochenko stands down. Détente would seem a reasonable compromise," Grozky said.

"For everyone, except General Koshygin," Metzov said.

"Koshygin has only himself to blame," Grozky said and stubbed out his cigarette in the crowded ashtray. He held

Metzov's stare, conscious the Grey Cardinal could snuff him out like a discarded cigarette.

Metzov stood up, the snap of his lighter triggering a fresh cigarette. He paced slowly around the room, exhaling in what sounded like a set of sighs. Grozky took stock of the room as he listened to the Grey Cardinal's footsteps. For a worker like Metzov, the ornate baroque wooden desk, the antique chairs, the Art Deco lamp and the French carriage clock on the mantelpiece struck Grozky as bourgeois. Above a fireplace a canvas dominated the wall. The picture was of a late-nineteenth-century town square, its church the centrepiece below which a dowdy crowd in a busy market had paused to listen to an orator atop a wooden crate, his brandished fist symbolic of injustice. The image could have been straight from a story by Turgenev.

In the window opposite, the outlines of the Kremlin buildings were being touched by the onset of dusk, the lustre fading from the golden domes.

Alone in the Grey Cardinal's presence, amidst the shadows grasping at the room's furnishings, Grozky saw the romanticism in Metzov's ruthlessness. Just as the USSR had survived Stalin's collectivisation in the 1930s, so the Russian Federation would survive Yeltsin's economic reforms. Russians endured hardships other nations could not imagine, from the slaughter of the Russian civil war to the twenty million sacrificed in the Second World War. Yeltsin's reputation might still be saved, provided Yanusk could be contained, otherwise the final chapter would be the flaws in his economic reforms providing nothing except shambolic deterioration to the lives of millions.

Behind him, the considered footfall of the Grey Cardinal creaked across the floorboards. Grozky prayed Metzov could see him as a faithful servant, not a traitor. The clock ticked, its beat seeming to warn against the proposed intrigue.

Outside, as the light dimmed through the window, the foreground of buildings faded against the backdrop of the Kremlin's brutal parapet. In the silence, it felt to Grozky like the onset of his incarceration.

Grozky sat in silence, conscious that speaking too soon might somehow incriminate him. He stared into the gloom until finally Metzov sat down.

"You think this will work?" the Grey Cardinal asked.

"The Subcommittee's righteousness is driven by the integrity of its witnesses. By destroying their reputation, the Subcommittee's own credibility falls away. The foundations upon which its conclusions depend become baseless. In contrast, how the Russian government has resolved Tomarov's criminality at Yanusk is documented and independently verified."

"What do I tell Ekomov? He's primed to strike in Washington."

"You can put Ekomov on hold. Why expose how secret Soviet funds were used to infiltrate the Senate? Trying to tarnish Gravell becomes secondary when we can use his subcommittee hearing to do our dirty work. We discredit their key witness and Archipelago's business practices while highlighting the extensive work overseen by the Ministry of Fuel and Energy in resolving the original fraud. Without a fire, there is no smoke," Grozky said.

Metzov nodded.

"Very well. Your counsel has merit. This is détente on my terms. Kochenko must hand over Zach Brown so he can be returned to the United States. Every day Brown stays missing embarrasses the Russian government. You are to notify the FBI's Inter-Agency Task Force immediately. Once we have this situation under control, I'll deal with Koshygin."

Grozky felt a wave of relief.

"There's one last thing. Kochenko will sign a non-disclosure agreement and that will be the end of it. He is to be under no illusion. If he crosses me, I'll destroy him," Metzov said.

Grozky nodded. Metzov's outward calm belied the threat of extreme brutality. The Grey Cardinal would scythe down anything to preserve the inner circle of the Russian Federation. The affairs of state required a lethal expediency to remain at the pinnacle of power. Aleksandr Metzov was more of a killer than the rest of them put together.

"Remind me, what did you do before you joined the FSB?" Metzov asked.

"I was an officer in the KGB's Third Directorate, sir."

"A survivor in the new order?"

"Barely, sir."

"Don't demean your intelligence. No one else in this operation has been able to offer a way out of this mess," Metzov said.

The Grey Cardinal's next question was almost gentle.

"After this is over, I take it you would prefer to remain in St Petersburg?"

"Truthfully, yes, sir. I would," Grozky said.

"That's a shame. I could use a man of your ability. Still, true talent deserves to be rewarded. I will see to that. Thank you for your efforts in this troubled affair. I know the President will be grateful for your contribution."

Metzov stood up, signalling an end to the meeting. He reached for the phone and dialled a number. Grozky managed a sharp salute before leaving the deathly office as quickly as protocol would allow.

Back in Red Square, he forced himself to march, using the momentum to calm his trembling legs.

32

Amidst the grand houses, one dominated the street, the original mansion expanded to absorb the plots either side. The trophy was the creation of Charles 'Chuck' Cowan, sole proprietor of Cowan Associates, whose dominance of political lobbying was matched by his fees. The scale of his home was in homage to Washington's Capitol building, the extensions representing the East Wing of Congress and the West Wing of the Senate.

While the light outside fought against the dusk, three men waited in the library on the second floor of the West Wing. A pair, comfortable in expensive suits and ties, sat in conversation, a giant holding court with a short, bald man puffing on a cigar. The third, General Peter Keefe, stood gazing from the bay window at the far end of the room, his vigil so still he might be awaiting an enemy.

The double doors to the library opened and two men entered. Chuck Cowan, beaming with the affluence of a grizzled power broker, clapped a hand around the shoulder of his latest guest.

"Bradley has come straight from the Dirksen building," Cowan said.

Amongst the veteran company, Senator Bradley Gravell, Chairman of the Senate's Permanent Subcommittee on Investigations, managed only a tired smile as he ran a hand through his hair and sank into a brown leather tub chair.

"Good evening, gentlemen. You'll have to excuse my tardiness. Washington traffic and it's been a hell of a week."

The two men looked up from their conversation, while Keefe remained at the window, still and silent.

Cowan looked across the familiar faces. He brokered many such meetings at his home. There was good reason why Eric Hesberger, a billionaire, Caspar Duncombe, a financier, General Peter Keefe and a high-flying senator should meet. Capitol Hill was the pinnacle of symbiosis where government, business and the military intersected, except this was not a political gathering. Hesberger, the leviathan of a man conversing with the cigar smoker, paid them all, an elite group referred to only as Tate. Hesberger's sobriquet of 'Minotaur' was fitting, Cowan thought, for aside from his bull head and brutal ambition, the billionaire industrialist was a patriarch without morality.

"Thank God I'm finishing this damn subcommittee hearing next week. Caspar's drink smells exquisite. I'll take a large brandy, Chuck. A *very* large one," Gravell said, using a hand to wrestle the tie from his neck and undo the top button of his shirt.

"When will you deliver your report, Bradley?" Hesberger asked, as Cowan walked to a drinks' cabinet recessed into the shelf of a bookcase. Around it, rows of aged spines relaxed behind leaded glass.

"By the end of April, except with Kochenko alive, that damned oligarch has all but destroyed my conclusion.

Kochenko's lawyers have sent hundreds of pages showing Yanusk to be a case study of effective corporate governance. Worse, the testimony of my primary witness has become a joke since the press reported his alleged ties to the Russian mafia. My report is hardly going to threaten Yeltsin now, is it?" Gravell said.

General Peter Keefe turned from the window and joined the group, his black shoes silent against the polished oak floorboards. He sat down next to Hesberger, his keen gaze fixed in rebuke at Gravell.

"What went wrong?" Hesberger asked.

Gravell sighed and when he said nothing, Duncombe spoke.

"The strategy was sound. Tate has had to be discreet in its pursuit of Yanusk because Yeltsin capped foreign ownership of Russian oil companies at fifteen per cent. None of us could have foreseen the precariousness of Tomarov's finances. We were within days of buying his stake in Yanusk…"

Duncombe paused, acknowledging the authority of Keefe's raised hand. When the general spoke, his voice was as measured as the buttons on his tunic.

"Tate's intermediaries made generous offers to Yevgeny Kochenko. When he refused to sell, we were forced to modify our plan. By using the Senate Subcommittee, we've forced the Russian government to take action against Kochenko. In counterintelligence, the best lies are based on truth and we leveraged a little KGB trick – *kompromat* or 'disinformation'. Tomarov was a crook and we embellished his fraud at Yanusk by creating the illusion of real commission payments between Tomarov and Lensky Bank," Keefe said.

"Except with Kochenko alive, Tate's ability to secure a stake in Yanusk is in jeopardy. Who is responsible?" Hesberger asked.

As Cowan handed Gravell a glass of brandy, he saw the richest group of corporate mercenaries around avoid looking at each other; Duncombe's detachment, Gravell's exhaustion and Keefe's coldness reflected where they stood in the post-mortem. Of all of them, the financier, Duncombe, was best protected from the front line, preserving Hesberger's public legitimacy from the private corruption of Tate. In his dark grey, three-piece suit, white shirt and speckled red tie he might have been at an investment board meeting. A plain, short man, the immaculate Saks 5th Avenue tailoring made him appear several pounds lighter. Duncombe took a puff from his Cuban half corona cigar as thick as his stub of a thumb, the rich smoke gently polluting the room.

"I am responsible," Keefe said. "We used a false cover to insert one of the best snipers on Tate's payroll. He confirmed the kill. Even the Russian government confirmed Kochenko was dead. In such operations, when strategies have to be modified, outcomes do not always go to plan. Mistakes happen."

"What are the odds of Tate purchasing Yanusk now?" Hesberger asked.

"We originally calculated there was more than a ninety per cent probability the Russian government would renationalise Yanusk, so it could be re-auctioned. Boris Nemtsov, the governor of Nizhny Novgorod, is an economic reformer who has proven the financial benefits fair auctions can bring. With Kochenko dead and the scandal of the Yanusk privatisation exposed…" Keefe said, before Hesberger cut him off.

"Except Kochenko's not dead, is he? With his survival and the improvements he's made to Yanusk's governance, how likely are the Russian government to renationalise Yanusk?"

It was Duncombe who responded.

"Less likely," he said, retreating to puff on his cigar.

Hesberger turned to Keefe.

"With what you're being paid, General, I expect more from the author of *The Boundaries of Anarchy*," Hesberger said.

Gravell stifled a smirk.

Cowan saw Keefe glower before he stood up and walked to the bar. The general's political fall was why Hesberger had hired him. Keefe was a ruthless military strategist who did not trouble himself with the collateral damage required to generate huge financial rewards.

Keefe returned to stand by his chair with a glass of whisky and stare at Gravell. With his eyelids tapering sharply downwards at the outer edges, he might have been a veteran boxer seeking satisfaction for the lean years spent in the ring.

Cowan saw Gravell shift in his chair, the pupil conscious of the teacher's displeasure. Gravell's brilliance in manipulating the Senate was in a lower league when it came to the Machiavellian grandmaster. A man insane enough to write *The Boundaries of Anarchy* was not to be gainsaid.

"With the mess this operation has become, you've been careful to leave no trail which might expose Tate?" Hesberger asked.

"No. The sniper travelled under a pseudonym. Someone who doesn't exist can't be found," Keefe replied.

Duncombe nodded.

"The offers made to buy Yanusk can't be traced. The myriad of entities roll into a *stiftung*, or secret foundation, in Liechtenstein which has a unique approach to banking secrecy. I am a paid trustee, while the beneficiaries are all nominee companies and need not be disclosed. We use various entities based in Geneva and even trusts in Nauru. A team of forensic accountants would struggle to piece together all the transactions, let alone make sense of them," Duncombe said, rewarding himself with a vigorous puff of his cigar.

The rest of the room watched the smoke curl slowly upwards, moving as mysteriously as the intricate financial structure Duncombe had just outlined. Keefe's plan now appeared simple in comparison. Hesberger grinned as he listened to the tortuous trail of companies hiding his brainchild.

"By exploiting the American political system we've shown how vulnerable the Russian government is to manipulation," Keefe said. "Until now, the US National Intelligence Council has avoided drawing attention to the scale of corruption in Russia because freeing the country from communism was such a foreign policy success. As Russia struggles with its free market reforms the American government doesn't want to be seen to be bayoneting the wounded. Our timing with the Russian elections could not have been better."

"I will remind you all when it comes to financial returns, the ends justify the means," Hesberger said.

"This isn't finished, Eric, it's just a delay," Keefe said.

"I agree with you, Peter," Duncombe said. "The economic opportunities in Russia have not been seen since the end of the American nineteenth century. Think of the robber barons like Rockefeller with Standard Oil or Andrew Carnegie in steel. They saw the potential to exploit natural resources and made fortunes. At these prices, Russia's assets are there for the taking."

33

Riding shotgun in front of Kochenko's convoy of three black Mercedes saloons, Grozky should have been driving the marked car he'd been assigned, an FSB Lada 'Sputnik', instead of the Chaser. Although the Sputnik's 1.5-litre Vaz-415 Wankel twin rotary engine was more than a match for the Chaser, the Sputnik's livery advertised his purpose. Kochenko had urged him not to be present, yet Grozky felt beholden to the oligarch and Metzov had approved of his suggestion. Casually dressed, the only evidence Grozky was an official outrider was the two-way radio handset on his passenger seat providing the shortwave communication with Kochenko's vehicles, and his AS Val rifle wedged into the opposite footwell.

They were less than a mile from their destination, the main administration for Internal Affairs on Suvorov Avenue, where Zach Brown would be kept out of sight until the city's deputy governor arrived to make a public statement crediting the St Petersburg police with his recovery and Brown would be paraded at a press conference. In private, Kochenko would sign the non-disclosure agreement, binding his silence, and all charges against him would be dropped. The Russian counteroffensive was already being felt: an American Senate spokesman forced to concede a US$100,000 payment received by Zach Brown was under review by the FBI. Koshygin no longer demanded constant updates. Borzoi had not seen him at GRU headquarters for days.

In a few minutes, they would park at the rear of the main administration for Internal Affairs, shielded by Karl Marx Park, and Grozky's role as a go-between would be over.

Driving past the small park at the junction with Moiseyenko Street, Grozky heard the splintering crack of a collision behind him. Pedestrians shrieked. Grozky braked and turned his head to see the lead Mercedes lying on its side in the middle of the road. A squat black Niva jeep was reversing from the side of the fallen car. At the corner with 9 Sovetskaya Street, men in urban camouflage, burdened by heavy automatic weapons, spilled from another jeep.

Grozky's hand scrabbled for the handset.

"It's a trap! Get out of there. Drive…"

Before he had finished his voice was drowned out by staccato gunfire. Grozky saw men firing PKM light machine guns, the heavy belt-fed 7.62 calibre 54mmR rounds smacking against armour plating, the bulletproof glass fracturing from the ferocity.

The remaining pair of Mercedes turned tail, their screaming tyres joining the barrage of sound. White smoke drifted across the road and Grozky smelled the scorched rubber of panic.

From a side street four black Niva jeeps launched themselves onto Suvorov Avenue, sirens wailing, and tore after the fleeing cars. The wreck of a Mercedes lay lifeless on its side, its windscreen finally shattering as armed men raked it with fire.

Grozky dropped the handset onto the passenger seat struggling with the betrayal. His hands shook and the V8 engine roared as he spun the Chaser. Shouts condemned him, weapons turning to track his passage, but the assailants' thrill was with the ruptured Mercedes and the Chaser escaped unscathed.

Ahead, he saw the jeeps haring after Kochenko's cars like wolfhounds and cursed as he tried to make up the ground. Passing Uprising Square, he swerved to avoid a car and then he was onto the long straight of Ligovsky Avenue and took advantage of the Chaser's power.

Grozky picked up the handset again.

"I'm about 150 metres behind the jeeps. What's your situation?"

"I'm alive and so is Zach Brown. I count four jeeps. We'll try and lose them," Kochenko replied.

Grozky left the handset on his lap, the bile in his throat as bitter as his failure to foresee his betrayal: Suvorovsky Avenue becoming the choke point in the trap. He could not tell the identity of the assailants – OMON, GRU, it made no difference. He was as much a target as Kochenko.

Ahead, the thinly colonnaded tiers and tall spire of the Cossack Church of the Exaltation of the Cross pinpointed the Bypass Canal. Crossing the bridge, Grozky saw a flare of red brake lights on the last of the jeeps and then the polka dot blue flashes on its roof stopped winking as it disappeared from view.

Joining the canal embankment, the path in the traffic left by the jeeps' wake had not yet closed and Grozky increased his speed, exploiting the gap to gain purchase on the pursuers' advantage.

At the junction with Moscow Avenue the approaching fury of the jeeps' sirens brought the vehicles crossing the lights at the New Moscow Bridge to a halt while the jeeps passed. As the traffic began to move, Grozky braced himself, his hand jammed against the horn. He prayed the blaring urgency would grant him safe passage. A truck stumbled forward and then stopped. Grozky accelerated, numb to his recklessness and then he was clear, leaving the traffic behind him in shock.

Once past the Baltic Metro station the city's grandeur faded. On either side of the canal the residential blocks competed against windowless industrial buildings and dark factories. Grozky's sense of foreboding grew as the surroundings became familiar, the hinterland of the port. Gutuyev Island was where he had staked out the docks. The murky fringe of the city was not a place to be cornered. Grozky reached for the handset.

"Yevgeny, you must cut north. If you can get back onto the Neva Embankment you can make a run for FSB headquarters. At least there I've got support. Out here we've got nothing."

"Valeri, stay back. Stay out of this, it's not your fight," Kochenko replied.

Even as the squat dome of the Epiphany church rose like a saracen's helmet from the far side of the Catherine's Court river, Grozky knew they were in trouble. Kochenko could not hope to outrun the sirens and, on the island, the close terrain was the worst place to get trapped into a gunfight.

Grozky threw the handset back onto the passenger seat and was stretching for his rifle when he saw the jeeps turn right across the canal. Kochenko had realised his error; provided he could keep running, he had a chance.

Crossing the canal, Grozky got a hand to the barrel of the AS Val. He pulled it to him and then wedged the rifle's stock against his hip and cocked the weapon. In another few hundred yards they would cross the Fontanka Canal and be back into the Admiralty District, fifteen minutes from the Big House.

Grozky caught his breath. The jeeps were turning left onto Riga Avenue, back to Gutuyev Island. He could not countenance Kochenko's decision. Perhaps the oligarch hoped to hide amongst the barracks of maritime warehouses, yet the half a square mile bordering the Baltic might as well have been a dead end.

Fifty yards from the Catherine's Court Bridge the silhouettes of cranes interrupted the skyline. Grozky crested the bridge to be met by the authority of the port, a broad square of ground guarded by a cluster of aged brick gatehouses. He reached the gap where the road was absorbed by the buildings and saw a jeep disappear between a pair of warehouses. He followed, struggling to keep sight of it amidst the warren of walls. Grozky wedged the rifle in the gap between the front seats as the pursuit became a cut and thrust of turns, Kochenko's vehicles exploiting the gridwork of roads.

His fears were confirmed as the gaps of light became more frequent and then the huge grey hulk of a container ship rose up and he was on the open quayside, the riveted panels of ships dwarfing the piles of metal containers stacked like pallets along the dock. Ahead, at the end of the quay, the sea was lost between a boundary of sky and hardcore.

The jeeps drew abreast of each other, spreading across the quayside to drive their quarry onwards. Grozky caught glimpses of the two Mercedes. The last of the ships could not be more than several hundred yards distant and still the vehicles raced along the quayside.

Grozky saw the jeeps sliding to a halt. They turned to form a perimeter, trapping Kochenko's vehicles against the sea. Armed men scurried forth, taking up positions behind their vehicles. Kochenko's vehicles were boxed into a killing ground. Grozky pulled up against the side of a container and grabbed his rifle and the radio handset as he left the car.

"I'm fifty yards or so behind the jeeps. You've got to get out of there. I'll cover you for as long as I can. Run for it once I start firing. It's your only chance," Grozky said.

He waited for a reply, taking up a position at the edge of the container. He saw the small army of men behind the jeeps. Grozky cursed at the hopelessness of the situation. He heard a voice he recognised issuing a command through a megaphone.

"Attention! We are here to arrest Yevgeny Kochenko on a matter of state security. You have thirty seconds to give him up. If you do not relinquish your weapons you will be fired upon."

Palutkin. Amidst the groups of camouflaged men Grozky spotted the Chechen veteran, one hand holding the megaphone, his other on the pistol grip of his AK-47.

Standing on the quayside was where Grozky would make his stand. His grandfather had taken three Germans with him on the Pulkov Heights, armed only with a bayonet. He took strength from Timur's memory. Sacrificing his life on unremarkable ground was a fitting end. At least he'd take Palutkin with him.

"Yevgeny, when I open fire, get out of there," Grozky said.

He put the handset to his ear as a sharp breeze buffeted the quayside, gusts of salt air marking time between the two groups. The pair of Mercedes remained sealed and silent.

Grozky saw Palutkin glance at his wrist before his voice boomed once more.

"Your time is up," Palutkin said.

The engines of the jeeps started up. Groups of GRU soldiers crept behind the armoured vehicles shielding their advance. Grozky raised the AS Val's stock to his shoulder. Despite the futility, he would make the GRU pay before they settled his account.

A faint vibration seemed to carry across the quay. Taking aim on Palutkin, Grozky attributed it to the eddying wind until the shaking rhythm grew in volume. The sound was intermittent, disguising its origin. The pitch rose to become the deep, earthy beat of a powerful machine close at hand, the muffled signature of rotors bouncing off walls. He saw the heads of the GRU turn as they sought to pinpoint the source.

Seconds later, the identity of the pulsating noise was revealed: a pair of Mi-24D Hind attack helicopters. Their recessed twin bubble cockpits, stubby wings and chin-mounted cannon marked them out as musclebound aggressors. They soared low, arrogant in their ability, and swung in an arc to face the cordon of jeeps.

In such open ground, Grozky saw a reversal of roles and the vulnerability of the GRU exposed. Palutkin screamed fresh orders, recalling his flanks and ordering his men to fire on the gunships. Then he dropped the megaphone and brought his assault rifle to bear.

Had the men stood together as Palutkin had ordered, they might have had a presence, but even as they engaged, the armour-plated predators drained their spirit. The experienced soldiers, confident of victory seconds before, knew the terrible power of the armed behemoths stalking them.

Fire spurted from the turret beneath one of the armoured cockpits, the efficiency of the four-barrel rotary gun shredding a jeep and the men behind it. Fear turned to panic and the

GRU killers scattered, desperate to escape the bloodlust of the beasts circling them.

One of the helicopters swung low and hovered. Grozky watched Palutkin rallying his men, his courage delusional, until a burst of quicksilver hit him square on, leaving him in several bloody pieces on the tarmac.

The remaining GRU men scrambled behind their jeeps, their heavy assault rifles no match against the titanium-armoured fuselage and rotors. The evil machines scoured for prey, their cannon shells indiscriminate, tearing through man and metal alike. By the end, the wrecks of jeeps and the debris of corpses littered the tarmac like an open grave. The supremacy of the Mi24-D Hind, vanquished in Afghanistan, had just been murderously reasserted.

Shocked by the scale of the deception, Grozky got back into the Chaser and drove across the quayside. The GRU's jeeps, reduced to mangled metal, paled against the damage to the men. Grozky gazed at a charnel house of a battlefield, the heads and limbs ripped from their torsos.

Parking the Chaser a few yards from the pair of Mercedes, Grozky left the car. He walked across to find a shaken Zach Brown supporting himself against a Mercedes, while Yevgeny Kochenko was being congratulated by his grinning subordinates.

"Ah, there you are, Valeri. I'm glad you're safe. I was just remarking on how Sergei Malievich would most definitely have approved," Kochenko said.

"How did you know?" Grozky asked.

From inside his overcoat, Kochenko retrieved a sheet of paper and handed it to Grozky.

"I'm afraid you'll discover what I found in Geneva makes for unpalatable reading."

Grozky snatched the paper and scanned the contents. It was not the neat analysis listing the names and numbers which caught his eye, but the identity of one recipient in receipt of several million US dollars: 'A. Metzov'.

"You knew."

"I realised Metzov could no longer leave this to chance. He has too much to lose. It isn't I don't trust you, it was better you didn't know," Kochenko replied.

EPILOGUE

In the Kremlin's dark corridors those who had betrayed Yeltsin redeemed themselves in death. Ivan Palutkin and his men received a hero's burial, fighting to the last man to recover Zach Brown after he was reportedly held for ransom by a Russian narco-military syndicate over a financial dispute. The Russian state media posted photographs of the aftermath at Gutuyev Island and Brown's release. Brown flatly denied the story and sued several newspapers though he could find no one to support his version of events. It only increased the FBI's interest in him since they were already looking into the funds received from an offshore account and, latterly, for passing confidential Senate Subcommittee materials to the Russian government. Brown also came under scrutiny from the US Drugs Enforcement Agency (DEA) after several significant seizures of heroin at American seaports. Following DEA raids on Brown's homes in Boston and Newport, the media circus continued.

Bradley Gravell completed his Senate hearing although without the conclusion he was asked for. His report was forced to acknowledge, despite the criminality of Yuri Tomarov, with the proper investment and management oversight the Yanusk Oil Company showed how the new economic reforms could work.

The FBI Inter-Agency's Task Force looked as closely as it could into the payment from a secret fund in Nauru without being able to trace the true source. Despite the assassination of Brown's professional reputation, there were few who could rival his experience. Spectrum Consulting continued to be the company of choice for those wishing to navigate the pitfalls of doing business in Russia.

Tate's failure to acquire the Yanusk Oil Company was a very costly mistake. When Caspar Duncombe showed Eric Hesberger the final bill, he was reported to be apoplectic and demoted General Peter Keefe. Several weeks later, Hesberger's bloated body was pulled from the Potomac river. A few miles away, from his office in the Pentagon, Peter Keefe watched the news break with cold satisfaction. Keefe had disliked playing second fiddle to Hesberger's insane ego. Tate was ripe for a new leader.

Anatoli Koshygin's double-dealing proved to be too much for him. He died of a heart attack, his body quickly cremated in case an autopsy might reveal the cause to be anything other than natural. His obituary omitted any mention of his role in a narco-military gang. He was buried with full military honours.

The payments received by Aleksandr Metzov never saw the light of day. If the Grey Cardinal expected leniency for his fanatical loyalty, he was very wrong. Although publicly much was made of an early retirement to the Black Sea, shortly afterwards Metzov was consigned to a private gulag to see out his days. As loose ends went, he fared better than Emile Rastich for the OMON major simply disappeared.

*

Grozky walked slowly up the steps, leaving the sunken centre of the Monument to the Heroic Defenders of Leningrad. He passed between the broken edges of the great ring in bronze and concrete encircling the centre, the missing piece symbolising the breaking of the Nazi blockade. On either side of the stylised jagged edges he saw the inscriptions, '900 days' and '900 nights', memorialising the city's suffering and endurance.

Reaching the top of the steps, he paused to look up at the statue of *The Victors*, a soldier and a worker at the base of the thin, red granite obelisk rising skyward.

He strode onto Victory Square to be greeted by rugged statues of partisans, infantry, pilots, sailors, metalworkers and civilians commemorating the one and a half million who had died during the siege. The defiant figures stood in small groups, arms outstretched, reaching out to help each other, timeless wraiths immortalised in bronze. Grozky walked among them. A few weeks previously he could not have envisaged he would return to the Big House as a colonel in the Division for Investigation of Criminal Organisations, URPO. Somehow, he had done the right thing and managed to survive, in that order. The city owed its life to the sacrifice of its people and men like his grandfather. He knew Timur would have been proud of his stand.

A series of short toots from a car's horn interrupted his thoughts. He looked across to where he had parked the Chaser at the top end of Pulkovo Park, opposite the square. He saw the three armoured Mercedes waiting behind his car.

Grozky jogged across the cobbles. He waited until there was a gap in the traffic and then ran across Pulkovo Highway. By the time he got back to the Chaser, Kochenko and Natassja were standing beside a Mercedes.

"I was killing time," Grozky said.

Natassja hugged him and they kissed.

"I hear you received a personal note of thanks from Yeltsin. That's more than I got. It sounds like congratulations are in order," Kochenko said.

"I've been very fortunate. I'm the one who has to thank you," Grozky said.

Kochenko extended his hand.

"I was joking. Even if Yeltsin escaped the political nightmare of Yanusk, he deserves everything he's got coming to him. I was congratulating you on your promotion. From what I hear about URPO, I'd better watch my step," Kochenko said.

They shook hands. It was the first time Grozky had seen Kochenko wearing the relaxed air of the victor.

"It's unusual to find an ex-KGB man prepared to stand up for what he believes in," Kochenko said.

"I thought it was time I redeemed myself."

"Everyone has a past. I'm glad you did," Kochenko said with a deferential nod. The oligarch grinned and Grozky thought there was almost a touch of humour in the cold blue eyes.

Grozky walked Natassja to the Chaser, their hands entwined. As they reached the car, she stopped and turned to him.

"Valeri, you have to stop living with the dead."

"I'm trying," Grozky said.

*

The first round of voting on 16 June was close with Boris Yeltsin and Gennady Zyuganov coming first and second with 35% and 32% of the vote respectively.

In the election run-off, on 3 July 1996, Yeltsin took 54.4% of the vote and was re-elected as the President of the Russian Federation.

1. Dramatis Personnae

1.1 Fictitious Characters

Name	Description
Abram	*Kommersant* newspaper photographer
Andrei Androvitch	Bodyguard of Yevgeny Kochenko (oligarch)
Dr Anosova	Doctor who treated Grozky's brother, Timur, for addiction
Major Nikolai Aristov	Police officer, Moscow Ministry of Internal Affairs
Viktor Baranov	Moscow lawyer for Irina Tomarov
Lieutenant Anton Bessonov	Police officer, Moscow Ministry of Internal Affairs
Kirill Blotski	Warehouse manager, Deviatkino
Lieutenant Dmitri Borzoi	Senior lieutenant, St Petersburg FSB
Zach Brown	Founder and CEO, Spectrum Consulting
Buzhkov	Warehouseman, Lensky Warehouse, St Petersburg
Nikita Chirkin	GRU captain, Moscow (see also Georgy Kramov)
Charles 'Chuck' Cowan	Political lobbyist, Washington DC (Cowan Associates)
William Danvers	Senator Bradley Gravell's office manager
General Donitsyn	Deputy Head of the St Petersburg FSB
Colonel Arkady Dratshev	GRU colonel, Moscow
Mikhail Dudin	Russian poet (1919-1993)
Iosif Dymov	Security guard at the Petrovsky Island marina

Name	Description
Galina	Wife of Abram, *Kommersant* newspaper photographer
Colonel Ilya Ekomov	GRU colonel, Moscow
Dr Feliks Fedorov	Doctor, St Petersburg FSB
Pasha Fett	St Petersburg FSB
Fadei Filimonov	Specialist, Federal Agency for Government Communications and Information (FAPSI)
Kostya Gagolin	St Petersburg FSB
Senator Bradley Gravell	Chairman, US Senate Permanent Subcommittee on Investigations
Marisha Grozky	Valeri Grozky's ex-wife
Keto Grozky	Valeri Grozky's father
Timur Grozky	Valeri Grozky's elder brother
Major Valeri Grozky	Major, Federal Security Bureau
Rolan Gubanov	St Petersburg FSB
Vasili Gorev	GRU Washington
Eric Hesberger	American businessman
Pavel Ikkonnen	Translator, GRU, Moscow
General Peter Keefe	US general, Washington DC
Milosz Klepin	Bodyguard of Yevgeny Kochenko
Yevgeny Kochenko	Russian oligarch (owner of the Lensky Group)
General Anatoli Koshygin	GRU general, Moscow
Katerina Kozhevnikova	Russian pathologist, Moscow
Georgy Kramov	Operational name of Nikita Chirkin, GRU captain, Moscow
Chief Inspector Matthias Lasola	Chief Inspector, Finnish police
Arnold Lennister	Chief Executive Officer (CEO), Archipelago Oil
Valentina Leskova	GRU Washington
Lyov	GRU Washington (Colonel Ilya Ekomov's driver)

Name	Description
Taras Lugin	Yevgeny Kochenko's lawyer
Sergei Malievich	Yevgeny Kochenko's business partner
Dr Oskar Markus	Finnish pathologist
Aleksandr Metzov	Deputy Chief of Staff in the Presidential Administration, Moscow
Lieutenant Stepan Nedev	Lieutenant, OMON Militia (Russian Ministry of the Interior)
Oleg	OMON Militia, St Petersburg
Iakov Osin	St Petersburg FSB (Economic Crimes)
Colonel Ivan Palutkin	Colonel, GRU, Moscow
Sergeant Bogdan Pavlova	Sergeant, St Petersburg FSB
Luka Peterkof	Bank manager
Natassja Petrovskaya	Journalist, *Kommersant*
Roza Petrovskaya	Natassja Petrovskaya's sister
Piotr Petrovitch	Special investigator, GRU, Moscow
Maksim Popov	Ex-OMON Militia, St Petersburg
Vadik Prigoda	St Petersburg lawyer
Sergeant Rakhimov	GRU sergeant, Moscow
Major Emile Rastich	Major, OMON Militia, St Petersburg
Stanislav Rusnak	Chief Financial Officer (CFO), Yanusk Oil Company
Andrei Simonov	Deputy Minister, Russian Ministry of Fuel and Energy
Borya Solokov	OMON Militia, St Petersburg
Irina Tomarov	Wife of Yuri Tomarov
Yuri Tomarov	General Manager, Yanusk Oil Company
Liliya Usova	Natassja Petrovskaya's editor, *Kommersant* newspaper

Name	Description
Vadim Vogorov	St Petersburg criminal
Grigori Zotkin	Prosecutor-General's representative, Moscow

1.2 Real people referenced in the story

Name	Description
General Viktor Cherkesov	Head of the St Petersburg FSB
General Pavel Grachev	Defence Minister of the Russian Federation
Vladimir Kryuchkov	Chairman of the KGB
Boris Nemtsov	Governor of Nizhny Novgorod
President Boris Yeltsin	President of the Russian Federation
Gennady Zyuganov	Head of the Communist Party of the Russian Federation

2. Acronym Summary: Soviet & Russian Federation Internal Security Services

Acronym	Russian	English
FAPSI	Federal'noe Agentstvo Pravitel'stvennoi Sviazi i Informatsii	Federal Agency for Government Communications and Information
FSB	Federalnaya Sluzhba Bezopasnosti	Federal Security Bureau
FSK	Federalnaya Sluzhba Kontrrazvedki	Federal Counterintelligence Service
GRU	Glavnoye Razvedyvatelnoye Upravlenie	Russian Military Intelligence

Acronym	Russian	English
GUBOP	Glavnoye Upravleniye Borbes Organizovannoy Prestupnostyu	Main Directorate for Combatting Organised Crime (MVD)
GUVD	Glavnoye upravleniye vnutrennikh del	Main Administration for Internal Affairs (MVD)
KGB	Komitet Gosudarstvennoy Bezopasnosti	Soviet State Security Committee
MB	Ministerstvo Bezopasnosti	Ministry of Security
MVD	Ministerstvo Vnutrennykh Del	Ministry of Internal Affairs
OMON	Otryad Militsii Osobogo Naznacheniya	Special Designation Police Detachment, a unit of the Ministry of the Interior (MVD)
OVO	Otdel Vnevedomstvennoy Okhrany	Department for Extradepartmental Protection (MVD)
URPO	Upravelenie Razrabotki Prestupnykh Organizatsit	The Division for Investigation of Criminal Organisations (FSB)
SBP	Sluzhba Bezopasnosti Prezidenta	Presidential Security Service
SOBR	Spetsial'nye Otryady Bystrogo Reagirovaniya	Special Forces unit of the Ministry of the Interior (MVD)
SVR	Sluzhba Vneshney Razvedki	Foreign Intelligence Service (Ex-KGB First Directorate)

3. Place Name Summary

3.1 St Petersburg

Russian	English
11-Ya Liniya Ulitsa	11th Line Street

Russian	English
Admiraltéyskiy Rayón	Admiralty District
Aleksandrovskiy Sady	Aleksandr ('Alexander') Gardens
Aleksandr Park	Alexander Park
Akademika Lebedeva Ulitsa	Academician Lebedev Street
Anichkov Most	Anichkov Bridge
Artilleriyskaya Akademiya Mikhaylova	Mikhaylov Artillery Academy
Avtovo Stantsiya metro	Avtovo Metro station
Naberezhnaya Arsenala	Arsenal Embankment
Baltiyskaya Stantsiya Metro	Baltic Metro station
Baltiyskaya vokzal	Baltic station (railway)
Belingskogo Most	Belinsky Bridge
Belingskogo Ulitsa	Belinsky Street
Birzhevaya Ploshchad	Exchange Square
Birzhevoy Most	Exchange Bridge
Bolshoi Dom	'The Big House' (FSB headquarters)
Bolshoy Petrovsky Most	'Great Peter' Bridge
Bolshaya Morskaya Ulitsa	Great Naval Street
Bolshaya Neva Peka	'Great' Neva river is the largest distributary of the Neva river
Bolshaya Nevka Peka	'Great' Nevka river is an arm of the Neva river
Bolshaya Pushkarskaya Ulitsa	Great Pushkar Street
Centralny Storona	Central District
Chernyshev Stantsiya Metro	Chernyshev Metro station
Chugunnaya Ulitsa	Cast Iron Street
Dobrolyubova Prospekt	Dobrolyubov Avenue
Dokhodny dom(a)	Tenement building(s)
Dvortsovy Most	Palace Bridge
Dvorstovy Prospekt	Palace Avenue
Dvortsovy Naberezhnaya	Palace Embankment

Russian	English
Espluatatsionnoye Lokomotivnoye Depo Sankt-Peterburg-Finlyandskiy	Finland-St Petersburg Operational Locomotive Depot
Finlyandskiy vokzal	Finland railway station
Fontanka Peka	Fontanka river
Gostiny Dvor	'Great Merchants' Court' shopping arcade
Grenadersky Most	Grenadier's Bridge
Kanal Griboyedova	Griboedov Canal
Khrushchyovka	Prefabricated Soviet apartment block
Gutuyevsky Ostrov	Gutuyev Island
Inzhenernaya Ulitsa	Engineering Street
Kanonerskiy Sudostroitel'nyy zavod	Gunboat Shipyard
Kamenny Ostrov	Stone Island
Kamennoostróvskiy Prospékt	Stone Island Avenue
Kazansky Most	Kazan Bridge
Kirochnaya Ulitsa	(Lutheran) Church Street
Kirovskaya Vyborgskaya Liniya	Kirov-Vyborg line (Metro)
Kontsertnyy Zal	Concert Hall
Krasnyy Oktyabr	Red October
Krestovsky Ostrov	Cross Island
Kresty Tyur'ma	Kresty ('Crosses') Prison
Krivusha Peka	Krivusha river
Kronverskiy Proliv	Kronversk Strait ('Rampart Sound')
Kanal Kruyokova	Kruyokov Canal
Khram Prepodobnogo Serafima Sarovskogo	Church of St Seraphim of Sarov (Serafimov Cemetery)
Kuybysheva Ulitsa	Kuybyshev Street
Knyaz'-Vladimirskiy Sobor	Prince Vladimir Cathedral
Lesnoy Prospekt	Forest Avenue

Russian	English
Liteyny Most	Foundry Bridge
Liteyny Prospekt	Foundry Avenue
Ligovsky Prospekt	Ligovsky Avenue
Malaya Neva Peka	'Little' Neva river (the smaller distributary of the Neva river)
Malaya Nevka Peka	'Little' Nevka river (the southern distributary of the Great Nevka river)
Mayakov Stantsiya Metro	Mayakov Metro station
Mendeleyevskaya Ulitsa	Mendeleev Street
Mikhaylova Ulitsa	Michael's Street
Moiseyenko Ulitsa	Moiseyenko Street
Moskovsky Prospekt	Moscow Avenue
Moskovskiy Park Pobedy	Moscow Victory Park
Motor-Vagonnoye Depo Sankt-Peterburg-Finlyandskiy	St Petersburg-Finland Motor Wagon Depot
Muzhestva Ploshchad	Muzhestva Square
Muzhestva Ploshchad Stantsiya	Muzhestva Square station
Moyka Peka	Moyka river
Murino Storona	Murino District
Nakhimovskaya Morskaya Akademiya	Nakhimov Naval Academy
Naberezhnaya Kanala Griboyedova	Griboedov Canal Embankment
Naberezhnaya Obvodnogo Kanala	'Bypass' Canal Embankment
Nevskaya Bukhta	Neva Bay
Neva Naberezhnaya	Neva Embankment
Nevsky Prospekt	Nevsky Avenue
Nepokoryonnykh Prospekt	Avenue of the Unvanquished
Novo-Moskovsky Most	New Moscow Bridge
Obvodny Kanal	Bypass Canal
Pestelya Ulitsa	Pestelya Street

Russian	English
Petropavlovskaya Krepost'	Peter and Paul Fortress
Petrogradsky Ostrov	Petrograd Island
Petrovskaya Ostrov	Peter's Island
Petrovskaya Ploshchad	Peter's Square
Petrovskogo Stadion	Petrovsky Stadium
Ploshchad Lenina	Lenin Square
Piskaryovsky Prospekt	Piskarev Avenue
Piskaryovka Stantsiya	Piskarevka station (railway)
Piskarevskoye Memorial'noye Kladbishche	Piskarev Memorial Cemetery
Pobedy Ploshchad	Victory Square
Ploshchad' Preobrazhenskogo	Transfiguration Square
Primorskiy Park Pobedy	Primorsky Victory Park
Pulkovskoye Ploshchad	Pulkov Square
Pulkovskoye Shosse	Pulkov Highway
Rechnoy Yakht-klub Profsoyuzov	Central Yacht Club
Rizhskiy Prospekt	Riga Avenue
Rustaveli Ulitsa	Rustaveli Street
Ryleyeva Ulitsa	Ryleev Street
Sadovaya Ulitsa	Garden Street
Sankt-Peterburgskiy Tramvayno-Mekhanicheskiy Zavod	Saint Petersburg Tram Mechanical Plant
Sampsoniyevskiy Most	'Sampson's Bridge' (also known as the 'Freedom Bridge')
Serafimovskoye Kladbishche	Serafimov Cemetery
Severny Prud	Severny Lakes
Shpalernaya Ulitsa	Tapestry Street
Siny Most	Siny Bridge
Smolninskiy Rayon	Smolninsky District
Smol'nyy Sobor	Smolny Cathedral
Spaso-Preobrazhenskiy Sobor	Transfiguration Cathedral

Russian	English
Sredny Prospekt	Middle Avenue
Stachek Prospekt	Strike Avenue
Suvorovsky Musey	Suvorov Museum
Suvorovsky Prospekt	Suvorov Avenue
Sverdlovsky Naberezhnaya	Sverdlovsk Embankment
Tavricheskiy Sad	Tauride Park
Tuckhov Most	Tuckhov Bridge
Varshavsky vokzal	Warsaw railway station
Vasileostrov Stantsiya Metro	Basil's Island Metro station
Vasilievsky Ostrov	Basil's Island
Vitebsky Stantsiya	Vitebsk station
Vladimirskiy Prospekt	Vladimir Avenue
Vosstaniya Ploschad	Uprising Square
Voyenno-Meditsinskaya Akademiya Imeni S. M. Kirova	Kirov Military Medical Academy
Voznesensky Prospekt	Ascension Avenue
Vyborg Storona	Vyborg District
Ya-Liniya Ulitsa	Line Street
Yekateringof Peka	Catherine's Court river
Yarmarka 'Yunona'	Yunona ('Juno') Fair
Yuzhnaya Dorogo	Southern Route
Zagorodny Naberezhnays	Zagorodny Avenue
Zakharyev Ulitsa	Zakharyev Street
Zhdanovka Peka	Zhdanov river
Zayachy Ostrov	Hare Island
Zhukovsky Ulitsa	Zhukov Street
Zimniy Dvorets	The Winter Palace

3.2 Moscow

Russian	English
Uglovaya Arsenal Bashnya	Corner Arsenal Tower
Berezovaya Roshcha Park	Birch Grove Park
Chkalovsky Voyennyy Aerodrom (Shchyolkovo, Moscow)	Chkalov Military Airfield (Shchyolkovo, Moscow)
Park Gor'kogo	Gorky Park
Filevskiy park	Filev's Park
Gosudarstvenny Universalny Magazin (GUM)	State Department Store
Aerodrom Khodynka	Khodynka Airfield
Khoroshev Shosse	Khoroshev Highway
Kazanky Sobor	Kazan Cathedral
Krasnyy Ploshchad	Red Square
Moskovskiy Kreml'	The Kremlin
Kremlevskiy Proyezd	Kremlin's Passage
38 Petrovka Ulitsa	38 Petrovka Street
Manezhnaya Ploshchad	Manezhnaya Square
Okhotny Ryad Stantsiya Metro	'Hunter's Row' Metro station
Polezhayev Stantsiya Metro	Polezhayev Metro station
Pushkin Stantsiya Metro	Pushkin Metro station
Voskresenskiye Vorota	Resurrection Gate
Spasskaya Bashnya	Saviour's Tower
Senatskaya Bashnya	Senate Tower
Gosudarstvennyy Istoricheskiy Muzey	State Historical Museum
Tagansko-Krasnopresnenskaya Liniya (Metro)	Tagansko–Krasnopresnenskaya line (Metro)
Borovitskaya Bashnya	Borovitsky Tower
Bashnya Kutaf'y	Kutafya Tower
Tverskaya Bul'var	Tversky Boulevard
Tverskaya Ulitsa	Tversky Street
Vernadskogo Prospekt	Vernandsky Avenue

4. Acknowledgements

4.1: The figures referenced in Chapter 2 are taken from page 75, *Violent Entrepreneurs: The Use of Force in the Making of Russian Capitalism* by Vadim Volkov (original source: Azalia Dolgiva, ed., Organizovannaya prestupnost'-4 (Moscow: Kriminalogicheskaya assotsiatsiya, 1998, 258).

4.2: The list of acronyms for the Soviet and Russian Federation Internal Security Services is broadly taken from 'A Glossary of Russian Police & Security Service Acronyms and Abbreviations' compiled by Dr Mark Galeotti, Organised Russian & Eurasian Crime Research Unit, Keele University (1997).

ACKNOWLEDGEMENTS

Without the grateful encouragement and support over the years, this story would not have made it onto the shelves. A very big thank you to:

Joel Tancer, Mike Roemer, Mike Parry, Mike Ashworth, Peter Ahrens, Mike Housden, Katherine Zhukoff, Andrew Slocum, Patrick Kalkotourian and the team at Bar Vanloo, Baptiste Kalkotourian, Philippe Gantelet, Gary Eaborn, Serena Morton, Alice Saunders, Pat McArdle, Shaiful Haque and the team at the Bengal Village (Richmond), Bernard and Danielle Genty, Philip and Sophie Butcher, Edward Boddington, Alistair Milward, Richard Bright, Rosa and the team at Villa Rosa and Café Leonardo (East Sheen), Kathy Ortiz, Whitney Wisely, Barry O'Byrne, Paul Haywood, Kevin Griffin, Joe Pizzuto, Craig Buick, Doug Scott, Charles Calthrop, Robin and Lysbeth Davies, Walter Davies, Ben Davies, Neil Graham, Al Coxall, Alan Stockey, Jeff Brooker, John Inglis, Robin Jones, David and Charlotte Jones, Harry Bingham and the team at Jericho Writers, Jo Marshall, Josey Wales, Vernon Waters, Malcolm Lee, Sam Mills, Howard Cunnell, Eve Seymour, Martin Toseland, Janet Laurence, Scott Halford, the publishing team at Matador Books, Joshua Howey, Sophie Morgan, Moira Hunter, Bill Ward, Café Mirabeau, the team at L'Amandine (Richmond).